THE FITZOSBORNES IN EXILE

Praise for *A Brief History of Montmaray*

"Once in a while, a special book will cross our paths and make us grateful for life and the ability to read. I'm talking about *A Brief History of Montmaray* by Michelle Cooper." —*Viewpoint* (Australia)

"An intoxicating romance fraught with tension and danger . . . *A Brief History of Montmaray* is one of the most enchanting novels I have read all year." —*San Francisco Book Review*

"This is a romance in the fuller sense of the word. The aristocratic poverty, eccentric family members and a scribbling heroine will remind readers of Dodie Smith's *I Capture the Castle*. Dare I say that *A Brief History of Montmaray* is even better than that much-adored book." —*The Source*

"This book has a bit of everything: romance, betrayal, a haunting, espionage, psychological discord, intimate liaisons, and murder." —*School Library Journal*

Praise for *The FitzOsbornes in Exile*

"This is top-shelf historical fiction." —*Booklist*

"There's adventure as well as history here, as the young royals take matters into their own hands. . . . A great read." —*January Magazine* (Australia)

"Despite the balls, the bores, and the frightening shadow of Hitler, Sophie never loses her lightness of touch in recording matters both serious and funny. Cooper's engagement of politics and her quick, inventive wit give the book its own captivating originality." —*The Horn Book Magazine*

THE FITZOSBORNES IN EXILE

Michelle Cooper

EMBER

Text copyright © 2010 by Michelle Cooper
Cover photograph copyright © 2011 by Corbis

All rights reserved. Published in the United States by Ember, an imprint of Random House Children's Books, a division of Random House, Inc., New York. Originally published in Australia by Random House Australia Pty Ltd., North Sydney, NSW, in 2010, and subsequently published in hardcover in the United States by Alfred A. Knopf, an imprint of Random House Children's Books, New York, in 2011.

Ember and the colophon are trademarks of Random House, Inc.

Visit us on the Web! www.randomhouse.com/teens

Educators and librarians, for a variety of teaching tools, visit us at www.randomhouse.com/teachers

The Library of Congress has cataloged the hardcover edition of this work as follows:
Cooper, Michelle.
The FitzOsbornes in exile / Michelle Cooper. — 1st American ed.
p. cm.
Sequel to: A brief history of Montmaray.
Summary: In January 1937, as Sophia FitzOsborne continues to record in her journal, the members of Montmaray's royal family are living in luxurious exile in England but, even as they participate in the social whirl of London parties and balls, they remain determined to save their island home from the occupying Germans despite growing rumors of a coming war that might doom their country forever.
ISBN 978-0-375-85865-9 (trade) — ISBN 978-0-375-95865-6 (lib. bdg.) —
ISBN 978-0-375-89802-0 (ebook)
[1. Exiles—Fiction. 2. Families—Fiction. 3. Great Britain—History—George VI, 1936–1952—Fiction. 4. War—Fiction. 5. Diaries—Fiction.] I. Title.
PZ7.C78748Fi 2011
[Fic]—dc22
2010034706

ISBN 978-0-375-85155-1 (tr. pbk.)

RL: 7.0

Printed in the United States of America
10 9 8 7 6 5 4 3 2 1
First Ember Edition 2012

Random House Children's Books supports the First Amendment and celebrates the right to read.

The FitzOsbornes of Montmaray

1850–1939

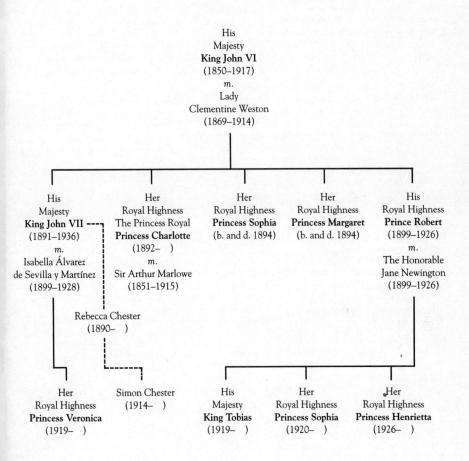

His
Majesty
King John VI
(1850–1917)
m.
Lady
Clementine Weston
(1869–1914)

His
Majesty
King John VII
(1891–1936)
m.
Isabella Álvarez
de Sevilla y Martínez
(1899–1928)

Her
Royal Highness
The Princess Royal
Princess Charlotte
(1892–)
m.
Sir Arthur Marlowe
(1851–1915)

Her
Royal Highness
Princess Sophia
(b. and d. 1894)

Her
Royal Highness
Princess Margaret
(b. and d. 1894)

His
Royal Highness
Prince Robert
(1899–1926)
m.
The Honorable
Jane Newington
(1899–1926)

Rebecca Chester
(1890–)

Her
Royal Highness
Princess Veronica
(1919–)

Simon Chester
(1914–)

His
Majesty
King Tobias
(1919–)

Her
Royal Highness
Princess Sophia
(1920–)

Her
Royal Highness
Princess Henrietta
(1926–)

Selected excerpts from the journals of

Her Royal Highness Princess Sophia of Montmaray,

1937–1939

These journals document the royal family's first years in exile
following the tragic events of 1936 and 1937 when His Majesty King John
the Seventh died, German planes attacked the Kingdom of
Montmaray, and the FitzOsbornes were forced to flee their home.

16th January 1937

I write this sitting at an exquisite little Louis the Fifteenth secretaire in the White Drawing Room, using a gold fountain pen
borrowed from the King of Montmaray and a bottle of ink provided by one of the footmen. Fortunately, the paper is just a six-
penny exercise book that I bought in the village this
morning—otherwise I'd be too intimidated to write a word.

It's interesting, though, how quickly one becomes accustomed to small luxuries—having an invisible maid whisk away
one's clothes in the night and return them freshly laundered and
mended the next morning, for instance. Of course, if she hadn't,
I wouldn't have had a stitch to wear today, other than the flan-
nel pajamas my brother, Toby, lent me. But Aunt Charlotte did
order us some things from London, and they're supposed to be
delivered soon. Is it *too* dreadful of me to rejoice in the prospect
of brand-new clothes—for once not handed down by older relatives? When the reason I no longer have any possessions is so

tragic? Probably. But as I can't do anything about the tragedy, I will continue to be quietly thrilled about the clothes.

Anyway. Here I sit, scribbling away in my journal on this first full day of my new life (writing in Kernetin, of course, our secret code, in case any grown-ups get hold of my book). I awoke at dawn, jolted out of a nightmare—or perhaps just a memory—in which I was running for my life as the world collapsed around me. As I stared up at the canopied bed and silk-paneled walls, it took me a moment to work out where I was. But then I remembered. Aunt Charlotte's house! Milford Park! England! I scrambled out of bed and rushed over to the window, but all I could see was a dense white mist, as though the house were swaddled in cotton wool each night and the servants hadn't got round to unwrapping it yet. This didn't help at all with the uneasy, dislocated feeling left over from my nightmare. I then decided to go and see Veronica—merely to check that *she* was all right, of course.

Her room, two doors down from mine, is more austere, decorated with bleak-looking landscapes and a cheerless charcoal study of Nelson's final moments at the Battle of Trafalgar. There *is* a vast marble fireplace, but all it contained early this morning was a mound of ashes. I was shivering in the doorway, peering at Veronica's half-drawn bed hangings and wondering whether I'd wake her if I moved any closer, when a sepulchral voice announced,

"She's not dead. She's still breathing."

I whirled about, hand at my throat.

"Henry!" I gasped. "Don't creep up on me like that!"

My little sister stood by my elbow, looking deceptively demure in a cardigan and pleated skirt. "I checked," Henry went on in her inexorable way. "Her chest was going up and down."

"Well, of course Veronica's not *dead*," I snapped, but I felt ashamed of myself at once. Poor Henry, stuck here for the past few days not knowing *what* had happened to us, the grown-ups rushing about in a panic and no one explaining anything to her. And then our dramatic arrival yesterday, Veronica being half carried out of the motorcar, her arm wrapped in bloodstained bandages. No wonder Henry was feeling anxious. "Now don't disturb her," I whispered, in what I hoped was a soothing manner. "Come back to my room and let me get dressed, then we can . . ."

But I wasn't sure what was expected of us. Were we supposed to gather in that immense dining room downstairs, or wait for breakfast trays to be sent up, or what? I had a hasty wash in the pink-and-white bathroom between my room and Veronica's (admiring yet again the fluffiness of the towels and the frothiness of the soap), then pulled on my old skirt and jersey. Meanwhile, Henry occupied herself opening and closing every drawer in my room, running her fingers over the wall panels, and fiddling with the window latch.

"Your room's bigger than mine," she declared as I searched in vain for a hairbrush. "And Veronica's is bigger than yours. But Toby's is absolutely *enormous*! It's got three windows and its own bathroom and a dressing room!"

"Well, he does have the highest rank of all of us," I pointed out, repressing a sigh. I could already tell that life here was going to be far more formal than at Montmaray. I hoped there wouldn't be too many mysterious forks and spoons at breakfast, before I'd had a chance to revise my dining etiquette. "I don't suppose *you* know where everyone has breakfast?" I asked, grimacing at my bird's nest hair in the looking glass.

"In the breakfast room, of course," said Henry. "At eight o'clock. But hurry up, I've got something to show you first." Then she bounded out of the room and down the corridor.

As my hair was a lost cause, and I was keen to start learning my way around the house, I hurried after her, towards the wide gallery that surrounded the Grand Staircase. There were a lot of heavily varnished gold-framed portraits here, as well as glass cabinets and statues on pedestals and Chinese vases large enough for a person to hide inside, all of which gleamed richly in the dim light. Past the staircase, Henry explained, were Toby's rooms and Aunt Charlotte's suite. Upstairs, apparently, were still more bedrooms, and above that were the servants' quarters.

But we went downstairs, leaving a trail of shoe-shaped indentations in the thick red carpet. I wouldn't have been at all surprised to glance over my shoulder and find a silent housemaid following us with a carpet sweeper. Everything was immaculate, and the scent of potpourri and lemon furniture polish hung heavily in the air. At the bottom of the staircase was about an acre of marble floor, with fluted columns running along either side, and massive brass doors leading off the hall to a myriad of drawing rooms. But Henry tugged me into an oak-paneled corridor be-hind the staircase. We plunged down a narrow flight of steps and into a room that made me feel instantly at home. There were macintoshes and straw hats in various states of disrepair dan-gling from pegs near the door, stacks of yellow newspaper tied up with string, walking sticks and wicker baskets and old brooms, and, best of all, a pile of blankets upon which lay a big black dog. He jumped up when we came in and flung himself at Henry.

"Darling Carlos!" said Henry, hugging him. "Did you miss me? Mean Aunt Charlotte, making you sleep down here! Never mind, I'll sneak you up to my room tonight."

But I didn't think our dog had minded the arrangements *too* much. He'd been curled up next to the boiler, and someone had already served him a hearty breakfast, judging by the bowl encrusted with gravy and the enormous bone he'd been gnawing. He demanded a pat from me, then went over to stick his nose in-side the Wellington boots Henry was trying to tug on. I'd thought that Carlos was the thing Henry had wanted me to see, but apparently "it" was "just down the drive."

The mist had lifted, I noticed, replaced with a gentle rain that fell without sound upon the gravel path. However, this obligingly stopped before we'd walked ten yards.

"Even the *weather*'s polite here," said Henry, giving the sky a contemptuous glance.

I gathered Aunt Charlotte had already Had Words with Henry about her manners.

"At Montmaray, it'd be bucketing down," Henry went on

wistfully, "*and* there'd be a howling gale. Probably a thunderstorm as well."

"They'll have thunderstorms here, too," I assured her. "You've only been here five days."

"Is that *all*?" she exclaimed. "It feels like weeks and weeks! Gosh, I hope Veronica gets better soon so we can all go home."

I stopped so abruptly that Carlos ran into the back of my legs. "Oh, *Henry*," I said.

"What?" she said, turning.

"We . . . we can't go home."

Henry stared at me, her blue eyes getting wider and wider. "But then . . ." Her lower lip trembled. "Then Veronica *is* dying, after all!"

"Don't be silly!" I said. "Of *course* she isn't." I reached out and folded Henry into an embrace (she was so thin, so tense, it was like hugging a bundle of twigs). "Veronica will be fine after she's rested in bed a bit longer. It's just . . . well, you *heard* us talking yesterday, about the Germans bombing the island. The castle was hit. The drawbridge was destroyed. Even the boats are gone."

"But the castle's not flattened, is it?" she said. "Even if it is, we can camp in the armory—and they couldn't have wrecked *everything* in the village! What about Alice's cottage?"

"The roof was damaged, and . . . Henry, you don't understand! It's too dangerous! The walls could collapse, there'll be unexploded bombs all over the place, the Germans could come back at any moment. That's if they're not already there—"

"But *why*?" she burst out, jerking away from me. "Why did

they do it? Is it because that German soldier disappeared? And that horrible officer Gebhardt blamed us? That's stupid!"

Veronica and I hadn't told her the awful truth about Hans Brandt's death, and I had no desire to burden her with it then, or ever. So I bent over Carlos, who'd just emerged from a hedge, and busied myself brushing twigs out of his fur.

"But they *can't* take over Montmaray like that!" Henry cried. "They just *can't*!"

There was a pause.

"Can they, Sophie?"

I looked up.

"I don't know," I admitted.

She turned on one foot and marched off down the drive.

"Henry! Wait! Where are you going?" I ran after her, but she went faster and faster, a furious whirl of limbs. She disappeared round a bend in the drive, and I didn't catch up with her till we'd both passed through a small stand of oaks and then a wooden gate.

"This is the Home Farm," Henry announced in a tight voice, not looking at me as I tried to recover my breath. "You have to close the gate behind you so dogs don't get in."

"Henry—" I started, but she turned away and pointed at a field.

"All the milk comes from those cows. There are three Jerseys and two Friesians. I thought the milk tasted strange at first, but that's just because it's from cows, not goats. They don't have any goats here."

"Henry, about Montmaray—"

She raised her voice. "The hens are in that shed, and there are ducks and geese, too. A goose attacked my leg yesterday, but I had Wellingtons on, so it didn't matter."

I'd never seen her face so guarded and still. My little sister had started to grow up, had begun to bury her thoughts and feelings deep down, out of reach, taking care to smooth over the surface afterwards. It made me feel terribly sad—and old. I bit my lip and followed her across the farmyard, Henry pointing out various features of interest.

"—and that's the milking shed, and over this way is—" Her voice brightened at last. "Oh, hello, Mr. Wilkin! This is my sister, Sophie."

A stout man took off his cloth cap and looked inside it. "Your Highness," he said.

I would have told him not to bother with the "Your Highness" bit, but I suspected this would get both of us in trouble with Aunt Charlotte, so I just said, "How do you do?"

"Have you already finished the milking?" asked Henry. "Has Mrs. Wilkin got the eggs in? Are the geese let out?"

"I hope Henry hasn't been bothering you, Mr. Wilkin, while you're working," I said.

"No bother," said Mr. Wilkin. "Been helping with . . ." And his wide face reddened.

"I've been helping feed Cleopatra," said Henry. "And scratching her back, because she can't reach."

"You have, at that," said Mr. Wilkin. Then he mumbled

something about the butter churn and went off. I hoped I hadn't said anything to offend him.

"Come on, she's in here." Henry dragged me into a low building and leaned over a railing. "There! Isn't she *beautiful*?"

Lying in a pile of straw was the most *enormous* sow. I had no idea they could grow that large.

"She's going to have piglets in a month or so," said Henry. "Only, Mr. Wilkin thinks it's rude to talk about that sort of thing in front of ladies."

"Aren't you a lady?" I asked.

"No," said Henry. "And I hope I never turn into one. Cleopatra's won five blue ribbons and a silver trophy at the Agricultural Show."

We gazed at her, and she gazed back. She had small, intelligent eyes and alert ears. I'd always read that pigs were dirty, but she was creamy white all over, except for where her pink skin shone through. She was really rather sweet, although I wouldn't have climbed in that pen for anything. I'd have been squashed flatter than a pancake if she'd accidentally sat on me.

This reminded me that I was starving, so we went back to the house for breakfast. It wasn't nearly as complicated as I'd feared. The cutlery was the usual sort, and we just helped ourselves from the sideboard. But, my goodness, what a lot of food! There were scrambled eggs, fried mushrooms, and grilled tomatoes, all in covered silver dishes kept warm over spirit lamps. There was game pie, cut into thick wedges, and a platter of cold chicken sprigged with parsley. There was an urn of porridge and a long silver rack with triangles of toast slotted into it. Then there were pots of jam and marmalade and honey and relish and mustard, and jugs of cream and treacle for the porridge. I ate and ate, and so did Henry. Aunt Charlotte sat at the head of the table, perusing the Court Circular of *The Times* while continuing to denounce the unfortunate policeman who'd turned up yesterday afternoon and tried to put Carlos in quarantine.

"The very idea," said Aunt Charlotte indignantly, "when Montmaray is free of every known canine disease and most of the human ones, too! They ought to be *thanking* me for bringing such an unblemished specimen of dog to this country. I shall certainly be having words with the Home Secretary about it when next I see him. Henrietta, elbows *off* the table. Ah, I see the Morland girl has finally announced her engagement. A baronet's son—and only a *second* son! Is that the best they can do, with all her father's money? He has factories, you know, makes hairpins or some such thing. Poor girl, she's been out at least three Seasons, and not even a proper title to show for it at the end!"

I suppose I should provide a description of Aunt Charlotte here. I'd always pictured her as a female version of Uncle John, only younger and nicely dressed and sane (so, not very like him at all, really). She certainly is just as grand as I'd expected, and very handsome, with curling chestnut hair parted to one side, piercing blue eyes, and the long, straight FitzOsborne nose. This morning, she wore a beautifully cut black-and-white suit with a cream silk blouse, black silk stockings, and black shoes with gold buckles. There were large pearls in her earlobes and around her neck, a diamond-and-sapphire horseshoe brooch pinned to her lapel, and an assortment of large, glittering rings on her left hand. And I could see that these were just her *everyday* jewels, laid out routinely on the dressing table each morning by her maid. I could only imagine what treasures Aunt Charlotte had tucked away in her safe, thanks to her rich, dead (and, according to Toby, unlamented) husband. Who hadn't had a "proper title," either, come to think of it, just a knighthood. It seemed a bit much for Aunt Charlotte to criticize the poor Morland girl, whoever she was. Although I suppose Aunt Charlotte had had more than enough title for both her *and* Uncle Arthur, being a king's daughter and everything.

At that point, a very good-looking footman came in and murmured something in Aunt Charlotte's ear. "Take *whom* to the station?" she said. "Oh, Simon Chester." I choked on my toast. "Well, tell Parker to have the car back by half past ten. No, eleven—*such* a lot of correspondence to attend to this morning. I shall need more black sealing wax, too. Now, has a breakfast tray gone up to His Majesty? And to Her Highness?"

The footman murmured a bit more, then departed. Luckily, the notion of a chauffeur named Parker helped divert me from any foolish speculation about where Simon was going, or how long he might be away.

"One needs to supervise every little thing," Aunt Charlotte sighed. "Even to ensuring breakfast gets sent up to Tobias.

Although I must say, I think *that's* sheer indolence on his part. If *I* can limp downstairs with my injured foot, then an energetic young man certainly ought to be capable of it."

"But Toby's leg is still in plaster," said Henry. "Your foot's not."

"It remains weak and frail," said Aunt Charlotte sternly. "But those of us with responsibilities do not have the luxury of dwelling on our infirmities. One struggles on, no matter how fragile one may be."

Since Aunt Charlotte looked about as fragile as Cleopatra, Henry did not bother to express any sympathy but only asked if we could visit the village this morning.

"The *village?*" said Aunt Charlotte with a frown. "Well, perhaps I could spare Barnes as a chaperone, although she does have that evening gown to hem and all my furs to—" Aunt Charlotte suddenly peered at her newspaper. "Good heavens, the Dowager Duchess of Dewsbury has died! In San Luis Obispo, wherever that is. How *very* eccentric of her."

"Well, Aunt Charlotte didn't actually say *no,*" said Henry an hour later as we set off across the park by ourselves. Veronica had shown no inclination to get out of bed, and Toby was unable to walk so far on his crutches. He did, however, give us detailed directions, lend me his comb and his smallest jacket, and press a handful of coins upon me, ordering me to buy myself something nice.

The park proved to be very pretty—almost *too* pretty. On one side was tame woodland, and on the other was a lake, far more pleasingly shaped than Nature could ever have managed. There were a lot of smooth, sloping lawns and then, wherever the beauty of this began to pall, avenues of trees and sculpted hedges. There were sundials and statues, fountains and follies and fishponds, all in the most fitting places.

The village of Milford was equally picturesque, although more rustic. I could just imagine Tess of the d'Urbervilles trudging down its narrow road on her way to some fresh disaster. Toby had said there was an actual mill, too, where the river narrowed, but we only went as far as the village green. This was edged by a row of stone cottages decorated with ivy, an inn called the Pig and Whistle, a shop, a lovely old church, and a Georgian vicarage (we waved at its front windows as we walked by, just in case the Reverend Webster Herbert was at home). The shop seemed the busiest—there were bicycles leaning against it, women clutching wicker baskets standing about the doorway, and boys playing marbles on the footpath nearby. Everyone stared as we approached—probably flabbergasted by my hair, which Toby's comb hadn't done much to improve—but then they all recovered and were very polite. Henry bought a pennyworth of sweets from a jar on the counter and ran out to share them with the boys. I chose the thickest exercise book they had, then looked around for something to cheer up Veronica. I couldn't imagine her showing much interest in gingham-capped pots of blackberry jam or little bags of dried lavender, which was all they seemed to stock in the way of gifts. But then the nice shopkeeper unearthed a dusty booklet about Milford, written by a local historian twenty years ago. The shopkeeper and I were both very pleased by my purchase. I hoped there'd be some historical inaccuracies in it for Veronica to get indignant at, she'd enjoy that—

Oh, Toby has just limped in and collapsed on the sofa beside me. Henry is settling his broken leg on a footstool and fetching him the newspaper. He needs another cushion, though. Just a minute . . .

Back again, hours later.

Toby explained that he and Henry had spent the past half an hour perched on Veronica's bed, trying to prod her into showing some signs of life.

"I even stole her pillow," Henry said, sprawling on the floor with her sketchbook. "But she just pulled the blankets over her head. Toby, can you please pass me the red crayon?"

Fearing for the well-being of the Aubusson carpet, I asked Henry whether this was really the best place for crayon-based activities.

"Course it is," said Henry. "It's a drawing room, isn't it?"

I explained that that was short for "*withdrawing* room," a place in which ladies and gentlemen could conduct civilized conversation, usually while sitting on chairs. Toby only laughed. At that moment, the butler, tall and terrifying, glided in to announce that "the Right Honorable, the Viscount Whittingham" had arrived.

"Yes, thank you, Harkness. Send him in," said Toby. I had

just enough time to cast a frantic look at my shabby skirt and wonder who on earth the Viscount Whittingham was before Henry jumped up.

"Anthony!" she cried, rushing over to the familiar figure stooping in the doorway.

"That's 'Lord Whittingham' to *you*, young lady," said Toby with mock severity. "Come and sit down, Ant. Sophie, could you ring the bell for tea?"

"No, I'll go!" shouted Henry, because she'd just discovered that the dumbwaiter—a little elevator used to convey dishes to the dining room—provided a quick and interesting route to the kitchen. She galloped off.

"Hello, hello! How *are* you, Sophie?" said Anthony, coming over to wring my hand. "Gosh, we were worried about all of you!"

"You saved our lives, Anthony," I said sincerely. "If you hadn't raised the alarm and sent someone for us—"

"Oh, no, no, no," he protested, stepping backwards. He narrowly missed Henry's crayon, slipped on a stray piece of paper, and landed in an armchair. "Oof! No, but, really, it was mostly Julia's uncle, you know, Colonel Stanley-Ross. And that Basque captain—what was his name?"

"You shall *all* be awarded the Order of the Sea Monster for personal services rendered to a Montmaray sovereign," said Toby grandly. "Once I've found out whether there *is* such a thing as the Order of the Sea Monster . . ."

"It couldn't possibly be called *that*," I said, although I knew our family did have some sort of jeweled decoration. I'd seen people wearing it in old portraits in the Great Hall at Montmaray.

"The Danish have an Order of the Elephant," said Toby. "Which is just silly. At least we *have* sea monsters at Montmaray. And then there's the British—the Order of the *Garter*!"

"Well, your cousin will know all about it," said Anthony, settling back in his chair. "In fact, Veronica's the reason I came over. You see, I realized this morning that I hadn't delivered her parcel as I'd promised. Terribly sorry about that! Got left in the aeroplane, and what with all the rush . . ."

I suddenly saw that he held Veronica's manuscript of *A Brief History of Montmaray*, as badly wrapped as when she'd thrust it at him that dreadful afternoon . . . could it *really* have been only six days ago?

"Where is she, anyway?" asked Anthony, setting the parcel on the gilded table beside him. "In the library, I suppose!"

Toby sighed. "In bed, actually, and no sign she's ever going to leave it."

"Oh!" said Anthony. "Oh, I do hope she isn't ill."

"No, no," said Toby. "Just sulking."

"Toby!" I protested. "She could have *died*! If Captain Zuleta hadn't arrived when he did, I don't know *what* would have happened."

"But . . . but your aunt didn't mention anything about *that*!" gasped Anthony. "Good heavens! Was it one of the bombs or falling rock or—"

"No, Rebecca tried to murder her with the firewood ax," said Henry, coming back into the room.

"Rebecca? You mean—your *housekeeper?*"

With unfortunate timing, the parlor maid arrived with the tea tray. She began to set out the silver teakettle, teapot, milk jug, sugar bowl, and tiered stand of scones, gingerbread, fruitcake, and finger sandwiches while Anthony stared at us, and her, in horror.

"Thanks, Phoebe, we'll manage the rest," said Toby after about half a minute of this. "Ooh, smoked salmon, we *are* lucky! No, no, that's fine. Sophie can pour."

The maid, a thin, sallow girl not much older than me, bobbed her knees and departed.

"Here, Henry," said Toby, shoving some fruitcake and half the sandwiches into her hands. "Take this down to Carlos. The poor thing must be lonely, and probably starving, too."

"You're going to *talk* while I'm gone, aren't you?" said Henry. "I don't know why you bother sending me off, I know all about it, anyway."

"Yes, but this way I can look Aunt C in the eye and swear I haven't said a word in front of you," said Toby. "Oh, and keep a lookout for her, will you? Give us a signal if you see the car coming up the drive. She's gone off to Lady Bosworth's for a chinwag, so she'll probably be hours, but one never knows."

"I'll give my special whistle," Henry said, cheering up. She provided us with an ear-piercing demonstration, then ran off.

"Rebecca?" repeated Anthony as soon as Henry had disappeared. "Tried to *murder Veronica?*"

"Well, perhaps not," said Toby. "It's possible that Rebecca just happened to be swinging the ax around and Veronica sort of . . . got in the way of the blade."

"And we think Rebecca was a bit mixed up," I added. "She might have thought that Veronica was her mother. Veronica's mother, that is, not Rebecca's mother. Veronica and Isabella do look awfully alike, and Rebecca always hated Isabella."

Anthony, not surprisingly, appeared even more confused.

"But the woman's been arrested?" he said. "She's in prison now?"

"Not . . . exactly," said Toby with a sideways glance at me (we'd already had one lengthy argument about this). "Because we're not quite sure what happened. Neither Veronica nor Rebecca is saying much, and no one else was there. Besides . . ."

Besides, there were a number of other complicating factors, including Rebecca's revelation that her son, Simon, was the eldest child of the late King of Montmaray. But I didn't think Anthony needed to know that.

"Anyway, for now, she's locked up in the attic," said Toby. "Only, Sophie's convinced she's going to creep downstairs one night like the mad Mrs. Rochester and burn us all in our beds."

I maintained a dignified silence and ate a scone.

"Well!" said Anthony. "It's all very, very . . ." He struggled for a while. "Odd" was the word he finally came up with.

"Never a dull moment with the FitzOsbornes," agreed Toby calmly. "Mmm, this gingerbread's good."

It certainly was, and so were the sandwiches, which had the crusts cut off and were filled with all sorts of delicious things. And the *scones*—I barely recognized them as such, they were so fluffy and high, so beautifully round. The few times I'd tried to make scones back home, they'd been reduced to cinders when our temperamental stove had flared up. Or else they'd emerged as desiccated lumps that had to be scraped off the baking tray, then sawed open with a carving knife.

I lifted my Spode teacup and was suddenly convinced that I was dreaming. What other explanation could there be for me sitting here, having tea with a viscount in an elegant drawing room? Unless I'd split in two a few days ago. Here I was, the new-made twin, set down in a fascinating, incredible world, while the old Sophie, the real one, was still in Montmaray, milking the goat and cleaning out the stove and setting buckets under the leaky parts of the castle roof when it rained. Perhaps Uncle John was still alive there. Perhaps Hans Brandt had never made his fateful midnight trip to the castle, perhaps he and Otto Rahn had never visited Montmaray at all . . .

My head felt fuzzy. I tilted warm, smooth china against my lips, the taste of bergamot and lemon and sugar rolling over my tongue. It wasn't enough to convince me that this was real. I concentrated on the voices.

"—and Julia sends her love, of course," Anthony was saying.

"She had to go up to London, sort out bridesmaids' frocks or some such thing." His voice took on a proud, tender note as he contemplated his fiancée. "But she'll be back tomorrow, and they're all longing to see you. Her mother wants to invite you to luncheon next week, although if Veronica still isn't well . . ."

"She will be," said Toby. "The doctor says she's perfectly able to get out of bed *now*."

"Oh! Well, I'm glad the doctor said . . . But then, it doesn't seem awfully like your cousin to, um . . ." Anthony trailed off.

I knew what Anthony meant. He'd been impressed—possibly even intimidated—by Veronica's intellect and energy. He, like the rest of us, had assumed she was invincible. It was disconcerting to think of her as even slightly broken.

"Don't worry. She'll be back to her usual self soon," Toby assured us. "I have a plan."

19th January 1937

One would think I'd have far more time for writing in my journal here than I ever did at home, now that I have servants to cook my meals, and wash my clothes, and even put an extra log in the fireplace if I wish (not that I'd ever ring the bell for *that*; the intimidating butler might turn up). But somehow, the hours seem to fly past, and now here I sit, *days* after my last entry.

There has been rather a lot happening, though. Firstly, our new clothes arrived, and it was like ten Christmases at once. *Two* suits for me, one a lovely, heathery tweed and the other a dark blue jersey, as well as a gray box-pleated skirt and a slim black linen one. Three silk blouses, two plain and one striped, and three Aertex shirts. A knitted jersey, a matching cardigan, a coat, two pairs of shoes, and a sweet little velvet hat that my unruly hair keeps shoving off my head—plus pajamas and vests and knickers and cotton gloves and handkerchiefs and lisle stockings. I'd only ever worn socks before, so the stockings make me feel very grown-up and sophisticated. Or they would if I could figure out how to use the mysterious devices that prevent the stockings from falling down.

There's also a black woolen frock for church, because we're all supposed to dress in mourning when we go out. Toby says I ought to be able to get away with white or violet as half mourning because Uncle John wasn't my father. I wholeheartedly agree with Toby, as black makes me look like a very faded ghost. Aunt Charlotte is not yet convinced by our arguments. She is thoroughly Victorian in such matters.

Veronica has the same clothes as I do, except one of her suits is black and she got brassieres as well as vests, on account of her having a great deal more bust. Veronica says the brassieres don't fit properly and need to be sent back. Aunt Charlotte says they're *supposed* to be uncomfortable. The two of them also had a spirited debate about girdles. Veronica is not willing to suffer on behalf of Modesty and Decency, let alone for the sake of Fashion—a stance that Aunt Charlotte finds both baffling and perverse.

But all that arguing came later. First, the doctor came back to check Veronica's stitches.

"Thank *heavens* debutantes wear long gloves," said Aunt Charlotte, frowning at Veronica's arm after the doctor had gone. Thin purple lines crisscrossed Veronica's right palm, and there was a three-inch puckered ridge, bristling with spidery threads, running along her wrist.

"Yes, that's my main concern—how I'll look in a ball gown," I could just hear Veronica saying sarcastically to herself.

However, as she wasn't talking out loud at that stage, she only pressed her lips together and stared out the window.

"It *is* a tiny bit gruesome, Veronica," said Toby, sitting on the end of her bed. "As though you tried to do yourself in. Except you're right-handed, so I don't know how you'd actually manage to—"

"Stop *babbling,* Tobias," said Aunt Charlotte, looking round to ensure Henry and all the servants were out of earshot. "Now, there are *matters* to be resolved. What have you done about getting rid of that dreadful woman in the attic?"

"Well, Simon's been investigating various . . . options," said Toby.

"I fail to see why *options* are needed," said Aunt Charlotte irritably. "The woman is a homicidal maniac. It's perfectly clear she needs to be taken away by the police and locked up in Holloway."

"But if Rebecca *is* mad, she's not liable for her actions," said Toby. "So she can't be sent to prison. Besides, we don't *really* want her going to court, do we? All sorts of things could come out."

Aunt Charlotte huffed. "There's absolutely no proof of her ridiculous claims about her son!"

"Well, there's Alice and the other villagers," said Toby. "They're all living in Cornwall now. They might know something about who Simon's father really—"

"Hearsay," interjected Veronica, unable to stop herself.

Toby shot me a triumphant glance—he'd made a bet with

me that she'd be talking by teatime if he kept mentioning Simon. Veronica sat up higher in bed and began ticking off points on her uninjured hand.

"Firstly," she said, "the law doesn't recognize evidence based on what has merely been *reported* to a witness by someone else. What does it matter if Rebecca repeated her absurd claims to Alice or Mary? Their evidence is inadmissible in court—they'd simply be repeating old rumors. Secondly, even if Simon *is* my father's son, he's illegitimate. Rebecca might claim there was a wedding, but it wasn't witnessed by anyone, let alone performed by a minister, and it certainly doesn't appear in any FitzOsborne records."

Aunt Charlotte gaped at Veronica, astounded by the sudden deluge of words.

"Thirdly," continued Veronica, "my father had twenty-two years to acknowledge Simon as his son, if he'd wished, and he didn't. Fourthly, the identity of Simon's father is irrelevant to the issue of succession when there already *is* a legitimate male relative of the late King." Veronica gave Toby a pointed look.

"But I'm underage," said Toby.

"You'll be eighteen next month," Aunt Charlotte said, finally recovering her powers of speech.

"But isn't twenty-one the age of majority?" Toby asked hopefully.

"King Stephen was only fifteen when his father died," said Veronica. "His mother ruled as Regent for the next two years, but he'd barely turned seventeen when he ascended the throne."

No one seemed to have noticed that we didn't *have* a throne anymore, nor a castle, nor a kingdom. But I wasn't going to be the one to remind them, not when Veronica had finally started talking again.

"I still think I'm too young," said Toby.

"Too lazy, you mean," said Veronica.

At that point, Aunt Charlotte's maid tiptoed in to whisper that the Earl of Dorset was on the telephone.

"About that horse, I suppose," said Aunt Charlotte. "Wait here," she ordered us, then stalked off.

"Actually," said Toby, lowering his voice, "it's not revelations about Simon's father that worry me. It's more what Rebecca might tell the police regarding that German soldier. Aunt C doesn't know anything about *that*, of course."

"Rebecca was there, too," I said. "She was the one who wanted to hide the body. She had as much to do with it as we did."

"Or even more than us," agreed Veronica. "*She* was meant to be keeping an eye on Father."

"Yes, well, this is Rebecca we're talking about," sighed Toby.

"What are you saying?" I asked. "That she's threatening to—"

"Of course," said Veronica, slumping back against the pillows. "She and Simon Chester think they can blackmail us into giving them what they want. And what they want is for Simon to be King of Montmaray."

"Oh, no . . . I don't think so," said Toby, not very convincingly. "It's more that Simon's worried about his mother and wants her to get some proper help. There are all sorts of clinics now for people who are, um—"

"Homicidal maniacs," said Veronica.

"I'm not denying she needs to be somewhere secure," said Toby. "But, Veronica, those old asylums were just awful! You don't want Rebecca locked up in a place like that."

Veronica only raised her eyebrows at this. *Oh, don't I?* was what she seemed to be thinking.

"What did Simon say in his letter this morning?" I asked Toby hastily.

"Oh, that he should be back by this afternoon, and that he inspected a place in Cornwall and another near Poole," Toby said, pulling a piece of paper from his pocket. "The one near Poole looked the best. Right by the sea and almost like a nursing home. They stay in bedrooms rather than wards, and therapists take them on outings and teach them how to weave baskets and so forth."

"It sounds expensive," I said.

"Don't worry, I'll talk to Aunt C," said Toby. "I think I can persuade her it'll be worth whatever it costs, to avoid a scandal."

"And you think that'll satisfy Simon Chester, do you?" Veronica said. "That once Rebecca's settled in a luxury loony bin, he'll happily go back to being a solicitor's clerk, carting files around and fetching people cups of tea?"

Toby and I looked at each other and then at the carpet. That was the problem. All of us—probably even Veronica—believed that Uncle John *was* Simon's true father, regardless of the arguments about Simon's legitimacy. And Simon had always been fiercely ambitious. Now he had proof, of sorts, that he'd been cheated out of his rightful place in Society. Even the most noble of souls would have felt some resentment about *that*.

"What *if*," said Toby, with the unmistakable air of one grasping at straws, "what if Simon was made, um, Regent? And looked after things till I turned twenty-one? Then I could be crowned King—"

"*Simon Chester*, give up the crown once he'd got his grasping fingers on it?" said Veronica.

"Anyway, Aunt Charlotte would never agree," I said.

"Yes, Toby, *you're* her favorite," said Veronica, with the slightest tinge of bitterness. "She'd never allow the mere son of a servant to get in *your* way."

There was another long, unhappy silence. Aunt Charlotte's unyielding sense of How Things Ought to Be Done colliding with Simon's determination to claim his rightful inheritance and Rebecca's sheer craziness—it seemed destined to end in catastrophe.

"It depends on Simon, doesn't it?" I said slowly. "If *he* could be persuaded to be reasonable—"

"I could talk to him," said Toby. "Well, I *have* tried, but it's difficult. He's hardly ever here and he's so distracted and . . ." He looked down at Simon's letter sadly, and even Veronica couldn't find it in her to make any more caustic remarks about Simon. In fact, she looked as though she wanted to pull the blankets over her head again.

Then Aunt Charlotte swept in, wearing a very pleased expression. "Bought that chestnut hunter!" she said. "Lord Dorset's sending over a pony, too—perfect for Henrietta!" Her gaze settled on Veronica. "Aren't you up *yet*? I'll send Barnes to draw a bath for you. I suppose the two of you will need your *own* lady's maid now." She sighed loudly. "Well, perhaps that parlor maid, the skinny one—what's her name?"

"Phoebe," said Toby, running his fingers along the crease of Simon's letter.

"What sort of name is *that* for a maid?" said Aunt Charlotte. "They used to have good plain names like Annie and Mary and Dot. What's her surname?"

"Oh, Westerdale or something. Isn't she the niece of one of the gardeners?"

"I shall call her Smith," declared Aunt Charlotte. "Barnes will have to train her. Really, what with trying to find a governess for your sister, dealing with that hopeless secretary of mine, and now *this*, it's a wonder I have time to *breathe*." Then she swept out again. Veronica trudged off to have her bath, and Toby and I returned to our respective bedrooms to brood.

Wondering whether writing things down might help, I seated myself at my desk. I jotted down all the reasons Toby should be King and then the arguments in favor of Simon. I added the names of those who supported Toby and those who supported Simon. This didn't get me very far, so I tried assigning points to supporters on the basis of how reasonable their claims were. Ten points to Aunt Charlotte for being head of the

FitzOsborne family. A grudging two points to Simon for being older than Toby, and probably having better leadership skills. Five points to Veronica for knowing more than anyone else about the history of the Montmaravian monarchy. Minus fifteen points to Rebecca for being insane and trying to kill Veronica. Arithmetic never having been my strong point, I got into a fearsome muddle with the figures, so I started doodling in a corner of the paper. I drew a crown and a sword, an island and a boat—and then a wisp of an idea appeared. An hour later, Henry stomped in to complain that Parker had gone to collect Simon from the railway station without telling her first, even though Parker had *promised* her a ride in the motorcar—by which time my wisp had coalesced into a very interesting-looking cloud.

I hastily changed into my dark blue suit and most business-like blouse. Then I ran downstairs and paced up and down the Marble Hall until Simon arrived.

"Oh, hello, Sophia," he said, tugging off a new pair of very stylish black gloves and looking over my shoulder. "Toby's upstairs, I suppose?"

"Yes," I said. "But before you see him, *I'd* like to speak to you."

There was a tiny pause as he took in my severe tone. He'd only heard it once before. *Then* it had astonished him, as if he'd been bitten by a butterfly. Now he merely handed his gloves to the footman, who was waiting, expressionless, with Simon's coat already folded over his liveried arm.

"Of course," Simon said to me. "Perhaps we could talk in . . .

the music room? As the Princess Royal appears to be interviewing governesses in the library?"

"Fine," I said.

"After you," said Simon with a half smile, knowing perfectly well I had only the haziest notion of where the music room was. The footman, bless him, inclined his head the slightest bit to the left and flicked his gaze at the double doors of the State Dining Room. I gave him a grateful nod, then marched off, glimpsing with relief an enormous gilded harp through an adjacent doorway. Once we were inside, I shut the doors and led Simon over to a pair of armchairs near the window.

"Please sit down," I said.

Simon did so, looking amused and extremely condescending. For the first time, I understood how Veronica often felt in his presence. I, too, had the urge to throw something at him. But I restrained myself, because there were Important Matters at stake.

"Do you want to be King of Montmaray?" I asked.

He leaned back in his chair, crossed one long leg over the other, and smiled. "Surely the question is not *Do I want to be King?* but *Who is entitled to be King?* I believe the honor usually goes to the late King's eldest son."

"It goes to the eldest *legitimate* male relative of the late King," I said.

"My mother says she was married to the late King. She certainly ought to know."

"So, she's of sound mind, then?" I said. "Quite able to face a

courtroom in order to answer charges of assault with a dangerous weapon?"

"I don't know that *that* would be a good idea," Simon said
gently. "For her or for the FitzOsborne family." It was as though
he were playing chess with a beginner and was—regretfully—
obliged to declare *Check* after half a dozen moves.

"So," I said, "deciding not to press charges against your
mother, paying for her to reside in an expensive clinic—is that
enough to buy your silence? I assume *you* want something, too."

"You ought to leave cynicism to your cousin, Sophia," he
said lightly. "It really doesn't suit you."

"You don't know me at *all*, Simon." I was proud of how steady
my voice was. "You've never even noticed me. But I've studied
you. And I know you won't be satisfied being plain old Simon
Chester, legal clerk, not anymore. I want to know what you'll
settle for—because you can be certain that Aunt Charlotte and
Veronica won't allow you to become King."

He was nettled but determined not to show it. "They may be
persuaded that I would do a better job of it—particularly as Toby
is still at school. And I believe Toby will support me in this."

"I don't think he will," I said. "Nor will the others, not when
I tell them that *you* were the sole reason the Germans came to
Montmaray."

"*What?*"

"Don't you recall?" I asked. "That dinner at Lord Bosworth's
where you pretended to be a diplomat? When you told the

German Ambassador all about the shipwrecks and the sunken treasures of Montmaray? And quoted Edward de Quincy Fitz-Osborne's 'Voyage of King Bartholomew'? The bit about the Holy Grail, surely you remember that?"

"What on earth does that have to do with anything?" he said, but he'd gone white around the mouth.

"They came in search of the Grail. That was the only reason they were there. And it all went horribly wrong, for them and for us, and now Montmaray is in ruins."

"You . . ." His fingers clenched on the armrests. "How could you *possibly* know what I did or said? Unless . . . Toby wrote to you, didn't he? About the dinner party."

"Yes," I said. "And Herr Rahn told me about his Grail quest. And Veronica had a copy of a monograph Herr Rahn had written, about the Nazi-funded organization that employed him. And I put it all together—"

Simon leapt to his feet. "Even if you're right! Even if they did . . . you can't possibly blame me! I had no *idea* what the consequences would be!"

"No, and neither did my uncle when he tried to defend the castle against intruders. Neither did your mother, I suppose, when she attacked Veronica."

Simon raised a shaking hand to his face. I watched, not as coolly as I would have liked. He was right. I couldn't blame him. Not for that, anyway. I didn't even blame poor Otto Rahn.

"Sophia, you have to believe me," Simon said at last. "I

never, ever wanted this to happen. Montmaray is my home, too. It broke my heart to see the castle in ruins that afternoon."

"I know," I said. "And you helped us escape." I considered for a moment. "Of course, we helped you escape, too."

"Yes," he said, sinking back in his chair. He was pale, but his voice was even. "But this doesn't change anything. Your aunt and cousin were never on my side. And Toby will support me— even when he knows about this. I'll tell him myself."

In fact, I'd mentioned it to Toby last year, but either he'd forgotten (understandably, given what was going on at the time) or he'd decided not to hold it against Simon. Still, I had to admire Simon's resilience. Perhaps he *would* have made a good king. But he had a lean and hungry look, as Caesar (or Shakespeare) would have said. Such men are dangerous.

"All right," I said. "And now we come to what I *really* wanted to discuss with you."

He gave me an incredulous look. "Good God, there's more?"

"I don't trust you with Toby," I said. "I think you're a *very* bad influence on him."

I folded my arms and waited for him to work it out. I held my breath, though, because I wasn't *entirely* certain I'd guessed correctly about their relationship. It took about thirty seconds. Then he gave a short, unamused laugh.

"You have been studying me," he said. "Because I know Toby didn't tell you *that*."

"I do make a habit of observing people," I said. "Not just

you. It's simply that there weren't many other people to observe at Montmaray."

He shoved himself to his feet and stalked over to the window, staring out at the lengthening shadows. I examined my fingernails, which looked as though they'd been attacked by a cheese grater. Of course, I *had* recently spent quite a bit of time hanging off cliffs by my fingertips. Thank heavens for gloves, as Aunt Charlotte would say.

"I can't believe I'm even discussing this with you," Simon said abruptly, glancing over his shoulder. "But I don't suppose you'd accept that Toby started it."

"I might," I said. (Actually, it seemed highly likely.) "But he's a schoolboy and you're not. Anyway, it's illegal."

"You'd be surprised how many gentlemen in the highest ranks of Society ignore that particular law," he said. His voice had taken on a jagged edge. "Of course, the rules are quite different for the upstart sons of housekeepers."

"I expect they are," I said. "But could you sit down? You're making my neck ache, trying to look at you from this angle."

He sighed, then returned to his chair. "All right, Sophia. What do you want?"

"Well," I said. "Firstly, I'm not sure that your job with Mr. Grenville is *quite* right for someone of your talents. I was thinking that, with your legal knowledge, you might consider becoming Montmaray's new Lord Chancellor. Or perhaps our Ambassador—but I think Lord Chancellor has a nicer ring to it, don't you?"

He nodded slowly, his dark gaze searching my face. "I think it does."

"And Aunt Charlotte's been complaining about how useless her secretary is, so perhaps you could do something about that," I went on. "I'm sure you'd have no trouble making yourself indispensable to her. You could live here or at Montmaray House in London—we'll be moving there ourselves for the Season." I paused. "Does all this sound sensible to you?"

"Very," he said. "Go on."

"That's about it," I admitted. "Did you have some other ideas?"

"Aren't you supposed to forbid me from ever being alone with your brother?"

"Would there be any point?"

"Not really," he said. "I could try to stay away from Toby, but I can't vouch for *his* actions. He's very stubborn. It seems to be a FitzOsborne trait."

We smiled at each other in a moment of perfect, mutual understanding.

"Anyway," I added, "it would make Toby sad, and we've already got enough to be sad about. But I do wish you'd encourage him to study a bit more, Simon. And try to persuade him that Oxford is a good idea. It'll make Aunt Charlotte happy."

"And we do want to keep the Princess Royal happy," he said.

"I think it would be wise," I agreed. "I hate it when people quarrel, don't you? Especially when they're all family." I stood and held out my hand for him to shake. He rose, captured my hand in his—and then lifted mine to his lips. I jerked my hand back, a couple of seconds too late, and gaped at him.

"It's been a most . . . *enlightening* conversation, Sophia," he said with his half smile. "Now, if you'll excuse me, I must have a word with Toby before dinner."

I ought to have accompanied Simon, but instead, I fell back into my chair the moment he left the room. I found I was trembling. It had been a nerve-racking and exhausting confrontation—but also rather thrilling. And the back of my hand still felt the press of Simon's lips, brief though it had been. Not that I gave any thought to *that* as I gathered myself together and went upstairs to dress for dinner.

"I didn't know you had it in you, Soph," said Toby as he, Veronica, and I sat in the Velvet Drawing Room later that evening—Simon having been summoned to the library for a "little chat" with Aunt Charlotte. "When did you become so *scheming?*"

"It's a fairly recent development," I said.

"Simon called you 'Machiavelli disguised as a debutante.'"

"Gosh," I said, not sure whether to feel flattered or insulted.

"What *are* you talking about?" asked Veronica, glancing up from her newspaper. It was the first time she'd dined downstairs since we'd arrived, and she looked extremely elegant in her black jersey dress, with her hair piled on top of her head—although I noticed she'd acquired a smudge of newspaper ink along one high cheekbone. I leaned over and wiped it off with my thumb.

"Sophie has persuaded Simon to drop his claim to the throne," Toby explained.

"Really?" said Veronica, astonished enough to let half of *The Times* flutter to the floor. "How did you manage *that?*"

"I simply reminded him of the importance of family loyalty," I said.

"And offered him the Lord Chancellorship instead," Toby added.

We braced ourselves for Veronica's explosion, but she merely stared at me a moment, then returned to *The Times*. Toby raised his eyebrows at me, and I shrugged.

"Well then, it's settled," Toby said. "We ought to have an official gathering of the new Court in Exile. Or is it called an Assembly? Veronica?"

"Privy Council," she said, not looking up from her newspaper.

"Right," said Toby. "Because, firstly, we need to decide what I'm called. I mean, do I have to be the next King John, or can I be King Tobias, or—"

"You can call yourself whatever you want," said Veronica, rustling her newspaper impatiently. "It's a monarchy, not a socialist democracy."

"'When Caesar says, "Do this," it is performed,'" I quoted.

"And look how *he* ended up—dead in the street with knives sticking out of his back," said Toby. "No thank you. *I* shall be the very model of a modern major monarch—"

Simon strode into the room and threw himself into an armchair.

"That was quick," said Toby.

"Wasn't much to discuss, really," Simon said. "I've always admired the Princess Royal. Remarkably *pragmatic* lady, when presented with the facts, and she was most appreciative of my offer to take over her appointment book. Her secretary seems to be making a terrible muddle of her charity luncheons and committee meetings and so forth."

"Excellent work," Toby said. "And you're just in time for the first Privy Council meeting of the reign of King Tobias of Montmaray. First item on the agenda—appointment of the Lord Chancellor. That's you, Simon."

"Thank you very much," said Simon, giving a little bow.

"Veronica, you can be Court Historian and Constitutional Expert," said Toby. Veronica rolled her eyes. "And, Sophie, what would you like to be?"

"Me?" I said.

"I know you're going to write all this down in that journal of yours," said Toby. "So you're already Court Scribe, but how about—"

"Ambassador?" suggested Simon blandly. "I happen to know she has excellent negotiating skills."

"Perfect," said Toby.

I gave Simon a narrow look. He smiled at me and leaned back in his chair.

"And Henry can be Commander of Defence," Toby went

on. "Next item! Finances. Simon? Any coins rolling around the bottom of the Privy Purse?"

"Well, it's complicated," said Simon. "I've barely started going through all the records in London, but my guess is that apart from the savings account, which has about sixty pounds in it, we're entirely dependent on the Princess Royal's private income."

"Good old Uncle Arthur," said Toby. "God rest his soul."

"Yes, but unfortunately, a large proportion of his fortune is derived from coal mining. If a Labour government got in again and nationalized the mines—"

"They'd pay compensation," said Veronica. "Besides, there's property as well. Most of the village of Milford, a hunting lodge in Scotland, warehouses and factories in Manchester and London. Plenty of rent coming in from them."

"*Naturally*, I'm aware of the Princess Royal's extensive property holdings," said Simon, scowling at Veronica. "I'm simply explaining that the Kingdom of Montmaray is essentially broke, and that if the Princess Royal were to, heaven forbid, pass away suddenly, her money wouldn't necessarily go to Toby. She could leave it all to the Cats Protection League if she so desired."

"Why would she do that?" asked Toby. "She doesn't even like cats. She likes *me*."

"She'd like you a damned sight more if you stopped getting expelled from schools," said Simon.

"It was only *one* school," said Toby. "Stop exaggerating."

"I'm merely pointing out," said Simon with studied patience, "that you ought to be as obliging as possible these next few months while I try to negotiate a permanent allowance for you and the girls. Do a bit of work for the entrance examinations, go up to Oxford, try not to get sent down in your first year—"

"Then marry an aristocratic young lady from a rich family and produce a couple of heirs," finished Veronica.

Toby pulled a horrified face and turned to me. "Soph, don't you *dare* fall in love with anyone with an income of less than a hundred thousand a year. And make sure you have sons, not daughters. Dozens of them, if you can manage it." He turned back to Simon. "Also, how am I supposed to pass exams when I won't be back at school for months?"

"*Months?*" said Simon. "Don't you mean 'a week or two'? Anyway, I'm going up to London in a few days, so I'll talk to your House Master and bring all your books back. Veronica can tutor you in Latin and History, Sophia can help with English Literature, then you just need to practice your music. Now, what's next on your agenda?"

"Simon, you are No Fun," Toby declared. "Hmm, what *is* next? Oh—Simon, could you find Alice and the other villagers, let them know what's happened, and give them our new address? And we really must organize honors for all the nice people who saved our lives. Ant, the Basque captain, and Colonel Stanley-Ross. We'll need to borrow Aunt Charlotte's Order of the Sea Monster—"

"Order of Benedict," Veronica corrected.

"—to have a few new ones made up. It's a sort of round silver thing with a blue sash, isn't it? We should probably have an official ceremony, but that might be difficult if the Captain's at sea. Can you track him down? His name's Captain Zuleta. Veronica, what's his first name?"

Simon was making a note of this in his little black memorandum book when one of the footmen came in and said that Aunt Charlotte needed Simon's help with some correspondence.

"Poor Simon," said Toby, watching him stride back down the corridor. "He'll never have a moment's rest now."

"Poor *Simon*!" repeated Veronica scornfully, picking up her newspaper. "I wouldn't waste any pity on him. He's *exactly* where he wants to be."

The next day, a car from the clinic in Poole came to collect Rebecca and Simon. It was thought Rebecca's departure might be more easily accomplished if the rest of us were out of the way. Lady Astley's invitation to luncheon had therefore been most welcome, although I still felt rather nervous about it.

"Who's going to be there?" I asked Toby as Parker shut my door and went round to the front of the car. "You have to tell me their proper titles and what we're supposed to call them. I always get barons and baronets mixed up."

Henry waved mournfully from the front door. Her new governess was due to arrive any moment, so Aunt Charlotte had insisted Henry stay behind with her. We all waved back.

"It's just the Stanley-Rosses and Ant, as far as I know," said Toby. "And Julia's father is Lord Astley—a baron, *not* a baronet."

"But what's the difference?"

"It's quite simple," said Veronica. "English peers are, from most important to least: dukes, marquesses, earls, viscounts, and barons. Then there are baronets, but they can't sit in the House of Lords, and knights, who can't pass on their title to their eldest sons."

"It's not simple at all," I said. "Why is he Lord Astley if his children are called Stanley-Ross?"

"The title's Astley, his family name is Stanley-Ross," said Toby. "Don't worry about it. *He* blusters a bit, but Lady Astley is awfully sweet, she'll adore you. As for the others—well, David's the eldest and he's married to the niece of Lady Bosworth. I don't know if he'll be around, though. Penelope, his wife, prefers London. There's a second son, Charles, but I've only met him once. He's the black sheep, off gold-digging in Ontario or Otago or somewhere. Then there's Julia, of course, and Ant—I mean, *Lord Whittingham.*"

"Only son of an earl, so he gets to use the courtesy title of Viscount," put in Veronica.

"And then Rupert's the youngest," said Toby. "Oh, I haven't seen him for *months.* I can't wait for you all to meet him!"

"Isn't he back at school now?" I asked. "Or does he still have the flu?"

"He's much better," said Toby. "But he had rheumatic fever when he was a baby and nearly died, so his mother tends to fuss a bit. Not that he's *all* that keen to return to school."

"Sounds like someone I know," said Veronica.

"What are you talking about?" said Toby indignantly. "I'm the *walking wounded*! Worse, the *limping* wounded. There's no way I could manage all those stairs at school. Besides, you haven't any idea how nasty and rough and *brutish* schoolboys can be. What if someone pushed me over in a dim, rarely used corridor, and I lay there like a tortoise on its back, neglected, forgotten, becoming weaker and weaker, until years later, my skeleton was discovered, one leg still encased in plaster—"

Veronica laughed, for what seemed like the first time in weeks, and Toby looked very pleased.

"But tell us more about Rupert," I said. "Does he really hate school? I thought you said he was clever."

"Oh, he is. He's always reading. But he's even worse than me at Games. And it doesn't help that both his brothers were in Pop—that's the Eton Society—and David was Captain of the Eleven and scored a century against Harrow. Still, only another six months and we're both free."

"Which reminds me," said Veronica. "When are the Oxford entrance examinations?"

"Around Easter, I think. Why? Are you putting your name down for them?"

"Yes, I'm sure Aunt Charlotte would be delighted to fund *my* university education," said Veronica sardonically. "I'm talking about *you*. Have you even picked up a book in the past week?"

"I *have* had other matters on my mind, you know!"

I tuned out their squabble, because the view was so much

more interesting. My only previous car trip had been at night. Now I gazed my fill, at farmland divided into neat shapes by hedges and stone walls, at velvety hills with the white chalk beneath showing through in patches, at clumps of dark old woodland. We motored past Salisbury, catching a tantalizing glimpse of the cathedral spire, and Toby promised he'd take us there once he could walk around properly.

"Do we go past Stonehenge on our way?" I asked.

Toby shook his head. "No, but it's not too far from here. We could visit it on the way back if there's time."

"I *do* feel sorry for Henry, missing all this," I said with a sigh, settling back against the leather seat.

"I feel sorrier for the new governess," said Toby. "I wonder how long she'll last."

We discussed this as we drove along beside a slate-green river. I thought at least six months, as Henry's behavior seemed so much improved lately. Toby said three weeks. Veronica felt it depended on the lady's employment history.

"If, for instance, she's worked in a prison or a zoo, she might have developed the appropriate skills and become a bit hardier," Veronica pointed out.

We turned off the main road, and Toby directed our attention to a large pile of gray stone with some chimneys poking out the top.

"Astley Manor," he announced, although it took another couple of miles of winding lane before we reached the gates.

"Is it really Elizabethan?" I asked, leaning forward.

"Well, the original part is," said Toby. "There's a Georgian wing and some hideous Victorian bits pretending to be medieval. Lady Astley wants to modernize the bathrooms and the kitchen, but I doubt they'll ever get round to it. With three sons to put through Eton and Oxford, it takes all their spare money just keeping the roof tiles on."

The car rolled to a stop near a doorway set into a thick stone wall. Shreds of bronze-colored ivy dangled from the lintel, where someone had attempted to cut the vines back. Further up, they grew unhindered, twining round a weathered coat of arms, half obscuring the diamond-paned windows, and seemingly holding one battered chimney in place. A couple of shabby evergreens reclined against the wall, and thistles popped their fuzzy heads out of the cracks in the path. As we climbed from the car, the door of the house was flung open and Julia rushed out, followed by a confusion of people.

"My dears!" Julia cried. "Have you had the most *dreadful* trip? That horrid, winding road—but, Sophie, what an adorable hat! And, Veronica, how *are* you? Ant told me—oh, Toby, you poor darling, do watch out for that paving stone, you *know* the place is falling to bits. Ant, take Veronica's arm, no, the other one. *Rupert!* Where is that—oh, there you are. Put that creature down at once, and come and meet the girls."

A thin boy with something brown and fluffy draped across his left arm hurried over. "Sorry," he panted. "I was just putting her— How do you do?"

He held out his right hand, which I shook. The brown thing

turned out to be the world's floppiest rabbit, who blinked at me, then went back to sleep.

"Is she all right?" I asked, looking at the neat bandage tied around her front paw.

"Oh, yes. It's just that she jumped off the sofa yesterday, knocked over a glass of sherry, and stepped on the—"

"Drunk *again*, I suppose," said Toby, limping over. He gave his friend a one-armed hug. "I've never known a rabbit to spend so much time getting blotto. Now, aren't you going to tell me how haggard and washed-out I look?"

"You look exactly the same as ever," said Rupert with a smile. "Except for a tiny bit of plaster on your leg. Stop fishing for compliments."

"Rupert only cares about injuries if they happen to poor dumb beasts," explained Toby.

"But why are we standing round out *here?*" wailed Julia. We instantly found ourselves in a long hall, maids divesting us of coats and gloves under the stern gaze of some Stanley-Ross ancestors rendered in dark, dusty-looking oils. Then the butler whisked us down a corridor into a cozy wood-paneled drawing room, where Lady Astley was waiting. Without rising from her seat or even saying very much, she gave the distinct impression she'd been looking forward to our visit for weeks. She was an older, languid version of Julia—warmhearted and very pretty, but lacking Julia's boundless energy. Julia seemed to have inherited that from her father, who stomped into the room in his tweeds, barking orders at the servants, organizing us into our seats, summoning up a footstool for Toby, marching over to poke at the roaring fire, then wheeling round to hurl questions at me.

I'd never before had to converse with so many new people at once. Faced with Lady Astley's amiable murmurs, Lord Astley's good-natured but brusque enquiries, and Julia's usual barrage of talk, I found myself sinking deeper and deeper into my armchair, my tongue tying itself in knots. On one side of me, Anthony was telling Veronica about his aeroplane's latest mechanical mishap; on the other, Toby and Rupert were deep in an equally unintelligible conversation about mutual friends and enemies at Eton. I could only be thankful that David and his wife were still in London.

After about twenty minutes of this, Julia jumped up and offered a tour of the house before luncheon. Lord Astley accompanied us as far as the library, where he was highly gratified by Veronica's interest in his diplomat grandfather's bound memoirs. Julia and I left them there and continued upwards, through a maze of rooms and corridors.

"It's all so poky and jumbled," apologized Julia, shoving open a door to reveal a bedroom that had been divided down the middle with a plywood wall, leaving a half window in each side.

"Oh, no," I said sincerely. "I think it's wonderful." I didn't say it reminded me of home, even though it did, because I was trying not to think too much about Montmaray.

"You *are* sweet," she said, beaming. "We adore it, of course, but it's hopelessly impractical, falling down round our ears. And compared to Milford Park—well! Everything's so beautifully designed there, *such* a sense of space and light, but not so large that it's impossible to run. Imagine, your aunt's dear old husband buying that entire estate for her as a wedding present! And then all the renovations and landscaping . . . Goodness, I wish *our* uncle had had the sense to buy up a lot of coal mines fifty years ago—but don't tell Ant I said that, he's awfully thingy about the poor old coal miners. Anyway, *this* was David and Charlie's room before they went off to school, but they kept trying to murder each other, so it was thought best to divide the room in two. David took a suite over in the East Wing after he got married, and now his wife wants to put in new windows and a glass bathtub, and she's driving Daddy completely mad. Here we are, *this* is mine."

We entered a narrow room into which had been squashed a four-poster bed, several wardrobes, and an immense glass-topped dressing table. "I have the *greatest* favor to ask," Julia said, yanking open a drawer. "Would you be an absolute angel and take some of these old things away with you? They'll fit *you*, with your tiny waist—oh, try this frock on. It has a beaded wrap, here it is . . ."

And Julia proceeded to off-load what seemed like half her wardrobe on me. I kept protesting, but she wouldn't listen. Instead, she rang for her maid, who pinned up some skirts for me and promised to have them hemmed before we left.

"Oh, Julia, I can't possibly—"

"But they're *ancient*, darling, and they don't fit me and I can't exactly pass them on to Rupert, can I? Besides, when I think of how it must have *been* for you, leaving all your things behind . . ." Her eyes welled. I didn't point out that the clothes I'd left behind had hardly been worth saving. "Well, thank *heavens* you're all safe now," Julia concluded with a sniff. "I just wish I had something that could fit Veronica, but she's so tall, isn't she?" Julia dropped her voice. "And of course, she doesn't love clothes and things as *we* do."

I had to admit this was true. Then the gong rang for luncheon, and we went downstairs. The food was wonderful. There was roast pork with sage-and-onion stuffing and applesauce and julienned vegetables, then rhubarb tart with custard, then biscuits and cheese. Lord Astley and Anthony discussed politics with Veronica, the men tactfully avoiding any mention of Germany. Lady Astley, Julia, and Toby gossiped about a lot of people I'd never heard of. Rupert joined in occasionally but was mostly silent. At one stage, I saw him lean down to check on his rabbit, who was laid out underneath his chair. It was difficult to detect anything of Julia in him; it made me wonder what his brothers were like. He had fair, straight hair that slanted across his forehead, big hazel eyes, and a sprinkling of freckles across his nose. He looked several years younger than Toby, although I knew he was actually five months older. I had a better chance to study him after luncheon, when Toby urged him to show me the garden (Julia having been called to the telephone and Veronica drawn irresistibly towards the library, as though it were a giant magnet and she were made of iron filings).

Being the middle of winter, the rose garden consisted of

spiky twigs sticking out of the ground, the daffodil beds were mounds of mud, and the herb garden was mostly wooden signs indicating where things might appear in three months' time. But there was a nice, long hothouse, with a fat-bellied stove at each end keeping the trays of seedlings and potted flowers warm. Next to the hothouse was a fishpond, and beyond that were the stables. As there wasn't much to say about any of this, Rupert and I crunched along the path in near silence, smiling shyly whenever we happened to catch the other's eye. Unfortunately, my tongue had knotted up again. I couldn't think of anything he might be interested in discussing; he probably felt the same about me. It was with a slight note of desperation that he asked if I'd like to see the birds.

"Oh! You mean your homing pigeons?" I asked.

"And yours. Well, Toby's. I've been looking after them for him."

He led me up a wooden staircase at the back of the stables, and we emerged into a large, light-filled loft. Soft cooing noises came from all around—from the rafters, from shallow boxes nailed to the walls, and from Rupert's shoulder, where a white creature with feathery legs and a fanned tail had just landed.

"Is that a *pigeon?*" I asked, wide-eyed.

"A fancy one, yes," he said, placing the bird beside a bowl of grain on a long wooden table. The bird pecked at a corn kernel disdainfully, then waddled off. "And a very spoilt one, as you can see. One of Julia's young men gave it to her. But most of the birds here are ordinary homing pigeons."

"Hardly *ordinary*," I said. "Flying for hundreds of miles in a single day! How many do you have?"

"Thirty-nine," he said, not even having to think about it. "But there are at least a dozen pairs that I'm hoping will nest this spring. Each hen usually lays two eggs, so—"

He stopped abruptly and blushed, perhaps remembering that such subjects weren't meant to be discussed in mixed company. I quickly looked around for another topic.

"Goodness, it's all so . . . so well organized," I said, which was quite true. Each metal feed-bin was neatly labeled, the floor was swept clean, the water in each bowl was clear. It smelled pleasantly of wheat and straw and feathers.

"We have a very good pigeon man," said Rupert, still slightly pink. "He does most of it, especially when I'm at school." Walking over to a nearby box, he peered inside, then lifted out a bird. "Here's one of Toby's. The first one to make it back with your message, actually. Hold out your hands."

I did so, and a soft, warm weight was lowered into them. A gray pigeon, vaguely familiar-looking, gazed up at me. I stared back, a heavy feeling growing in my chest.

"She's four years old, one of my very first chicks. I remember training her."

"How . . ." I cleared my throat and started again. "How can you tell one bird from another?"

"That little metal band on her leg. And she remembered exactly which box was hers, she headed straight to it. After I'd fed her, of course."

"She must have been so hungry," I said. "And, and so *tired*, flying all that way—"

Then I burst into tears.

Poor Rupert. When he'd agreed to show me round the garden, he had no idea he'd be forced to deal with *this*. The pigeon fluffed out her feathers, wondering why it had suddenly started raining inside, and Rupert stepped forward to rescue the unfortunate bird. Then he pulled a handkerchief from his pocket and held it out to me.

"I'm *so* sorry," he said, looking almost as distressed as I felt. "I'm such a *clod* . . . Won't you sit down?" He led me over to a bench and sat beside me as I sobbed and sobbed. It was the sort of crying that I knew from experience wouldn't stop just because I wanted it to—in fact, trying to control it only made it worse. After about five minutes, which felt like five hours, I ran out of tears and oxygen.

"Sorry," I gasped.

"No, it's *my* fault," he said. "I was so thoughtless, reminding you of—"

"Montmaray," I said. I blew my nose into his handkerchief.

"Mummy told me not to mention it," he said miserably. "That it would be too awful for you, and then I went and—"

I took an unsteady breath. "Although it *is* supposed to make one feel better, having a good cry," I said.

"*Do* you feel better?" he asked.

"Not just at the moment, no," I admitted. "I feel much worse."

"As though you'd stuffed a whole lot of things into a

cupboard, far too many to fit, and you were worried the door would burst open? And then it *did*, at the worst possible moment, and everything fell out on the floor and smashed?"

"Well . . . yes," I said, staring at him.

And indeed, I *did* feel empty inside, and it *did* seem that my memories of Montmaray had been shattered beyond repair, that even my oldest, happiest recollections were tainted by the way things had ended. But I was surprised that a near stranger, a *boy* at that, could understand this so well.

"How does it burst out for you?" I asked, curious. "Toby never cries anymore. At least—he did a bit when he broke his leg, but he was barely conscious at the time."

Rupert looked down at his hands. "Well, I haven't had anything *nearly* as dreadful as what you've had to deal with, of course. Just . . . well, just being homesick and hating school. But I *do* cry. I try to save it up for when no one's around, though. It's difficult at school. Sometimes one has to save it up for *weeks*, and by then, it's stopped being sadness and become a sort of . . . irritation with everything and everyone."

"I can't imagine *you* stomping about, kicking and swearing at people," I said with a watery smile.

"No, it's more snapping at them—usually at friends because they're the closest and most convenient," he said. "Which makes one feel even worse. I think it would be easier to be a girl, to be *expected* to cry."

"Veronica doesn't."

"What, *never*?"

"Never. Not even when she was very little."

"Gosh, Julia does it about once a day," he said. "She doesn't even have to be sad. She cried when Ant gave her her Christmas present, and then when our grandmother said Julia could borrow her tiara for the wedding . . ."

We discussed whether crying was an involuntary reflex, like sneezing, and whether animals cried. The conversation was so interesting that I almost forgot to be upset. But I kept needing to blow my nose, and a glance out the window revealed the afternoon light had suddenly grown much dimmer. Rupert jumped up and showed me the sink, and I washed my face and dried it on my sleeve. It didn't do much good—I knew my eyes would stay red and puffy for hours. We went back into the house, where everyone stared, then decided the most courteous thing to do would be to ignore my woebegone countenance. Lord Astley had been called away to his study to speak with a tenant, so the rest of us sat around the drawing room for a while, Julia and Toby reading bits of *Tatler* and *Country Life* out loud to each other in silly voices and Rupert dabbing ointment on his rabbit's paw where she'd gnawed off her bandage. Then Parker brought the car to the front, and we went outside, and Lady Astley kissed us all goodbye in a very motherly way, which nearly made me start crying again. In the car, Toby put his arm round my shoulders, and Veronica took my hand and squeezed it. Nobody said anything. I was so exhausted, I slept most of the way back.

I mean, most of the way *home*. I have to start thinking of it as that.

22nd January 1937

Surprisingly, I have felt better since my outburst—not right away, because when I got back to Milford, my primary emotion was severe embarrassment over what the Stanley-Rosses must have thought of me. But that night, for the first time since I'd arrived, I didn't dream—or I didn't recall what I'd dreamt, which I took to be a good sign, since the ones I did remember were so horrid. I told Veronica this when I went in to see her before breakfast. I've got into the habit of sitting on (or in, if it's especially cold) her bed while she goes through the process of waking up, which seems to take her about ten times as long as it did at Montmaray.

"So," I concluded, "I've decided it's better to *talk* about things. Otherwise it just bursts out some other way, in nightmares or fits of weeping."

"You sound like that Freud-obsessed tutor we used to have," Veronica said, her eyes still closed.

"Oh, yes—what was his name? Francis? Fergus? Something

like that. But, Veronica, that reminds me! Have you written to Daniel Bloom yet?"

"No."

"But what if he's still sending letters to Montmaray and they're being Returned to Sender! He'd be so worried!" Another thought occurred to me. "Do you think it was in the newspapers? The bombing, I mean. The British government knows we're here, because that policeman came round just after we arrived and told Aunt Charlotte we needed registration cards. Not that she paid the slightest bit of attention to him. But do you think people know *why* we're here?"

Veronica finally opened her eyes, but only to glare at me.

"I suppose Daniel might have heard about it, anyway," I went on, not allowing the glare to deter me. "Doesn't he work as a journalist now?"

"Not that sort of journalist," she mumbled, closing her eyes again.

"What sort? Veronica, don't go back to sleep!"

"He writes for some little weekly in the East End," she said, and turned over on her side.

"Perhaps we can see him when we go to London," I said. "Did you know it's a quarter to eight? Are you getting up today?"

"Is there any point?"

"*Yes*. We get to see the new governess in action! And Henry's pony arrives this morning."

Veronica groaned.

"Aunt Charlotte wants *us* to have riding lessons, too," I said.

"She says it's an essential part of a young lady's education, that one can't even *begin* to take part in Society if one can't ride. That's how most meet their future husbands, apparently—at a hunt or the races or a polo match. Or at dinner parties, where everyone *talks* about hunts and races and polo matches."

"All the more reason not to learn to ride, then," she said.

"They are awfully big, aren't they?" I said, biting my bottom lip. "Horses, I mean. It's such a long way down if one falls off."

"Yes, I expect people die of it all the time."

"You're not being helpful," I told her. "Sit up, and I'll brush your hair while you finish waking up."

She submitted to this, and then to me twisting the thick, dark waves into a knot at her nape. It was as I was pinning this in place that I returned to my original topic, the one that had been battering against the sides of my head for days, even though I'd made a very good attempt at ignoring it for a while.

"What are we going to *do*? I mean, about Montmaray, about the Germans."

"Nothing," she said.

"*Nothing?*"

But she'd shrugged into her dressing gown and was stalking off to the bathroom. Unfortunately, having a policy of talking about things doesn't mean one's conversational partners will actually *answer*, or even listen properly. I also happen to know that Veronica shoved her *Brief History of Montmaray* parcel at the very bottom of her wardrobe. Unopened.

Another person who is not very interested in discussing

Montmaray's invasion is Aunt Charlotte, who seems to assume "the authorities" will deal with it. But *what* authorities? I daren't ask. Aunt Charlotte regards the whole subject as entirely unsuitable for young ladies. I also suspect she simply doesn't *care* as much as we do. She hasn't been back to Montmaray since my grandfather's funeral in 1917, before I was even born, and she seems thoroughly entrenched in English Society now. Perhaps Montmaray is one of those childhood things she has put aside, along with hopscotch and teddy bears and Beatrix Potter.

I suppose that when she arrived here in England as a young bride, torn from her home and unable to do a thing about it, she just got on with it—threw herself into Society life, and then, after her husband died and there was no longer any possibility of children, channeled her relentless energies into managing her estate and building up her stable of racing horses and bossing around people on her charity committees. She had a responsibility to her husband, to her new country, not to look back. It was what her parents would have expected of her. It was the Sensible Thing to Do.

My aunt is extremely Sensible.

Anyway. Henry came down to breakfast that morning dressed in her new riding jacket and jodhpurs, trailed by her governess, Miss Thompson. I've never seen anyone wear so much pink at once; she'd even pinned a pink silk rose to her lapel, and every time Toby glanced in her general direction, her whole head blushed to match. Aunt Charlotte had apparently chosen the most girlish governess available, in the hope that all the pinkness would rub off on Henry.

"Did I say she'd last three weeks?" Toby muttered. "I meant three *days*."

To make up for this, I gave her an especially encouraging smile, but I don't think she noticed—she was too busy being terrified of Aunt Charlotte.

Simon wasn't at breakfast, but he joined Veronica, Toby, and me in the library before luncheon. While Veronica and Toby grappled with Gibbon's *History of the Decline and Fall of the Roman Empire*, Simon sat beside me on the window seat and told me all about Rebecca's introduction to the clinic, which hadn't been entirely smooth.

"Still, the therapists are very experienced," he said, a little line appearing between his brows. "And she has a lovely bedroom, with a view of the sea. I think that will help, don't you?"

Just as I succeed in hardening my heart towards Simon, he reveals something of himself that makes me adore him. To care so deeply about Rebecca—a *most* unlovable person—is surely the mark of a kind soul, even if Simon does his best to disguise it. I was agreeing that sea views were extremely soothing when Henry burst into the room.

"What are you all doing in here? *Talking*, I suppose!"

"How was your first riding lesson?" Toby asked.

"Well! You won't *believe* it!" exclaimed Henry. "I had to put both my legs on *one side*, in this silly girls' saddle! I thought it would be like pictures of cowboys, a leg on either side of the horse. How else is one supposed to stay on? But Aunt Charlotte says that only boys get to ride like that! It's the stupidest thing! It ought to be the other way round. It's boys who have dangling bits between their legs—*they* ought to be the ones riding sidesaddle!"

"Quite right," said Toby. "Especially if they have really *large* bits. The first time I got off a horse, I couldn't walk properly for hours afterwards."

Simon was suddenly overcome by a severe coughing fit and had to leave the room in search of a glass of water.

"*Please* tell me you didn't say that in front of Aunt Charlotte," I begged Henry.

"Why?" she asked.

"Because it isn't very ladylike," said Veronica, straightening her face. "Nor gentlemanly. Come here, you've got mud all over you."

"I fell off twice," said Henry proudly as Veronica helped her out of her filthy riding jacket. "That was mostly the saddle's fault, though. I do love my pony. He's called Lightning. Isn't that a good name? And the groom is called Ericson, and he's going to see if he can find a proper saddle for me tomorrow."

"Where's Miss Thompson?" I asked.

"Lying down in her room," said Henry. "She got dizzy when I fell off the first time. You'd think it was *her* who'd fallen on her head. Then she had a screaming fit because Carlos jumped up on her. He only wanted to see what was on her hat, and do you know what it was? Pink rabbit fur! No wonder he was confused."

"Did I say three days?" Toby murmured to me. "I meant three *hours*."

"Anyway," said Henry, "have you come up with a plan yet? For getting Montmaray back from the Nasties?"

"Nazis," I corrected.

Veronica got up and walked out.

"Why does she always do that?" said Henry, her face falling. "Whenever anyone mentions Montmaray—"

"Never mind, Horrid Hen," said Toby quickly. "Because we need her out of the room while we figure out what to do for her birthday."

"Aunt Charlotte's giving her a three-strand pearl necklace," said Henry. "I overheard her talking to Barnes about it."

"You shouldn't have been eavesdropping," I told her.

"It's practice for when I become a private detective," said Henry. "Toby, can I borrow a shilling? I know what I'm getting her, but it's a secret."

"What are *we* getting her?" I asked Toby as he handed over a coin. "Books, I suppose."

"Probably," he said. "But I do have one surprise up my sleeve—I got Simon to look up the address of her Communist paramour."

"Don't call Daniel *that*," I said crossly. I was starting to regret ever having told Toby about Daniel. "And we don't even know if he *is* a Communist."

"Well, apparently he runs a newspaper distributed by the International Alliance for the Promotion of Socialist Beliefs, so I doubt he'll be campaigning for the Conservatives at the next election. You'd better write to him—he doesn't know me."

After further debate about Veronica's birthday present, Toby and I decided on a subscription to *The Manchester Guardian*, because she'd complained that *The Times* was biased and kept spelling the names of Spanish towns incorrectly. However, given the current state of the world, I hardly think a newspaper will cheer her up. And I *so* want her to feel better—if not actually happy, then at least as though there's a point to getting out of bed in the morning. I do think I understand a *little* of how she must feel. Montmaray would have ceased to function if Veronica had stayed in bed all day, but here there's Aunt Charlotte to make all the decisions, and a small army of servants to take care of the house and grounds. To feel superfluous, on top of everything else . . .

For now I wonder if Veronica actually blames *herself* for what happened to Montmaray. It would explain her refusing even to talk about it. She's so used to being responsible for everything, perhaps she thinks she could have, should have, done something differently, something that would have changed how it all turned out. Which is absurd, of course. The Germans were *always* going to come up to the castle, regardless of what she said or did; her father was bound to go berserk when he discovered them; and whether we'd told the truth about Hans Brandt's death or not, Gebhardt would still have been determined to make us pay for it . . .

How depressing, the image of the greatest tragedy of one's

life as a series of toppling dominoes, the whole thing started off by the careless nudge of an elbow, and not even one's *own* elbow. It almost makes me want to climb into bed and pull the covers up over *my* head, too. I shouldn't be surprised that Veronica can barely muster the energy to have a decent argument with Simon nowadays.

It might be easier for Veronica if she enjoyed some of the activities *I* use as distractions—experimenting with new hairstyles, for instance, or talking Barnes into letting me try on all Aunt Charlotte's jewelry. But feminine frippery merely serves to remind Veronica that here her value lies in her looks, not her brain (that, indeed, her brain will be a serious liability when it comes to husband-hunting, unless she's clever enough to disguise how clever she is). But fortunately, Toby has talked Parker into giving Veronica driving lessons. So, between that and Veronica trying to prepare Toby for his exams, she should be too busy to succumb to despair—I *hope*.

I also wrote to Daniel explaining our new circumstances and reminding him that Veronica's birthday is on Saturday, adding a subtle hint that he send something cheering, or at least intriguing enough to be a distraction. I then spent some time puzzling over the conundrum of Rupert's linen handkerchief, now washed and ironed (although not by me). In books, weeping females are often lent handkerchiefs by gallant gentlemen, but hardly ever does the reader find out what happens to the handkerchief afterwards (unless it sparks off some catastrophe, as with poor Desdemona). What's the correct etiquette for such an occasion? Should I post it back to Rupert with a letter of thanks? Or is he desperately trying to forget all about the incident, and me? He was so easy to talk to, once we got started, but the whole thing's really quite embarrassing . . . I suppose I should just give it to Toby and ask *him* to return it, but I'll need to brace myself for the teasing that will probably result. In any case, subsequent events pushed such trivial matters as handkerchiefs from my mind.

Firstly, Miss Thompson bolted (on the same early-morning London train as Simon, it turned out). Her resignation letter, brought in at breakfast by a footman, cited a mother who'd suddenly developed a grave illness. While Miss Thompson's departure came as no great surprise, it did make Aunt Charlotte very cross, because it meant she had to find another governess. The situation, already tense, was not improved when Henry started shrieking at Toby, who'd just put a rasher of bacon on her plate.

"But it comes from pigs!" she cried. "*Dead* pigs! Pigs who've been *killed*!"

"Better than coming from pigs that *haven't* been killed," he said. "And what about the ham you've eaten every Christmas for the past ten years?"

"But I hadn't *met* any pigs then!" she wailed. "I didn't know they had personalities, like dogs! You wouldn't eat *Carlos*, would you?"

Toby sighed. "I suppose sheep and cows have personalities, too?" he said, peering inside the remaining silver dishes. "What about chickens?"

"Spartacus had a personality," she sniffed, recalling our ferocious rooster at Montmaray. "Remember how he teased the cats? Oh, poor, poor Spartacus—do you think he was squashed by the bombs?"

Aunt Charlotte was becoming more and more annoyed, and Veronica looked as though she were about to throw down her newspaper and do a bolt of her own, so I hurried Henry into her seat and handed her my piece of toast.

"There's scrambled eggs," mused Toby, still at the sideboard. "They're not actually chickens. *Potential* chickens, perhaps . . ."

After some thought, Henry decided fish didn't have personalities unless they were extremely large, like Moby Dick, so she had half of Toby's kippers. Aunt Charlotte, muttering under her breath, stomped away to telephone the agency about a new governess, and Toby and Veronica returned to the declining Roman Empire. I went off to the music room, where I was trying to teach myself to waltz with the aid of Aunt Charlotte's gramophone and a booklet Julia had lent me. Unfortunately, transforming little black shoe-shapes and curly arrows on a page into actual movement was proving difficult. I was deep in a dizzy muddle when the footman came in to announce I was wanted on the telephone.

"Me?" I gasped, dropping the tasseled bolster I'd been using as a dance partner.

"Mr. Simon Chester expressly asked for Your Highness," he said.

I followed him to the little room under the stairs where the telephone was kept and gingerly picked up the speaking part.

"Hello?" I shouted, first in one end, then the other.

"Oh, there you are," said Simon, sounding as though he were in the next room instead of all the way up in London. "Sophia, the clinic called—I'm afraid Mother's not at all settled, so could you please go over and sort it out? Parker can drive you—"

"What?" I said, aghast. "Simon, how would I be any help? Your mother hates me!"

"No, no, it's Veronica she can't stand. And Toby's supposed to be studying, and I'm stuck here, meant to be meeting the bank manager at noon . . . But you're much the best person for the job, anyway. The matron's expecting you, and there's a therapist wanting a chat, too."

"But I don't know anything about—"

"The address is in the green book, on the Chippendale table in the library—"

"Simon! Are you listening?"

"—and could you please remind your aunt about that dinner invitation from Lady Bosworth?"

"But—" I started again.

"Pip, pip, pip!" said the telephone.

"Sorry, my three minutes are up," said Simon. "Must go— thanks awfully, Sophia. See you in a few days." And he was gone, leaving me spluttering into the silence.

I couldn't see any way out of it. What if they sent Rebecca back? If it were possible to be expelled from a mental asylum for bad behavior, Rebecca could probably manage it. So I ran downstairs to find Parker, quite forgetting that we were supposed to ring the bell to summon a footman if we needed anything. Bursting into the kitchen, I startled half a dozen maids sitting at the table with their midmorning mugs of tea. They all jumped to their feet and started curtseying.

"Oh, I'm so sorry!" I blurted. "I was just looking for—"

"Quick, fetch Mr. Harkness!" hissed the cook at the tiniest maid, who shot off through a doorway.

"But I only wanted—"

"Mr. Harkness will be here presently, Your Highness," said the cook, crossing her hefty arms across the bib of her apron and not quite looking me in the eye. "Ethel, stop that racket! Show some respect!" A maid, abashed, put down the bowl of eggs she'd been beating. Meanwhile, I stared helplessly around the room at all the pale faces frozen into deferential masks. At Montmaray, we'd practically *lived* in the kitchen. It had been the warmest, most welcoming place in the castle. But in *this* kitchen, I was a fearsome stranger. Fortunately, the butler arrived almost at once, straightening his cuffs.

"May I assist, Your Highness?" he intoned.

I stammered out what I'd wanted, and the bootboy was sent off to find the chauffeur. And I retreated upstairs, my face burning, having learned an unpleasant lesson about Milford Park protocol.

Eventually, Parker sent a message back that he would drive me to the clinic after luncheon. Veronica said she'd come, too, to watch him change gears and deal with traffic. "Don't worry, I won't go in," she assured me. "I'll wait outside. And we can visit

Shaftesbury on the way! King Canute died there!" It was the most enthusiastic I'd seen her since we'd arrived—there's nothing quite like long-dead kings to cheer up Veronica.

Shaftesbury turned out to be a little town on a steep green hill, its rows of historic houses looking as though they might tumble down into Blackmore Vale. It was all very pretty and Veronica had a lot of interesting things to say about its Anglo-Saxon founders, but I was too anxious to listen attentively. Rebecca had nearly *killed* Veronica last week, and the woman wasn't all that fond of me, despite what Simon had said. Of course, there were unlikely to be axes lying around a clinic, but still . . . The car plunged on towards the coast, and all too soon, the sea appeared, a gray-blue blanket scrunched up on the sandy seafront. It wasn't the same sea as the one I'd known, though—it was too mild-mannered. It didn't even *smell* right.

The clinic was a friendly-looking white building, the front path edged with seashells, a bird feeder dangling from the bare branches of a nearby tree. Inside, however, were the unmistakable signs of an institution—a notice board reminding residents about fire drills, a reception desk littered with ringing telephones, and a lot of women marching about in crisp white uniforms (it was some comfort to think of all those highly trained professionals standing guard between Rebecca and me). It turned out Simon had given them my full royal title, which got me an immediate audience with the matron but also meant lots of heads popping out of doorways to stare as I was escorted to her office. Several people bobbed curtseys and looked mildly awestruck as I walked past, and one woman (presumably a patient rather than a member of staff) asked why I wasn't wearing my tiara.

The matron's mind was on sterner matters. "Mrs. Chester is delusional," she said, frowning over a file. "As are many of our patients, but she's rather . . . *insistent* that others go along with her beliefs, no matter how ludicrous. She got into a very nasty argument this morning with our receptionist, claiming that her son was the King and demanding he be addressed as *Your Majesty*."

"Ah," I said. "Er . . . well, she's lived with our family for a very long time, and she may have been a little confused about—"

"She threw a *stapler* at the girl," said the matron, giving me a severe look.

"Well, that was *very* wrong of her," I said, my voice somehow taking on the exact tones of the matron.

"Indeed," she said. "And so we really must— Oh. Here's our head therapist."

I shook hands with the head therapist, thinking that surely *all* the therapists must deal with heads. At any rate, she was very enthusiastic about her job.

"Well, Your Highness, this is lovely!" she cried. "To take such an interest in the well-being of your . . . I believe Mrs. Chester was your housekeeper? You see, we find our residents settle more easily if they can take part in familiar activities, so I was wondering if Mrs. Chester might like to help out in the kitchen. Do you think that's a good idea?"

Not if you want your meals to be edible, I thought. And the image of Rebecca let loose in a room full of sharp knives gave me the shivers. The matron must have been thinking along the same lines.

"I really don't think—" she began, peering over her spectacles.

"Or hobbies?" the therapist went on, leaning forward and tucking her clasped hands under her chin. "What gives Mrs. Chester *pleasure* in life?"

Screaming at people? Throwing staplers at them? "Well, she is very fond of her son, Simon," I offered. "Perhaps if she could have some photographs of him in her room . . ."

"Oh, but she does! And her son is most welcome to telephone or visit as often as he likes. I must say, she also seems to be getting on very well with her roommate, which is *wonderful*, because her roommate can be rather . . ." The matron cleared her throat, and the therapist hurried on. "But is there anything else? Does Mrs. Chester enjoy music or nature walks or sewing?"

I thought hard. "Um . . . well, she's quite religious. Is there a church service she could attend on Sundays? And if a clergyman could visit her, I'm sure she'd pay attention if *he* told her not to throw staplers at people."

"Of course!" said the therapist, beaming. "She can join the group that walks over to St. Jude's each Sunday—they're supervised, of course. And I'll ask the vicar—a lovely man—if he can pop in and see her. What an excellent idea!" And then she went on about the clinic choral group that Rebecca might like to join, and how she was thinking of converting the old scullery into a meditation room.

"I expect you'd like to see Mrs. Chester now," interrupted the matron. I couldn't think of any polite way out of it, so I was shown into a sitting room that smelled of disinfectant, where I had a short, strained conversation with Rebecca.

"Do you need anything?" I asked. "More clothes or . . . or books or anything?"

"My *son* brings me everything I need," she said haughtily. She was wearing a sober gray dress and had her hair scraped back and coiled in braids above each ear, which made her resemble the second Mrs. Rochester more than the first. I can't say she looked happy, but when had she ever? She seemed well fed and clean, and she hadn't thrown anything at me. Was happiness— the long-term sort of happiness, not momentary bursts of it— even possible for Rebecca? I had a glimpse of what it might be like to be her: to have given up everything for love and then be tossed aside, to have been taken up again by one's lover when he'd been abandoned by everyone and everything, even his sanity—and then to be forsaken again, this time for eternity. Contemplating Rebecca's life was like peering into a bottomless coal pit. But imagine being *in* the pit, peering up at an impossibly distant speck of daylight! Poor Rebecca! No wonder she spoke to people who weren't there and lashed out viciously at those who were—and I suddenly recalled that Saint Jude was the patron saint of lost causes. It was all so disheartening that I was relieved when she said an abrupt farewell and stomped out.

The therapist then insisted on giving me a tour and outlining the clinic's philosophies (all of which sounded very impressive, although now I come to write them down, I can't remember a word). I had the distinct impression that she had mistaken me for a member of the British royal family, or at least for someone far more important than I actually am. In the recreation room, we came across Rebecca and a tall, ferocious-looking woman, presumably her roommate, standing by a barred window. They were looking out towards the road, where Parker was pointing out bits of the car engine to Veronica. Rebecca was muttering in a low voice, no doubt pouring vitriol into her roommate's ear (I could almost see it, a poisonous blue-green stream). Which did make me feel slightly less sympathetic towards Rebecca. But at least she seemed to be enjoying herself, in a Rebecca-ish sort of way. The therapist and I moved on to the music room and the dining room, and then finally, after a cup of milky tea and a digestive biscuit, I was able to make my escape.

"About time," Veronica said. "We were just about to storm the barricades and rescue you. So they haven't thrown her out yet?"

"No," I said. "And the place is very nice."

"It ought to be, with the fees they charge," said Veronica. Then we drove home, Parker letting Veronica steer in the flat areas, while I thought about the human mind. I wondered whether mad people would be better off if their memories could be neatened up, or taken off the shelves on which they were stored and replaced with nicer ones, and if they'd be the same people then or completely different ones, and whether dreams were like a vandal rampaging through a library of memories, tearing out random pages and turning them into paper boats . . . and then I fell asleep and dreamed of the sea, and when I woke up, we were home.

23rd January 1937

It was Veronica's birthday today. The cook made a chocolate cake, decorated with sugar roses and eighteen pink candles, and Julia and Anthony came over for tea. Julia brought a gorgeous black silk evening gown, which she claimed she'd snapped up for a bargain in the sales, then taken home before realizing it was the wrong size, "so please, Veronica, *do* take it off my hands." Anthony gave her a book by Karl Marx, and Lady Astley sent hothouse roses and an enormous box of chocolates. Henry's present turned out to be a magnifying glass, "because you've probably got eyestrain from too much reading, although when you're not using it, can I borrow it?" And Veronica insisted that Toby's and my newspaper subscription was "perfect," exactly what she'd wanted, although I must say it didn't look very impressive next to the other presents (especially as the actual newspapers won't start being delivered until next week, so it was just an invoice from the newspaper office).

But I think the parcel she was most pleased about was

Daniel's, which arrived in the morning post, wrapped up in brown paper. He sent a thick letter and a couple of books about politics, one of which he'd actually written himself. Anthony was a bit condescending over Daniel's book, because it was about Socialism rather than Communism. I'd thought they were pretty much the same, and Anthony's explanation didn't really clear up matters. I'd just about grasped the idea that Socialism was a milder form, with less emphasis on violent revolutions, when he and Veronica got into a debate about it ("But *Engels* said . . ." "Yet didn't *Trotsky* . . ." "Well, what about *Stalin?*").

So the rest of us left them to it and talked about the forth-coming Season. I'm not officially old enough to make my debut into Society this year, but I'll be doing so regardless—Aunt Charlotte has put up my age by six months in order that Veronica and I can come out at the same time. It's unlikely the Palace officials will find out. I don't have a birth certificate for them to check, and Julia's uncle pulled strings so that we didn't need to acquire British registration cards. (Apparently, all new arrivals to this country are meant to register as "aliens" and have to carry identification cards around and inform the police every time they change their address or start a new job.) I'm beginning to feel rather nervous regarding this whole Season thing, though, so I asked Julia about her experiences as a debutante.

"Oh, the dances are lovely, and you meet *such* a lot of new people, which is awfully stimulating," she said. "Of course, it's a bother remembering their names, especially the men, all dressed exactly alike, whereas at least with the girls . . . although one does look at everyone else's beautiful dresses and turn *green* with envy. Then there's the presentation at Buckingham Palace, which makes one go green all over again, from sheer *nerves*. The girl in front of me was sick into an equerry's top hat, another girl started gnawing on her Card of Command, and when she got to the Lord Chamberlain, he couldn't read a word and sent her to the back of the line, then someone else's bouquet fell apart, fern leaves and pink carnations scattered all over the carpet of the Throne Room—"

Which really didn't do much to relieve my anxieties.

Toby also used the occasion to present Anthony with his Order of Benedict. (It turned out Aunt Charlotte had half a dozen of them in her safe—the family must have had them made up in bulk at the jeweler's, decades ago.) I was worried Anthony might not believe in accepting royal honors, being a Communist and everything, but he seemed very pleased and gave a nice, rambling speech in return. We decided to get Julia to pass along her uncle's Order of Benedict to him, as he was abroad doing top-secret government things, and no one was sure where he was or when he'd be back. Unfortunately, Simon hadn't yet located Captain Zuleta.

"Because he's resigned from the shipping company," Toby explained after Julia and Anthony had left. "And they wouldn't give out his address."

"He told us once that all his family lived in the ancient Basque capital," I said. "The town with the historic oak tree—I forget its name."

"Guernica," said Veronica.

"Perhaps he's got his own ship now," said Henry, lying on the carpet. She was sharing her crumpet with Carlos, who'd been allowed upstairs as a special birthday treat. "Simon should look for a ship called *Veronica.*"

"Well, if the new ship's registered in Spain, it might be difficult to get details," said Toby.

"Oh, yes, Spaniards are quite impossible," said Aunt Charlotte absently, not looking up from the letter she was reading. "Erratic, unreliable—"

"I just meant with the war going on and everything," said Toby hurriedly, glancing at Veronica.

"Exactly," said Aunt Charlotte. "All due to their excitable temperament. Wouldn't be *having* a war if they were capable of discussing things calmly and rationally amongst themselves."

"It's rather difficult to have calm, rational discussions with Fascist thugs," snapped Veronica.

"Thugs?" said Aunt Charlotte, putting down her letter. "Nonsense! Look at Mussolini, getting the trains to run on time. Not in the least thug-like. Pamela Bosworth met him in Venice years ago, says he was absolutely charming." Aunt Charlotte frowned at Veronica. "You know, you always seemed such a *sensible* girl from your letters, Veronica, and now here you are, spouting Communist slogans. It's the influence of young Whittingham, of course. He's been such a worry to his poor father . . ."

Veronica, looking as though she wanted to throw her copy

of Daniel's *Principles of Evolutionary Socialism* at Aunt Charlotte's head, instead gathered up her books and stalked out.

"Takes after her mother," said Aunt Charlotte, highly gratified by this evidence of Spanish excitability. "Who, I notice, didn't bother to send so much as a birthday card."

Toby and I exchanged looks. Aunt Charlotte had no idea Isabella was dead. I was just glad Veronica hadn't stayed around to hear her mother mentioned. If it ached to hear about Montmaray, then the subject of Isabella was a raw, gaping wound. I wondered if I should tell Aunt Charlotte—but Toby and I had agreed between ourselves that it should be up to Veronica.

"And what about me, Aunt Charlotte?" said Toby quickly. "Whom do I take after?"

"Ah—now, you're the very *image* of your father," she said, giving him a fond smile. "Poor dear Robert, my little golden-haired brother, wrenched away from us at such a tender age . . ."

"And me?" cried Henry, kneeling up. "What about me?"

"You," she said, peering over at Henry, "remind me of a monkey your Great-uncle William brought back from India."

Henry hooted with glee and rolled around on the floor with Carlos. I didn't ask about myself. I was afraid she'd say, "Oh, I expect you're like your mother—what was her name? Jean? Joan?" Everyone remembers my father—he was so lively and affable, so open, so uncomplicated. But my mother, Jane, tended to fade into the background even when she was alive—just as I do. Although this might simply be because the other members of my family are so *very* conspicuous. It will be interesting to see if I fare any better in a crowd of strangers . . .

To take my mind off *that* terrifying prospect, I will now describe Henry's latest governess, who arrived this afternoon. Miss Bullock is not pink but a steely shade of gray. Her tweed suit is cut like a uniform, her felt hat resembles a helmet, and her voice is raspy, probably from shouting at her charges.

"I don't go in for modern, namby-pamby ways," she told Aunt Charlotte. "I won't *stand* for children who don't do as they're told."

"Quite right," said Aunt Charlotte. "And how do you—"

"I lock naughty children in their rooms," she said. *"Without any supper!"*

This didn't sound like much of a punishment to me. We often went without supper at Montmaray, if the supply ship was overdue and there hadn't been much luck with the fishing nets or lobster pots that day. Besides, Henry is more than capable of climbing out a window and down the drainpipe, then raiding the kitchen— or else catching a fish in the lake, scaling and gutting it, and cooking it over an open fire. Also, I don't think Henry is *deliberately* naughty, not very often. Mostly it's that she doesn't consider the consequences of her actions before she plunges in, or doesn't understand social conventions (especially the ones that don't even make much sense to grown-ups). I didn't point this out to Miss Bullock, though. She doesn't seem the sort to welcome the advice of others. She'll figure it out eventually—and if not, Henry's pretty good at standing up for herself.

Still, I should disregard any uncongenial first impressions and make an effort to be kind to Miss Bullock, because the life of a governess does not seem to have improved much since Jane Eyre's day. They are regarded as neither one of the servants nor part of the family, so she eats breakfast with us, luncheon with Henry in the schoolroom, and a solitary supper off a tray in her room. She isn't permitted in the drawing rooms except when she brings Henry in, can't join the staff in their sitting room off the kitchen unless expressly invited, isn't provided with a uniform but can only wear clothes approved of by her employer . . . No wonder she's crabby after years of being treated like that.

I'm starting to understand more of the other unwritten household rules now—not that I agree with them. For example, we're not supposed to say "please" and "thank you" to the servants, but I do, anyway, because it seems awfully rude to pretend they're not people with feelings. Aunt Charlotte says they're paid good money to do their job invisibly, that that is the *point* of a servant—although I notice she treats Barnes, her lady's maid, as a trusted confidante, so she's not being entirely consistent there.

The servant we have most to do with is Phoebe, Veronica's and my lady's maid. I expect she'd be fairly good at her job if she had a mistress who could tell her exactly what she needed to do, but we know even less than she does. Unfortunately, Phoebe is the one held responsible if Veronica comes down to dinner with her hair lopsided or if I'm late to breakfast because I can't find two clean, matching stockings. Barnes is not as patient as she could be when explaining things, which makes Phoebe more and more anxious, and then she spills talcum powder on the carpet or knocks over a vase of flowers, and gets into even more trouble. It doesn't help that the poor thing is homesick. Her village is about fifteen miles away, and her single day off a fortnight doesn't always coincide with the bus timetable. She has two brothers and three sisters, and I think her father drinks, or is dead, or something—anyway, he doesn't seem very helpful. Her mother takes in laundry, all the children older than fourteen are in service (apart from a brother who works on the docks up north, which sounds even worse than being in service), and the little ones are taken out of school anytime they are needed in the fields, which seems to be six months out of every year. It's like something from a Thomas Hardy novel, the way she tells it.

Of course, Aunt Charlotte would say they oughtn't to have so many children if they can't afford them, but firstly, isn't it rather difficult *not* having children if one is married? And secondly, surely it's obvious that some people start off with far less in life than others and that for *them* a minor bit of bad luck can quite easily turn into catastrophe. Even if Aunt Charlotte says it's bad management, not bad luck—well, children can't develop into good managers unless they have a decent education and proper food for their growing brains . . . But now I'm starting to sound like a Socialist (or is it a Communist?).

And speaking of Communists—while Julia was saying goodbye to Veronica and Toby, I pulled Anthony aside and asked if he'd happened to fly anywhere near Montmaray recently. I was suddenly stricken with a desperate desire to find out whether the Germans were there, if the castle was really as badly damaged as I remembered, that the island still existed . . . *anything*. Anything at all.

But it was silly of me to ask—he explained he was still working on those engine problems he'd been having and hadn't been able to fly anywhere. I ought to have known that; he told Veronica all about it when we visited Astley Manor. And anyway, I'm supposed to be behaving *sensibly* about Montmaray, not pining over things that are gone. Still, Anthony was very sweet about it, and patted me on the shoulder, and said he'd ask his pilot friends if they'd seen anything. He's such a kind man.

By the way, I gave Rupert's handkerchief to Julia to return to him. *He's* very nice, too. It's a relief, in fact, to find there are so many good people in the world, after all. I was really beginning to doubt that.

26th January 1937

Last night we went to our first proper dinner party, and it was a disaster. Or rather, a series of disasters.

Firstly, Aunt Charlotte sprained something in her foot as she was getting off her horse in the morning. The doctor said nothing was broken but that she wasn't to stand on it for forty-eight hours because it was the foot that had been in plaster.

It was awful luck, especially as I then received Julia's note saying she'd rather eat her own head than endure another dinner at the boring Bosworths, and thank God, she and Ant had been invited elsewhere. I'd been hoping Julia would be there to give me clandestine signals across the table if I picked up the wrong fork.

"Don't worry," said Toby as I fretted over what shoes to wear. "They won't even notice you."

It was depressing to consider he was probably correct, given that Veronica looked absolutely stunning in her clinging black silk, worn with Aunt Charlotte's rubies. In contrast, I had on an old bridesmaid's frock of Julia's, mauve chiffon with puff sleeves and a white organza sash. It was pretty enough, but hardly the height of sophistication. Worse, the satin shoes that went with the frock were slightly too big for me, and one of the heels was loose. I hadn't even *thought* to try walking in them till then. But the only other shoes I owned were my everyday pairs—tan lace-up brogues (out of the question) or black Mary Janes with no heel whatsoever.

"Can you see my feet if I'm standing up?" I asked Toby, tugging my dress down in a vain attempt to cover the Mary Janes. But they poked out beneath the hem like a pair of fat black beetles emerging from under a leaf.

"Here, give me the others," Toby said.

He stuffed some cotton wool in the toes of the satin shoes, and I tried them again. It was *slightly* better, although I was forced into a weird shuffling gait.

"You won't have to walk far," he said consolingly. "And at least there won't be dancing. It won't even be a very late night. Wiltshire in January isn't exactly High Society."

It may have been dull by London standards, but there was more than enough noise and dazzle to frighten me into speechlessness. Lady Bosworth swooped down on Toby the moment we arrived ("Ah! Your *Majesty!*"), settling him into an armchair and shoving her daughter in his direction. The daughter seemed more interested in Simon, although he quickly shook her off. A moment later, I saw him leaning against the chimneypiece, lighting a cigarette for a raven-haired beauty in a strapless scarlet gown (I caught Toby glowering at both of them). Meanwhile,

Veronica and I stood in a corner, sipping our glasses of lemonade and trying to make polite conversation with David Stanley-Ross and his wife, Penelope. It was heavy going. David was nothing like Rupert in looks or manner. He had little to say in response to Veronica's openings on the subject of Amelia Earhart's plan to fly around the world, the forthcoming coronation of King George the Sixth, or the state of President Roosevelt's health. He merely gazed around the room, tilting his head back so he could stare down his long, aristocratic nose. I fared no better with Penelope.

"That's a lovely dress," I said brightly.

"Oh—*this*," she said, glancing at herself with disdain. "Had it made in Paris." There was a pause as she looked me up and down. "I recognize *your* frock, of course." Which was when I realized my bridesmaid's dress was from *her wedding*. I know there are worse things than being discovered wearing a hand-me-down frock, but I wanted to sink through the floor. I twisted round, searching for an escape, and found myself nose to nose with Lady Bosworth's daughter, Cynthia.

"Hellooo," she brayed. "Hunt much?"

"Er, I'm afraid I don't ride," I said. She looked at me as though I'd announced I was from the planet Mars. I quickly added, "My little sister does, though, and she says it's lots of fun."

"What's she ride?"

"Um . . . a pony?"

Fortunately, there was a flurry at the door at that moment and several men stomped in, calling out greetings.

"Ah, Tom!" cried Lord Bosworth. "There you are, late as usual, ha-ha!"

"Who's that?" I whispered, nodding at the tallest, most important-looking one. He had sleek black hair, extremely mobile eyebrows, and a rakish mustache.

"Mummy's cousin Tom," said Cynthia, waving at him. "You know—Sir Oswald Mosley." Veronica suddenly stiffened, like Carlos catching sight of a rabbit. Mosley's appraising glance landed on her, then brushed past me, unseeing. I shivered. I didn't like him then, and I liked him even less when Simon explained who he was.

"Leader of the British Union of Fascists. Amazing speaker. Riles up his Blackshirts, then they rampage through the East End, getting into fights with the Communists."

I gave Simon a horrified look.

"So keep Veronica away from him," Simon hissed as we went in to dinner. Of course, there was nothing I could do about our placement at the dining table, which was determined by social rank. Toby was up one end between Lady Bosworth and a wizened duchess, and Veronica down the other next to the Marquess of Londonderry and across from Mosley. Simon was between Penelope and the Scarlet Woman, and I was in the middle of the table, perfectly placed to watch the whole catastrophe unfold. I didn't even have a conversation of my own to distract me, the two middle-aged gentlemen either side of me simply talking over the top of my head once they realized I knew nothing about horses or gambling. The soup and fish courses passed without incident, but then Lord Bosworth asked what Mosley thought about reports of Fascist atrocities in the Spanish war.

"Pure invention," Mosley said promptly. "A pathetic attempt by Red propagandists to cover up their own barbarities and generate some sympathy for their doomed cause. And of course, our Labour Members of Parliament are wringing their hands, on cue."

There was some sniggering, then a voice rang out.

"How very interesting," said Veronica. "For weren't *you* a Labour Member of Parliament, Sir Oswald?"

"Certainly," he said, with a little bow in her direction. "And I was appointed a minister, and I developed an innovative—and, if I may say so, quite brilliant—plan for tackling the crippling unemployment problem. Sadly, the party was in the crushing grasp of the trade unions and voted against my plan, so I realized I must turn my back on their petty games and power plays."

"Is it only the *Labour* Party that engages in such games?" Veronica enquired, in carefully innocent tones that had Simon and me exchanging worried glances. "Because you were a member of the *Conservative* Party before that, I believe? And, after that, the New Party?"

"My dear girl, I'm afraid *all* the parties have fatal flaws."

"Now, Tom," chided Lord Bosworth, clearly a dyed-in-the-wool Conservative.

"I'm afraid you must bow to my considerable breadth of experience on this matter, Bosworth," Mosley said, raising his glass and smirking.

"*Some* might salute your breadth of experience," agreed Veronica. "Although others might call you a political dilettante."

There was a sudden muffled oath from Lord Londonderry, who glared in Simon's direction. I was fairly sure Simon had tried to kick Veronica under the table and missed. Penelope gave Simon a suspicious sideways look, then turned to Mosley.

"It's so fascinating, though, isn't it?" she trilled. "That your experiences inspired you to set up your own British movement! Awfully smart uniforms, and that emblem of yours—a sort of lightning bolt, isn't it?"

"We call it the flash of action in the circle of unity," said Mosley proudly.

"Also known as a flash in the pan," said Veronica. "Tell me, why do you insist your movement is British when your black shirts, your salute, the name 'Fascism'—probably even your funding—come from the Italians?"

"How . . . gratifying to see young ladies taking an interest in world affairs," Mosley said slowly, doing something very odd with his eyes. The pupils seemed to get bigger, then smaller, as though he were trying to hypnotize Veronica into submission. It had no discernible effect on her, although Penelope fluttered a bit. "But I'm afraid you're sadly misinformed about our funding," he continued, "which comes from sales of our newspapers and other literature—and of course, from those in England who see our good work and are moved to contribute in whatever way they can. But you'll find all this information in our publications. May I recommend *Fascism: 100 Questions Asked and Answered?*" He spoke in mocking tones, but there was real anger bubbling below the surface. He was not a man used to being questioned, I felt.

"I've read that," said Veronica. "Although I doubt I'm the intended audience—it appears to have been written for people whose critical faculties are severely impaired. For example, how can you insist in one paragraph that your movement is *not* anti-Semitic, when in another you claim that all the ills of the world are the result of greedy Jewish bankers and shopkeepers? And according to you, even though the Jews are the evil face of capitalism, they're also busy running the Communist movement and trying to *destroy* capitalism—"

"The Jews are irrelevant," he said, waving his hand impatiently. "The press insists on going on about that, but I assure you, it's of no importance to me. I have a number of Jewish friends."

"Yet you write that Jews should not be allowed the full rights of other British citizens, that they must have their possessions confiscated and be deported—"

"Successful new political movements are based on engaging the emotions, not the intellect!" he snapped. "They require *something* for followers to hate."

"Then how clever of you to choose to hate a traditional enemy of both the undereducated masses *and* your foreign backers," Veronica said coldly.

"*Speaking* of foreign places," burst out the Scarlet Woman, "we had such a lovely time in Venice last summer, but I have thoughts of *branching out* this year, and I wonder if anyone has visited—"

Penelope quickly took up the topic, but several of our dining companions preferred to stare at Veronica in icy silence. My appetite had quite disappeared, even though a footman had just set in front of me an exquisite creation of meringue, preserved cherries, and whipped cream. Simon, avoiding my gaze, drained his wineglass and joined in the Vichy versus Biarritz debate. I poked at my pudding, relieved that at least dinner was nearly over. But a further calamity was just around the corner. As all the ladies rose to leave the gentlemen to their cigars and port, my shoe got caught in the leg of my chair—*and the heel fell off.*

I crouched there for a second, staring at the little wooden thing lying on the carpet, wondering if I could possibly retrieve it. But the longer I stood there, the more attention I attracted, so I was forced to half shuffle, half tiptoe towards the door. The eyes of the nearest footman widened and his mouth grew tight as he tried his hardest not to burst into laughter. I limped into the drawing room and sat down on a chair near the door, whipping my feet under my skirt and wondering wildly what to do.

"Are you all right?" asked Veronica. I whispered my dilemma, although I needn't have bothered lowering my voice. The others were all giving us a wide berth. Mosley seemed a great favorite of one blonde in particular—she kept shooting Veronica very offended looks.

"Give me your shoe," Veronica demanded, still fired up from her argument. "*I'll* go and find the other bit!"

"What?" I hissed. "I can't take it off here! And you can't go in *there*."

"Oh, come on," she said, dragging me up. Under the pretense of visiting the loo (although why we'd need to go *together*, I've no idea), we escaped into the hall. Luckily, the footman was coming out of the dining room, looking for me—he'd rescued my poor heel. I thanked him profusely.

"And if Your Highness will permit me, the shoe can be mended."

So I sat on the marble staircase like Cinderella, one shoe on and one shoe off, waiting for the footman to return, while Veronica stalked along the hall, gazing up at the paintings.

"Look, Sophie!" she kept saying. "It's a Caravaggio!" Or a Rubens. Or a Van Dyck. It seemed extraordinary that people who'd grown up with such beautiful, thoughtful pictures could enjoy the company of that horrible Mosley man. The footman eventually came back, and I slipped my shoe on, apologizing to him for all the trouble I'd caused. Then, thank heavens, the gentlemen filed back into the drawing room and we were able to depart.

"*What* an eventful evening," said Toby once Parker had stowed away his crutches and gone round to the front of the car. "We never had dinner parties like that before the girls arrived, did we, Simon?"

"Hmm," said Simon.

"*I* mixed up the name of Cynthia's brother with that of her horse, so she glared daggers at me all night," said Toby. "Veronica insulted the leader of a gang of vicious hooligans. Simon, what did you do to poor old Lord Londonderry? He kept giving you the filthiest looks."

"I kicked him in the shin when I was trying to get Veronica to shut up," said Simon.

"Soph, how was *your* evening?"

I recounted my shoe saga.

"I was wondering why you smelled of glue," Toby said. "Well, an excellent evening all round for the House of FitzOsborne. Unless—" He slid open the glass window separating us from the chauffeur. "Parker, how did you go at cards tonight?"

"Lost three bob, sir," said Parker.

"Oh dear," sympathized Toby. "It wasn't to one of those Blackshirts who drive Mosley around, was it?"

"Indeed it was, sir," said Parker. "Indeed it was."

"Rotten luck," said Toby, then leaned back in his seat. "We'll probably never get invited back to the Bosworths' again." He smiled broadly. "So, well done, all of you!"

Of course, Aunt Charlotte was absolutely furious when she found out. Lucky for us that she's too busy with preparations for our London Season to do much reprimanding. She is trying to compile a guest list for our coming-out ball in May (a *most* arduous task, as she keeps reminding us) while supervising the packing and trying to run a household with two-thirds of her staff (several carloads of servants have already been dispatched to London to open up Montmaray House). At least Henry has now calmed down about being left behind at Milford Park with Miss Bullock—her pony and the impending arrival of Cleopatra's piglets seem to have helped, and of course, Carlos will stay here . . .

Oh dear, Phoebe has just knocked a bottle of cologne into my handkerchief drawer. Never mind, they'll smell extra-nice now!

It's no good, the poor girl's still oozing tears. Better go and cheer her up . . .

25th February 1937

Their Royal Highnesses
Princesses Veronica and Sophia of Montmaray,
accompanied by the Princess Royal,
Princess Charlotte of Montmaray,
have arrived at Montmaray House
in anticipation of the Season.

It seemed an extraordinary thing for *The Times* to print on
their front page—who on earth would care? (Especially as hardly
anyone here seems to know where Montmaray *is*, let alone
what's happened to it. Toby says that people at school were always mistakenly thinking he came from Montenegro or
Montserrat, or getting him mixed up with Prince Rainier of
Monaco.) But then this morning, an absolute *avalanche* of envelopes descended upon Montmaray House. Advertisements
from dress shops and tea shops and businesses that hire out gilt
chairs and marquees; offers of free sittings with photographers;

letters from dance schools and florists and "hair artistes." And then there were the invitations.

"What's a fork luncheon?" asked Veronica, staring at one engraved card as we sat around the breakfast table. "And who's Mrs. Douglas Dawson-Hughes, and why would she invite us to one?"

"We've got *eleven* invitations to tea parties," I said, counting. "One of them promising consultations with 'Madame Zelda, the famous fortune-teller.'"

"She can't be all that famous if they need to explain who she is," said Veronica.

"Everyone's hoping for invitations to your coming-out ball," explained Toby. "There haven't been any big parties at Montmaray House since before the war—probably not since the last Montmaravian Ambassador lived here, decades ago—so they're all wondering what it looks like inside. And I bet they're madly curious about you two."

"They're more interested in *you*, Toby," said Simon. "Wondering if you'll do for their daughters. Here, Sophia, give me those." He began sorting the invitations into two piles. "Definitely *not* Mrs. Dawson-Hughes—her husband's about to be declared bankrupt. Yes to the Marchioness of Elchester, yes to the Fortescues . . ."

"I suppose Lady Redesdale's youngest girl is out this Season, too," mused Aunt Charlotte. "Poor child, I don't suppose she can help having such scandalous sisters. One divorced and now one run off to Spain with that awful Romilly boy . . . Is that in the newspapers yet, Simon?"

"Not this morning's, ma'am," said Simon.

"Lady Bosworth told me all the details yesterday. Dreadful thing. Well, girls, what are you doing today? Do you need the car?"

"Julia's coming over at eleven to take us shopping, then there's dress fittings and a Court class in the afternoon," I said.

"Theater this evening?" asked Toby.

"Can't, I don't have any proper evening shoes yet," I said. "Ask me again in a week's time."

"Glad I was born a boy," said Toby. "Aren't you, Simon?"

"Very," said Simon.

I was very happy to be a girl, though, when Julia swept us into Harrods and showed us all the beautiful things girls could wear. Chiffon scarves and exquisite little straw hats and strings of pearls and bright silk tea dresses and silver evening sandals . . .

"Right," said Julia. "Gloves first." And we bought three pairs each of long white kid gloves for evenings ("because you need to have them cleaned each time you wear them, and they stretch and split so quickly") as well as black leather gloves for everyday, with clutch purses to match. Then we bought silk stockings and lipstick, and looked at hats. I fell in love with an elegant black pillbox with dotted veil, but I knew it would look ridiculous perched on my frizz of hair. Julia pronounced the frocks "tedious" and "far too expensive" and whisked us off to Peter Jones, where we bought a couple of silk afternoon frocks for "only" nineteen shillings each. I didn't dare calculate how much we'd already spent—pounds and pounds, I was sure, but it all got charged to Aunt Charlotte's account. Phoebe, laden with bags and boxes, staggered off to the car and was driven back to the house by Parker while Julia took us to Claridge's for luncheon.

"Ant's mother's arriving from New York this afternoon, so now I have to go and meet her, but I promise I'll be back tomorrow to help you look for evening shoes—remember to get fabric samples at your dress fittings—and oh, Sophie, I *must* introduce you to the man who does my hair, he's an absolute magician."

"He'd need to be, to make something of my bird's nest," I said.

"Nonsense, it just needs a trim! Now, long hair is terribly old-fashioned, but if anyone can get away with it, it's *you*, Veronica—just pile it up and stick a tiara on top."

"Yes, Julia," said Veronica, who finds Julia highly amusing, although too frivolous for words.

After that, we went to order evening dresses, and the designer went into raptures over Veronica's face and figure. His enthusiasm was dimmed somewhat when Veronica insisted on wearing mourning dress for her presentation at Court, but he rallied quickly. "Simple, yet elegant," he cried, holding up lengths of black satin against her. "Nothing to distract from the natural beauty. No frills, no frippery, no furbelows." (He actually said that, "furbelows"—one of those words that make less and less sense the more one repeats it, until finally one starts to wonder if it *is* a word.) For me, though, it was felt that frills and furbelows would be a very *good* idea. After much frowning and tongue-clucking, he decided on a gathered bodice with thin straps and a full skirt, in a shimmering silk that was halfway between violet and pale blue. We were meant to choose two more evening dresses each, but even I'd had enough by that stage, and besides, we were due at the Vacani School of Dancing, just around the corner.

"Oh, I'm not going," said Veronica. "I've already arranged to meet Daniel for tea."

I stared at her, horrified. "You can't go wandering off into the East End by yourself!"

"No, he's meeting me at Lyons Corner House, near Marble Arch. You can come, too, if you'd like."

"But we've got to practice curtseying! And Parker will have a fit if he comes to pick us up and you're not here! And what if Aunt Charlotte—"

"Oh, look, there's the bus! Meet you at quarter to five in the Harrods car park," she said, and she dashed off, swinging herself up the stairs of a tall red bus as though she'd been doing it all her life.

My first class with Miss Betty went very badly, which I'd like to blame on anxiety about Veronica, although I suspect it was simply my innate lack of coordination. We had to line up against a wall, holding the barre with our right hand, place our right foot (or was it our left?) against the wall and the other foot behind that, sink almost to the floor, then rise without wobbling or falling over sideways. I got my left and right confused, my knees cracked, I plunged downwards too fast and too far, and couldn't get up again. The other girls tittered behind my back. Then Miss Betty had one of them demonstrate the procedure at Court, while Miss Betty sat in a chair, pretending to be the King.

"To be presented, Miss Lucinda Adams-Smythe." And Miss Adams-Smythe, a curtain pinned to her shoulders to simulate her train, descended gracefully, bowed her head, and rose, beaming throughout.

"Keep your eyes on the King, kick your dress out of the way, three steps sideways, smile at the Queen, curtsey again . . . Excellent!"

If she was so excellent at it, what was she doing in this class? I stomped out as soon as we were dismissed and was further irritated to find Veronica calmly reading *The Evening Standard*, right where she said she'd be.

"You've no idea how worried I've been," I said crossly. "Running off by yourself, *anything* could have happened! You could have been abducted by white slavers and shipped off to the Argentine!"

"What, in the middle of Mayfair?" she said.

"*Yes!* Phoebe was saying she'd heard that women disguised as nurses wander round London injecting young women with morphine. And taxi drivers are in on it, too. A quarter of taxis have *no handles* on the inside doors, so the victims can't—"

"How was your lesson?" she asked, folding up the newspaper.

"Awful," I said. "How was Daniel?"

"Very well, though rather thin," she said. "He sends his

fondest regards to you and wanted to know how your writing was going."

My *writing*! Imagine him remembering those earnest little stories I used to labor over when I was twelve! (I fancied myself a budding Brontë.) Now the only thing I write is my journal, and I haven't even managed to do *that* for weeks. I haven't done a very thorough job of today's entry, either—I forgot to mention all the arguments over Toby's eighteenth birthday. Aunt Charlotte yearns for a grand ball in London to celebrate, as well as a party in the village (with fireworks) for the Milford tenants, whereas Toby just wants a quiet family tea.

I also meant to note down my first impressions of London. Ponderous buses swaying round Piccadilly Circus, looming shopfronts plastered with flashing advertising signs, rows of houses in Park Lane jostling against one another, each trying to look taller and more impressive than its neighbors . . . And *so* many people! Bowler-hatted businessmen who never seem to unfurl their black umbrellas, not even when it's pouring; slender young ladies in sable coats stepping out of Rolls-Royces, and stout old ones in plaid shawls selling bunches of violets on the footpath; nannies stuffing red-faced infants back into their perambulators; footmen walking poodles; deliverymen balancing crates of fish on their heads; cloth-capped newspaper sellers shouting the day's headlines . . .

Oh! I forgot something else—that Daniel gave Veronica a clipping from *Action*, the Fascist newspaper. (Daniel keeps a close eye on the enemy's propaganda, ever since the Blackshirts hurled a brick through his office window.) And the paper had a whole paragraph about *Veronica* in it! As she points out, Mosley couldn't decide whether to attack her for being a dangerous foreign Bolshevik trying to stir up trouble or to poke fun at her for being a silly debutante, parroting ideas she didn't understand. So the whole thing was rather incoherent—but definitely offensive in tone. That *hateful* man! I gather Daniel suggested to Veronica that she refrain from denouncing Fascism in public, for her own protection—but Daniel ought to know that this would just make her want to give weekly lectures about it on top of a soapbox in Hyde Park.

I have to stop there, the dinner gong has sounded. I *do* resolve to make more of an effort with my writing, though . . .

17th March 1937

Well, so much for my resolution to write more—although the following account of my activities might provide *some* excuse. In the past three weeks, I have:

—attended seven debutante teas and had my palm read twice by Madame Zelda (the first time, I was told I'd marry a lord and have three children; the second, that I would overcome my "tragic past" to find true happiness in love, which Veronica said showed Madame had finally got around to doing some research on us)

—been to five fork luncheons (which turns out to mean standing in an overheated drawing room eating creamed chicken with a fork)

—learned how to curtsey without falling over and worked without much success on the waltz, the polka, and the fox-trot

—attended numerous fittings for my Court dress; also ordered three evening gowns and three pairs of satin shoes, dyed to match

—had my hair cut and shaped into a style that instantly

made me look five years older (Julia was right, Monsieur Raymond *is* a magician), although the sophisticated effect only lasted till the next time I washed it

—been shopping with Julia three times

—watched *Romeo and Juliet* with Toby at the Odeon (Aunt Charlotte wouldn't let us see *Camille*, because apparently Greta Garbo is "not at all ladylike" in it)

and

—visited the British Museum with Veronica, Simon, and Toby, where we were followed around the Roman Gallery by a party of American tourists who mistook Veronica for a guide.

Toby and Aunt Charlotte also managed to reach a compromise about his birthday celebrations. We ended up having a nice quiet dinner at the Savoy with Lady Astley, Julia, and Anthony—although Aunt Charlotte, who always has to have the last word, then presented Toby with the keys to a crimson Lagonda coupé, which is so sleek and stylish and speedy that Anthony wants to buy one now. Toby's not allowed to drive it till he gets his license, though.

I must say, London is just as impressive as I'd always imagined. So vast, so important! So full of history, yet so bustling and modern. I adore the shops and the cinema, I long to explore all the museums and art galleries . . .

Except there are days when I step out into the street and step right back inside again, cringing away from the blaring horns and sharp lights, the stampeding pedestrians, the taxis and buses and lorries hurtling past at inhuman speeds. Some days, I can scarcely breathe, the air is so dense and gray and evil-smelling. London stops being exciting then, and turns cold and menacing—"an ever-muttering prisoned storm," as John Davidson called it.

Then, at other times, sliding through the city in the motor-car, gazing up at the buildings through a thick pane of glass, I can't help but think that the tall facades are mere sets on a stage, flat sections of painted plywood, that one good shove would send them clattering backwards to reveal . . . What? Nothingness? At those moments, London simply doesn't feel *real*—not compared to Montmaray. It doesn't help that returning to Montmaray House is like walking into a museum, or perhaps a very grand hotel in its declining years. There are a lot of dim, cavernous drawing rooms filled with antique furniture and portraits of long-forgotten statesmen, then some dark little offices decorated in a manner that was probably very fashionable when Queen Victoria was a young bride, topped by a couple of floors of vast, icy bedrooms redolent of camphor and old velvet. Montmaray House has been owned, if not always occupied, by the FitzOsborne family for hundreds of years, so it ought to feel more like home—but I really think I prefer Milford Park. Perhaps it's just that I'm more a country girl than a city girl.

Or perhaps I feel so disconnected from this place because I haven't made a single new friend, despite all our frantic social activity. Who would have thought it was possible to feel lonely in the midst of hundreds of people? But all the other debutantes seem to know one another and move in noisy packs, like hounds. Either they've been to the same finishing school in Paris or they've hunted together or their fathers sit next to one another in the House of Lords. And their conversation! Whenever I summon up the nerve to walk across the room and introduce myself, they're talking about clothes. I've as much interest in clothes as the next girl (far more, if the next girl happens to be Veronica), but there's only so much one can say about them. If it isn't fashion, it's horses or hunting, neither of which I know anything about. No one appears to read anything except *Tatler* or *The Queen*. And those who aren't standoffish or silly are downright spiteful. Last week, I was sitting in a window seat, half hidden in the folds of the curtain (which happened to be the same color as my dress), trying to work out how to dispose of my horrible creamed chicken, when I overheard a girl sneeringly describe Veronica as "clever."

"Yes, but she's awfully good-looking, don't you think?" said another.

"No, no, *far* too tall," said the first. "Don't you know, men much prefer the petite, *dainty* ones."

"Like us!" They shrieked for a bit.

"Yes, but have you seen the *King* of Montmaray? *Too* divine! He was at Eton with my brother."

"Mmm. How *did* he end up with such a mousy sister?"

I wanted to sneak into the cloakroom and pour my creamed chicken into the pockets of their coats, but I didn't know their names or what their coats looked like. What was worse was that they came up to me later and pretended to be friendly, asking me all sorts of questions. What a sweet frock—had I made it my-self? Did I have any brothers? Would he be at my coming-out dance? I was so furious, I spluttered at them, which no doubt gave them more things to be catty about afterwards ("mousy *and* a half-wit"). Unfortunately, it was only hours later, back in my bedroom at Montmaray House, that I thought up a lot of bril-liantly cutting responses.

Veronica finds these events equally unpleasant now that Aunt Charlotte has forbidden her from wandering off to the library (if it's at a private house) or going down to the lobby to scrounge a newspaper (if it's in a hotel, and many of them are). She isn't as shy as I am, but she's bored and that makes her irritable—and she'd rather avoid people altogether than snap at them.

"It's *most* ungrateful of you girls," Aunt Charlotte said in the car home yesterday after Veronica and I had spent yet another afternoon skulking around the walls of a Belgravia drawing room. "I bring you to London, get you invited to these things—not *everyone* has the chance to take tea with the Marchioness of Elchester, you know—and what do you do? *Mope.* I'll say this for your mother, Veronica—she may be feckless and disloyal, but at least when *she* was eighteen, she could walk into a room and turn every head."

If the car hadn't been moving, Veronica would probably have been out the door in an instant and stomping down Sloane Street; as it was, she merely scowled ferociously.

"That's exactly what I mean," said Aunt Charlotte. "What

a face! What girl is going to invite you to her dance, or her next house party, when you look at her like that? And *then* how are you going to meet her brothers or her male cousins or even her widowed uncles?"

I do feel for Aunt Charlotte. Here she is, three recalcitrant nieces having been dropped on her doorstep (well, two recalcitrant nieces, plus a well-intentioned but awkward one), and it's not as though our aunt adores young people. With the exception of Toby, I really think she much prefers horses. But she honestly does *try*—introducing us to the crème de la crème of London Society, buying us lovely clothes, instructing us in the rules of ladylike behavior. For example:

"A lady always wears a smart hat when lunching at a restaurant."

"A lady never powders her nose or applies lipstick when in a public place."

"Young ladies do not drink or smoke, and they are *certainly* never seen in nightclubs."

"Never permit a gentleman to kiss one anywhere except upon the back of the hand, unless one is engaged to him and the notice has appeared in *The Times*—and even then, never allow a kiss to last for more than a minute, and always keep both feet firmly on the floor."

"Why?" asked Veronica.

"Because," said Aunt Charlotte darkly, "men—even gentlemen—have *urges*. And it is the lady's responsibility to *restrain* those urges."

"If men are at the constant mercy of their uncontrollable *urges*," said Veronica, "why are they allowed to run the country? Don't they get distracted awfully easily?"

"Please try not to be so *contrary*, Veronica. Young ladies do not argue with their elders and betters."

When we got back to Montmaray House yesterday, Veronica stormed straight up to her bedroom, although she managed to stop herself from slamming the door. I went to unburden myself to Toby, who was playing Chopin in the largest of the drawing rooms.

"I feel so *horrible*," I said, slumping beside him on the piano bench. "Poor Aunt Charlotte, she's spent all this money and made such an effort, and we're complete failures before the Season's even officially begun! I haven't made one single acquaintance. I can't even find anything to *talk* to them about."

"I can't say I'm surprised," he said. "Whenever I've gone to house parties, the debutantes have always seemed so silly and giggly—or perhaps they're just that way around me. But look on the bright side, at least you don't have to go to school with them. And in a few years, they'll probably be much improved."

"That's no help to me now," I sighed.

"Do you know what it is?" he said thoughtfully. "It's that they haven't had anything really *awful* happen to them. No wonder they seem so superficial and unfeeling."

It was certainly an interesting theory. But *some* of them must have had tragedies in their pasts—a brother who'd died in infancy, or a house that burnt to the ground, or a father who'd gambled away the family fortune (well, probably not the last, because it costs such a lot of money to make one's debut). And in any case, surely one didn't need to have suffered in order to possess empathy for those who had? All it required was a bit of imagination and a well-stocked library. Where were all the quiet, sensible girls who loved books? Perhaps they were hiding behind curtains. Or were too sensible to allow themselves to be drawn into the froth and frivolity of the Season in the first place.

I was also surprised to hear Toby sounding so philosophical—for him to acknowledge that human suffering even *exists* is bizarre in the extreme. But then, as if reading my mind, he launched into a loud rendition of "Yes, We Have No Bananas." So the universe was restored to normal.

Luckily, we're in regular contact with Henry, and she always manages to cheer me up. She is conducting a battle of wills with Miss Bullock, the score currently standing at something like nineteen to seven in Henry's favor. Today, Henry was very excited because she'd sneaked off to the Home Farm to watch Cleopatra have her piglets, all fifteen of them.

"And Mr. Wilkin says I can have the runt, and bring her up and show her if she turns out a good'un!" Henry cried down the telephone. "Oh, *wait* till you see them! They're so lovely and pink, and they squeal and squeal! I'm going to call mine *Julia*."

"Er . . . I don't know if that's such a good idea," I said. "Some people prefer not to have pigs named after them."

"Really?" said Henry, surprised. "I'd *love* it. The other name

I thought of was Antonia, but I suppose that's out, too. Sophie, could you think of a really *excellent* name? You'll have to meet her first, though, so you can get an idea of her character."

I promised to consider the matter carefully, said goodbye to Henry and Carlos (he always leans against her to listen in during her calls—I can hear him snuffling), and handed the telephone receiver to Aunt Charlotte. Then I went to join Veronica and Toby, who were sitting by the fire in the little drawing room, opening their post.

"Rupert sends his regards," said Toby, looking up as I came in. "And—"

Veronica suddenly crumpled up the letter she'd been reading and hurled it into the fire.

"Ooh!" said Toby. "Lovers' quarrel?"

"It wasn't *from* Dan— Oh, very clever," she said as Toby smirked. "No, it was just some rubbish. I've no idea where it comes from."

"I wish people would send *me* letters," I said wistfully. "Although I suppose I can't expect to receive them when I never write any."

"You could write to Rupert," said Toby. "He always asks after you. And *I'd* write to you—if I were away at school, that is."

"When *are* you going back to school?" asked Veronica, because he had his leg cast taken off on Friday.

"Never, hopefully. I'm sure I can talk Aunt C into letting me stay at home. Anyway, I'm getting through far more work here with you than I ever did at school," he said. "Ouch!" he added, because the fire had just spat at him. He leaned over to push a singed bit of paper back into the flames, then frowned and picked it up. "What the . . . Veronica, is this *your* letter?"

She glanced up. "Oh, yes. Throw it away."

"But . . . it's *dreadful!* Who sent it?"

I peered over his shoulder. The paper was scorched, but I could still make out a few typewritten words—"traitor" and "harlot" and "get what's coming." Veronica snatched it out of Toby's hand and tossed it back into the fireplace, where it was devoured in a flash of red. "Oh, *really*, Toby," she said as he continued to protest. "They're simply not worth thinking about."

"Wait, *they*?" I said. "You've had more than one?"

It took a while, but eventually we got it out of her. She'd received at least three that she could remember, all addressed to "HRH Princess Veronica," all filled with offensive epithets and vague threats.

"And you didn't think to mention this to anyone?" said Toby incredulously. "Or call the police?"

"The police!" she scoffed. "It's just some madman who picks names at random out of the Society pages of *The Times*—or else it's schoolboys playing a prank. If it were anything serious, he'd have attacked me by now."

I wasn't entirely convinced, and we kept arguing about it until Aunt Charlotte came in for tea, at which point the whole subject was dropped by instant consensus. Aunt Charlotte won't even let us go shopping without a chaperone, so *this* would probably give her a heart attack.

It's all very tedious, especially for Veronica, who's longing to go and visit Daniel's newspaper office. So am I, actually. He sounds just as nice as ever, from the bits of his letters that Veronica reads to me, and he seems to have a very interesting job. I don't think Veronica is in love with him, though, which is probably a good thing, because he's what Aunt Charlotte would regard as "completely beyond the pale." Apart from being poor and a Socialist and our former tutor, I think he might be Jewish. Although he doesn't believe in God—and is it possible to be a Jewish atheist? I don't know very much about it, but perhaps being Jewish has more to do with race or ancestors than with one's personal religious beliefs? That's what the Nazis seem to think—which probably means it's complete rubbish. Anyway, Daniel's grandparents came here from Vienna decades before he was born, so he's far more English than we are . . .

Well! Just as I was pondering Veronica's love life, or lack of it, she knocked on my door, wanting to talk about *Toby's* love life. Or lack of it.

"Aunt Charlotte had me trapped in the drawing room for what felt like *hours*," she said crossly. "Apparently, Lady Bosworth is demanding to know why Toby hasn't proposed to her daughter yet, or at least fallen head over heels in love with the girl."

"Toby thinks she looks like a horse," I said.

"Yes, I said that. So then Aunt Charlotte wanted to know if he was enamored of some *other* young lady, and who she was, and how much her father's estate was worth! Why ask *me*? Well, of course I know why—Toby's been evading all her questions on the subject, and I can't say I blame him. Whenever she starts up with *me*, I get the strongest urge to run away and join a nunnery—and I don't even believe in God."

"Just like Daniel," I said.

"What?" she said, giving me a distracted look. "No, but, Sophie, listen. It did set me wondering. Don't you think it's a bit odd? A friendly, handsome boy like Toby, showing not the slightest bit of interest in all these females who keep throwing themselves at him? Of course, most of the girls are completely idiotic, but do men really mind about that?" She sat down beside me. "I know he's always flirting with Julia, but neither of them takes that seriously, of course—even Anthony just laughs about it. Still, there *are* other women Julia's age—smart, attractive ones. At least, Simon Chester seems to find them attractive. Is Toby just being contrary because Aunt Charlotte keeps badgering him? Or do you think he's harboring a secret passion for one of the scullery maids?"

"There definitely isn't any scullery maid involvement," I said. "And I don't *think* it's Toby being contrary. At least, not in the way you mean . . ."

"Go on," she said when I hesitated. "Unless he's sworn you to secrecy, of course."

"In which case, you'll ambush him when he least expects it, sit on him, and threaten him with a feather."

"Well, there *are* benefits to being taller and older and knowing all his ticklish spots," she said. "I'd be interrogating him *now*, except he's gone off somewhere with Simon Chester. I really don't see why *I* should have to put up with Aunt Charlotte's nagging about him, not without a very good reason."

So I took a deep breath and told her that while Toby hadn't discussed the matter with me, I suspected he was rather more interested in boys than girls.

"Oh! Like King James the First!" she breathed. "No *wonder* Toby's avoiding Aunt Charlotte." She sat there a moment, lost in thought. "Still, it didn't stop King James fathering seven children. Or possibly nine, depending on which source one consults. Of course, there *is* controversy about the exact nature of the King's relationship with George Villiers—"

"*Veronica*," I said, because she tends to wander rapidly off topic whenever she starts contemplating history. "It's also *against the law*. Men go to prison for it if they're caught. Look at poor old Oscar Wilde."

"Who? Oh, right." She frowned.

"Besides, it's simply not *done* in Society," I said. "Most people think it's disgusting and depraved. Or else regard it as some sort of illness. Toby could get into terrible trouble. And Aunt Charlotte would have a fit if she ever found out."

Veronica's frown deepened. "Then I suppose we'll just have to hope that he's careful."

"Hmm," I said doubtfully. (Although, now I come to write this down, I realize that's a bit unfair—Toby's been extremely discreet so far.)

"And perhaps he'll grow out of it," said Veronica.

"Perhaps," I said. "Just as long as he doesn't lose his heart to someone completely unsuitable in the meantime."

Like, say, Simon Chester. Not that I said this aloud. I had mentioned my suspicions about Simon and Toby to Veronica months ago, before we left Montmaray, but fortunately she hadn't been paying much attention at the time.

Mind you, I'm in no position to talk about unsuitable men, as I've been known to have some rather unsuitable feelings for Simon myself. One would think his constant presence would make my heart grow less fond, and there are certainly times when he irritates me nearly to death—when he's baiting Veronica, for instance. And yet, he's so *very* charming when he wants to be! And so good-looking and clever and kind to his horrible mother. He's also one of the few people I can really talk to about Montmaray—he even wrote to the shipping company we used to deal with, to see if they had any news of Montmaray (they didn't). It's difficult to define my relationship with Simon. We're not quite cousins, not quite friends, certainly nothing approaching lovers (apart from all the other complications, I'm not *nearly* glamorous enough for his tastes, judging by the women who attract his attention at parties). But sometimes I catch him giving me a considering look across the dinner table . . .

I'm stopping that train of thought right there.

I think I'll go and try on my new hat again, and endeavor to make my hair stay *underneath* this time, instead of springing out all over the place like a very tenacious type of garden weed . . .

29th April 1937

Fussing over silly crushes and hats and hairstyles—how *petty* that all seems now, how contemptibly insignificant, in the light of what has just happened. Well, I realized the Spanish war was still going on, of course—wars don't stop just because I'm too busy to read about them in the newspapers. And yet, *this*. Even the most hardened war correspondents are shocked.

Veronica was the first to learn of it. She was hunched over the newspaper when Toby and I came in to breakfast yesterday, her face white, and I knew something was terribly wrong . . . but let me find *The Times*, so I can write down exactly what she read to us.

" 'Guernica, the most ancient town of the Basques and the centre of their cultural tradition, was completely destroyed yesterday afternoon by insurgent air raiders. The bombardment of this open town far behind the lines occupied precisely three hours and a quarter, during which a powerful fleet of aeroplanes consisting of three German types, Junkers and Heinkel bombers and Heinkel fighters, did not cease unloading on the town bombs weighing from one thousand pounds—'"

I sank into a chair as Veronica read on and on. "'The whole of Guernica was soon in flames . . . Guernica was not a military objective . . . The market was full and peasants were still coming in . . . The whole town of seven thousand inhabitants, plus three thousand refugees, was slowly and systematically pounded to pieces . . . Next came fighting machines which swooped low to machine-gun those who ran in panic from—'"

"Stop it!" said Toby, snatching the paper away. "That's *enough!*"

"Montmaray was the rehearsal," Veronica said in a voice I hardly recognized, it was so choked. "The Germans practiced on *us*. And then they—"

And I saw something I'd never seen before. Veronica was crying.

Oh God, I thought. Captain Zuleta. His whole family lived there. They couldn't possibly have survived this massacre.

"Where did the aeroplanes come from?" said Simon, who'd brushed past me and seized the newspaper. "There were *waves* of bombers, where did they refuel? If they came from the north—"

"They're using *Montmaray?*" said Toby, horrified.

"Why wouldn't they? Now they have control of an island off the coast of Spain, they've got a natural landing strip and deep waters for their ships to anchor—"

"Shut up!" I shouted, turning on Simon. "Stop being so . . . so *rational!* People we know are *dead*, shot and burnt and crushed to death, and you're talking about how clever the Germans are at military strategy! They're not even supposed to *be* in the Spanish war!"

"We have to do something," said Veronica, wiping her face with the back of her hand as she stood up. "We *can't* let the Germans get away with this any longer. We can't pretend it only affects us, not when they're using Montmaray to attack others, to kill our *friends*—" And she strode out of the room, straight past Aunt Charlotte.

"What on earth . . . ?" said Aunt Charlotte, stopping in the doorway and staring. Simon began to explain as I ran after Veronica, who'd headed straight for the library.

"Where *is* it?" she muttered. "Was it in yesterday's *Times* or—" She was rummaging through the newspapers on the big, round table. "Ah, here it is! The National Joint Committee for Spanish Relief." She turned to me. "Some women from the Committee have gone to Bilbao. They're hoping to evacuate children from the area and bring them to England."

"Oh, Veronica . . . ," I said helplessly.

She grabbed a pencil and started jotting notes on the back of an invitation to yet another fork luncheon. "We need to take action, we need to make the British *government* take action against the Germans," she said, almost snapping her pencil point, she was scribbling away so fiercely. "But first of all, we need to do what we can to help the Basque people. I'll write to the Committee, offering our assistance. They'll probably need Spanish-speaking volunteers, don't you think? And then write—

no, I'll go and *see* Daniel. He'll probably know some of the Labour politicians involved with the Committee. And we should telephone Anthony. His mother's from Texas, isn't she? I wonder if *she* speaks Spanish."

"I wouldn't think so," I said, picking up a very crumpled *Manchester Guardian*, which Aunt Charlotte thinks inappropriate for young ladies and Veronica keeps rescuing from the wastepaper bin. "Look, the Mayor's launched an appeal for food for Spanish children. Actually, they prefer money, but they'll accept condensed milk, canned soup, dried cereal . . . But isn't there a Fascist blockade? How are they getting the food into Spain?"

"They're not," said Anthony grimly, that afternoon. He'd come round for tea, although he was as fired up as Veronica and barely able to stand still long enough for me to hand him a teacup. "There are half a dozen British freighters hanging round the harbor of Saint-Jean-de-Luz, crates of food rotting below-decks. Can't get past the Fascist gunboats into Bilbao. Worst of it is, there's a British warship sitting right next to them, but that blasted government of ours won't let it do its job! Can't intervene in a Spanish civil war! That Potato Jones fellow is a darn sight braver than any of our navy admirals, that's for certain!"

"I know I shouldn't even ask," said Toby. "But *who?*"

"Oh, they're all named Jones, the captains of the freighters. Awfully confusing, so they're called after their cargo. Potato Jones, Ham and Eggs Jones, Corn Cob Jones—"

"You're making this up," said Toby.

"No, it's true," I said, looking up from the newspaper. "It says here that a Labour MP shouted at the First Lord of the Admiralty, 'Is the First Lord aware that the entire British fleet is now toasting Potato Jones?'"

"Britain will have to overturn its non-intervention policy *now*, surely?" said Veronica.

"Don't be ridiculous," said Simon. "The Prime Minister doesn't even support this evacuation of Basque children, I've heard. He thinks even *that* might be a breach of the non-intervention policy."

"*You've* heard?" repeated Veronica scornfully. "What, when you went round to 10 Downing Street for tea?"

"Now, now," said Toby. "Remember, peace begins at home."

"It's *charity* that begins at home," said Veronica. "Speaking of which, your job is to talk Aunt Charlotte into giving us a house for the children when they arrive."

"What children?"

"Haven't you been listening? The Basque children being evacuated!"

"But I thought they were setting up a camp at Southampton for them," Toby said.

"They can't keep thousands of children in tents *permanently*. The children will need to be moved to proper houses once they've been organized into groups. There's bound to be somewhere suitable in Milford. Oh, and I must write to the Reverend Webster Herbert. He can organize his parishioners into helping . . ."

Of course, Aunt Charlotte disapproves heartily of all of this. Refugees, Basques, Communists, Labour MPs, they're all "beyond the pale"—and yet, even she couldn't fail to be moved by the thought of starving children being bombed and machine-gunned. Toby was also cunning enough to point out that the National Joint Committee for Spanish Relief was a respectable charity organization, presided over by a *duchess*. So Aunt Charlotte has grudgingly agreed to let the Old Mill House in Milford be used to accommodate Basque children ("but only if there's absolutely nowhere else for them to go, and only for a short while, mind you"). She's forbidden Veronica from visiting Daniel but otherwise has been remarkably obliging. I *think* Aunt Charlotte believes Veronica will lose interest once the Season officially starts next week—that the exciting, exhausting round of cocktail parties and dinners and balls will push all thoughts of refugees from Veronica's mind. This just demonstrates how little she knows Veronica.

For while I would rather none of this had happened, I can't help but rejoice at the change in Veronica as I sit here in the library this evening. She is almost back to her old self—writing lists of provisions, listening to the BBC news, and bossing Toby around, all at the same time. She's even got Simon culling our pile of invitations, as we'll need to go back to Milford to organize things.

"But *all* the debutantes attend Queen Charlotte's Ball," Simon protests. "It's supposed to be one of the highlights of the Season."

"What is it?" she asks, turning to me.

"It's run by Lady St. John of Bletso and held at Grosvenor House," I explain. "We have to wear white and, er . . . curtsey to a giant cake." Toby snorts with laughter.

"I'm not going to *that*," says Veronica firmly. "Not when there are *important* things to be getting on with."

"Well, you can't get out of the Elchester dance," says Simon. "It's the first ball of the Season, and your aunt would have a fit if you missed that."

"And there's a bachelor nephew they have in mind for you, Veronica," says Toby mischievously. "Only thirty-eight, most of his own teeth, heir to the Elchester fortune—"

"If meeting bachelors is the whole point of this Season business," Veronica says, "then Aunt Charlotte ought to let me go and do volunteer work for the Committee in Southampton. Plenty of young men *there*. Of course, they're all trade unionists and Labour Party members . . ."

"I'd rather see you die a spinster than marry a Red!" shrieks Toby, doing a creditable imitation of Aunt Charlotte.

"Nothing wrong with spinsters," says Veronica. "Just look at Queen Elizabeth the First."

"We don't need to, we've got *you* to look at if we want to see a royal tyrant in action," mutters Simon. But I don't think he really minds. I think he's missed having a worthy debating opponent.

18th May 1937

Goodness, I've been busy these past few weeks—yet somehow scrubbing floors and whitewashing walls has proved to be far less tiring than standing round a drawing room eating creamed chicken and trying to make polite conversation. Why *is* that? Perhaps it's simply that being useful always makes one feel better.

We are now back in London, but only for a few days. I felt bad about poor Parker having to drive us back and forth between Milford and London, but things will be easier now that Veronica has passed her driving test and appropriated Toby's Lagonda. I'm not sure what Aunt Charlotte will think about two young ladies zooming around the countryside in a red sports car, all by themselves—no, actually, I have a fairly shrewd idea of what she'll think. Perhaps we should just forget to mention it to her . . .

The Old Mill House, the reason we were in Milford, is now looking much improved. Its last tenant departed ten years ago, and although the roof and walls were sound, the insides were rather depressing—mildewed plasterwork, dirt caked on the flagstone floors, and not a stick of furniture. It took us ("us" being the Reverend Webster Herbert's housekeeper, half a dozen village women, Veronica, and me) five days just to clean the place, then another couple of days to paint the walls. We brought over some tables and chairs from the attics at Milford Park, and Anthony has arranged for the delivery of two dozen camp beds and a couple of boxes of kitchen equipment. When Veronica and I left yesterday morning, the Milford Park handyman had just arrived to fix the boiler, and some of the women were making curtains out of the bunting used to decorate the village for King George's coronation. I'm afraid the house will still be fairly primitive—only one bathroom, no rugs, and heaven knows what we'll do for heating upstairs. But perhaps there'll be good news from the Spanish front, and the refugee children will only need to stay a few months. Besides, spring is sweeping so beautifully across the countryside at the moment that it's hard to imagine winter will ever make an appearance.

In London, spring is rather more subdued. The sky is still ash-gray, any flowers daring to unfurl their petals are immediately showered in soot, and the trees seem yellowish and stunted after our week in Dorset. It *is* a little warmer than before, and the afternoons do seem a bit longer. And of course, *the Season* has officially begun . . .

I attended my first ball last week, but I must admit it was more exciting to anticipate than to experience. Getting dressed up was probably the most enjoyable part. I wore a violet gown with a white lace overskirt and white kid gloves that reached nearly to my armpits (it took Phoebe and me twenty minutes to tug the gloves on and get all the pearl buttons fastened). Aunt Charlotte lent me a sapphire-and-diamond necklace with matching bracelets, I had my hair done by Monsieur Raymond, I curled my eyelashes with little tongs as Julia had shown me, and I painted my lips Pearl Pink. I really did look quite pretty, I thought, as I inspected myself in the long looking glass in the hall at Montmaray House. Toby started to agree, then got distracted by Veronica descending the marble staircase in a swish of black taffeta.

"Oh, absolutely *not*," he exclaimed. "Those shoes have *got* to go."

With her long hair heaped on top of her head and her two-inch heels, she towered over him, to his indignation and her great glee (the two of them have been comparing heights ever since they were old enough to stand up straight).

"Well, don't expect *me* to dance with you," he said. "I'll look ridiculous."

He was joking, of course. He had the first waltz with Veronica while I danced with Simon, then we swapped partners. I sat out the next dance (trying not to think about how warm and firm Simon's hand had felt resting on my waist). Anthony and Julia arrived fashionably late, and Anthony asked me if I'd care to join him for the fox-trot, although he was so bad at it that we quickly agreed to sit down. Toby was swamped with girls wanting his initials on their dance cards but managed to fight most of them off. He waltzed with Julia, though, three times, and they looked superb together, whirling around the floor. Later I found out they'd practiced for a whole winter, rolling up the rug in the drawing room at Astley Manor and trying to get Rupert to join in. I half wished Rupert could have been at the ball—not so much to dance with but to talk to—except he was at school, of course. Julia was busy catching up with her friends, Veronica got embroiled in a political debate with two elderly gentlemen from the Foreign Office, and Simon was occupied with Aunt Charlotte, keeping her supplied with champagne and vital information ("He's the Brazilian Ambassador, you met him at the Londonderry dinner . . . She's the niece of the Chancellor of the Exchequer. No, yellow *isn't* her color, you're quite right . . . That's Miss Rosalind Christie, her mother writes those detective novels . . ."). So I spent quite a lot of time perched on my gilt chair watching the dancers, hoping no one was watching *me* and thinking what a wallflower I was.

At about eleven, there was a great surge from the ballroom into a smaller room next door, where a sit-down supper of caviar, lobster, quail, asparagus, strawberries, and cake was served. I forgot to mention how hot and stuffy the ballroom was, with all the lights blazing away and the hundreds of sweaty dancers, and how noisy, with the band and the chatter. The supper room wasn't much better, so Julia and I climbed out some French windows onto a balcony for a breath of fresh air. Normally, London balconies are too sooty to go anywhere near, but this one had been draped in red felt for the occasion.

"That's better," said Julia, fanning herself. "Well, Sophie, what do you think of Society?"

As I hadn't talked with anyone new, apart from the maid in the cloakroom, it didn't seem I was any more a part of Society than before. Julia laughed and said it would get better, then teased me about a young baronet she claimed had been gazing across the ballroom at me.

"More likely gazing at Veronica," I said. We both looked back through the window to where Toby, Veronica, and Simon were leaning into each other over the tablecloth. Veronica and Simon were squabbling about something, and Toby was laughingly trying to insert himself between them. Veronica looked especially beautiful, her eyes sparkling, her cheeks flushed, her lips as red as the rubies glowing at her throat.

"What a *very* good-looking family you have," sighed Julia. She tilted her head towards me. "And they *are* all family—aren't they?"

I paused. The Stanley-Rosses are our closest (really, our *only*) friends, so it seemed silly to keep secrets from them. Yet Julia *did* love to gossip . . . But I'd hesitated too long.

"I *knew* it," she said triumphantly. "Veronica and Simon are so awfully alike."

"Don't say that around Veronica," I warned her. "And Aunt Charlotte isn't exactly thrilled about it, either."

"Oh, of course," Julia assured me. "My lips are sealed. Although I think it's rather romantic—it gives him a mysterious, brooding air." This certainly seemed to be a view shared by others, because after supper, Simon was dragged onto the dance floor by a succession of glamorous women. Not that I paid any attention to that. Well, not much.

Veronica and I went back to Milford the next day, but Toby and Aunt Charlotte stayed because they'd been invited to King George's coronation at Westminster Abbey. Toby gave a very funny account of watching the peers shuffling into the Abbey with packets of sandwiches concealed under their coronets and flasks of whisky tucked inside their robes. He said he wished *he'd* thought to do the same, because the ceremony seemed to go on for hours, enlivened only by a couple of mishaps. The Archbishop of Canterbury fumbled with the crown at a crucial moment, and a bishop stepped on the royal robes as the new King was trying to get out of his chair. Little Princess Margaret, watching from the royal gallery, squirmed about, tapped her feet, poked her sister Elizabeth in the arm, yawned widely, and otherwise made her boredom very clear. It was some consolation to hear that there are other badly behaved princesses in these parts, because Henry, we discovered when we arrived at Milford Park, had just chopped all her hair off with the garden shears.

"Much easier to manage," she said cheerfully. "This way I don't have to curl it or comb it or whatever it is Miss Bullock keeps trying to make me do."

Henry's governess had also ordered a lot of new summer clothes for Henry, but as they are mostly frilly and pastel-colored, Henry refuses to wear them. She stomps around in her riding gear or Toby's old trousers, which aren't nearly as long as they used to be on her—she's shot up at least three inches this year. It must be all the good food. She certainly seems happy, spending hours hurtling over fences on her pony or taking Carlos and her piglet, Estella, for long walks. (Estella's name comes from *Great Expectations*—she's a very haughty-looking piglet.) I must say Henry was also very helpful at the Old Mill House, washing our paintbrushes, running errands, and chopping wood for the stove. And I suppose there's still another six or seven years before she needs to put on a frock and start practicing Court curtseys.

Our curtseys at Buckingham Palace, I should note, went off rather well last night. I did wobble a bit coming up from one of them, but I don't think anyone noticed—certainly not the King or Queen, who were propped like little wax dolls upon their thrones (and quite possibly asleep, in the case of the King). It was interesting to see Buckingham Palace from the inside. The furniture and paintings and chandeliers were certainly very grand, but it was disappointing to see how *grimy* everything was. Perhaps it was just the week I'd spent at the Old Mill House, but I found myself longing to give the walls of the Throne Room a good going-over with a bucket of soapy water and a scrubbing brush.

After our official presentation to the King and Queen, we all trooped down some red-carpeted stairs for a champagne supper in the basement of the Palace, where Toby and Simon were immediately surrounded by admiring debutantes. The boys both looked very dashing in Court dress—black velvet coat with white lace jabot, blue sash and medallion of the Order of Benedict worn on top of that, black knee breeches, and black silk stockings (with black cotton ones worn underneath, so their hairy legs didn't show). There'd been a lot of good-natured bantering between them over who had the better legs, although Toby said it wasn't a fair competition, with one of his calves skinnier than the other after being squashed in plaster all that time. It was nice to see them getting on so well, because they were *very* formal and polite with each other for quite a while after the Elchester ball. I think Toby felt Simon had spent a bit *too* much time dancing with one particular lady. They must have made up while Veronica and I were in Milford. I am not going to speculate on *how* they managed this—although it may just have been that Toby felt sorry for Simon, who had to rush off to Poole to calm down Rebecca (she'd thrown a massive tantrum after her roommate was declared "cured" and sent home).

We'd been invited to several debutante dances scheduled for the same night as our Court presentation, but Veronica was most insistent that we attend one *particular* dance. I couldn't understand why, as it was the coming-out ball for one of the most poisonous debutantes we'd encountered thus far (I shan't call her *catty*—that's unfair to cats). It turned out the girl's godmother was a friend of Aunt Charlotte's, so we didn't have a hope of avoiding the occasion. The house in Cadogan Square was rather too small for the number of guests, and I lost Veronica in the crush soon after our arrival.

"Who's that interesting-looking chap with Veronica?" Toby asked nearly an hour later, nodding towards the doorway. "The one in the baggy suit. He's been talking to her for ages."

I glanced over my shoulder and nearly dropped my plate of salmon. "It's *Daniel*!" I whispered.

"Is it *really*?" said Toby, brightening. "Excellent!" He stood up and waved both arms over his head until he'd caught Veronica's attention (as well as the attention of nearly everyone else in the room).

"Aunt Charlotte will be *furious*," I groaned, but fortunately, our guardian didn't seem to be anywhere nearby. "So *that's* why Veronica was determined to come to this dance! She must have told him to meet her here."

Veronica was leading Daniel over by then, and he looked exactly as he had four or five years ago, the last time I'd seen him. He wore the same round spectacles, which were still slipping down his nose and being shoved back into place with a long, ink-streaked forefinger; his warm brown eyes were still peering out at the world through the smudged lenses with amusement and a very gentle sort of cynicism; his dark hair was still straggling around his ears and down his neck, badly in need of the attentions of a barber. He wasn't the slightest bit handsome, and yet he was undeniably pleasant to look upon. I couldn't help grinning back at him as he arrived in front of me.

"Sophie, I would never have recognized you!" he said, grasping my hand with both of his. "All grown up, I see! And you must be *Toby*—I've heard so much about you!"

While Toby was complimenting Daniel on his suit ("You'll start a new trend, like Oxford bags in the twenties." "Well, actually, I borrowed it from my cousin—"), I pulled Veronica to one side and gave her a pointed, enquiring look.

"He was hungry, poor thing," she said unrepentantly. "His landlady doesn't feed him properly, and there's always far too much food at these events. Besides, I needed to discuss the Basque refugees with him. He's spoken to the Committee and got us a letter of introduction to the children's camp. They're supposed to be arriving on the twenty-third now . . ."

"I think I might write an article on this," said Daniel a short while later, between mouthfuls of roast chicken and asparagus. "'The Decadent Life of the Debutante.' As careworn maids slave away in furnace-like kitchens, aristocrats loll about upstairs, stuffing themselves with lobster and caviar . . ."

"And don't forget the footmen," said Toby, who was getting along famously with Daniel. "Servingmen staggering under silver salvers of sumptuous sustenance. And the chauffeurs, shivering in the chill air as they chafe their chilblains."

"You should write an article yourself," said Daniel. "You've a definite flair for alliteration. I think a talent for words must run in your family."

Then he turned to me and we had a nice long discussion about poetry, until Veronica spotted Aunt Charlotte at the far end of the room and Daniel decided to make a hasty exit. Although not before jotting down the names of some contemporary poets for me on the back of my dance card—he was horrified when I admitted I'd never even *heard* of W. H. Auden.

Oh—and that reminds me to note that Toby has just received a letter offering him a place at Christ Church, Oxford, to read History. He'd already reported that he'd managed to get through the entrance examination all right, thanks to Veronica cramming facts and theories into him for weeks beforehand, and that his interview had gone extremely well—mostly because one of the dons had been the tutor of our father and another, very elderly don recalled our grandfather with great fondness. Toby sounded rather resigned about it all, but then he found out that Rupert got in, too, and became a bit more cheerful. (Apparently, Rupert had been trying to talk his father into letting him go to the Royal Veterinary College instead of Oxford, but without success.)

I should also mention how magnificent Aunt Charlotte looked last night at Buckingham Palace. She wore a full-skirted midnight-blue satin gown heavily embroidered with gold, and she was absolutely ablaze with diamonds. A few of the gentlemen seemed quite dazzled, and not just by the jewels, which made me wonder, not for the first time, why she never remarried. She might seem ancient to us, but she was barely in her twenties when poor old Uncle Arthur died during the war (he wasn't a soldier; he just had a heart attack while inspecting one of his factories). And she was even more splendid-looking then—I've seen the photographs—so she must have had lots of suitors. Perhaps she thought they were just after her money. Or perhaps her experiences with Uncle Arthur made her decide that men simply weren't worth bothering about. Amongst all her advice to us, she has dropped a hint or two that, for women, the physical side of marriage is mostly a matter of duty rather than pleasure. Of course, Uncle Arthur was so old—in his sixties, according to Veronica—that he probably couldn't do anything at *all*. It's no wonder they didn't manage to have any children.

I suppose it's lucky for us that Aunt Charlotte *did* keep her fortune to herself, given that none of us have any money of our own. Simon has just negotiated a monthly allowance for each of us. Veronica's and mine are very generous (though not half as generous as Toby's, but he'll have more expenses, being at university). We're expected to pay for everyday clothes and hairdressing appointments and things like that out of it, but Veronica has already spent all hers on supplies for the Old Mill House.

And now I really *must* go to bed, as I can barely keep my eyes open. We didn't get home till half past three this morning. Being part of Society is such an exhausting business . . .

27th May 1937

The Basque children arrived on the SS *Habana* on Saturday evening, and on Monday, Veronica and I drove across to Southampton to visit their camp. It was an amazing sight— hundreds of white tents had sprouted on what had been a bare field only a few weeks ago.

"Just like the tepees in that cowboy film," breathed Henry, who'd insisted on coming along. "And look at all the people!"

There were nurses pinning back the flaps of a marquee, Boy Scouts carting buckets and benches, young men inspecting a freshly dug drain, and lorry drivers unloading crates of food. And then there were the children, *thousands* of them, ranging in age from about four years old to fifteen, running in and out of tents, straddling benches, clustered round a water pipe.

"The camp organizer's called Mr. Sams," said Veronica as we got out of the car. "I need to speak with him or Mrs. Manning. Henry, what's that?"

"Just some things for the children," said Henry, hugging a large, roughly wrapped parcel.

"Oh, that's very thoughtful of you," said Veronica.

"Wait a minute," I said, suddenly suspicious, but Henry had already skipped off and accosted a young lady with a clipboard, who beamed, accepted the parcel, and marched away with it. (Later, of course, I discovered Henry had given away her entire collection of summer frocks.)

Veronica was very warmly welcomed, as few of the British volunteers spoke Spanish. In no time, she was translating in the medical tent while I offered to help serve the children's first English luncheon. It was heartbreaking: The children were *so* thin, so used to subsisting on whatever they could scrounge. They were astonished by the quantity of food and, in particular, all the soft white bread—one girl grabbed a piece and stuffed it in her pocket, announcing in a loud voice that she was saving it for her mother back home. As I washed up afterwards, another small child attached herself to my skirt and started sobbing for *her* mother. Luckily, Henry had brought along her skipping rope and a football, which were well received by a large group of children.

There was a bad moment later in the afternoon, when some aeroplanes from nearby Eastleigh Aerodrome thundered overhead. *Instant* panic—all the children screamed in terror and bolted for cover, and I have to admit my first instinct was to join them. The whine of the engines brought back such dreadful memories—half an hour later, I was still trembling. Veronica said afterwards that she dropped a thermometer and almost dived under the table when *she* heard them, which made me feel a bit better. It made it seem less like cowardice and more like a normal reflex, like one's knee jerking when a doctor hits it with a little rubber mallet.

We could only spend a day at the camp, because we had to go back to London for our coming-out ball. Montmaray House, when we arrived, was also a maelstrom of activity, although of a rather different type. A battalion of servants was busy polishing everything from the enormous crystal chandeliers to the marble floors. Footmen bustled around the ballroom arranging chairs along the walls while maids snapped lengths of damask over the tables in the largest drawing room and set out the sparkling glasses and china, the monogrammed linen napkins, and the antique silverware stamped with the FitzOsborne crest. Immense arrangements of white lilies were carried into the hall, white climbing roses were twined around the banisters and secured with white satin bows, and vases of white tulips were set upon each table, along with hundreds of white candles in silver candlesticks. Aunt Charlotte had also decided Veronica and I would be wearing . . . white.

"She might as well stick a sign on us," grumbled Veronica. "*Virgin nieces—all reasonable offers of marriage considered.* She could hold a double wedding tomorrow morning in the drawing room, we wouldn't even need to change our dresses."

"It's all right for you," I said. "*You* look wonderful in white. I look as though I'm dying of consumption."

Toby, who was perched on the end of Veronica's bed,

suggested I put on a pink-lined sash and asked Barnes to fetch all Aunt Charlotte's amethysts—which did improve matters somewhat. I asked him whom I'd be sitting next to at dinner.

"Lord Londonderry, I think," he said. "Veronica's beside Lord Elchester."

"Not *again*! I'm always stuck with that ghastly old Fascist!" exclaimed Veronica. Phoebe, who'd been trying to fasten Veronica's pearls, squeaked and dropped them on the carpet, whereupon they slithered under the dressing table.

"Never mind, Phoebe. I'll get them," I said hastily. "We're pretty much finished, anyway. Why don't you go down and have supper now?" Phoebe ran off, sniffling.

"What is *wrong* with that girl?" said Veronica, staring after her.

"Perhaps she's in love," suggested Toby. "Suffering from some unrequited passion—that always turns everything tragic."

"Or else she's still worried about her brother," I said as I retrieved the pearls. "He was in some sort of trouble in Liverpool. She started to tell me about it once, then Aunt Charlotte came in and she got scared off."

"Well, if she ever manages to explain it, *please* do something to help her," said Veronica. "She's getting more dim-witted by the hour. I caught her fumbling through my post the other day—said she was looking for the shopping list Barnes gave her. Why on earth would it be on *my* desk?"

"Speaking of which, you haven't had any more of those poison-pen letters, have you?" asked Toby.

"Not really," she said, which of course meant "Yes, but stop fussing about it." I finally got the diamond clasp secured on her necklace, and she leaned forward to straighten her coronet. "Anyway, Toby, I meant to ask you about—" There was a knock on the door. "What do *you* want?"

This last was addressed to Simon, who walked into the room looking very elegant in his tails and white tie. He ignored her and held out his wrist so that Toby could fasten his cuff link. "You look very nice, Sophia," he said, smiling at me.

"Thank you," I said. "Now tell Veronica how lovely she looks."

She scowled at him in the looking glass.

"She looks as though she's on the verge of tearing up the furniture and running amok with a table leg," he observed.

"I may well resort to that," she snapped. "If Lord Elchester starts up again about how wonderfully organized the Berlin Olympics were, and how this country could do with a man like Hitler!"

"Agree to marry his nephew, then your aunt might stop seating you beside him at dinner parties," suggested Simon, holding out his other wrist to Toby.

"If I married his nephew, I'd be spending the rest of my *life* listening to foul Elchester opinions," said Veronica.

"Besides, that nephew's never going to ask *anyone* to marry him," said Toby. "He's a confirmed bachelor. He made a pass at me at the Fortescue ball."

"Ugh," Veronica and I said, because the nephew is *vile*.

"He did not," said Simon. "You think everyone makes passes at you."

"They do," said Toby calmly. "But I can't help being irresistible."

While I have no desire to encourage Toby's vanity, I must admit it was his irresistibility that saved the evening. It certainly didn't start well. Aunt Charlotte read us the riot act before we went downstairs. "There will be no haranguing people about *politics* at dinner, is that understood?" she said, glaring pointedly at Veronica. "Otherwise there will be *consequences*."

"I can't believe we were dragged back to London for *this*," hissed Veronica in my ear two hours later as we left the dining room. Lord Londonderry had droned on about his trip to Germany and what a marvelous host Göring had been; Lord Elchester said that if only the press here weren't controlled by Jews, the man in the street would realize Hitler was on the same side as us, against those blasted Bolsheviks; and everyone else talked about horses.

"Never mind—it'll be better when the ball starts," I whispered. The dinner was just for fifty of Aunt Charlotte's oldest, most important acquaintances, but three hundred people had been invited for the dance, including our own friends—that is, Julia (Anthony had sent his apologies, as he had to escort his mother to some family function, and Rupert was at school). What I'd forgotten was that we were expected to spend another hour standing on the Grand Staircase, shaking hands with all our guests. And when we finally staggered into the ballroom, flexing our numb fingers, it was too crowded to locate anyone we wanted to see.

For once, I had no shortage of dance partners—Aunt Charlotte had browbeaten half a dozen eligible bachelors into submission on the issue. But as this involved being jerked silently across the floor, a clammy hand sliding around my bare back, clumsy black shoes occasionally coming down hard on my toes, I did not find it a particularly pleasant experience. It occurred to me, not for the first time, that this whole Season thing was a very haphazard and inefficient way of finding a spouse. It was with some relief that I heard supper was announced. I escaped into the drawing room, where I collapsed onto a sofa beside Toby.

"Having fun?" he enquired, twisting a stray tendril of my hair back up behind my coronet.

"Not really," I said. "You? Did you dance with anyone nice?"

"Just Julia," he said, glancing towards her table. She was surrounded by people, mostly men, and as I watched, she threw back her head and laughed uproariously.

Toby frowned. "She's not happy," he said quietly, and as I looked back, I could see what he meant. There was a forced quality to her gaiety that I'd never observed before. "She told me she had her final wedding dress fitting this morning," Toby added.

"Well, she's probably getting nervous about the big day, then," I said.

"More likely, she's wondering what on earth she's got herself into."

I stared at him. "But she *loves* Anthony."

"Oh, *everyone* loves Ant," Toby said impatiently. "He's terribly sweet and earnest and so on. But he's all wrong for Julia—especially as a husband."

"Did she say something to you?" I demanded.

"Heavens, no! She's too busy reminding herself how rich he is—and telling herself over and over how wonderful 'Lady Whittingham' will sound."

"Don't be so cynical," I said crossly. "Anyway, you can't deny Anthony's madly in love with her."

"Is that *enough?*" he said, as much to himself as to me. He stared across the room. "To have one person in love but not the other . . ."

Just then, Veronica threw herself on the other side of Toby. "Hide me, quick! There's a horrible little man who keeps following me around. He claims he knew my mother, says he painted her portrait or something."

"Probably longing to paint *you,*" I said. Over Toby's shoulder, I saw what he was gazing at—Simon, deep in conversation with a willowy blonde. I poked Toby in the ribs and told him to stop it.

"I'm not doing anything," he said, sitting up straighter. "Besides, it's Veronica you ought to be telling off. Her behavior tonight's been very disappointing."

"What *are* you talking about?" she said. "Ow, these shoes pinch."

"Well, you claim to care about the poor old Spanish Republicans, you're supposed to be against Fascism, yet here you are, a roomful of Conservatives to convert to your cause—and you haven't said a word. If men are following you around, hanging off your every word, why aren't you taking *advantage* of their fascination?"

Veronica snorted. "Don't you recall? Aunt Charlotte threatened to cut off all our allowances if she catches me, in her words, 'haranguing people about politics.'"

"She only said 'at dinner,'" I pointed out.

"Sophie's right," said Toby. "How much did you say it'd cost to feed a Basque refugee child for a week?"

"Ten shillings," she said severely.

"And *look* at this crowd," he tutted. "Swilling champagne, stuffing themselves with caviar, the ladies dripping with diamonds . . ."

A dangerous gleam had appeared in his eye.

"Toby," I said. "What are you . . . ?"

"Dare me," he said. "Go on."

"I dare you," said Veronica at once.

Toby leapt up and caught the elbow of one of the footmen, spoke into his ear for a moment, then strode over to the largest table. Bounding onto a chair, then the table itself, Toby raised both arms.

"If I may have your attention!" he shouted. "Ladies and gentlemen! We are gathered here this evening to welcome my adored sister and cousin into Society—a Society that has ruled over England wisely and bravely since the Magna Carta. But, my friends, you mustn't be ashamed to show the *other* qualities for which the English are famed—that is, true compassion for those in need and a fervent belief in justice. For not far from this peaceful nation stands a proud country, who asks only that we shelter a few—a pitiful few—of her little souls while she defends her land from brutal invaders."

For one wild moment, I thought he was talking about Montmaray. But he went on, clasping his hands near his heart.

"I know that every single one of you is filled with sadness at the thought that this evening an innocent, helpless Basque child is shivering with cold, wondering where her next meal will come from, praying that her poor mother will be spared a savage, senseless death."

Beside me, a footman emptied a silver ice bucket into a vase.

"These little children have been wrenched from the arms of their parents and brought here to a temporary haven. Yet they sleep on straw, they shelter under lengths of canvas, they eat dry bread—"

A stout matron in gold lamé sniffed and raised her lace handkerchief to the corner of her eye.

"If only England's finest knew these details!" cried Toby. "They would rush to the aid of these children! When a mere ten shillings could feed and shelter a tiny orphan for an entire week . . . That is why I venture to ask that you spare a coin or two—perhaps a little more—for this worthy cause!"

He gave a small nod, and footmen began to move around the room with a variety of empty silver receptacles. Ladies delved into their evening bags and a few gentlemen patted their pockets.

"Every penny will go towards helping a hungry child," Toby said, turning his sorrowful gaze upon a cluster of wide-eyed debutantes. Then, observing the scowls of the older, more recalcitrant members of his audience, he hurriedly went on. "Of course, the relief efforts so far have been run by . . . well, members of the *Labour* Party. And, ugh, *trade unionists*! Will we stand by and allow *them* to take all the credit? Will we stand silent while they claim the upper classes no longer *care* about the underprivileged? Let us prove them wrong!"

Toby jumped down from the table, grabbed a champagne bucket, and made a beeline for the debutantes. One of them flung her diamond bracelet into the bucket, earning a dazzling smile from Toby; at this, the others began stripping themselves of jewels as fast as they could. I could see Aunt Charlotte over by the doorway, staring frantically round the room and clutching her pearls as though a Basque peasant were about to snatch them from her neck. However, her horror at the situation was tempered by the fact that it was her beloved nephew at the center of it. In the end, she settled for pretending she'd been behind the whole thing.

"One does get tired of the *usual* sort of dinner and dance," she agreed when several ladies congratulated her on turning the evening into a surprise charity ball. "A theme does make things seem less *tedious*."

This morning, of course, we had dozens of telephone calls from young ladies desperate to retrieve earrings and bracelets and necklaces that they'd recklessly given away the previous evening, and which turned out to have been borrowed from their (now very irate) aunts and grandmothers. Fortunately, they all agreed to give hefty sums of cash in return.

"That's better, anyway," said Toby. "Saves us having to sell the jewelry."

"You mean, saves *me* having to sell it," said Simon rather grumpily (he'd been the one to deal with most of the telephone calls).

Toby patted his arm consolingly. "How much have we got, Veronica?"

She looked down at her piece of paper. "Two thousand three hundred and seventy-nine pounds and eight shillings," she said. "Plus a couple of silver cigarette cases and a silk handkerchief—although I think the handkerchief fell in by accident. And I still think you could have at least *mentioned* Montmaray in your speech, Toby. We've been invaded, too, you know."

"But that would have sounded as though we were asking for money for ourselves," he explained. "It would have been terribly impolite. Not that we need money. We need . . . Actually, what *do* we need? I mean, what exactly are we supposed to be *doing* to get Montmaray back from the Germans?"

"I haven't quite decided yet," said Veronica, raising her chin. "Besides, the Basque children are our priority at the moment."

"You mean, you haven't got a clue where to start," said Simon, curling his lip. "In *my* opinion—"

Veronica glared at him. "I don't recall *asking* for your opinion."

"Oh, here's the post!" said Toby quickly. "Perhaps people have sent checks!"

There was silence as we opened dozens of thank-you letters, many of which had clearly been posted before the ball. There were no checks, but Veronica suddenly gave an exclamation of what sounded like disgust.

"What?" said Toby. "It's not one of those poison-pen letters, is it?"

"*Worse,*" said Veronica, thrusting a piece of paper at him. He stared at it a moment, then burst into peals of laughter.

"It's not funny," she said irritably. I reached over and took it from him. A company that made face cream was offering Veronica a small fortune if she'd agree to be photographed in her white ball gown for a newspaper advertisement.

"Think of all the Basque refugee children that would feed," Toby managed to gasp.

"Really, Toby," she snapped. "As if I'd do anything to encourage women to spend their money on such *rubbish*!"

"And Aunt Charlotte would think the whole thing too vulgar for words," I said a little sadly. I could only dream of someone catching sight of me and wanting to take *my* photograph for a newspaper. At that point, a footman came in and announced there was a telephone call for me from Miss Stanley-Ross.

"Sorry, didn't get you out of bed, did I?" said Julia. "But heavens, what a triumph last night was! You looked so sweet, and wasn't *Toby* the hero! The expression on your aunt's face when he jumped up on that table—but listen, Sophie, I have the most *enormous* favor to ask, and do say no if you can't possibly, I'll quite understand, but you see, my wretched little cousins have come down with measles, and the eldest was supposed to be one of my bridesmaids, but that's out now, obviously, and the dress is almost done and I *can't* have an uneven number of bridesmaids—imagine walking down the aisle of St. Margaret's with five bridesmaids, it would look *too* ridiculous, and besides, there'd be thirteen in the bridal party, it simply won't *do,* and she's almost exactly your size, and would you please, please consider it?"

"You . . . you'd like me to be your bridesmaid?" I stuttered. "Oh, but, Julia, I—"

"Oh, bless you, Sophie! You're an absolute angel!" she cried. "I'd much rather have you than my horrid cousin, anyway—she pushed Rupert's puppy in the fishpond years and years ago, and he still hasn't forgiven her—Rupert, that is, not the dog, I'm sure the dog's forgotten. Can you come for a fitting this afternoon? I'll pick you up at three-ish, all right? Oh, and tell Toby I've posted him a check! Goodbye, darling!"

I stood there a moment, stunned, then went back to the drawing room and told the others.

"Well, we're all invited, anyway, and now you don't have to worry about what to wear," said Toby.

"And stop imagining you'll drop your bouquet or step on

Julia's train or whatever it is you're thinking," added Veronica, doing her usual mind-reading act. "You'll be fine."

"Yes, look at when you were presented at Court," said Simon. "Last night went well, too."

"That's what I mean," I said glumly. "Things have been going *too* well. It's about time I tripped over my hem or did something really embarrassing."

"All the better if you do, it'll make the bride look extra-graceful in comparison," said Toby, grinning.

On that comforting note, I came upstairs to write this down—and start fretting in earnest.

If *only* tripping over my hem were the worst that could have happened at Julia's wedding! I am beginning to think we Fitz-Osbornes have been hit with that "May you live in interesting times" curse. Perhaps one of us accidentally smashed a Ming vase in the Great Hall at Montmaray years ago, unleashing a malignant Chinese spirit that has pursued us across the seas— although I must say it wasn't *all* our fault. A wedding day that begins with the bride in floods of tears is always going to struggle to turn out well.

"Now, that's enough, Julia," said Lady Astley, roused out of her habitual languor by the incessant weeping. "Goodness, Anthony will think you don't *want* to marry him! And consider what it's doing to your poor eyes!" Julia went on sobbing, and Lady Astley gazed around helplessly at the rest of us.

"Never mind. All brides get like this," said the matron of honor briskly, marching in with a bottle of witch hazel and a handful of cotton wool. "I was sick in the chapel foyer myself, before *and* after. And one of my cousins came out in hives, red welts everywhere . . . Do sit up, Julia! Here, take my handkerchief. It's nerves, that's all, worrying about what married life will be like. But honestly, a week later and it seems as though one's been married for *years*—it all seems quite normal and ordinary."

It occurred to me that *that* was what was bothering Julia. Until this moment, her future had been a vast sweep of thrilling possibilities. Now it would narrow to being the wife of a devoted but rather dull man, and her life would go on getting narrower and narrower until she suffocated.

"It's not that I don't love him," she whispered to me, after her makeup had been redone and her veil fixed in place, and the others had gone down to make sure the cars were ready. "And it's not as though I love someone else *more*. It's just . . ."

She sighed heavily.

"But then I imagined poor Ant standing there at the altar, waiting," she went on. "And he *would* wait, wouldn't he? For ages and ages, thinking the motorcar had had an accident or something. Oh, he *is* a dear, isn't he, Sophie?"

"He's a very nice man," I said.

"I *know*," she said. "Even if he sometimes . . . Oh, my eyelashes are falling off again. They really ought to make the glue waterproof." She poked at her face for a moment. "There! How do I look?"

"Absolutely beautiful," I said with complete sincerity. The

clouds of white lace, the roses in her hair, the beaded ivory silk billowing across the carpet—all made any slight puffiness under her eyes quite unnoticeable.

"Now, tell me I'm doing the right thing," she said.

I considered for a moment. "You're doing the *sensible* thing," I said.

She laughed till she choked. "Oh, bless you, Sophie!" she cried, hugging me and rumpling both our dresses. "Toby's right, he always *said* you were the best listener—"

"Julia!" bellowed her father up the stairs.

"Coming!" she shouted back, and off she went, pausing only to wrench her skirt free of the chair leg.

"So she hasn't changed her mind, after all," said Toby when the bridal party eventually arrived at St. Margaret's, Westminster. He and Rupert were ushers—I could see Rupert inching down the side aisle with an ancient female relative attached to his arm. "Floods, I suppose?"

"Mmm," I said. "Anthony all right?"

Toby rolled his eyes. "I'll leave it to your imagination. Heavens, why do people *put* themselves through this sort of thing? If I were them, I'd elope. Oh, and by the way, try to steer clear of Aunt C and Veronica till they've both calmed down. They had the most enormous row over Veronica's dress."

I sighed. "She did say last week that it didn't fit."

"Well, apparently it *does* fit, if one also wears some sort of laced-up whalebone thing that Barnes dug out of the depths of Aunt C's wardrobe."

"What, a *corset?*" I asked, starting to giggle.

"Aunt C called it 'stays,' and Veronica called it 'a medieval torture device' and claims she can barely move in it—but look, the matron of honor is ordering you over. How much do you want to bet *she* was a prefect at school? Well, I suppose we're starting, then."

The ceremony went surprisingly smoothly, apart from Anthony dropping the ring, and the smallest page boy growing bored and crawling off under a pew. In an extremely short time, the newlyweds were wandering back down the aisle to the thundering chords of Mendelssohn, Anthony dazed with happiness, Julia clinging to his side and beaming round at the congregation. We spilled out into the gray London afternoon to find a small crowd of onlookers being held back by a harassed-looking policeman.

"Oo is it, then?"

"Lovely, ain't she?"

They were all women, except for a single gentleman in a Burberry coat, who stood on tiptoe and craned his neck for a glimpse of the bridal party. A romantically minded passerby, I thought—unless he was one of Julia's spurned suitors, come for a final, tragic look before he threw himself off Waterloo Bridge. Julia sailed down the red carpet, tugging Anthony in her wake, waving away confetti and the flash of the newspapermen's cameras, and then the two of them were carried off by the chauffeur.

"Come on," said Toby, appearing beside me. "We're going in Rupert's car."

"You'd better drive," said Rupert. "Hello, Sophie, you look very nice."

"Thank you," I said. The last time I'd spoken with him, I'd been bawling my eyes out, but it wasn't nearly as embarrassing as I'd feared, seeing him again—probably because it had been so long, and also, we weren't alone. I was about to compliment him on the Bible reading he'd done during the service when I was distracted by his top pocket, which had suddenly . . . *twitched*. A small pink nose appeared, followed by some white whiskers. "Rupert, is that . . . is that a *rat?*"

"No, no, a dormouse," he assured me. "She's due for a feed." He took a tiny medicine bottle from another pocket and shook it.

"Oh," I said weakly. "Right."

Veronica hurried up, clutching her side, as I was climbing into the car.

"Sorry, just wanted another look at that east door," she panted. "There's a marvelous window dedicated to William Caxton—he printed the very first English book, you know—and he's said to have been buried in the churchyard."

"Samuel Pepys and John Milton got married here, too," said Rupert, now holding an eyedropper to the little flannel-wrapped bundle he'd propped up in one hand. "Er, not to each other, obviously."

We moved off, surrounded by dozens of Rolls-Royces and Daimlers, as well as a couple of taxis, and made our slow way to the family's town house, which they'd temporarily repossessed from their tenants. Veronica seemed to have recovered from any bad temper occasioned by the corset, and she chatted away cheerfully about whether the new Prime Minister, Neville Chamberlain, would be any better than Stanley Baldwin (probably not, she decided) and whether Mrs. Simpson was already regretting having married the abdicated King Edward (very likely, judging by their gloomy wedding photographs).

"Park over there, Toby," said Rupert, tucking the baby dormouse back in his pocket as the house finally came in view. "We can go through the side gate."

Now, I've been careful to write everything I can remember up till this point, no matter how trivial, but *this* is where it gets confusing. There were such a lot of people milling about, most of the ladies wearing enormous straw hats laden with flowers and feathers, and the gentlemen in tall top hats, all of which made it rather difficult to see. I know a taxi pulled up behind us and someone got out—but was it someone visiting a house further down the street, someone entirely unrelated to subsequent events, or was it someone who followed us inside? We pushed through the crowds and made our way to an empty corner of the main hall, where Toby tried unsuccessfully to flag down a waiter. Through an archway, I caught a brief glimpse of Julia surrounded by babbling aunts before the whole group of them moved into a large drawing room to inspect the wedding presents. Then Simon, who'd escorted Aunt Charlotte to the house, appeared halfway up the first flight of the main stairs, clearly looking for us. I waved, but he didn't notice. At that moment, a harsh voice cried out.

"Veronica FitzOsborne!"

Veronica, slightly apart from the rest of us, turned. There was a sudden pop, like that of a champagne cork, and the smell of fireworks. Then Veronica staggered backwards.

"Oh," she said, sounding more surprised than anything else. Her arm knocked against a marble pedestal, upon which was balanced a large and very ugly vase. Veronica and the vase hit the floor at the same time—the vase made rather more noise. There was a scream from near the front door, and then Simon's voice, raised above everyone else's, "Get him!"

But all I cared about right then was Veronica. I threw myself down beside her, although she was already starting to sit up.

"Veronica, are you all *right?*" I cried, taking her arm and helping her lean against the wall. She looked down at herself.

"Well, I think so," she said. "I mean, I don't seem to be bleeding or anything. What *was* that? It felt as though I'd been punched in the side by an invisible fist."

"Good God," said Toby, who'd gone white. "That's a *bullet.*" He pointed at the floor with a trembling finger. We all stared. Then Veronica started shaking and gasping.

"Don't worry!" shouted Simon, running up. "There's a doctor coming. We just need to— Someone get a blanket, she's gone into shock!"

"Don't be an idiot!" spluttered Veronica, and I realized she was laughing. "It's this *corset.* The bullet bounced off!"

"It's nothing to laugh at!" snapped Simon. "You could have been *killed!*"

Rupert appeared with a cashmere wrap, which he tucked around Veronica, then he and Toby raised her to her feet—with some difficulty, as she was weak with mirth. Leaving her to Toby and me, Rupert darted off to unlock an empty drawing room. There we sat Veronica down on a chaise longue and she examined herself more carefully. There was a small charred hole in the left side of her dress, just above where her ribs ended.

"Look, you can see where the whalebone's cracked," she said. "But the bullet can't have been traveling very fast, otherwise it would have gone straight through. Let me see, Toby." He held out his hand—he'd scooped up the bullet in his handkerchief before it could get lost. "Yes, the front bit is flattened. Isn't it *tiny*? I always imagined bullets were bigger than that."

"You mustn't touch it, there might be fingerprints," said Simon. "I've marked the spot where it fell, and the butler's roping off the area. The police have been called—no one caught that man."

"What exactly did you see?" I asked.

He pushed his fingers through his hair and shook his head. "Just someone who seemed out of place. He wasn't wearing a morning suit, just a coat and an ordinary hat, and he was looking around for someone. Then he shouted and pulled a gun out of his pocket—"

Rupert came back in with a maid, who carried a robe of Julia's and a silver ice bucket. "There's a powder room through that door there," he said. "You ought to put some ice on that, Veronica, you'll have an awful bruise otherwise. I brought some arnica, too." He pulled a bottle from his pocket, and the dormouse poked her nose out hopefully at the clink of glass. "Oh, and, Toby, your aunt wants to know what's going on," Rupert added apologetically. "She doesn't know it involved Veronica, just that there's been some sort of incident . . ."

"Oh dear, I'd better try and head her off," Toby said. "Can we keep all this from Julia, do you think? It's hardly what one wants to hear about on one's wedding day."

"That'll be difficult," said Rupert. "There are ladies fainting all over the place, now that they've found out what happened."

"At least they'll give the doctor something to do," said Toby. "Veronica, are you sure you don't need him to—"

"Of course not," came Veronica's muffled reply from the powder room. "I'm perfectly— Ow! No, don't worry, I just stabbed myself with a bit of whalebone. Sophie, can you give us a hand with this thing?"

Aunt Charlotte stormed in five minutes later, just as we emerged from the powder room. Toby followed, sending us rueful looks from behind her back.

"Really, Veronica!" our aunt said crossly. "If it's not *one* scandal, it's another! First Communism, then refugees—and now *this*!"

"She didn't do anything!" I cried indignantly. "It's not *her* fault that—"

We were interrupted by a portly policeman, who introduced himself as Inspector Sykes.

"Who?" said Aunt Charlotte, glaring at the hapless

inspector. "I've never *heard* of you. Where's the Chief Inspector? In any case, I *refuse* to allow my niece to be interviewed. If you *must* ask questions, you may address them to me. She's in shock, in a delicate frame of mind—"

"I most certainly am not," said Veronica, pulling Julia's dragon-embroidered black-and-gold silk robe tighter around herself and sitting down on the chaise longue. The two constables who'd appeared behind the inspector goggled at her.

"*And* is in a state of *undress*," hissed Aunt Charlotte in Veronica's direction.

"Do have a seat, Inspector," said Veronica, ignoring her.

"Well, Your Highness, if you could explain—in your own words—the events as they transpired," said the inspector. "*Ahem!*" He turned around and glowered at the constables, who stopped gaping at Veronica and hurriedly flipped open their notebooks.

They took a statement from her, then from Toby, Rupert, Simon, and me. Phoebe was summoned by Aunt Charlotte to bring a change of clothes for Veronica and arrived looking far more upset and fearful than the victim of the crime. The policemen interrogated the waiters, the Stanley-Ross butler, and the two gentlemen who'd unsuccessfully pursued the mysterious assailant down the street. A footman handed round mushroom vol-au-vents, smoked salmon sandwiches, and glasses of champagne. Lord Astley came in to see how Veronica was and said *he* was no expert, but the bullet looked to him like a .41 rimfire cartridge, fired from one of those Remington double-barreled derringers. More policemen arrived to inspect the scene of the crime. Julia discovered what had happened after overhearing some waiters, rushed in, and threw herself upon Veronica with shrieks of alarm, until she was finally persuaded by everyone to go back upstairs for the wedding speeches.

It was almost dusk by the time the policemen gathered back in the little drawing room, where we were all eating wedding cake—except for the dormouse, who was licking milk from the end of the eyedropper.

"Well?" said Aunt Charlotte impatiently. "What have you discovered?"

"It appears," said the inspector, "that Her Highness was shot."

"Yes, we'd worked that out for ourselves," said Veronica. "But have you identified the pistol? Can the owner be traced?"

"It's probably a small handgun," he said, peering at his notes. "Likely to have been manufactured, and perhaps purchased, in America. Either single-barreled or else . . . not. A fairly old gun, if it's single-barreled. If it were double-barreled, the assailant would have fired a second bullet."

"Or else he fired the first bullet outside, to test the gun was working," said Veronica. "Or thought I was mortally wounded after one shot, and knew if he stayed any longer, he'd be caught. What about fingerprints?"

The inspector shook his head. "Now, if the gun itself were found . . . but it doesn't appear the assailant threw it away."

"So, you haven't discovered *anything* useful?" said Simon, exasperated.

"Well!" huffed the inspector in offended tones. "If certain persons hadn't destroyed *valuable evidence* . . ." Toby had told them about the poison-pen letters.

"And what would *that* have shown you?" snapped Veronica. "That they'd been typed using a small Olivetti that was probably purchased somewhere in Europe, on a brand of writing paper available throughout the world?"

I did feel a bit sorry for the policemen. When they'd asked for the names of any person who might have reason to dislike Veronica, Simon said, "Anyone who's ever sat next to her at a dinner party, the majority of this year's debutantes, and the entire readership of the Fascist newspaper *Action*." Toby, upon being informed that ladies who were shot were generally the victims of rejected suitors, provided them with the name of Lord Elchester's nephew. Aunt Charlotte berated the youngest constable for spelling "FitzOsborne" incorrectly and nearly made him cry. And . . .

Oh! I've just thought of something!

Back again, hours later. Glancing over my journal entry, I suddenly had an idea about the man Simon had seen from the staircase, the man in the ordinary coat and hat. What if the gunman had been the same man I'd seen outside the church, and he'd been waiting for a glimpse of *Veronica*, not Julia? Comparing descriptions, Simon and I agreed that the men were of similar height and wore similar clothes, so Simon and Toby went off to the newspaper office to see if the wedding photographs had been developed. Luckily, they had. Even more luckily, the sub-editor accepted Toby's improbable story about being the photographer hired by the Stanley-Rosses, having a whole roll of film over-exposed, and needing to purchase some newspaper photographs to save his professional reputation from utter ruin.

"But couldn't you just have told the police and had *them* requisition the photographs?" asked Rupert, who came round this afternoon for tea.

"What, send PC Plod after them?" said Toby. "And have him drop them in the street or accidentally file them in the wastepaper bin?"

"Anyway, we *did* give them the photographs, after we'd had a good look at them," said Simon. "The man's face wasn't very clear—he had his hat pulled down low and his collar up—but Sophia recognized him."

"I said he looked familiar, but I couldn't think where I'd seen him," I corrected.

"Yet none of us recognized his voice," said Veronica, frowning. "Although I suppose he could have been trying to disguise it. It was rather hoarse, wasn't it?"

"And quite high-pitched," said Simon.

"Definitely English, though, not German or anything like that," mused Veronica. "Of course, we only heard two words."

So, it's as much of a mystery as before—but it was rather exciting, for a moment, to think that my journal had provided a clue, however small. And I might yet recall *why* he seems familiar . . .

After that, Simon was summoned to the library to type some letters for Aunt Charlotte, and Veronica went off to telephone the Reverend Webster Herbert about the Basque children, two dozen of whom are due to arrive in Milford in a few days. Toby, Rupert, and I sat around the tea table, discussing the bits of the wedding we'd missed. Anthony, it turned out, had become rather drunk after his best man laced his champagne with vodka; an elderly aunt got her tiara caught in an elaborate floral arrangement, knocked over a candle with her elbow, and set fire to the tablecloth; and a scandalous divorced second cousin, whom nobody could remember inviting, had caught Julia's bouquet.

"Oh, and I forgot to ask," said Toby. "How was the Fourth of June?"

Apparently, this is some big day at Eton, when there are speeches and cricket matches and a procession of boats and fireworks, and all the families turn up with vast picnic hampers.

"Everyone was busy with the wedding preparations, so it was just David and Penelope this year," said Rupert with a sigh. "Well, I don't blame the rest of them for wanting to stay away. Poor Mummy must have been to a dozen of them by now."

"I suppose David loved it," said Toby.

"All those fellow Old Etonians slapping him on the back and reminiscing about the best days of their lives," agreed Rupert. "If *I* ever have a son, I won't be inflicting any of that rubbish on him. He can go to the local secondary school."

"Do you suppose even *they* have ridiculous, pointless rules?" asked Toby. "Remember that time I sat on the—"

Whereupon both of them collapsed in giggles, and their gasping attempts at explanation just left me bemused. Apparently, Toby, in his second year, had sat upon a certain wall at Eton, causing widespread horror and disbelief because only a select few were allowed to rest their behinds on that particular stretch of brickwork. It all sounded rather silly to me.

"Very silly," said Toby, taking a deep breath and wiping his eyes. "Oh dear. Do you suppose Oxford will be as bad?"

"It couldn't possibly be," said Rupert. "And even if it is, it's only three years, not six." He took the dormouse out of his pocket for a feed just as Toby was called away to the telephone.

Rupert proceeded to tell me a lot of interesting facts about dormice—that they spend most of summer up in trees and most of winter fast asleep in nests on the ground; that they love honeysuckle and hazelnuts; and that their tails are so fragile that often the skin and bones fall apart, which is why some dormice seem to have such short tails. They're really quite adorable, I've decided, with their enormous dark eyes and shell-like ears and extravagant whiskers—not at all rattish.

"Sorry!" cried Toby, coming back in ten minutes later. "Aunt C suddenly realized you two were alone in here, so I've been ordered back to chaperone you. Don't mind me, I'll keep my eyes shut and my fingers stuffed in my ears. Carry on."

I started to laugh—both doors were wide open, and maids had been marching in and out to clear the tea things, so it was hardly the place for a bit of romance, even if the idea had entered either of our heads, which it most certainly had *not*—but Rupert went a bit pink and said he had to be getting along, anyway. Once he'd departed, I was sent for by Aunt Charlotte and subjected to one of her "little chats."

"Quite an old family, the Stanley-Rosses, good breeding on both sides," she said loftily. "But, my *dear* child, there's hardly *any* money. I believe they're thinking of selling that London house—too expensive to keep up and not much point now Julia's married off—but regardless of all that, the boy's a *third* son. He won't inherit a scrap of land. You can do far better than *that*, Sophia."

Although she then gave me a rather dubious look, taking in my ink-stained fingers (my pen leaks) and bird's nest hair (the hairdresser's lacquer spray from yesterday proved very difficult to wash out, and hanks of my hair are still sticking out at odd angles).

I couldn't think of anything to say in my or Rupert's defense, it was all too idiotic. The situation wasn't helped any by Simon coming in halfway through with some letters to be signed, realizing what was going on, trying to back out, then being ordered by Aunt Charlotte to sit down and find that address she'd been looking for. He gave me a sympathetic grimace, then rustled noisily through the papers on the desk, feigning deafness but clearly trying not to laugh. The moment I could get away, I rushed upstairs to my room, to the comfort of my journal—although now I'm far too irritated to write any more. I think I'll go and have a very long soak in the bath, using the rose-scented bath salts I bought with my first month's allowance. They're supposed to be soothing. Besides, they might help dissolve some of this hair lacquer.

7th June 1937

I was still indignant about Aunt Charlotte this morning and spent half an hour unburdening myself to Veronica, who was very sympathetic.

"She's given up on me, you see," Veronica said, nodding. "I'm causing far too many problems. She thinks you'll be easier to marry off."

"But I'm *sixteen*!" I said. "I don't *want* to get married! Well, not at the moment, anyway. In about ten years' time would be perfect . . . And poor *Rupert*! We were just sitting there, talking about dormice! Something embarrassing happens every single time I see him. He'll probably run away and hide the next time he catches sight of me."

"I'm sure he won't," said Veronica. "He seems very sensible—and he's excellent in a crisis, isn't he? I mean, look at how he was at the wedding. And if he isn't already used to mothers and aunts inspecting him as possible husband material, he soon will be."

"'It is a truth universally acknowledged, that a single man in possession of a good fortune, must be in want of a wife,'" I said, sighing.

"*Is* it?" said Veronica, looking surprised. "*Universally* acknowledged? Surely that presupposes life similar to human societies beyond this planet, and besides—"

"No, no, it's a quote from . . . Never mind," I said. "Anyway, Rupert's not in possession of a good fortune."

"Well, he's more likely to earn one than either of us," said Veronica, scowling. She jumped up from my bed and began pacing the room. "We've received no education to speak of, no training for anything but marriage—and not even much training for *that*. It's appalling the way sex is treated as some sort of dark, mystical secret."

"I *know*," I said. I wondered if Julia could be persuaded to tell whatever she knew when she got back from her honeymoon.

"Discouraged from attending university, kept out of the professions, paid half a man's wages if we *do* take a menial job," Veronica went on, her voice rising. "Expected to be *grateful* that women have finally been given the vote, then criticized when we take an interest in politics, because we can't possibly *understand* what we read in the newspapers. Forbidden from doing *anything* because we're such fragile little creatures—"

Veronica is confined to Montmaray House until her would-be assassin is caught, so she's behaving a bit like a bear in a zoo. I'm sure bears are quite good-natured if allowed to wander round the mountains, doing as they please—but even the nicest bear would soon become very cross if locked in a cage and bombarded with stones by small boys.

"And now *this!*" growled Veronica, brandishing the latest stone, otherwise known as *The Times*, which was the reason she'd come in to see me in the first place. The newspaper contained a letter written by Lord Elchester, who complained that the refugees at Stoneham Camp were thieving little hooligans and ought to be shipped straight back home.

"How would he know if they *were?* He doesn't live anywhere *near* Southampton!" Veronica exclaimed. "He's just using it as an excuse to proclaim his despicable political opinions!"

"Do you think some of the children *are* behaving badly?" I asked anxiously. After all, two dozen of them were about to arrive in Milford.

"With their experiences in the war, I wouldn't be surprised," said Veronica. "Although I doubt any of them are worse than Henry."

At that point, Phoebe sidled into the room, for no apparent reason. Perhaps she'd been told to keep a close eye on us, in case assassins started climbing through the windows and concealing themselves in the wardrobe or under the bed. If they do, I can't think of anyone less likely to deter them than Phoebe, especially at the moment—she's even paler and thinner than usual.

"Are you ill?" asked Veronica, not unsympathetically. But Phoebe only shook her head and trembled even more. (She finds Veronica rather intimidating.) Looking round, she caught sight of a crumpled handkerchief under my dressing table, scooped it up, and vanished as quickly as she'd appeared. I wondered if she'd been hoping to have a word with me alone, so I cornered her later in the bathroom. She was laden with a stack of towels, so I knew she wouldn't be able to make an easy escape.

"Is everything all right?" I asked. "You're not worried that an assassin will attack us, are you? Because there's no way any-one could get inside this house, and even if they did, Harkness was in the war—he'd soon sort them out."

"I know, Your Highness," she said, setting the towels on a chair. "He's got his old pistol out of its case and polished it up." She looked even more miserable at this.

"Then, is your family all right?" I said. "Your mother's not, er . . ." She couldn't possibly have had *another* baby, could she?

"Oh, no, Your Highness. I mean, she's well, Your Highness."

"And your sister, the one who's just gone into service in Salisbury?"

"She's . . . she's all right, thank you, Your Highness."

If I went on enquiring about every member of Phoebe's fam-ily, we'd be there for hours. I pondered for a moment as she hung up the towels. Perhaps she just needed a holiday. She'd had every second Sunday off since we'd arrived in London, but it would take a whole day to travel to her village by train and bus. She'd no sooner get there than she'd have to leave, and even then, she'd be late coming back.

"Do you need a week off?" I ventured. "To go and see your family?"

Her whole face lit up, but she demurred. "Oh, but I couldn't,

Your Highness," she said. "I haven't any leave due to me. I've not worked long enough."

"Never mind about *that*," I said, making a mental note to get Toby to ask the housekeeper (as she, like everyone else, adores him and indulges his every whim). "If you *could*, would you like to go and see your family?"

"Ye-es, Your Highness," she said—very reluctantly, as though I were dragging a confession of murder out of her. Then I understood. She wouldn't be paid for the week if she didn't work, and there'd be the train ticket and the bus fares, and I knew she sent most of her earnings home. Poor Phoebe! It made me want to join Daniel's next march in support of Fair Working Conditions for All—but as that's impossible, I made a silent vow to use my allowance, and Veronica's and Toby's, too, if necessary, so that Phoebe could have a proper holiday.

"If it's what you want, I can try to arrange it," I said. "And don't worry about the train fares or anything. Of course, if you don't want to go, that's all right, too."

"Well," she said, wringing her hands. I stood there a bit longer, smiling encouragingly, but eventually gave up and turned to go. *Then* the dam burst. Oh, she *would* like to go home, please, because her favorite brother—the one who'd been in trouble in Liverpool—was back, having lost his job up north.

"What sort of trouble?" I asked, madly curious.

"It weren't his fault," cried Phoebe, in full flow by then. "It's the police—they've got it in for Blackshirts . . ." Her eyes widened and she clapped her hand over her mouth.

"Your brother's joined the *Blackshirts*?" I said, goggling at her.

"You won't tell Her Highness, will you?" she begged.

I assumed she meant Veronica rather than Aunt Charlotte. But before I could say anything to reassure her, Barnes came in to see why Phoebe was taking so long with the towels, and it was probably only my presence that saved Phoebe from a tongue-lashing. Phoebe shot off downstairs and I walked back to my room, my thoughts whirling.

A *Blackshirt*! No wonder Phoebe gets into such a fluster whenever Veronica starts railing against the Fascists! But why would a nice village boy (I assume he's nice if he's Phoebe's favorite brother) want to dedicate himself to someone like Mosley—especially if it caused the poor boy to lose his job? Why would *anyone* want to be a Fascist? I thought of asking Veronica, but she'd only tell me he must be a complete idiot. She is not very balanced on the subject of Fascism. Although, I must admit, she thinks fanatical Communists are idiots, too. Actually, anyone who blindly follows *any* form of dogma, whether written by Marx, Hitler, or God, is regarded by Veronica as a complete idiot.

So I decided to go and ask Simon. I'd been eager to learn more about his political views, anyway. Sometimes he appeared to agree with Chamberlain, the Conservative Prime Minister, and other times he favored Winston Churchill (also a Conservative, although Churchill seems to be Chamberlain's sworn enemy these days). Then, on other issues, Simon supported the Labour Party. Of course, mostly Simon argued the opposite of whatever Veronica had just said. I waited till Aunt Charlotte had left for one of Lady Bosworth's interminable luncheon parties and Toby had gone for a walk in Kensington Gardens with Rupert. Then I went looking for Simon, eventually finding him in an armchair in the library, engrossed in a thick leather-bound volume. I tilted my head sideways to read the gold lettering on the spine.

"What's 'tort'?" I asked.

"Aarrgh!" he said, jolting upright. "Oh, it's you." He started to shove the book under a cushion, realized I'd already seen the cover, and blushed.

"Is it something *scandalous?*" I asked, intrigued.

"It's perfectly proper," he said. "Oh—*here* you are, then, if you don't believe me." And he held out a page, which consisted of a lot of complicated legal language, quite unintelligible to me.

"Hmm," I said. "So why did you try to hide it?"

"Are you going to pester me until I tell you?"

I pulled a footstool closer, sat on it, and stared up into his face. "Perhaps," I said.

He sighed.

"Or I could just ask Toby," I said.

"No, don't!" he said quickly. "All right, then. If you promise not to tell anyone."

"I can't promise till I know what it *is*," I said. "But I won't tell if there's a good reason to keep it secret."

It was destined to be a Day of Astonishing Revelations. It turns out that Simon has enrolled in night classes, to study law.

"But why would you want to keep *that* a secret?" I asked, bemused.

"For one thing, I doubt the Princess Royal would approve. She prefers me to spend every waking moment engaged in official duties."

"Oh. Yes, I see what you mean. But Toby wouldn't mind."

Simon fiddled with the cover of the book. "I don't want him to know, Sophia, in case . . ." He took a deep breath, then spoke in a rush. "In case I don't do very well. I haven't been to school before, I'm not used to working for examinations, and you know Toby doesn't take *any* kind of study seriously."

Gazing into Simon's face, I was filled with an intense but confused emotion. Admiration mixed with pity might be the closest way to describe it. I thought of how Simon must have felt, watching Toby open that acceptance letter from Christ Church, knowing how little Toby valued it . . .

"I swear, I won't tell *anyone*," I said fiercely—perhaps a little *too* fiercely, because Simon looked surprised, then slightly worried. I hastened to change the subject. "But, Simon, you distracted me. I came down to ask you a question."

Simon seemed relieved when he realized all I wanted to know was why people became Fascists. First he explained about German Fascism—how Hitler had taken advantage of the terrible conditions in Germany after they lost the Great War, how he'd ruthlessly eliminated other political parties and the free press, had set up storm-trooper armies and secret police and propaganda units and youth societies, so that now it was difficult and dangerous for a German to choose *not* to be a Fascist.

"Yes, I know about that," I said. "But why do *English* people become Fascists? Why would they want a Fascist dictator instead of a Parliament they could elect?"

Simon looked down at the book in his lap and drew his brows together. "You know, I once heard Mosley speak, years ago, in Trafalgar Square. It wasn't so much *what* he said but how he said it. He really knew how to use his voice. All that practice in the House of Commons, I suppose. And then there were his men in their black uniforms, flinging their arms up in salutes and waving their banners. It seemed so impressive." Simon glanced at me, giving me his half smile. "And he's said to be very good-looking, by those who care about such things. There are quite a few *lady* Fascists, you know."

"Ugh! I think he's creepy," I said with a shudder. (Mosley personifies the word "cad" to me. The words "scoundrel" and "rake" and "knave" also come to mind. Well, perhaps not "knave," that's a bit too medieval. Mosley is a thoroughly modern villain.) "So, it's just having a charismatic leader, that's all there is to their popularity?"

"It's also what he promises. Everything will become perfect the moment he takes over. Industry will be more efficient, there'll be jobs for all, workers will get paid more for working less, education and health care will be freely available. It's all a lot of nonsense, of course. None of his ideas would actually work, and half of them contradict the other half. But for people without much education, with badly paid, backbreaking jobs—or no jobs at all—it must sound wonderful. And he's careful to say exactly what his audience wants to hear. He promises to get rid of the idle rich when he's talking to unemployed miners up north, then he vows to abolish the Communists and trade unions when he's talking to his fellow idle rich. But the *main* thing is that he claims he's the only one who can save Britain from war."

"By letting Hitler do whatever he wants," I said, disgusted.

"Well, it's not that different from Chamberlain's policy of appeasement," Simon pointed out. "And who wants to go to war? You know how terrible it was last time. Imagine how much worse it'd be with modern armies, with aeroplanes able to bomb entire cities to rubble."

I felt sick, thinking of Guernica, of Montmaray.

"Sorry," he said quickly. "I didn't mean to . . . And anyway, there *won't* be a war, Sophia, everyone hates the idea of it, here and everywhere else. Besides, Hitler can't possibly think he could attack the rest of Europe and *win*. That would be crazy."

"Yes," I said, trying to get dreadful images of broken buildings out of my head. Then I asked Simon whether he thought a Blackshirt had shot Veronica.

"It's as likely as anything else," he said grimly. "So you haven't recalled where you saw him before?"

"No," I said. "And not for want of trying. Simon, you don't think he'll have another go at it, do you?"

"Let's see if he sends any more letters."

"If he was the one who *sent* those letters," I said. It's a sad day when we sit around *hoping* Veronica will receive threatening letters—but they're the only clue we have.

"Oh, and speaking of letters," said Simon, getting up and going over to the desk, "I had one from Alice in Cornwall—the Montmaravians are all well, and they send their regards."

I think Alice finds it easier to stay in contact via Simon— she always was very old-fashioned when it came to her dealings with us "Royal Highnesses." Her son Jimmy works on his uncle's fishing boat now, and Alice and her sister Mary seem to have settled comfortably into their new life—not that surprising, I suppose, when half the villagers either came from Montmaray originally or married Montmaravians or have Montmaravian relatives. Most of them consider themselves Cornish now, just as their ancestors were, and they're probably all British citizens, anyway, after all these years.

Simon was still shuffling through the papers on the desk. "Unfortunately," he continued, "I also had one from your sister's governess, threatening to resign. I haven't shown the Princess Royal—I'm still trying to figure out what to do about it. It won't be easy finding another governess at this time of year."

He picked up the letter and handed it to me.

"It sounds as though she's hoping for a raise in her wages," I said, scanning it. "Otherwise she wouldn't bother *threatening* to leave—she'd just go. Although it could be that she's worried what Aunt Charlotte will say once Aunt Charlotte gets back to Milford Park and sees Henry running wild and still practically illiterate. Miss Bullock might just want to be out of the way before that happens, and feels guilty enough to give us a few weeks' notice."

I gave the letter back to Simon.

"I think we ought to go to Milford and see which it is, then offer the poor woman a raise and a holiday," I said. "She deserves it, putting up with Henry all these months. Then Veronica can get Henry's behavior under some sort of control and settle in the Basque children before Aunt Charlotte arrives. Veronica needs to get out of London, anyway. She'll do something desperate if she's cooped up here too long . . ." I broke off, because Simon was giving me an odd look. "What?" I said.

"Have you been reading Machiavelli again?" he said.

"No, I'm reading *Regency Buck* by Georgette Heyer. It's about a beautiful heiress who conquers Society despite her unconventional manners, and it's got Beau Brummell in it. But, Simon, the thing is, *you'll* need to come with us to Milford as a chaperone and bodyguard, and I don't think Aunt Charlotte will agree to it just yet. She needs to get over the whole shooting incident—I should give her till next week. By then, she'll be caught up in Ascot Week and she'll be too busy to worry about anything else."

"You used to be such a sweet, guileless girl," Simon said, shaking his head.

21st June 1937

Milford Park is heavenly in summer. The garden is spilling over with warm, ripe fruit—raspberries and strawberries in the kitchen garden, plums and peaches and nectarines in the orchard, grapes and melons in the hothouse—and the flower beds are ablaze with color. Even more beautiful than the fifty-seven types of roses and massed plantings of lavender and scented lilies are the meadows full of wildflowers. I walk back from the village gathering armfuls of cornflowers and larkspur, marveling at the variety of hedges—hawthorn and blackthorn and holly, all tangled up with wild roses, ivy, and honeysuckle. The birds crowd into the trees and sing from dawn till dusk, and the long grass rustles with the frantic activity of little furry creatures—Rupert would know all their names, but I think they are mostly field mice and shrews, with the odd stoat. Once I even thought I saw a hedgehog curled up in a nest of leaves—although it may just have been a pile of twigs.

The Basque refugees are not quite as enamored of Nature as

I am, being mostly city children, but they're doing their best to cope with its less appealing aspects—the mice in the pantry, for instance, and the bats that swoop past (and sometimes through) the windows each evening. There are seventeen children, ranging from five years old to fifteen. The Stoneham Camp organizers were very good about keeping the children grouped in families, so we have six Labauria siblings, five Morenos (who are related to the Labaurias), five Martínezes, and a López (who is cousin to the Martínezes). Two of the boys are named Jesús, which makes the Reverend Webster Herbert twitch a bit—he calls one Jim and the other Johnny. The girls are mostly Henry's age or younger, with enormous dark eyes and wide, bright smiles. I don't know the boys as well, because they disappear whenever it's time to wash up after dinner or hang out the laundry. The group's elected spokesperson (they are very democratic about that sort of thing) is a glowering, chain-smoking fourteen-year-old named Javier. His father is (or was; no one knows if he's still alive) someone very important in the Basque government. I find Javier rather daunting, but he gets on well with Veronica, now that he's interrogated her at length about her political views and judged them acceptable.

All the children are vehemently anti-Fascist, of course. I saw an angelic six-year-old named María Teresa spit on the ground when Franco's name was mentioned, and there was widespread rejoicing when General Mola, the leader of the attacks on the Basque Republic, died in an aeroplane crash a few weeks ago. But I really can't say I blame the children—I feel much the same as they do, now that they've confirmed our worst fears about the Basque captain's family. We asked the children if they knew him, and one of them said her cousin had gone to school with the Zuleta girls, and she'd heard they were all killed in Guernica when the church in which they were sheltering was hit by an incendiary bomb. I try not to discuss the war with the children anymore, especially now that the news from Spain is so bad. Yesterday was dreadful—we learned that Bilbao had fallen to the Fascists. Javier and two of the older boys immediately marched off down the road in the direction of Southampton, determined to commandeer a southbound boat and join the fighting. Veronica went after them in the Lagonda and only managed to persuade them to return by reminding them of their responsibilities towards their little sisters and cousins.

"And I'm not sure I did the right thing," she said to me last night. "Who am I to tell them to stay when their friends and families are being slaughtered over there?"

"They're *children*," I reminded her. "Their parents sent them here to keep them safe." Then I asked her how long she thought the Basque Republic could hold out.

She shook her head. "Maybe another month or two," she said. "They're cut off from the Spanish Republicans, they've no weapons thanks to that non-intervention policy, they're running out of food and fuel, the towns are being bombed into oblivion—it's hopeless. They say they'll never surrender, but . . ."

I know she's very upset about Captain Zuleta's family,

although she doesn't talk about it. My growing suspicion, too horrible to be spoken of aloud, is that Guernica was singled out for destruction by the German bombers *because* of the Basque captain; that SS-Obergruppenführer Gebhardt is continuing his scheme of retribution against us; that anyone who is known to have helped us, anyone who might have witnessed what happened to Montmaray, is marked as a target. Sometimes this idea seems like wild surmise, but at other times (in the dark hours before dawn, when I wake, shuddering, from yet another nightmare), I know the Nazis are capable of *anything*, anything at all.

I think Veronica's also unhappy about her lack of progress on the Montmaray campaign. Where does she even start? A letter to the Prime Minister? But if all those Labour MPs haven't succeeded in changing the Prime Minister's mind about the Germans in the wake of Guernica, then what hope do *we* have? And how will we ever get Montmaray back without the British government's support?

And then, at times (when being laced into a new silk evening dress by my maid, being served dinner on Spode china by liveried footmen, slipping between fine linen sheets at night), I wonder if I could ever go back to our old life on Montmaray, even if it *were* possible . . .

And then I feel terribly disloyal.

"All we can do right now is look after the children as best we can," I told Veronica firmly last night, pretending I wasn't full of guilt and apprehension myself.

"I know," said Veronica, chewing her lip.

"And keep them all too busy to think about the war," I added.

So we give them English lessons, and join in their football games, and take them on long nature walks. Ericson the groom offers them pony rides, the boys go fishing with the villagers— and the girls get bossed around unmercifully by Henry, leader of the newly formed Girl Guide Eagle Patrol.

I regret to say the whole Girl Guide thing was my idea. I read about Princess Elizabeth and the 1st Buckingham Palace Company, and thought it might be a good way to keep Henry occupied while Miss Bullock is on holiday. It all sounded so civilized, with those neat blue uniforms and little badges and solemn pledges. I ought to have known that Henry would seize on the quasi-military aspects with fervor and ignore all the ladylike bits—hence her obsession with marching drills and acquiring proficiency badges in archery, tracking, and signaling. Needlecraft, hostessing, and child nursing might as well not exist in the Girl Guide handbook as far as Henry's concerned. A Guiding Lady wearing a navy suit and plumed hat came over from Salisbury last week to inspect our girls, and she suggested a change of name.

"What about *Robin* Patrol?" she said sweetly. "Or Lark? Or Dove?"

"No, I don't think so," said Henry decisively. "I wanted Vulture or Buzzard, but Sophie looked in the handbook and said it had to be a bird found in this area."

"Er . . . yes," said the lady, glancing over at me. "Well,

Guiding will certainly provide you girls with *wonderful* opportunities to develop new skills! Our company's been having a lovely time this month learning Scottish country dancing!"

"What I really want to learn," said Henry, "is how to defuse a bomb. But there doesn't seem to be a badge for that."

I did insist that participation be on a voluntary basis, and several of the Basque girls decided after the first meeting that they'd rather stay at the Old Mill House, helping Mr. Herbert's housekeeper bake scones, than crawl through the woods on their knees and elbows evading imaginary pursuers. But, surprisingly enough, four of the Basque girls and a couple of village girls have stuck with it. Perhaps we've been underestimating Henry's leadership skills all this time. At any rate, it's keeping us all busy— and no one's sustained any permanent injuries. Yet.

It's been quite good having it as a distraction, because, apart from my anxiety about the Basques and the Germans, I'm still troubled about Veronica's attacker. Phoebe accompanied us to Milford, and then I sent her off to her mother's for a fortnight. They needed an extra hand for the harvest, and she might be able to talk some sense into her brother. I deliberated for ages over whether to tell anyone about him. I didn't want Phoebe getting into trouble and losing her job, and it was clear that she, at least, thought he was responsible for the threatening letters. Why else would she be going through Veronica's post? But would a boy who'd left school at fourteen to work on the docks *really* be capable of typing those letters? Would he own an expensive Burberry coat, as the man outside the church had worn? Would he know how to use an old-fashioned American pistol? It seems unlikely. And yet, there hasn't been a single poison-pen letter since Phoebe spoke to me about him. Is that just a coincidence, or is it cause and effect? Perhaps the gunman seemed so familiar to me because he looked like *Phoebe*. Should I telephone the inspector to tell him my suspicions? But what if it came to nothing and got poor Phoebe into trouble? And on and on my thoughts whirled. Eventually, I did what I ought to have done straightaway and discussed it with Veronica.

"But he doesn't know me," she said, bemused. "Why would he go to all that bother?"

"Perhaps he read about you in *Action*," I said. "Or he thinks we're exploiting his sister. Maybe he feels she ought to have better working conditions."

"He's a Fascist, not a Communist," she pointed out. "Besides, we've just given her a fortnight's leave with pay. Honestly, Sophie, don't worry about it. It was just some madman who's now seen the error of his ways. Or else he's been recaptured and locked up again in his asylum. I hope so, anyway—I'm certainly not wearing a corset in this weather. Oh, that reminds me, you *must* read Daniel's latest letter. It's absolutely fascinating—did you know that a bulletproof silk vest saved King Alfonso from an assassin's gun in 1901?"

"King Alfonso of Spain? Your second cousin once removed, or whatever he is?"

"Yes, but don't tell Javier that Alfonso and I are related. Apparently, layers and layers of silk slow down bullets. Isn't that interesting? Archduke Franz Ferdinand heard about it and bought a silk vest, too. He was wearing one in Sarajevo when *he* was shot in 1914."

"But didn't he die? And start off the Great War?"

"Well, yes," said Veronica. "Because they shot him in the neck, not the chest. If only he'd been wearing a silk balaclava. Goodness, one could write a *book* about how the silkworm has altered the course of world history. When one considers the Silk Road . . ." And on and on she went for a good quarter of an hour, but I think we were both desperate to talk about something other than our problems for once.

Sometimes I think Life is best summed up as

(a) Awful Bits

and

(b) Things That Successfully Distract One from the Awful Bits.

However, I'm still working on this theory. Will write more later.

6th August 1937

Well, let's get the awful bits over with first. The Basque Republic is on its knees, on the verge of total surrender. Most of the children at the Old Mill House have no idea what has happened to their families, but the Basque leaders all seem to be dead or in prison, apart from the few who've escaped into exile. Lord Elchester continues his campaign to deport the "little Basque hooligans" from England. Further east, the Japanese have invaded Peking and Miss Amelia Earhart remains missing without trace somewhere in the Pacific, having crashed her aeroplane.

It seems heartless of Nature, but here, the sun continues to beam, the fruit to ripen, the flowers to bloom, the birds to chirp, and the little furry creatures to scamper about in the undergrowth. The lake is our most successful distraction right now— we spend half our day either in it or lying beside it. Carlos is permanently damp and smells of waterweed. Estella the piglet, now almost as big as Henry, wallows happily in the ditch she's dug near the jetty. Veronica and Simon have turned the color of butterscotch, Toby and Henry have sun-bleached curls and a golden glow, and I have a new crop of freckles.

We held a birthday picnic for Henry down by the lake, inviting all the Basque children, and they loved it (except Javier, who hates everything at the moment). And not even Javier could keep up his scowl when Estella stole his little sister's cupcake out of her hand—the expression on Carmelita's face as she tried to work out where it had gone was priceless. Goodness, even Aunt Charlotte found it difficult (although not impossible) to maintain her disapproving expression as she watched Toby lead the children in manic versions of Musical Cushions and Blind Man's Bluff. She has made it clear to Henry that none of the Basque children, not even the Girl Guides, are to come within fifty yards of the house. She thinks they all have lice, or worse.

Perhaps I ought to have included Aunt Charlotte's arrival at Milford Park amongst the awful bits. She's in a very grumpy mood because her best horse narrowly lost some important race, beaten by one of the horses of her most loathed rival, a parvenu industrialist without so much as a *knighthood*. She's a terrible snob—she wouldn't have minded nearly as much if it'd been Lord Rosebery's horse that had won. Still, I suppose our aunt *is* a distraction. It's impossible to do anything *but* pay attention to her when she's in the room, especially as she's renewed her campaign to get at least one of us engaged to be married by the end of the year. She pores over *Debrett's* in the manner of a horse trainer scrutinizing the studbook.

"There's Billy Hartington, heir to the Duke of Devonshire," she said this afternoon as we all sat around the tea table. "He'd do nicely for you, Veronica—apart from his many other advantages, he's very *tall*."

"He's very *dull*," said Veronica. "If he's that Cambridge boy you made me sit beside at the Fortescue ball."

"Although he's probably *too* eligible," Aunt Charlotte went on, right over the top of her. "The Palace is said to have him in mind for Princess Elizabeth."

Toby pointed out that Princess Elizabeth is eleven years old.

"They grow up so quickly," said Aunt Charlotte, turning pages. "Now, there's Earl Fitzwilliam's boy. Oh, I forgot—he married the Plunket girl. And really, when one's nieces insist on getting tangled up with Communists and Basques and who knows what else"—she paused to glare at Veronica, who glared back—"and fail to accept a *single* house party invitation throughout the entire summer—not that there *were* very many invitations to begin with—then, sadly, one must accept that most of the decent English families are out of reach." Heaving a sigh, Aunt Charlotte tossed *Debrett's* aside in favor of the *Almanach de Gotha*. "Hmm, King Alfonso's children are all of age now—"

"*Firstly*, I'm related to them," said Veronica through gritted teeth. "And secondly, all the boys are either deaf-mutes or hemophiliacs."

"Nonsense! The youngest boy's perfectly normal—married already, unfortunately—but I was thinking of his sister. For Tobias."

Toby, who'd been quite enjoying the conversation up till that point, choked on his cucumber sandwich.

"Infanta María Cristina," said Aunt Charlotte, peering at the page. "Catholic, of course—not that we FitzOsbornes worry too much about that sort of thing. Still, it wasn't such a success with *your* mother, was it, Veronica? I don't know if one can blame it all on religion in her case, though—"

"Blame all *what?*" said Veronica, her eyes narrowing to dangerous slits.

"Oh, look, everyone!" cried Toby desperately, waving his newspaper around. "The Rector of Stiffkey's been mauled to death by a lion!"

"I wouldn't be surprised at *anything* that dreadful man gets up to," snapped Aunt Charlotte. "And you know quite well what I mean about your mother, Veronica. As if finding a suitable husband for you isn't difficult *enough*, without you running about dressed like a maid and acting like a chauffeur—there was no reason those children couldn't have taken the bus to the dentist—not to mention writing that letter to *The Times* about Lord Elchester, I've never been so embarrassed in my life! And even if one could find a respectable family willing to ignore all *that*, there's your scandal of a mother, bolted off from a perfectly good husband and who knows *what* she's currently—"

Veronica stood up, sending her chair crashing backwards. "He was *not* a perfectly good husband!" she cried. "He had a vile temper, he treated her contemptibly, and now she's dead!" Then she whirled on one heel and stormed off.

"What?" cried Aunt Charlotte, letting her teacup fall. "Dead? Why wasn't I informed? Simon! Where is that young man? *Simon!* It is your responsibility to keep me advised of— And how did that *dog* get in here?"

Carlos looked up from the rug, where he'd been busy chewing burrs out of his paws. It was obvious to everyone that he'd had the run of the house while we'd been away—he knew his way round better than I did. But I jumped to my feet to lead him outside, grateful for the opportunity to escape. I decided against trying to find Veronica—I was fairly sure she'd prefer to be alone just then. Instead, I opened a side door for Carlos and followed him down towards the lake, my copy of Ernst Toller's *Seven Plays* tucked under one arm. Daniel had sent it to Veronica, telling her she needed to read something other than newspapers once in a while, and she'd passed it on to me. It's rather depressing, though. The author was exiled from Germany after his books were burnt by the Nazis, and his plays are full of war and suffering and death, all of which he describes in gruesome detail. The book isn't really much of a success as a distraction, but I feel I ought to persist with it, for poor Herr Toller's sake. I was wandering along, flicking through the pages and trying to find my place, when I nearly stumbled over Javier.

"Oh!" I said. "Sorry."

He grunted what I presumed was a greeting. He was sitting on a rock, scowling at the lake. The sparkling water, the fluffy clouds drifting through the pale sky, the gently waving grass, all seemed to mock his misery.

"No word from your family, then?" I ventured, sitting down beside him.

"Word?" he repeated with an angry laugh. "No. No words." He gave my book a scathing glance. "What good are words, anyhow? Or books, or writings."

"Sometimes," I said carefully, "they can be a comfort. *I've* found. When things get very bad."

His glare softened. He knew about us, about Montmaray. I think the Basque children found it a strange comfort to know that we, too, had lost parents, had lost our home. He sighed.

"But words are no good against enemies," he said, turning back to the lake. "They are not guns."

"Well," I said feebly, "guns are certainly very . . . Except they're rather . . ."

I really didn't want to think about guns. My gaze fell upon my book, and I suddenly recalled Herr Toller's introduction, which I'd read the night before.

"But, Javier!" I said. "Wait, listen to this." I fumbled for the right page. "This writer has just escaped from Germany, so he knows what he's talking about, and he says, 'The power of dictators is limited. They can kill the mind for a time and they can kill it in any one land. But across the border, they are impotent; across the border, the power of the word can save itself . . . the *word*, which in the long run is stronger and greater than any dictator, and will outlast them all.'"

I looked up, but Javier remained silent, staring out at the lake. We both watched Carlos paddle through the blue-green water, his bearded chin held high, a line of ducklings bobbing in his wake.

"You think that?" Javier said at last. "About . . . across the border?"

"Sometimes, across the border is the *only* place where one can fight dictators," I said.

Carlos reached the bank, shook himself vigorously, then flung himself into the soft grass to squirm around. Estella trotted over to join him, grunting happily. I saw that Carlos, at least, had adapted to this new life with ease. Why did humans insist on clinging to the past, to things that were lost, probably forever? Why were we so stubbornly territorial, so uncompromising—and so *savage* to one another—when animals managed to get along quite nicely, wherever they were?

Of course, the rabbits of Milford Park might have quibbled with my benevolent view of Carlos.

"You are right," Javier said abruptly. "Words help. Mr. Herbert shows me the letter."

"What—oh, Veronica's letter in *The Times*."

"That man, he tells lies about us."

"Lord Elchester? Yes, he's horrid."

"*I* would write a letter—no, not a letter, a long story with the truth. But my English is bad."

"Write it in Spanish," I said. "Veronica will translate it."

"No, they will not put it in the newspaper."

"Well, *The Times* is awfully Conservative. But there are other newspapers."

Javier shook his head impatiently. "No, I am bad at writing. Even at school, my best teacher said . . ." His voice broke. Was his teacher in prison now or turned traitor or dead? I didn't know, and neither did Javier, and he probably never *would* know. How *cruel* war is, I thought, for the hundredth time. Not just for killing soldiers by the thousands, not just for murdering women and children, but for tearing apart everything that makes up a normal, civilized life—children growing up with their parents, going to school . . .

Javier suddenly lurched to his feet, turning his face away from me, towards the village. "I am late."

"Well, good—" I said. But he was already slouching through the grass, his shoulders hunched, his dark head bowed. As though he felt even the word "goodbye" was useless.

23rd October 1937

I am seventeen years old today but feel about a hundred and two. This morning, in a fit of nostalgia and homesickness, I read over my old journal—the battered, sea-stained one I started last year. Goodness, who *was* that person writing it? She seems so young, so pathetically hopeful, dreaming of her debutante dance and sighing over Simon. I should like to travel back in Mr. Wells's Time Machine and give her some helpful advice, except I don't have any to offer. Besides, I think the Time Machine only went forward, into the future. And I don't think I want to know about *that*, especially if there's nothing I can do to avoid the awful bits.

I *am* in a gloomy mood, aren't I? A lot of it's to do with missing Toby, now up at Oxford, and Simon, who's gone to London, on Aunt Charlotte's orders, to continue sorting through the mess of FitzOsborne financial records and investigate whether Isabella left Veronica anything in her will. (The latter task is, of course, quite pointless. Isabella's family may have been Spanish aristocrats, but they weren't particularly rich and they didn't leave her a penny. Also, the idea of Isabella doing anything as organized as writing a will is laughable.)

Meanwhile, Veronica has decided she needs a thorough understanding of the British parliamentary system before she can even *begin* to convince the British government to help Montmaray, so she's started working her way through the library's bound volumes of *Hansard's Parliamentary Debates*. Which apparently date back to 1830. Veronica never *used* to procrastinate like this. But if she *does* believe she was, in part, responsible for Montmaray's destruction (which is absolute rubbish, but no use telling her that), it might explain why she's so reluctant to act now. Better to do nothing than do something if there's the slightest chance her actions might end in disaster. Except we've already lost Montmaray, so how could things possibly get any worse? Not that I have a clue about where to begin, either.

Aunt Charlotte, who knows nothing of all this, has insisted Veronica take over Simon's job while he's away. Veronica is just as capable as Simon of writing letters and keeping track of Aunt Charlotte's committee meetings, but is not very good at being cheerful and obliging—hence the shouting that erupts at intervals from the library. I try to steer clear of that part of the house.

Toby and Rupert did invite Veronica and me to luncheon at their college last week, which might have cheered us up—if it had happened. We'd planned to stay in London at Montmaray House and do some shopping, then take the train up to Oxford. But Aunt Charlotte said no, because Veronica's would-be assassin is still on the loose. Even though, as Veronica pointed out, we haven't heard anything from him, or the police, for months and months. Then Aunt Charlotte said that "Smith" (as she persists in calling Phoebe) wasn't a suitable chaperone for us (too young, too incompetent—it's just lucky our aunt doesn't know about Phoebe's Blackshirt brother), and that Barnes was needed at Milford, so that was that. I think Aunt Charlotte was just annoyed *she* hadn't been invited to luncheon (which was a bit tactless of Toby, I must admit).

Most of my indignation was on Veronica's behalf, because I'd thought seeing Oxford might provide some enjoyable distraction for her. But she told me she'd probably feel sick with envy if she caught sight of a lady undergraduate, so perhaps it was better she stayed away, at least until she got used to the idea of Toby being there. Apparently, Oxford has *eight hundred* female students now—almost one for every six men! Goodness, that's eight hundred sets of parents who are progressive enough (and rich enough) to send their daughters to university! And that doesn't include the girls who go to Cambridge or . . . Actually, girls aren't awarded degrees at Cambridge, Veronica has just told me, nor are they permitted to join any Cambridge clubs, nor wear caps and gowns—although they *are* allowed to attend lectures, as long as they don't speak or applaud.

So I suppose it's a good thing I don't want to go to university. I don't think I have the right sort of mind for it, anyway, judging by Rupert's letters. He is reading English Literature and says it's like school, only worse. He says the tutors are all obsessed with analyzing things. For instance, it isn't enough to read a poem about Nature, and think it beautiful, and feel happy while reading it, and then drift off into a lovely memory of a summer's day just after a sudden rainstorm, with the flowers still dripping and the warm, rich scent of new life rising from the black earth. No, one is expected to tear apart the stanzas and lines and words and even the spaces in between the words, and inspect all the broken pieces, and then write a long essay, with footnotes, about how and why the poet put it together in the first place. I think university would make me never want to read anything ever again.

I wrote back and asked Rupert why he wasn't studying Agriculture or Biology or something like that. He replied that his father told him only a fool would try to learn that sort of thing from books, and if Rupert wanted to manage a farm, he could work on one of theirs—*after* he got a proper degree. Rupert also said he'd much rather be reading English than Economics, as his brothers did (or started to do—Charlie got sent down at the end of his first year for being drunk all the time and not turning up to exams). The rest of Rupert's letter was about him finding the cook's cat in the quadrangle after a fight with a terrier, and the veterinarian having to shave the cat's hind legs in order to stitch up the cuts, so the poor thing now looks as though she were wearing a pair of long pink socks and is too embarrassed to be seen in public. It did not surprise me to learn that she is recuperating in Rupert's room, sharing the space with three pigeons (in a box nailed above the window, in case the cat makes a sudden recovery) and the dormouse (on top of the wardrobe).

Rupert writes very good letters—not as funny as Toby's, but more revealing of what he actually thinks and feels. In my letter to him, I just described what I'd been doing, which was not much—helping at the Old Mill House, mostly, and desperately trying to think of some indoor activities for the Guides. (Autumn has descended upon us like a wet gray blanket, and it's not much fun shivering in the mist, icy raindrops trickling down the back of my neck, watching the girls practice their archery.) There *was* my article in *The Evening Standard*, but I thought it would be boasting to mention it to Rupert. Actually, it's probably boasting to mention it *here*, except no one could possibly read this (my Kernetin is now so abbreviated that even Veronica would have problems deciphering it).

The article was all about the Basque children at Milford, and how beautifully behaved they are, and how well they've adapted to village life. I made sure I described them doing lots of wholesome English activities, like baking Victoria sponge cakes and going to church. I also explained how awful things were in Spain due to the war, especially with all the German bombing, but unfortunately, the editor took that bit out. (So it's probably a good thing I didn't follow Toby's suggestion and send in something about Montmaray as well—they'd never have printed that.) Still, the children pinned up a copy of the article in the Old Mill House kitchen, and Veronica sent a clipping to Daniel, so I feel quite proud and almost like a proper writer.

There—recalling pleasant things *does* make one feel more hopeful about life! So I shall now list all my birthday presents—

a string of seed pearls with matching drop earrings from Aunt Charlotte; a portable typewriter in a caramel-colored case from Veronica, Toby, Henry, and Simon; a copy of W. H. Auden's *Look, Stranger!* from Daniel; a box of chocolates from Lady Astley; a bottle of Shalimar scent from Julia and Anthony, now returned from their honeymoon in France; and a blank journal with marbled sky-blue covers from Rupert, because I'd mentioned that I'd used up nearly all of my exercise book. And then the Basque children gave me a lovely birthday tea at the Old Mill House, and the Girl Guides presented me with a walking stick that they'd carved themselves, which will certainly come in handy, given Henry's determination to get her tracking badge. I adore all my presents—but I think the typewriter and journal are my favorites, because they show that the others take my writing seriously (probably more seriously than I do).

I forgot to say that Daniel also sent us a newspaper clipping about Oswald Mosley getting hit on the head with a "metal object" after his Blackshirts started a riot in Liverpool, and Mosley having to go to hospital to see if his brain was all right, which is not really funny, but if anyone deserves to be hit on the head, it's Mosley. The Blackshirts threw another brick through Daniel's window, and his neighborhood has a lot of disgusting anti-Jewish slogans chalked, and even painted, all over the walls . . .

Oh, I'm back to the awfulness of life again. Bother. I think I'll go to bed.

20th December 1937

We've just arrived back at Milford after a week in London. Henry desperately needed new clothes (one can almost *see* her sprouting upwards, like a bean plant), and the rest of us had Christmas shopping to do. Miss Bullock took Henry to the Zoo and the Natural History Museum, and I accompanied them to watch the Changing of the Guard at Buckingham Palace.

Veronica and I also had luncheon with Julia, at the Park Lane flat where Julia and Anthony are living while their house in Belgravia is being done up. Julia apologized for how small and squashed the flat was, but *I* didn't think it was, not at all. It took up an entire floor of the building and seemed even larger because it was so bright. All the furniture was white, except for a chrome-plated sideboard, and the wallpaper was ivory with silver stripes. There were big vases of iceberg roses set everywhere, huge looking glasses on the walls, and a set of towering windows framing the wintry expanse of Hyde Park. It seemed as though everything should be freezing to the touch, but there was also a ferocious central heating system pouring hot air through vents in the floor.

"It's like living inside a lightbulb," said Julia. "Ant's mother had it done up ten years ago, when I'm sure it was horribly fashionable, but . . . Oh well! Beggars can't be choosers!"

There couldn't possibly be anyone who looks *less* like a beggar than Julia. She brought back three trunks of clothes and jewelry from Paris, and all her new outfits are extremely chic, fit her superbly, and appear to have cost thousands of pounds. She has lost some weight (even her eyebrows seem thinner) and has stopped being pretty in favor of being glamorous. She also seemed more than a bit tired. Anthony was rushing off to a meeting at his club as we arrived, and Julia snapped at him, telling him his tie was appalling and to go and change it at once, which he did. He didn't seem to mind being bossed about. Perhaps he likes it? But Julia didn't seem to enjoy it much.

"Finally," she sighed, sinking into a shiny white sofa once he was gone. "Now we can have a lovely chat. You must tell me *everything* you've been up to."

Veronica talked about the Basque refugees for a while, but I thought Julia probably got enough of that from Anthony, so I told her about Henry saying she didn't think much of the security arrangements at Buckingham Palace, and being very disappointed when Piccadilly Circus turned out to be utterly devoid of clowns, elephants, and acrobats.

"Heavens, that *child*!" said Julia, starting to laugh and looking slightly less weary. "And how's our darling Toby?"

Veronica said he was his usual lazy self. He's only attended two lectures all term (neither of which had anything to do with the subjects he's supposed to be studying), he failed to hand in his last essay, and he spends most of his time having very long luncheons and even longer dinners. I did wonder why Julia didn't already know this from Rupert's letters.

"*Rupert's* letters!" snorted Julia. "Goodness, a couple of sentences about the weather and his work and how are *we*? He might as well send a postcard. Do you mean to say you get proper letters from him? With actual paragraphs? Well, my *dear*! You *are* privileged—"

Veronica saw me starting to blush and quickly asked whether Julia and Anthony had visited the Louvre during their time in Paris, and was it true that it had a better collection of Roman art than the British Museum? Julia said she had no idea, but that the *Mona Lisa* was so tiny and dark she couldn't understand what all the fuss was about. The Eiffel Tower, on the other hand, seemed far *larger* than in pictures, especially when one's husband insisted on one climbing hundreds of steps to the second level.

At that point, the maid came in to announce luncheon was served, but the subject of Paris was fascinating enough to last us all the way through the spinach soufflé and then the pheasant à la Normande.

"Actually, I'm surprised your aunt hasn't sent you two over to Paris for finishing school," said Julia, nodding at the maid to bring in the next course. "Or at least to do some shopping."

Veronica explained about the FitzOsbornes not being very keen on France, on account of Napoleon shooting a hole in our castle wall, and then the disaster of the Great War. "Besides, she wouldn't trust us over there by ourselves," Veronica said as we were served slivers of an exquisite tarte au citron.

"What, she thinks you'd elope with an Anarchist?" asked Julia.

"Something like that," I said, giving Veronica a meaningful look so she wouldn't mention the Crazed Assassin. After all, the attack had occurred on Julia's wedding day—had almost ruined the event entirely for her. And then, of course, I couldn't help recalling Julia's floods of tears that morning. I was longing to ask whether she now regarded her doubts beforehand as silly and schoolgirlish, or perfectly sensible. Was it wonderful to be married, I wanted to know, or terrible, or simply a *relief* after all the trouble everyone took to get girls married off? But it seemed rude to ask, and if Julia believed she *had* made a colossal mistake, she'd hardly admit it a mere six months later. I did ask what she did all day in London, as it turned out Anthony was often away at the family estate, learning how to manage it.

"Oh, darling, you wouldn't *believe* how busy I am," she said. "Supervising the maids and sorting out the menu with Cook— not that she pays the slightest bit of attention to me, just says, 'Yes, m'lady,' and goes on with whatever she'd already planned— and then there's invitations to answer, having one's hair and nails done, dress fittings . . . Then luncheon out, usually, and in the afternoon, meeting friends at the Forum—my club, you

know, *far* more modern than the poor old Alexandra Club, I suppose your aunt belongs to that one—or else a fashion show or an
art exhibition, generally some charity thing, then tea, then it's
time to dress. Dinner, then a concert or the theater, then supper
and going somewhere to dance—"

The maid set biscuits and five sorts of cheese in front of us.

"—and so by the end, one is simply *longing* to collapse into
bed and never get up again!"

I took a piece of the blue-and-white cheese, because I'd always wondered what mold tasted like, and discovered it was
nicer to look at than to eat. So I had a wedge of Camembert
with a buttery biscuit, which was glorious.

"Not that I'm complaining," Julia went on. "Heavens, when
I think of how it was at home! Perishing of boredom, forbidden
from doing *anything* interesting . . ."

"But, Julia, you did lots of things!" I couldn't help protesting.
"You were always going up to London, or off on flying trips with
Anthony."

"Only after I got engaged, and really only one proper flying
trip—well, you know about that one—and Daddy had a fit when
he found out. No, no, it's *much* better being married," she said,
but in tones that made me wonder if she was trying to convince
herself. Then she told the maid we'd have our coffee in the drawing room, and the coffee was black and deliciously bitter and
came in gorgeous little pink-and-green Sèvres cups with a bowl
of chocolate truffles.

And now writing about all the scrumptious food Julia gave

us has made me ravenous. Aunt Charlotte and Toby have gone to the Bosworths' for a luncheon party (Veronica and I weren't invited), Simon is in Poole, and Harkness the butler is at his sister's wedding in Bristol, so the servants are having a bit of a holiday, except for the kitchen staff, who are frantically busy with Christmas preparations. (How odd, the idea that stirring the Christmas pudding or decorating the Christmas tree is just another chore on a busy servant's list. I wonder if they look forward to it, and find it as much fun as we used to do? Although I may be romanticizing Christmas at Montmaray a bit. Last year's was actually pretty awful, if I'm being honest with myself.) Anyway, due to the kitchen staff being rushed off their feet, we just had the nursery luncheon today, boring old shepherd's pie and not much of it, either. It's at least another hour till teatime, so I think I'll go downstairs to try to find a biscuit and see what Veronica's doing . . .

Well! What Veronica was doing was GETTING ATTACKED BY THE CRAZED ASSASSIN! My hand is shaking too much to write neatly . . . and now Aunt Charlotte's back, judging by the shouting. Yes, it must have been her car that I heard a moment ago. I'd better go . . .

Later. I am now tucked up in bed and Barnes has brought in a pot of hot chocolate, "for the shock." I explained that I'm not in shock anymore, and suggested she give it to Phoebe, who collapsed in hysterics again after the police left, but Barnes only pursed her lips and stalked off. Poor Phoebe. At last, there is silence . . . Except Henry and Carlos have just burst through my door.

"Hot *chocolate!*" Henry cries. "*I've* only got a glass of warm milk with disgusting skin on top. I do think that's unfair, *considering.* Are you writing everything down? You ought to use your typewriter and send it to the newspaper!"

If I were typing this, I'd still be on the first line, searching for the full-stop key. (I'm teaching myself out of a book, but the keys seem to be arranged in a very illogical manner.) Henry has gone off to fetch my tooth mug so she can share my hot chocolate. No, she's back. I've said they may stay, *if* they don't disturb me. Now Carlos is drinking Henry's no-longer-hot milk from my saucer, as quietly as he can. The skin of milk is plastered to his whiskers, and he's shaking his head and pawing at his nose . . .

Is it obvious I'm trying to put off reliving this afternoon's terrible events?

All right, here goes. So, I went down the staircase into the Marble Hall and was about to turn into the corridor that leads off the Hall, towards the dining room and the door to the kitchen stairs, when I heard Veronica's voice. She was using the imperious tone she keeps especially for Simon.

"How did *you* get in here?" she demanded.

But Simon wasn't due back till after tea, and he would've come in through the front door, as he always did. Who *was* she talking to? Without much thought to the matter, I charged on, round the corner, into the corridor—and then came to an abrupt, horrified halt.

For there stood Veronica, her back to me, and there, a mere five feet away, was the Crazed Assassin, pointing a silver pistol straight at Veronica's heart. Veronica's head whipped round at the sound of my footsteps, her expression switching from anger to alarm when she saw me—as though only a threat to someone *else* counted. But I barely registered this at the time. The gun had such a mesmerizing effect that it was impossible to focus on anything but those two gaping, malevolent holes, one on top of the other, an ominous gleam discernible deep within their darkness. With a supreme effort of will, I jerked my gaze away, up into the face of the person who held the gun.

"Why, it's *you!*" I cried out.

"Who?" asked Veronica—clearly not the most pressing issue at that particular moment, but I quite understood her curiosity.

"It's Rebecca's roommate from Poole! She saw you that day we—"

"Quiet!" barked the woman. Her voice was hoarse, and she was as tall as Veronica, though much broader in the shoulders. In her bulky overcoat, she might easily be mistaken for a man—*had*, in fact, been assumed to be one, by me, outside St. Margaret's, and by all of us at Julia's wedding reception. "But I don't need to kill you," the woman spat at me. "Just *her*." And she tilted the gun barrels towards Veronica's face.

"*Kill* me? With that thing?" scoffed Veronica, nevertheless edging backwards. Her arm came up to shove me behind her, but I wasn't having any of that. If Veronica was the target, it made sense for me to be in front. "I mean, it wasn't very successful last time, was it?" Veronica went on as I tried to step around her arm. "You really ought to—"

"Shut up! Shut up!" shrieked the woman. "Don't tell me what to do!"

How on earth could they have let her out of the clinic? I thought desperately. *Anyone* could see she was stark raving mad! But wait—what would that head therapist have done to calm her down?

"Just a minute," I said, raising my palm. "First, we need to explore exactly how you feel about Veronica."

Veronica looked at me as though *I* were mad, but at least the gun barrels lowered an inch or two.

"I mean, *why* do you dislike her?" I asked the woman as I continued to struggle, surreptitiously, against Veronica's restraining arm. "You haven't even met her—well, not properly. Is it something Rebecca said about her? We ought to consider whether Rebecca was slightly . . . confused at the time."

"Oh!" cried the woman. "Oh, it's not just her being a harlot! And a liar! And stealing other people's husbands!" (Heavens, Rebecca really *had* gone completely round the twist.) "No, it's her being a disgusting *Red*! Messing about with filthy Spanish hooligans! And disrespecting the *Leader*!"

And, with a dramatic flourish, she tore open her coat lapel to reveal her black shirt, black breeches, long black boots—and shiny British Union of Fascists badge.

"I . . . I didn't even know ladies *could* be Blackshirts," I said faintly. "At least . . . not with uniforms and everything."

"The Leader says that under Fascism, women will be valued and honored!"

"Who's . . . Are you talking about Mosley?" I asked.

"The *Leader* says every true British citizen, male and female, must fight for Britain! The Leader doesn't want war, but he won't back away from taking on the Russians! And beating them!"

"Er . . . but Veronica's not Russian," I said. I was having difficulty following her logic, which was only partly due to the terrifying presence of the gun. I wondered if Mosley was as crazy as his followers, or whether he simply happened to attract people who were violently insane. Meanwhile, I could sense Veronica shifting from foot to foot beside me as she weighed up our options. The gun, if it was the same one Lord Astley had described, held two bullets and could only kill at fairly close range. Which was . . . what, five or six feet? More? Unfortunately, neither of us were wearing corsets or bulletproof silk vests. If we turned and ran, would we be able to get far enough away before she pulled the trigger? How good was her aim? I could tell Veronica was considering lunging forward and wrestling the woman to the ground. With the element of surprise, Veronica and I stood a fair chance against her—but who could say where the gun might be pointing if it accidentally (or otherwise) went off? Surely the best thing would be to keep her talking—perhaps we could actually talk her into *surrendering*.

"That's very interesting," I said. "About, um, your Leader." Veronica slid one foot forward and I caught hold of her sleeve. "Could you explain more about him being against war?" I went on, trying to keep my voice even. "I think that's an awfully good philosophy, don't you, being *against* violence?"

The Crazed Assassin glared at me. "The Leader isn't a coward, he's a *hero*! He was in the last war, and he understands *everything* about—"

Veronica suddenly made a tiny sound, almost a squeak, and clapped her hand over her mouth. "Yes!" she agreed loudly, dropping her hand. "Fascinating! *Do* go on about his ideas."

Over the woman's shoulder, I saw what Veronica had seen, and my heart, hammering at twice the normal speed, seemed to stop altogether. Because in the paneled wall ten feet behind the woman, the dumbwaiter doors had just slid open to reveal Henry in full Girl Guide uniform, bow in hand, a quiver of arrows slung over her shoulder.

"Get help!" I mouthed at her, trying not to move my lips too much. I was terrified the Crazed Assassin would turn and see what we were trying not to stare at. But Henry just dropped silently to the floor and began fitting an arrow to her bow. Behind her, the dumbwaiter platform descended without sound (and I blessed the footman who'd kept it so well oiled) while I frantically tried to think of a way to remove my little sister from this horrible situation.

"—and get rid of filthy Jews and foreigners—" ranted on the Crazed Assassin.

"Quite right, Britain's *much* better off without those sorts of people," said Veronica (fortunately, the Crazed Assassin was in no state to recognize sarcasm). "But don't you think that sometimes, it's better to *take no action at all?*" Veronica raised her voice, hoping Henry would take the hint. "Or to *call* on the *authorities?*"

The dumbwaiter platform reappeared, supporting the curled-up figure of Carmelita Labauria, Javier's ten-year-old sister, who climbed out and raised her own bow and arrow. I nearly groaned aloud. If anything happened to her, Javier would *kill* us. If there was anything left of us, that is, after we'd been shot to pieces by this crazy Fascist . . .

"—keeping Britain racially pure, and eliminating all the bloody Reds—"

There was an outraged exclamation from behind me, the voice of an angry child.

The Crazed Assassin's mouth hung open, but the flow of words ceased as she stared past me. Then the hand holding the gun jolted upwards, her fingers twitching.

"Down!" cried Veronica, shoving my shoulder. We both dived to the floor, Veronica sliding far enough to grab the woman's ankle and yank it sideways. There was a tremendous explosion somewhere above my head, and then assorted crashing noises. The Crazed Assassin fell to her hands and knees, and Veronica hurled herself across the woman, wrenching her wrist backwards. The gun clattered across the floor, trailing wisps of sulfur-scented smoke.

"Don't touch it!" I screamed at Henry and Carmelita, who'd dashed forward, bows raised. "And put those arrows *down!*" I twisted round to assess the damage and saw wave upon wave of Girl Guides pouring into the hall—through the front doors, around the staircase, even out of the White Drawing Room. Actually, there were only about half a dozen of them, but the uniforms made it seem like far more. I gaped at them, dumbstruck.

"Don't worry. No one got shot," said Henry cheerfully. "Well, except for poor old Edward de Quincy."

The bust of our only ancestor of note, I saw, now lay in jagged shards across the floor. Veronica and Carmelita had forced the Crazed Assassin onto her front by then and were twisting her arms behind her back. I started crawling over to secure her thrashing legs, but then Phoebe appeared with a pile of towels, stared at the writhing black-booted figure on the floor, and began screaming. Luckily, Carlos had turned up and was quite willing to sit on the woman's legs in my place while I attempted to calm Phoebe down.

"Don't worry. It's not your brother!" I shouted over Phoebe's wails and the Crazed Assassin's strident and rather creative cursing.

"Ana Luisa, the rope!" called Henry, and a tiny Basque girl hurried over. "We were in the folly, practicing knot-tying," Henry explained as little Ana Luisa expertly looped a piece of rope round the woman's wrists. "And then this man walked past, on his way to the house—but he went *off* the path, through the woods. *Very* suspicious, anyone could see that. So we tracked him—well, her—as far as the driveway. Then I told everyone to split up and use the side doors, and Carmelita and me went through the laundry room."

"And you didn't think to tell any of the *servants?*" exclaimed Veronica, rubbing her face where the woman had just hit her.

"We didn't see any," said Henry. "I think they were having their tea, and anyway, they'd just say we weren't allowed to play in the house. And there was no point calling the *police*, they'd have to come all the way from Salisbury. You'd all have been *dead* by then."

"We could all have been dead, anyway, thanks to you waving those arrows around!" snapped Veronica. "As if it isn't bad enough that *you* could have been hurt—I can't believe you put these children in danger as well!"

"We *wanted* to come!" protested Carmelita. "Anyway, that woman's a Fascist. I *heard* her." And all the Guides nodded ferociously, even the girls from the village. One or two looked as though they wanted to spit on the floor, but fortunately, they restrained themselves. A footman, alerted by Phoebe's screams, then rushed in to help with the still-wriggling assassin, and he sent Henry to summon the other servants.

"But, Sophie, you're bleeding," Carmelita said, pointing at my hand. It turned out I'd been injured by a sharp piece of Edward de Quincy, although I hadn't even noticed till then. I picked up a towel from the pile Phoebe had dropped and wiped away the blood. The cut looked fairly shallow, but the Girl Guides made me sit down on the stairs, in case I fainted.

"We haven't done our first aid badge yet," said one of them, frowning at my palm. "So I'm not sure what else to do." Veronica, on her way back from telephoning the police, suggested that doing that badge *before* the archery one might have been more prudent.

"But not as interesting," said Henry.

The police sergeant and two constables eventually arrived, and Phoebe started crying again, because she was worried they'd discover her Blackshirt brother had a criminal record and think that *she'd* let the Crazed Assassin in the house. But of course, the police didn't care about that—it was perfectly obvious that *anyone* could have walked in, anytime he (or she) wanted. Who locks their doors in the country? So I patted Phoebe on the back a bit more and gave her my handkerchief. The police took the Crazed Assassin away, the maids swept up the remains of Edward de Quincy, and the Girl Guides were taken down to the kitchen for milk and biscuits. I made Veronica put some ice on her face, and Barnes bandaged my hand, although it had already stopped bleeding. Then I ran up to my room for my journal, because I thought I should jot down as much as I could remember, in case the police needed a detailed statement later on. I had just sat down at the secretaire in the White Drawing Room when I heard the shouting—not Aunt Charlotte and Toby, as it turned out, but Simon and Veronica. A moment later, Simon flung open the door.

"My God!" he cried. "Are you all right? I saw the police at the gates as I was driving in, and then Veronica told me . . . She said it was someone from *Poole!*"

I closed my journal and went over to join him.

"Yes, your mother's former roommate," I said. "It's all right, no one was hurt."

"But someone *could* have been!" he exclaimed. "Veronica's right, someone could have been killed! How *could* they have let her leave Poole like that? Why didn't any of the staff realize she was dangerous? My God—why didn't *I* realize?"

He sank onto the sofa and stared at me, raking his hands through his hair.

"*I* chose that place," he said. "And I *knew* Mother was still obsessed with Veronica's mother and . . . and still *confused* about everything. Why didn't I think of that when we were trying to work out who might want to attack Veronica?"

His hair was in total disarray by now.

"I knew Mother was in Poole, and of course, it wasn't *her* at the wedding—but how could I not have recognized that woman?"

"I didn't, either," I said. "I looked and looked at those photographs, and I didn't figure it out."

"But you only saw her once! I saw her three or four times, I had *tea* with her, and— Sophia, you're injured!"

He took my hand by the fingertips and drew me closer.

"It's just a cut," I said as he gently turned my hand over. "I must have put my hand down on something sharp when I was on the floor. I didn't even notice at the time, it was all such a blur—"

"Well, of *course* it was," he said, gazing at me with sympathy. My hand, which had started shaking when I'd sat down to write, felt very odd. Actually, I felt odd all over. The trembling had spread, up my arm, into my chest, and down my legs, a horrible, cold, shivery feeling. "Good Lord, the whole thing must have been terrifying," Simon continued, still holding my hand.

"It *was*, a bit," I whispered, because I was worried my voice would start shaking, too. "Especially when Henry . . . when I thought she might . . ."

He leapt up and put his arms around me as I started to cry.

"I thought Henry was going to get *shot*," I sobbed into his chest. "And . . . and Veronica, when she—"

"Of course you did," he murmured into the top of my head. "It must have been awful. You've been very brave."

"No, I wasn't!"

"Yes, you *were*. Veronica said if you hadn't turned up when you did and acted so calmly, she'd probably have been shot dead in the first minute."

"She said that?" I sniffed.

"Oh, yes," he said, his hands rubbing slow circles on my back. "But that didn't surprise me. I know how sensible you are in a crisis."

The shaking feeling was beginning to subside, but I was grateful nonetheless for his warm, solid presence. I thought that if he took his arms away, I might just crumple to the floor.

Perhaps he'd been taking mind-reading lessons from Veronica, because the next thing I knew, he'd sat me down on the sofa. He gave me his handkerchief but kept his arm around me. As soon as I'd blown my nose, I smelled his cologne or the soap he used or perhaps just *him*. It was a wonderfully complex scent, like dried lavender stored in a sandalwood box, or cinnamon and vanilla and pepper spilled on a pantry shelf. I couldn't help leaning into him a bit as he brought his hand up to smooth my hair out of my eyes.

Then Barnes walked in.

"Her Highness is suffering from shock," Simon announced, sitting up straighter. He could just as well have been referring to Barnes, who'd nearly dropped the cup of tea she'd been carrying and was now giving him the look of extreme disapproval she usually reserved for Phoebe. "She ought to have been taken *straight* up to bed after that terrible experience," Simon added, frowning right back at Barnes. "Where's her maid?"

"*I'll* see to it, sir," said Barnes indignantly, setting down the teacup and bustling over to help me up. "I'll take Her Highness upstairs at once."

And now here I am, writing this in bed and waiting for dinner to be brought up on a tray. Veronica has just come in and said she'll have it with me. She has a darkening bruise on one cheekbone but claims she can hardly feel it. Henry is sprawled across the end of my bed, working away at a labeled sketch of the Crazed Assassin ("in case she escapes and the police need to put up WANTED posters"), and Carlos is looking very smug because no one has made him go downstairs yet. It turns out Aunt Charlotte and Toby went off to visit the Stanley-Rosses after luncheon, which is why they still aren't back (one of the footmen telephoned the Bosworths to see where they'd got to, just in case *they'd* been attacked by the Crazed Assassin). As long as *I'm* not the one who has to recount the whole thing to Aunt Charlotte— I couldn't bear to go through it again. I expect that task will fall to Simon . . .

Speaking of whom, at least there'll be no difficulty returning *his* handkerchief, which is still balled up in my pocket. Oh, wait a moment—it's *Toby's,* I can see the monogram!

Well. It's a good thing I'm not the slightest bit infatuated with Simon anymore. Considering how *close* he and Toby still are. To the extent that their *personal belongings* are mixed up with each other's!

I think I *am* feeling a bit emotional after today's crisis.

Oh good, dinner's arrived.

12th January 1938

More tears today—sometimes it seems I consist of nothing but salt water. Actually, I didn't cry *very* much, not compared to the children. Even Javier's eyes were suspiciously shiny when he said goodbye to Veronica, although I'm certain he'd deny it. He didn't even hug her, just shook hands in a very gruff and masculine manner. I *did* see the two of them having what looked like a rather intense conversation beforehand—though, knowing them, it was probably a political argument.

The Labauria siblings and their Moreno cousins are now on a ship bound for Mexico, having received word that Javier's father and uncle arrived there safely two months ago. The letter announcing this, written in mid-November, had unfortunately been sent to Southampton, then Birmingham, before someone finally located the correct Labaurias. It was such a relief for the children, to discover their fathers were alive—I'd never before seen Javier's face lit up in quite that way, with joy rather than anger. But he immediately sank back into gloom. How *could* the men have given up on their homeland like that? Surely it would be better to be hiding in the mountains, even to be in *prison*, than to have crawled off to the other side of the world! What about when the Republicans triumphed over Franco? They would all need to *be* there, to help clear the Basque homeland of Fascists! The Basque government might have surrendered, but he, Javier Moreno Labauria, had not! And so on.

Until Carmelita uncrossed her arms and shouted across the kitchen that *she* was not going to spend another second listening to him, because she needed to pack her things so she could join their papa. And perhaps when Franco was dead, they would go back to Bilbao, but right then, home was where the whole family was, or what was left of it, and did Javier think that their mama, God rest her soul, would have wanted them to argue with what Papa said? Then she stomped upstairs. She used to be such a shy, mild-mannered child. I think she's spent a bit too much time with Henry.

Anyway, that was that. The other six children at the Old Mill House decided they would move to one of the large Basque colonies in Manchester, as they had friends there from their old neighborhood. They might even return to Bilbao with their friends, although that depends on how things go (the news from Spain is as bad as ever). Veronica went to the bank and found there was almost seven hundred pounds left over from the donations we'd received, so we divided the money equally amongst the seventeen children, down to the last penny. There was a flurry of shopping for suitcases and new shoes, a hurried final visit to the dentist, and then one last party at the Old Mill House, with most of the village turning up with little farewell presents (and how I wished Lord Elchester could have been there to see *that*).

And now they are gone. There is a new tenant moving into the Old Mill House next week, thanks to us having made it habitable again (so Aunt Charlotte really ought to be *grateful* to the children), and I need to go down to check that all the borrowed furnishings have been returned to their original owners. It will be so sad walking round the empty, echoing rooms, though. Perhaps Veronica will come with me . . .

Evening now, and I never *did* get down to the Old Mill House, after all. I walked into Veronica's room and found her kneeling on the floor beside her wardrobe, the carpet scattered with papers.

"What are you—" I started to ask.

And then I saw what it was.

"Oh, *Veronica*," I breathed. Because it was her *Brief History of Montmaray,* or at least the few bits that Anthony had managed to save. I knelt down beside her and stared at the pages. They were all different sizes, whatever she'd been able to scrounge at the time, and the handwriting was so tiny, in order to conserve paper, that it was almost indecipherable. "Do you think . . . Is it possible to go on with it?" I asked quietly. "I mean, can you continue your research here?"

Veronica picked up a scrap of paper and considered it. "I don't know," she said at last. "There's certainly nothing about

Montmaray in the library here at Milford. Well—apart from a dozen copies of Edward de Quincy FitzOsborne's *Collected Works*."

I smiled at her, and she at me, each of us trying to be cheerful and brave for the other's sake. For today is the anniversary of the day we left Montmaray—a year ago, exactly, that we watched our home being destroyed.

But why *should* anniversaries be so significant? Why should a year hurt more than eleven months or thirteen months or thirty-seven? Surely I could choose how I felt and when I felt it. I took a deep breath.

"Poor old Edward!" I said, a little too brightly. "Gosh, do you think anyone alive's actually *read* his book, apart from us?"

"I hope not," Veronica said. "Imagine people associating us with all that terrible poetry."

"Oh, be fair. Not *all* his verse is terrible," I said. (I'd just about got my tone right now: rueful but gently amused.) "There's that sonnet about the sun setting over South Head."

"The sun does not set in the south."

"Well, no. But that lovely simile, where he compares—"

"Do you think the library at Montmaray was *completely* destroyed?" said Veronica abruptly.

I stopped smiling. The last time I'd seen the library, it had been a pile of broken granite. "I think . . . I think it was very badly damaged," I said.

"Still," she said slowly, "I doubt it caught fire. There was hardly any wood in that structure. Even some of the bookcases were stone. I expect there are whole shelves of books on the lower floors that escaped damage. They'd be buried under a lot of rubble, of course, but at least they're protected from the weather that way."

"Veronica—"

"I keep wondering about that man, Otto Rahn," she said. "He was a scholar. *He* would have a proper respect for books. I'm sure he went back and tried to retrieve some of them, even if he was only looking for information about the Holy Grail. But oh, Sophie . . ." Her voice faltered. "The *thought* of those Germans trampling through our home!"

She turned to me, and her eyes were blazing.

"We need to get Montmaray back," she said. "We need to . . . to work together, all of us, to get rid of those Germans. I've been stalling, I know I have, because . . . well, because I knew we'd need Simon, and I simply couldn't face asking him for help." She hesitated, worrying at her bottom lip. "Sophie—*do* you think he'll help?"

"Of course he will," I said. "He cares just as much about Montmaray as we do."

"I know," she said, nodding. "After all, he *is* one of the family."

I stared at her. "What on earth did Javier *say* to you?"

"How did you know that he—"

"I didn't," I said. "But I do now."

She looked at the floor and began to gather her papers

together. "Well, it wasn't just him. I'd been considering . . . and then when he said . . ." She sat back on her heels and sighed.

"He said that if *he* were in my position, he wouldn't be sitting around feeling helpless. He said if *he* had money, and was an adult, and didn't have a lot of younger brothers and sisters to look after, he'd be fighting in every way he could to get his home back. He wouldn't let *anything* stop him."

"Although we *don't* actually have any money of our own," I pointed out. "And you *do* have younger brothers and sisters—well, cousins—and we're not really adults till we turn twenty-one. And we're *girls*."

"But you know what he means," she said. "And you know he's right."

I gazed back at her. "Yes," I said, and it felt as solemn as a vow. "Yes, I know."

She stood up and tapped the papers against the glass top of the dressing table. It made a crisp, business-like sound. "I need," she announced, "to write a list."

She wore an expression of such grim resolve that, for a moment, I almost felt *sorry* for the Germans. But that soon passed.

21st February 1938

Veronica, Simon, and I have arrived at Montmaray House brimming with fresh purpose, charged with determination. And so it is fitting that I set aside my tattered old exercise book, filled cover to cover with my blotchy scrawl, and turn to the first page of my beautiful, new sky-blue journal. I even have a nonleaky pen, a Christmas present from Toby. I do believe that, as a result, everything I write this afternoon will be significant and hopeful—and unsmudged.

The weather, it must be admitted, is not very encouraging. Yesterday, we were shrouded in a thick gray fog. This morning, an icy gale arrived, direct from the Arctic. Now sleet is splattering itself against the sooty windows, making the library even dimmer and colder than usual. Perhaps in an attempt to counteract this, Veronica and Simon are embroiled in yet another blazing row. (Just because they've agreed to work together on the Montmaray campaign doesn't mean they agree on anything else.) This argument seems to be about . . . the Prime Minister?

No, apparently they're debating which government department is most likely to be helpful to our cause. Simon thinks the Ministry for Coordination of Defence will have the greatest interest in us, given the Germans seem to be using Montmaray as a military base.

"Where's our proof of *that*?" says Veronica. "Besides, everyone knows the Minister of Defence is completely useless. 'The most cynical appointment since Caligula made his horse a consul,' that's what they said when the PM announced Thomas Inskip had the job. He was *chosen* to do nothing."

"Inskip!" says Simon scornfully. "Who said anything about approaching him? It's the senior civil servants who make all the decisions in that department. If we talk with them, they'll get in contact with the navy and the air force—"

"And then they'll do *what*, exactly?" says Veronica. "Send a battleship to Montmaray? So it can sit there, doing absolutely nothing, just like that ship they sent to Spain?"

Simon scowls at her. "The mere *presence* of a battleship might make Germany have second thoughts. There'll only be a few Germans actually on the island; they won't be capable of offering any real resistance."

"Oh, for heaven's sake! They'll know it's a bluff!" snaps Veronica. "This is a crisis requiring international *diplomacy*. It's the Foreign Office we need to target! First of all, we need the British Ambassador to deliver an official letter of protest to Berlin. Now, who's the new Permanent Under-Secretary for Foreign Affairs?"

"Sir Alexander Cadogan—and give me back that pen! I'm not letting *you* draft that letter! What *you* know about diplomacy and tact could be chiseled on the head of a pin—"

And so on. Oh good, the footman's just come in to announce that luncheon is served. Now they'll have to call a temporary truce . . .

Much later. We had apple dumplings with butterscotch sauce and clotted cream for pudding, and even *that* didn't improve Simon's mood. He's stomped off down the corridor to the little room Aunt Charlotte uses as her office, after announcing that Veronica was driving him mad. Poor Simon. In addition to working on our Montmaray campaign, he's still sorting through the records at Mr. Grenville's, and I don't think it's going very well. I get the distinct impression Mr. Grenville's employees resent the fact that a former clerk has been elevated to the status of valued client. They can't openly express this, of course, but they keep "misplacing" keys to cabinets and "accidentally" dropping files, then stuffing all the papers back in, upside down and in the wrong order.

"But what exactly are you looking for?" I asked Simon this afternoon.

He sighed heavily. "Oh, Sophia, you wouldn't believe what a mess things are in, once one goes back more than a few years. I've already found a bank account set up in 1897 to pay for subscriptions to some club that doesn't even *exist* anymore. There was a grand total of seven shillings and sixpence in that account, by the way. And then I keep coming across documents that ought to be here at Montmaray House, nothing to do with legal or financial matters—bundles of personal letters, for instance, and a diary belonging to some long-departed princess."

"Really?" I said, intrigued. "Who was she?"

"Heaven knows. It was half eaten by mice, and I think it's in French. But what I'm really hoping to discover is a fat pouch of diamonds, or some secret trust fund that's been accumulating interest for decades."

"That *would* be exciting," I said. "Would you like me to come down and help?"

"That's kind of you, Sophia. But really, it needs someone who's familiar with the filing system, and it's a task more grubby than glamorous. I can't imagine your aunt would approve of— Good Lord!"

"What?" I said, peering over at the newspaper the footman had just delivered.

"Anthony Eden's resigned!"

"Isn't he the Foreign Secretary?" I asked. "The one with the nice suits? Why did he resign?"

"He probably heard Veronica was planning to target the Foreign Office and wanted to get out of the way first."

"*Simon!*"

He glanced up and smiled. "No, I expect he disapproves of Chamberlain's policy of appeasing Hitler and Mussolini."

"But how would resigning help? Now he won't be able to influence Conservative policy, and they're the ones in charge."

"Hmm? Oh, yes," said Simon, thoroughly absorbed in his newspaper, so I left him to it and went back down the corridor to tell Veronica.

"Oh, *blast!*" she exclaimed, looking up from a messy draft of a letter. "I was counting on Eden supporting us." She shoved her hair back, leaving another smudge of ink on her forehead, and sighed. "Well! I wonder what Churchill will have to say about this."

"Churchill's against appeasement, too, isn't he? Do you think they'll both leave the Conservatives and start up a new party together?"

"Hmm. No, I wouldn't think so," Veronica said. "They might both be worried about the threat posed by the Fascist dictators, but that's about all they have in common. Churchill wants a war, any war—ideally against the Soviet Union—but Eden's strongly in favor of the League of Nations and collective security." And Veronica gave an approving little nod.

The effectiveness of the League of Nations is one of the topics most hotly debated by Veronica and Simon. The League is a sort of club for all the nations of the world, and it's supposed to resolve disputes between countries by helping them negotiate. If negotiations don't work, and if a country's done something really awful, like invading another country, the others are meant to band together to impose sanctions, which means cutting off trade and eventually even travel and diplomatic ties to the country.

Simon thinks the League has been a failure. Look at Italy,

he said. It paid no attention whatsoever to the League's warnings, and went on bombarding poor little Abyssinia with mustard gas and flamethrowers, until the Abyssinian Emperor was forced into exile. Veronica frowned at Simon and said Italy would have retreated with its tail between its legs if only Britain and France had stood firm on collective sanctions, instead of messing about with secret pacts that had nothing to do with the League. She then reeled off a long list of conflicts that *had* been successfully resolved by the League, but the only one I can recall is the 1925 War of the Stray Dog—not that I remember much except its name. I think it was between Greece and Bulgaria. Neither Veronica nor Simon knew what had happened to the dog.

Personally, I think countries working together with regard to negotiations and sanctions sounds very sensible, so I wondered why Veronica didn't just write directly to the League of Nations and tell *them* what the Germans had done to Montmaray. However, it turns out that the League of Nations is like most clubs, whereby one needs to be a member to use its services—and we simply can't afford the fees. Apparently, they're so high that even countries like Nicaragua and Honduras, much bigger and richer than us, are withdrawing their membership. Countries also need to be *invited* to join, and Veronica can't recall Montmaray ever receiving an invitation. Of course, it could have been lost in the post (quite a few things from the supply ship got washed overboard, especially in winter, when we lived at Montmaray). But regardless, it seems the League won't be of much help to us. We'll simply have to work away at the British government.

After a bit more discussion about Anthony Eden, Veronica returned to her letter, and I went upstairs to practice my typing. However, it was so cold that I was forced to don my fur-lined gloves, which were a bit of a hindrance as far as finger flexibility went. I soon gave up and started sorting through my wardrobe, because Aunt Charlotte has said Veronica and I will be having a second Season this year.

"And I sincerely hope *this* one will be more successful than the last," she said, giving us both a severe look. "Still, at least you've finally given up wearing head-to-toe black, Veronica. Perhaps that will help a *little*. Gentlemen are not attracted to gloominess, you know. They prefer cheerful, sparkling young ladies. Filial respect is all very well—and of course, mourning needed to be observed for a *few* months—but enough is enough."

Filial respect! I almost laughed out loud at that when I considered Veronica's relationship with her father. "Troubled" is probably the politest way to describe it. I don't think Aunt Charlotte ever grasped that Veronica was not in mourning for her father, or even for her mother, but for her home. And no doubt still *is* in mourning, although her grief appears to have taken on a less passive form now, thank heavens.

Aunt Charlotte remains at Milford Park, by the way, recovering from a bad cold. She caught it while doing what Henry called "shooting peasants."

"*Pheasants*, Henry," said Toby. "Those squawking, feathery things."

"Oh! I did wonder about that," said Henry. "Because I didn't think there *were* any peasants left in England."

"Oh, darling, there *are*, thousands and thousands of them," said Julia. (This conversation took place at Veronica's birthday tea.) "It's just that we call them the proletariat now."

"And nobody shoots them, Henry," I said firmly. "Not in England, anyway."

"No, just in Spain," said Veronica. "And the Soviet Union—although they don't usually shoot them there, just starve them to death."

It was a good thing Anthony was away at an air show—he hates hearing the Soviet Union criticized. In any case, Julia must be a bit tired of Communism by now, because she quickly diverted the conversation to the far more entertaining topic of *Me and My Girl*, which she saw in the West End just before Christmas. Pretty soon, she'd taught us her favorite song and dance from the show, and we were all strutting round the Velvet Drawing Room doing the Lambeth Walk. I must say, Julia is excellent at distractions. And we certainly needed some distraction at the time, what with the departure of the Basque children (Henry misses them dreadfully) as well as the ongoing saga of the Crazed Assassin.

Veronica's attacker, it turns out, is the niece of a wealthy baronet—not *all* that surprising, I suppose, given how high the fees are for the Poole clinic. However, much as her family would have liked to hide her away again in a more secure private institution, she'd actually been arrested this time, so proper legal procedures needed to be followed. Aunt Charlotte was horrified at the thought that Veronica or I might have to appear in court as witnesses ("The scandal! Mere months before the Season begins! Why, you won't be invited *anywhere*!"). Luckily, Veronica's attacker was found to be "of unsound mind" without any need of our testimony, and was rapidly packed off to Broadmoor "for her own safety and the safety of others." Aunt Charlotte then decided Rebecca should also be moved somewhere more secure (and less expensive). But, after all, *Rebecca* hadn't tried to kill anyone (not recently, anyway), and it's not illegal to say mean things about other people.

"Yes, it is," said Veronica. "It's called slander. Or libel, if it's written down."

Then she and Simon got into an argument about legal definitions. However, even Veronica and Aunt Charlotte acknowledged that moving Rebecca would only agitate her, just when she finally seemed to have settled in at Poole—and no one wants to deal with an agitated Rebecca. So Simon went down to have yet another talk with the matron and the therapists, who'd already been interviewed by the police, and it was agreed that a very close eye would be kept on her. So perhaps anxiety over his mother is contributing to Simon's grumpy mood . . .

Oh, there's the dinner gong. Hmm, wasn't this journal entry supposed to be hopeful and happy? Well, at least it's unsmudged.

15th March 1938

We have not had any response from the government about Montmaray, even though we've written two letters to the Permanent Under-Secretary for Foreign Affairs. I've a sneaking suspicion that the letters, sent to Toby for his official King of Montmaray signature, are lost on his desk at Oxford, buried under a pile of dinner party invitations and unread textbooks. However, Veronica has decided that the whole of the blame lies with Simon, for having edited her "forthright, well-argued missives" into "meaningless drivel."

"No wonder the Foreign Office hasn't paid any attention," she said at breakfast this morning. "An urgent issue of international injustice, and *you* made it sound like a spot of bother over a disputed right-of-way!"

"I don't suppose it's occurred to you that the Foreign Office might have *other* matters to deal with at the moment!" snapped Simon.

"And I don't suppose it's occurred to *you* that if the Foreign

Office had been aware of the cold, hard facts about Montmaray's invasion—as opposed to your pale, insipid version—they might have recognized Hitler's ruthlessness earlier. They might have taken some *action*. And perhaps Vienna wouldn't have Nazi storm troopers goose-stepping through its streets today!"

"Oh, of course," he said. "The Anschluss is all *my* fault!"

"Don't say 'Anschluss.' It's not a union, it's an *invasion*." She stood up, threw her napkin on the tablecloth, and glared down at him. "Although I concede the invasion of Austria isn't entirely your fault—you don't have *that* much influence over world affairs. After all, you can't even get me the names and addresses of those senior civil servants in the Foreign Office, which I requested a week ago. Which is why I am going *out*, to Whitehall, to obtain the information myself."

"No, you're not," said Simon. "Your aunt said you're not to leave the house without a chaperone, and I'm busy."

"Coming, Sophie?" Veronica said, sweeping out of the room.

I raised my eyebrows at Simon.

"I'm *busy*, Sophia," he said somewhat defensively. "I have a meeting at the bank at eleven o'clock, and I need to spend the afternoon at Grenville's."

I sighed and followed Veronica down the corridor. Simon got up and stuck his head round the door in a final (and quite futile) attempt to assert his authority.

"And don't think you're taking the car, because I've got the keys!" he shouted after Veronica.

"Never mind. There's this amazing invention called the bus," said Veronica.

"But do we have to do this *today*?" I asked as we went upstairs. "It's pouring! And is it really worth all the trouble we'll be in when Aunt Charlotte finds out? Couldn't you just telephone the Foreign Office to get that information?"

"Possibly," she said. "But I've asked Daniel to meet us for luncheon, so we may as well pay a visit to Whitehall first."

"Oh!" I said. "Well then!" Because I was very keen to see Daniel again and, in particular, to see him with Veronica. His letters have been arriving very frequently of late, and they've taken on a tone that might be regarded as distinctly affectionate by some—although not by Veronica.

"Of course he knows you read them," she said after she tossed over one of his letters to me yesterday, and I suggested she might prefer to keep them private. "Well, I assume he does. He's got some very interesting things to say about the Pope and Italian anti-Semitism in that one—it's on the second page, have a look."

Veronica really is *hopeless*. I asked her this morning why she wasn't wearing her new outfit (a tight-fitting black dress with scarlet bolero-style jacket and matching hat; she looks sensational in it), and she just glanced down at herself in bemusement and said her old jersey and tweed skirt were much warmer. But I made her change—even if Daniel wasn't going to pay any attention to what she was wearing, the receptionist at the Foreign Office would. Then we walked outside and caught a bus to Trafalgar Square.

One certainly feels closer to the beating heart of London when traveling by bus than when motoring about in a chauffeur-driven Daimler—not that this is *entirely* a good thing. People kept hitting my legs with their dripping umbrellas, and a heavy-set young lady stood on my foot (she did apologize very nicely, but I'd rather have had unbruised toes and no apology). Then we realized after we'd got off the bus that we were at the wrong end of Whitehall. Still, it was a pleasant walk, despite the drizzle. We were just in time to see the end of the very colorful Changing of the Guard, although I'm not sure whom they were meant to be guarding, as there didn't seem to be any royalty around (except us, of course). The guard horses were lovely, though—I've decided I quite like horses, as long as I'm not expected to ride them. The people who designed Whitehall must have been fond of them, too, because every time I turned around, there was another statue of a horse, usually with a sternly triumphant bronze soldier balanced on top. Veronica pointed out lots of other interesting things: Great Scotland Yard, where the Metropolitan Police used to have their headquarters; the old Admiralty, where Nelson's body lay in state after the Battle of Trafalgar; and Downing Street, where the Prime Minister lives. Right in the middle of the road was the Cenotaph, the memorial to the Great War.

"'The Glorious Dead,'" said Veronica, reading the inscription. "*Glorious!* What's glorious about dying in agony in a foreign land?"

I thought of all the poor Montmaravians buried in France—

or not even buried, simply left to rot in the trenches where they'd been blown up. I said that it was as though the government had been certain there'd be another war, sooner or later—

"And figured they'd need to persuade a new generation to die for their country," finished Veronica grimly.

We stood frowning at the memorial a bit longer, then turned our backs on it and marched over to the vast edifice that housed the Foreign Office. It had far too many doorways, none of which seemed to be the one we wanted. First we found ourselves in the India Office, then a broom cupboard, then Veronica got distracted by a set of gaudy conference rooms.

"Look, Sophie!" she cried, grabbing my arm. "It's the Locarno Suite! This is where the Locarno Treaties were signed in 1925. Imagine, three Nobel Peace Prizes were earned inside this *very* room."

"Gosh," I said, peering at the scarlet silk walls and glittering chandeliers, wondering how anyone could negotiate anything peace-related in such a garish setting.

"It was *here* that all the western European nations agreed to respect one another's borders," said Veronica, looking around eagerly.

"But didn't Germany occupy part of France a few years ago?" I asked.

"What? Well, yes, the Rhineland. After the Nazis came to power."

"And now they've invaded Austria, too."

"Yes."

"So, the treaties are worthless."

I instantly regretted this statement, because Veronica took the sort of deep breath that signals the start of one of her long, largely incomprehensible historical lectures. I quickly tugged her forward, even though I hadn't a clue where we were headed.

"Now, that's a *very* interesting question," Veronica began. "Although I'm not sure I'd use the word 'worthless,' not when France and Britain are still committed to helping Poland and Czechoslovakia, if Germany were to—"

A young gentleman darted in through a side door, shaking raindrops from his brilliantined head. He carried a greasy paper bag and was scurrying along in a manner that seemed oddly familiar. I stared at him as Veronica went on.

"—and, having redrawn the map of Europe, some might say the Allies had a responsibility to—"

"Wait a minute!" I said to Veronica. "It's that diplomat, the one who came to Montmaray!"

"Who . . . Oh!" said Veronica. "Mr. Davies-Chesterton!" she called out.

He glanced up, saw Veronica, and froze, like a rabbit caught in the glare of headlights as a car bears down upon it at great speed.

"Hello," I said as we hurried over to him. "You visited us at Montmaray last year. Do you remember?"

"Er," he said. "Yes . . . How, how do you do?" He shook hands with both of us, giving Veronica a very nervous look. He'd been a day late for her father's funeral, and Veronica had been extremely unimpressed at the time. However, she now generously decided to forgive his past transgressions.

"You're *just* the person we were hoping to see!" she said, beaming at him. "Someone who knows his way around the Foreign Office—because I need the names and addresses of a couple of civil servants . . ." She'd already extricated her notebook from her bag, and now she clasped his elbow and began propelling him down the corridor, all the while firing questions at him. Poor boy, he'd sneaked out to get an iced bun for his morning tea, and look where it had landed him.

"Your Highness," he gasped, "if, if you'd allow me to show you to the reception desk—"

"*Very* kind of you, but I don't think that's necessary," she said. "Oh, what a magnificent staircase! I wonder where this leads?"

A quarter of an hour later, we'd visited seven offices, jotted down a dozen names, titles, and addresses in Veronica's notebook, and watched a young lady in a fluffy pink cardigan type half a page in less than a minute.

"Goodness, how did you get so *fast*?" I said admiringly. She explained her secretarial teacher had made them do keyboard drills with their eyes closed, rapping them over the knuckles with a ruler whenever they tried to peek.

"Anyway, fifty words a minute is nothing. You ought to see Miss McIntosh upstairs," she said, whipping another sheet of paper out of her typewriter and setting it on the towering stack beside her elbow. "Seventy-five wpm, and twice as fast with shorthand."

"Miss McIntosh . . . she's not Sir Julius Pemberton's secretary, is she?" asked Veronica, perusing her list.

"That's right. Down the corridor, first staircase on the left, door next to the big glass case full of photographs."

"Thank you," we chorused, and trotted off, trailed by a now-whimpering Mr. Davies-Chesterton. Surprisingly, no one had attempted to stop us at any stage, not even when Veronica marched through a doorway marked STAFF ONLY. It must have been the presence of our unofficial escort—unless it was Veronica's regal demeanor and extremely expensive outfit.

"Thank you *so* much," said Veronica after a quick chat with Miss McIntosh. "You've been *most* helpful. Is this the way out? Excellent."

Mr. Davies-Chesterton said a hasty goodbye and scuttled off down a staircase, his iced bun now rather squashed and sad-looking. We stepped back out onto the damp footpath just as the Little Bens began hammering out the half hour from the Houses of Parliament. There was a bit of a wait for a bus, then we had to change to another bus halfway there. The Underground would probably have been quicker, but I'm not too keen on tunnels, so Veronica had kindly neglected to mention this option. I don't think we were very late, but Daniel looked as though he'd been waiting for a while and was peering near-sightedly in quite the wrong direction when we arrived.

"Oh! Hello!" he cried, jumping up and shaking hands. He wore shapeless gray trousers and a jacket patched at the elbows, and the frames of his spectacles had been mended with sticking plaster.

"Sorry we're late," said Veronica. "We've been at Whitehall."

"Browbeating some hapless clerk into giving you information, I suppose," said Daniel, clearly up to date on the Montmaray campaign. "Is that why you're dressed up like the Duchess of Kent? Shall I take your coat? What is it, sable?"

But Veronica had already dumped it on the spare seat.

"It's *wool*, as you ought to know," she said. "And before you say it, yes, I'm aware it cost more than it'd take to feed and house a family in Bethnal Green for a month. Anyway, when did you become an expert on the Duchess of Kent? Have you taken out a subscription to *The Queen?*"

He snorted and told her to hurry up and order, he was *starving*, but as Veronica studied the menu, his gaze kept straying to her face, his expression softening. Then he caught me observing him and went a bit pink, so I quickly asked why he ought to know about coats.

"Well," he said, clearing his throat, "unless she's commenting on my sad lack of sartorial taste, I expect your cousin is mocking my background in *trade*—as your aunt would say in horrified tones. My father has a business importing furs, you see, and my mother's family owns a dress factory."

"I'm not mocking you because your family makes and sells things instead of lazing about on country estates," said Veronica. "And I'd be as badly dressed as you if it weren't for Sophie telling me what to wear. I'm just amused that you're using your considerable intelligence to try and bring down capitalism, when it was capitalism that bought your education, and very expensive it must have been, too. I'm going to have the cutlets."

"Oh, you think my intelligence is *considerable*, do you?" he said airily. "I *am* honored." But he fought back a smile. "And what are you having, Sophie?"

I'd never had Irish stew before, so I decided on that, although when it arrived, it was just ordinary beef and potato stew, which is often on the nursery menu at Milford. I suspect Aunt Charlotte instructed the staff not to call it "Irish." She tolerates Catholics if they're Spanish and aristocratic, but the Irish are "beyond the pale," along with colonials, Jews, Americans, and people in *trade*—with a few rare (and very rich) exceptions.

As we ate, Veronica and Daniel discussed the news from Europe. It turned out Daniel still had some relatives in Vienna— an elderly uncle, who'd played in the orchestra at the Vienna State Opera, and a couple of cousins.

"Oh, Daniel, I didn't know that!" said Veronica, letting her fork fall with a clatter. She stared at him with an expression that seemed, to me, far graver than Daniel's information warranted. "Are they in immediate danger, do you think, now the Nazis have taken over Austria?"

"Why?" I asked, looking from Veronica to Daniel. "Are your relatives involved in politics, too? Are they Communists?"

"They're Jewish, Sophie," said Daniel gently.

"Oh. But . . ." A dozen questions were twittering around

inside my head, but I didn't want to sound a complete bird-brain.

"No, no, go on," said Daniel in his encouraging tutor's voice.

"Well, I know the Nazis—all the Fascists, really—keep saying horrible things about Jews," I said slowly. "Like in that disgusting German newspaper Unity Mitford wrote to, the one where she said she wanted everyone to know she was a Jew hater. But when you talk about *danger*, I'm not sure . . . I mean, why would the Nazis care about an elderly gentleman? Or even your cousins?"

"Why?" Daniel said. "I'm not sure I understand it myself. Is it just the personal mania of a dictator? Combined with the political expediency of using a small and historically despised group of people as a scapegoat for all the country's problems? As for *how*, that's much easier to answer. By banning Jews from working in the civil service—not just in government departments but schools, universities, clinics, even the State Opera. By boycotting Jewish businesses, by banning Jews from parks and restaurants, by passing a law that makes it a crime for a non-Jew to marry a Jew. And when anti-Semitism is not just a normal part of everyday life but actually *encouraged* by the government . . . well, there are always young men with a tendency towards violence. So, why *wouldn't* they take the opportunity to enjoy themselves, to deface the walls of a synagogue, or smash up a store owned by Jews, or attack a family walking along the street—"

He suddenly seemed to become aware that his hand had clenched itself on the tabletop.

"Sorry, I'll climb back down from my soapbox now," he said, loosening his fingers and making an effort to smile.

"Why do the Jews stay?" I asked softly. "Why wouldn't they all . . . well, go somewhere safe, somewhere they're welcome?"

"And where's *that?*" he said. "No, of course you're right, Sophie. That may even be the aim of the Nazis, to make all the Jews want to leave. And quite a few *have* moved here, or gone to America. But it takes money and contacts, and not everyone has those. And some, like my uncle, will never leave. He refuses to believe there's any real threat to *him*, a gentleman of culture and education. How could a change of government be enough to make him abandon everything—his apartment and his French poodles, his friends, his daily walk in his favorite park, his evenings at the opera? So . . . But my mother has hopes of convincing her cousins to come here."

"I'm sorry," I said. "About your relatives—and for asking. I honestly didn't know it was that bad. I thought it was just the Nazis *saying* terrible things—not that that's all right, either," I added hurriedly.

"You mustn't ever apologize for asking questions," Daniel said firmly. "Why *should* you know? How else can you find out? You've never visited Germany, you don't have family in Europe writing to you about it—and it's not exactly making huge headlines in *The Times*."

The waitress brought our pot of tea, and Veronica ordered treacle pudding for Daniel, because he still looked hungry. She asked if I wanted anything, but I shook my head. My stomach was weighed down with an uncomfortable lump that was half Irish stew and half guilt. Daniel was *wrong* when he said I had an excuse for being ignorant. The harassment of German Jews may not have been in the center pages of all the newspapers, but *I* had Veronica, better than any newspaper. The fact was, I'd not *wanted* to hear awful things. I had enough nightmares about German soldiers as it was. I'd deliberately clapped my hands over my ears and squeezed my eyes shut . . .

I brooded over this while my tea went cold, and when I next looked up, Daniel and Veronica's discussion had moved on.

"—Czechoslovakia?" Veronica was saying.

"Yes, I'm afraid that's next. With that riot in the Sudeten-land last year—"

"Well, they are actually *Germans*, aren't they, most of those Sudeten people? Czechoslovakia didn't even exist until 1918."

Daniel nodded. "The question is, will Hitler be satisfied taking over just the Sudeten part of Czechoslovakia?"

"Where *is* the Sudetenland?" asked Veronica. "Is it that bit north of Prague?"

"Yes, on the border of Germany and Poland. Here—" Daniel moved the mustard pot into the middle of the table. "Look, this is Germany. And the sugar bowl is Czechoslovakia, and this spoon can be the Sudetens—"

Soon the saltcellar, sauce bottle, two empty teacups, and a milk jug were jostling for European domination on our tabletop.

"But you're leaving out France, aren't you?" said the man at the next table, leaning across. "Don't tell me that's not in Herr Hitler's sights! And just you wait, we'll be going over there to rescue them French, just like before."

"Ooh, don't say that," sighed the waitress, who'd come over to see if we wanted more tea. "That were awful, that was. My mum lost her three brothers over there, and her fiancé. Hang about, where's Belgium? I met a gentleman from there just last week—ever so nice, he was."

The man at the next table donated his saltcellar to stand in for Belgium.

"But you haven't taken into account the Maginot Line!" huffed a beefy, red-faced man who'd been on his way to the cashier. "The Huns won't be getting past *that* in a hurry, let me tell you! I've seen it with my own eyes. Huge concrete forts and lookout posts and barbed wire—"

"No, see, that's my fork," said Veronica, indicating the bit of cutlery guarding France from Germany.

"And great, big underground chambers—why, the French army could live down there for months!"

"But . . . doesn't that Maginot Line stop at the border with Belgium?" I asked. "I mean, couldn't the Germans just go round the top of it if they wanted to attack France?"

There was silence as half a dozen people stared at the fork.

"Let's hope there aren't any Germans listening in right now," remarked Daniel after a moment.

"Course there aren't," said the Maginot Line expert heartily.

"Besides, there's no need for you young ladies to worry your pretty little heads about all *this* business, is there?" Veronica began to bristle, so Daniel hurriedly asked for our bill. The man lumbered off, and Veronica and Daniel had a brief scuffle over the bill. Veronica won.

"I invited *you* to luncheon," she said. "Anyway, I've got money and you haven't. Just think of it as an equitable redistribution of wealth. Marx would approve."

We went outside and Daniel was surprised, and slightly worried, to discover that Parker wasn't waiting for us, so he offered to see us home. However, as he was going east and we were going west, we declined firmly. He waited with us till our bus came, then shook hands with each of us, lingering noticeably over Veronica's, then waving till we were out of sight.

He is *definitely* in love with Veronica.

"What a productive day!" she said, taking her notebook out of her bag as soon as we'd found a seat and examining her list of names with great satisfaction. Then she produced a pencil and began drafting a letter to Sir Julius Pemberton, without even a backwards glance through the window.

She is definitely *not* in love with Daniel.

11th April 1938

I sit here in the drawing room, surrounded by my family, and consider what a lovely picture this would present to a stranger peeping through the window (assuming the stranger were able to hover outside the second floor of Montmaray House and had managed to clear a space in the grimy windowpane). Observe, then, stranger: the dignified aunt, presiding over the embossed silver teapot; the handsome blond nephew, down from Oxford for a few days; two genteel young ladies, one reading, the other writing in her journal; the family's loyal retainer, a good-looking young man in his early twenties, handing round a plate of pastries; and an innocent, curly-haired child, sitting on the rug with her faithful pets.

Of course, the stranger might be *slightly* surprised to observe that one of the pets is a large pink pig. If very attentive, he might also notice that the more attractive of the young ladies is reading not *Tatler* or *Vogue* but a crumpled left-wing newspaper she has just fished out of the wastepaper bin, and that the nephew is gazing glumly at the tablecloth while the aunt delivers a blistering lecture.

"I have better things to do, Tobias," she thunders, "than correspond with your tutor, who claims you've failed to attend a single meeting with him all term! Now, *I* don't mind if you're not the academic sort—your dear father wasn't, God rest his soul—but what, may I ask, are you *doing* with your time? Pamela Bosworth's nephew reports you haven't joined *any* of the right clubs at Oxford, that you're never seen at the Union, that when you appear in public, it's with a *most* disreputable crowd—"

Toby accepts a pastry from Simon and shreds it on his plate; Veronica frowns at *The Manchester Guardian*; and Henry scratches vigorously behind Estella's ears. The pig's eyes are squeezed shut with pleasure, and she leans into Henry so heavily that Henry is in danger of tumbling over backwards.

"And now I discover you've exceeded your allowance yet again!" Aunt Charlotte continues with rising indignation. "What *do* you spend it on? Champagne, I suppose, and cigars, and extravagant dinners with unsuitable young ladies!"

It's a measure of how cross she is that she's berating Toby, her favorite, in front of the rest of us. In her defense, she's just back from a long luncheon with Lady Bosworth, who was overflowing with "helpful advice" on the subject of disobedient nephews. Toby would usually have said something placatory by this stage, but perhaps he feels it's better that Aunt Charlotte wear herself out, and she *does* appear to be running out of steam . . .

No, she's merely switched topic.

"As for you, Henrietta, I thought I told you to take those animals downstairs. *How* your governess didn't notice you loading them into the luggage car is quite beyond me . . . Henrietta! Do not walk away while I'm speaking to you! Where are your manners? Remember, you are a FitzOsborne, not a peasant! What *will* they think at Buckingham Palace?"

For Henry, improbable as it seems, has been asked to tea at Buckingham Palace on Wednesday, hence her presence in London. A dozen Girl Guide patrol leaders from across the country will gather with Princess Elizabeth and Princess Margaret for a stroll through the Palace grounds and a picnic tea, weather permitting.

"If *only* they'd asked us a couple of months ago," Henry sighed when the invitation arrived at Milford Park. "I could have brought the others. Carmelita would have *loved* to see London."

"You are sadly mistaken if you believe the Palace would ever invite a rabble of Communist refugees to a garden party," said Aunt Charlotte coldly. "Simon, who else will be attending?"

"I'm afraid the letter doesn't specify, ma'am," said Simon.

"Only girls from titled families, one would *hope*," said Aunt Charlotte. "Wouldn't you agree, Simon? One can't imagine the King and Queen would want their daughters associating with, well . . ."

"Riffraff, ma'am?" suggested Simon blandly.

"The *lower classes*," said Aunt Charlotte, giving Simon a

suspicious look. Then she turned on Veronica. "You, I am saddened to report, are not invited. Only Sophia is mentioned. Perhaps if you'd made yourself more agreeable last Season—or if you'd helped supervise the little girls, as Sophia charitably did—then you, too, would have been included in this gathering at the Palace."

"How *will* I endure the torment of being overlooked?" murmured Veronica, busy opening her own post, which consisted of a single official-looking envelope.

"Then perhaps this will teach you a lesson," said Aunt Charlotte, her mind too fixed on the dazzling prospect of Buckingham Palace to perceive Veronica's sarcasm. "Perhaps you will learn that there are *rewards* for young ladies who behave in a manner—"

"Damn," said Veronica, staring at her letter.

"*What* did you say?" cried Aunt Charlotte.

"Oh, sorry," said Veronica, looking up with a frown. "It's just—"

"Damn," muttered Simon, peering over her shoulder—although, fortunately for him, his utterance was lost in Aunt Charlotte's outraged exclamations.

"Veronica FitzOsborne! Such unladylike language! And in front of your little cousin!"

"Oh, I don't mind," Henry said earnestly. "My friend Jocko says much worse things. *He* says—"

"I do not want to hear it!" said Aunt Charlotte, drawing herself up to her full and rather imposing height. "I do not want to hear whatever vulgar expressions are employed by *Jocko*, whoever he may be!"

"You don't know who Jocko is?" said Henry. "He lives in the village. His father's the pigman." Which prompted another explosion from Aunt Charlotte. Veronica went to Henry's rescue, and Simon passed the letter to me. It was, at last, a response from the Foreign Office. Alas, it was not encouraging.

"But it's not completely awful," I said to Simon in a low voice. "Look, it says they're referring the matter to a review committee."

"That's civil service code for 'We are going to file this away in a cabinet in the basement and hope that you forget all about it.' See the signature? I doubt our letters got anywhere near an official with real authority."

"Oh," I said, crestfallen. "Now what?"

"Well, I did say right from the start that I thought the Ministry for Coordination of Defence would be more helpful than the Foreign Office," began Simon, but then Aunt Charlotte ordered him to go off and locate Miss Bullock and find out why the governess had been permitting Henry to consort with the offspring of pigmen. Aunt Charlotte then went back to chastising Veronica for her unladylike conduct, although Veronica was so disheartened about the Foreign Office letter that she barely listened to a word, which made Aunt Charlotte even more annoyed.

"I don't know," Aunt Charlotte says now. "I *do not know* what I am to do with you children. Unruly, undisciplined, unmannerly—"

Her rant does appear to be winding down, though. Toby

quickly pushes the plate of pastries closer (he stopped in at her favorite patisserie on his way here), and, eventually, she sighs and takes an éclair.

"So, Veronica!" Toby says, judging it safe to speak once Aunt Charlotte's mouth is full of pastry, cream, and chocolate. "What's in the news? Anything interesting?"

Veronica looks up. "Well, Unity Mitford turned up at a Labour Party rally in Hyde Park wearing her swastika badge, assaulted a couple of people, and nearly got tossed in the Serpentine."

"There," says Toby cheerfully. "See, Aunt Charlotte, how much worse it might be for you? You could be poor old Lady Redesdale."

"Oh, *yes*, all those dreadful daughters of hers," muses Aunt Charlotte, dabbing at the corner of her mouth with a napkin. "At least *you* children manage to keep out of the headlines. Unity's the enormous blonde one, isn't she? Most peculiar girl. I remember seeing her at a debutante dance with a white rat on her shoulder. And then, after her Court presentation, she apparently wrote to a lot of people on Buckingham Palace stationery. Stolen! As a *joke*!"

"You needn't worry Henry will do that," Toby reassures Aunt Charlotte. "She's quite illiterate."

"Imagine, purloining His Majesty's stationery as a *prank*," Aunt Charlotte says, shaking her head. "Such an act of disrespect! When one considers the King is the ultimate authority in this land—"

Veronica's teacup clatters in its saucer, and Aunt Charlotte frowns at her.

"Veronica, do put that appalling newspaper away. It's very ill-mannered to read at the tea table, anyway, and now you've knocked over the sugar."

Veronica only leans forward eagerly, her elbow narrowly missing the butter. "But he *is*, isn't he? The King *is* the executive authority throughout Britain! That's why it's called *His Majesty's government*."

"Of course it is," Aunt Charlotte says irritably.

Simon catches on before I do. "That's just a name," he says. "The reigning British monarch hasn't any real power."

"Nonsense!" says Veronica. "He opens Parliament, he needs to approve each bill passed, he's the only one who can declare the country at war with another."

Aunt Charlotte looks thoroughly bewildered at this turn of the conversation.

"*Only* on the advice of his ministers," says Simon.

"Whom he has the right to warn and encourage!" says Veronica.

"Even *so*," says Simon, "there's no reason for him to help *us*."

Veronica beams. "Oh, yes, there is!" she says triumphantly. "There's Queen Elizabeth the First's promise to send her navy to Montmaray's aid whenever we need it!"

"You mean that letter written after we helped them defeat the Spanish Armada?" says Toby incredulously. "That no one could read because her handwriting was so awful?"

"A letter that is *no longer in existence!*" adds Simon heatedly.

Aunt Charlotte gives up, shakes her head, and goes off to telephone Lady Astley, to see when she's coming up to London . . .

Evening, written in bed. I am getting very speedy with my ab-breviated Kernetin, but not quite speedy enough to keep up with an argument between Simon and Veronica, particularly if I want to contribute to it.

So, to summarize the rest of this afternoon's discussion: Veronica wants to direct our campaign towards King George. Simon thinks this will be a waste of time, as Queen Elizabeth's letter pledging England's assistance is now buried under a pile of rubble at Montmaray. Veronica is certain there must be *some* mention of Montmaray's contribution to the defeat of the Span-ish Armada in other texts and is planning a visit to the British Museum's Reading Room tomorrow. She also notes that a hun-dred and fifty-eight Montmaravian soldiers gave their lives for the Allied side in the Great War a mere twenty years ago, and *that* ought to count for something. Simon says that she's ignor-ing the fact that King George is of German descent and no doubt in favor of appeasement. Simon also repeated that the King has no real legal power in this country. Veronica asked when Simon had become an expert on British constitutional law, whereupon I gave Simon a very pointed look, but he stubbornly withheld the fact that he's taking classes in law (and came top of his class in his last exam). Then Toby tried to talk us all into sneaking out to a nightclub this evening, but Veronica said she needed to spend the evening in the Montmaray House library, and I didn't want to risk the wrath of Aunt Charlotte, even though I'm wildly curious about what goes on at a nightclub. Besides, I don't think I have any suitably decadent clothes. Oh, Veronica has just come in . . .

Veronica wants me to use my visit to Buckingham Palace on Wednesday to convert King George to our cause.

"*What?*" I said, not certain I'd heard correctly.

"You may need to give him some background information before you get to the bit about the Nazis. I'm not sure how familiar he is with the Kingdom of Montmaray. Try to avoid any mention of King Henry the Eighth if you can possibly help it— his family might still be a bit sensitive about Catherine Howard having an affair with our ancestor. And make sure you tell the King how Montmaray fired upon Napoleon, he ought to approve of that—"

"Veronica!" I said. "Do you honestly think I'm going to start lecturing King George about Montmaravian history at a garden party? Why on earth would he listen to a word I said?"

"Why wouldn't he?" she said. "You're at least as articulate as I am, and certainly more charming. And you don't need to convince him beyond reasonable doubt—just soften him up a bit, then we'll hit him with a couple of letters. Next thing you know, he'll be telephoning Downing Street, urging the Prime Minister to take action!"

I stared at her. "Have you gone *completely* mad?"

"All right, it may not happen quite as smoothly as that. But it's a step in the right direction, don't you think?"

She gave me a pleading look that I found difficult to resist.

"But . . . but is doing something that's bound to fail *really* better than doing nothing?" I asked weakly.

"Oh, Sophie!" She grasped my hand. "Listen. I admit, I was thrown into despair when I got that awful Foreign Office letter. Especially as Simon kept saying 'I told you so' in that infuriating manner of his. But then I decided to take a leaf out of your book. And do you know what I did?"

I shook my head, dumbfounded.

"I turned to the poets and the playwrights," she said. "I went to the library and took down that big volume of Shakespeare, and I opened it to a random page in search of inspiration and hope."

I was thrilled. "And what did it say?" I breathed.

"Well, it fell open at that idiotic *Romeo and Juliet*. And then to the even more idiotic *Taming of the Shrew*. So I kept flipping pages until I came to something based on actual history."

"It's not supposed to work like that," I protested. "You're meant to leave it up to Fate!"

"Funny you should say that!" she said. "Because you know what I came to? 'Men at some time are masters of their fates!' Cassius, urging Brutus to take action!"

"Urging Brutus to *kill someone*," I pointed out. "An action that Brutus bitterly regretted for the brief remainder of his life."

"All right," Veronica said. "How about this, then? 'The abuse of greatness is when it disjoins remorse from power.' That's Hitler, obviously, and that Nazi officer, Gebhardt, as well—all power and no remorse. 'Think him as a serpent's egg . . . and kill him in the shell.'"

I wasn't sure how *that* applied to us—unless Veronica and Daniel were secretly plotting to assassinate Hitler, which wouldn't actually surprise me. However, I agreed aloud that *Julius Caesar* was full of powerful phrases.

Veronica nodded thoughtfully. "Mind you, I *did* keep getting distracted by all the historical inaccuracies in that play. Clocks striking the hour, when the ancient Romans didn't have clocks! And people reading books rather than scrolls—"

We had a short discussion in which we failed to agree about poetic license, then Veronica said she had to get back to the library. At the doorway, she turned and added, "Anyway, you're *not* bound to fail. I have complete confidence in you."

Well, she might, but I haven't.

Still, what's the likelihood of King George attending a garden party for Girl Guides? Extremely low, I hope.

6th May 1938

Well, I didn't get to talk to King George, because he didn't make
an appearance at the Buckingham Palace tea party. However,
His Majesty is now very aware of the FitzOsbornes of Montmaray. Just not in any positive sort of way.

This, I must emphasize, is not my fault. It's not even Henry's
fault—well, not entirely. She was provoked from the very start
by little Princess Margaret, who spilled her milk on Henry's
shoes, scoffed at Henry's name and the name of our Girl Guide
patrol, refused to believe any such place as Montmaray existed,
and (worst of all, in Henry's opinion) laughed at the notion that
Henry's brother might be King. Then, while I was caught up in
conversation with a Guiding Lady, Henry explained to Princess
Elizabeth in graphic detail how London would be annihilated
by German bombers once war was declared, which made a dozen
Guides cry and no doubt condemned them to weeks of screaming nightmares.

"How dare you upset the little ones with such lies!" cried

one of the mothers, clutching her weeping child. "The Germans are our *friends!*" Whereupon Henry (in her usual strident tones) replied that that was a load of rubbish, all Germans were bloody Fascists, weren't they, Sophie? At which point, everyone realized Queen Elizabeth, resplendent in feathery pink, surrounded by ladies-in-waiting, was standing, horrified, in the doorway of the summerhouse, having dropped in unexpectedly on what was *supposed* to be a decorous tea party for the crème de la crème of junior Society.

The row that followed our misadventures at Buckingham Palace was the worst yet. Aunt Charlotte even threatened Henry with boarding school (an indication of just how upset our aunt was, because she believes sending a girl to school is like trying to teach a monkey to cook—not only a waste of time, money, and effort but extremely dangerous). Henry and Miss Bullock were packed off back to Milford Park at once, as if they needed to be quarantined. In fact, one of Julia's stuffier aunts reported that Henry is now blacklisted in the nursery rooms of at least seven aristocratic families, although I'm not sure this is solely due to Henry's outburst at Buckingham Palace. It may also be connected with an incident that same morning when she took Estella and Carlos for a walk in Kensington Gardens. We only found out about that later. Estella dug up a nasturtium plant and ate it, and Carlos went for a splashy swim in the Round Pond, overturning someone's valuable toy yacht and then shaking himself dry beside a couple of venerable nannies and their infant charges, one of whom was the granddaughter of a duke.

Veronica and I are also in disgrace, Veronica for inciting Henry to misbehave, with all her talk of Fascists and bombs, and I for not supervising Henry more closely at the garden party. Suitably chastened, we are now putting on very good impressions of dutiful and well-bred nieces. We attended the opening of the Royal Academy's Summer Exhibition and then, without a word of complaint, a cocktail party hosted by Lord Elchester's vile nephew (Toby was also invited but claimed to be working so hard towards his examinations that he was unable to leave Oxford). We have also gone to three tea parties, five luncheons, and a dance in Berkeley Square, and behaved impeccably at each event. Veronica even agreed to accompany Aunt Charlotte, Lady Astley, Julia, and me to a charity fashion show this morning, where she made polite (that is, nonpolitical) conversation with several ladies. Then, as the mannequins stalked along the stage, I saw her jotting something on the gilt-edged cards they give out, on which ladies are supposed to mark down which outfits they wish to purchase. Of course, when I leaned over, I saw she was writing, *Letters to: Secretary of State for Air; First Sea Lord; W. Churchill* . . .

I probably don't need to add that the letter we sent to King George did not bear any fruit—or rather, the fruit it produced was so shriveled and bitter that Veronica wanted to throw it straight into the fire, except Simon made her keep it for our records. Simon has won quite a few battles with her lately. In particular, Veronica has come round to his view that we need to convince the government that Montmaray's invasion poses a genuine military threat to Britain.

"After all, Montmaray's right next to France, their main ally," said Simon. "And not far from the Channel Islands, either, and they're British crown dependencies. It's in Britain's military interest to help us."

"But where's our *evidence?*" asked Veronica. "How do we know the Germans have armed forces stationed at Montmaray? We don't even know for certain that they used it in the raids against Guernica."

"What we need are some contacts in the British navy and air force," said Simon, frowning at his papers. "*They'd* have some idea of what's going on at Montmaray, surely."

"There's Julia's uncle," I said. "Isn't he something in intelligence?"

"Colonel Stanley-Ross is still overseas—I checked," said Simon. "I can't even find out what he *does.* It must be something terribly important, but that's no help if we can't get hold of him. Anyway, as I was saying, the navy and air force are both overseen by the Ministry for Coordination of Defence. So, in theory, we ought to start working away at the Minister, Thomas Inskip—"

"You mean, Caligula's horse," Veronica said.

"I said, *in theory,*" said Simon. "But I do know a young lady whose father's a senior civil servant, rather high up in Defence. I may be able to convince her to put in a good word for us."

"What, using your legendary Lotharian charms?" said Veronica with a snort.

And I couldn't help adding, "Really, Simon, it doesn't sound very . . . gentlemanly."

He just smirked.

Then I found out via Julia that this particular young lady has Quite a Reputation—which made the whole thing even *more* distasteful. Toby also disapproves heartily, not that *I* told him. He had a loud fight with Simon about it over the telephone. Still, perhaps I won't mind too much if it produces results . . .

Oh, yes, I *will*—the end never justifies the means! But the whole thing is too repugnant to consider further, and besides, I need to go and pack (that is, watch Phoebe pack) for this Bosworth house party to which Veronica and I have inexplicably been invited. I'm certain it will be *dire*. Oh dear, I wish Toby were coming, too, at least we'd have someone friendly to talk to, but he claims he *cannot tear himself away from his textbooks* . . .

How wrong can one be? All the way to the Bosworths on Friday afternoon, Veronica and I were moaning about how awkward and tedious and pointless the whole thing would be, and wondering whether there'd be any way we could escape before Monday morning.

"They don't even have a decent library," said Veronica. "All the books are about *horses*."

"And Lady Bosworth loathes us," I said.

"Well, no, she only loathes me," Veronica said.

"She ignores me," I said. "Which is almost as bad. I bet she only invited us because she thought Toby would come. Or else she's invited some Americans and she wants to impress them with a bit of royalty. Oh . . . I just had a terrible thought! Cynthia will probably make us go *riding!*"

"Perhaps we could escape on *horseback*," said Veronica. "How far is it to Milford, do you think, cross-country?"

Unfortunately, Simon had taken the Lagonda in order to

promote his nefarious schemes—I think he was planning to whisk the Girl with the Reputation away on a picnic—so Parker had to drop us off, having arranged to collect us again on Monday morning. I suppose the Lagonda would have been a bit of a squash, anyway, what with Veronica and me, two big trunks, several hatboxes, and Phoebe. (Phoebe was the only one who was thrilled by the idea of staying with the Bosworths. I think she's in love with one of their footmen.)

It was even worse than I'd imagined, walking into the Bosworths' drawing room for tea that afternoon. Over by the table was a loud, tomato-faced baronet, who'd danced with me at my coming-out ball (if one could call jerking my arms about and stomping on my feet "dancing"). He was being shrieked at by two horrible girls who'd once spent an entire luncheon party sneering at Veronica. Blocking all the warmth of the fire was a very broad Elchester cousin, who was arguing about rugby with a former dorm-mate of Toby's (Toby had pointed him out at a dance last year and warned me away from him). To top it all off, there by the window, leafing through *Vogue*, was Penelope Stanley-Ross, Julia's snooty sister-in-law.

"At least Oswald Mosley's not coming," muttered Veronica. "I asked the butler."

We gazed into the room like swimmers contemplating an ice-encrusted pool in the middle of winter. Then, with a couple of deep breaths, we plunged in. Veronica was immediately snagged by Toby's dorm-mate, but I floundered alone in the deep end for quite a while. Lord Bosworth eventually took pity on me and "introduced" me to the two horrible girls, whose names I pretended to have forgotten. We made desultory conversation for a quarter of an hour, then Cynthia stomped in, brushing mud off her jodhpurs. She asked if Simon was with us, scowled when I replied in the negative, and proceeded to ignore me. Meanwhile, Lady Bosworth was in a flap, because she'd just discovered her son was bringing his party of young gentlemen the next morning instead of that afternoon, which meant an excess of females at the dinner table that evening. Horrors! For a moment, I thought she was going to make me have supper upstairs on a tray to balance out the numbers, but in the end, the vicar and an ancient bachelor neighbor came to her rescue.

Dinner was interminable, although at least there wasn't any discussion of politics this time. Afterwards, I sat and watched the older couples play bridge while the Elchester cousin plinked out some "music" of his own composition on the grand piano. Beside me, the two girls flirted with the red-faced baronet, Cynthia flipped through *Horse & Hound,* and Toby's dorm-mate, Geoffrey, described his hunting exploits to Veronica in excruciating detail.

"No doubt you'll find it more lively tomorrow, when the rest of the boys arrive," Lord Bosworth said to me in kindly tones as we went upstairs. "Fun and games! Or, as you young people say, *high jinks!*"

He really is a dear old thing. I just hoped he hadn't overheard Veronica telling me how she'd coped with Geoffrey's monologue.

"I simply recited to myself the names of all the British kings and queens, in chronological order, starting with Egbert," she said. "Whenever I came to a new dynasty, I'd say out loud, 'Gosh!' or 'Really?' When I reached the House of Windsor, Geoffrey was still going on about a five-mile point, whatever that is, so I did them all again, backwards, with the dates of their reigns."

"I *thought* you looked a bit too absorbed for it to be real," I said.

"It's all those Ethelbalds and Ethelberts that are tricky," she mused. "The Tudors are so much easier, only six of them."

The next morning, I managed to avoid being included in Cynthia's riding party by hiding in the loo for half an hour. Veronica wasn't as lucky—she was forced into a two-mile walk to the Roman ruins (a couple of fragments of mosaic floor she'd already seen) with Geoffrey, Penelope, and the Elchester cousin. I waited till everyone had gone, then crept up to the Long Gallery. I was happily ensconced there by the fire with *Persuasion* when a commotion downstairs announced that the party from London had arrived.

"Ah, *there* you are, Your Highness," said Lady Bosworth, pouncing on me a few minutes later. "Where *has* everyone disappeared to? Well, you'll show this young lady around, won't you, while I find— Darling! Where have the boys gone? The *billiards* room? Oh, for heaven's sake!" And Lady Bosworth stalked off, leaving me to entertain the American Ambassador's daughter, Kathleen. I looked at her with interest because I hadn't met any Americans before (apart from Anthony's mother, and her only briefly, in the chaos of Julia's wedding). At first glance, this girl appeared much like anyone else, except for having more teeth, all of them very large and straight and white. They were noticeable because she smiled so often—indeed, I'd never before met a girl of my own age who was so friendly and relaxed. I liked her at once.

"Call me Kick," she said, demonstrating her nickname by kicking off her shoes and curling her feet beneath her on the sofa. "All my friends do. Are you *really* a princess? Gosh! So, are you making your debut this Season? I'm being presented at Court next week, and boy, you should *see* my Court dress! It's gorgeous! White tulle with silver threads, from Lelong in Paris. My sister got hers from Molyneux."

I asked about her sister.

"Rosemary's two years older, and then I've got three younger sisters, but they're all still at school, and four brothers." She laughed at my expression. "Don't you *have* proper-sized families here in England, then?" she teased. She went on to tell me all about her life, which sounded fascinating—a father on first-name terms with Hollywood stars and the American President; a couple of dashing older brothers at Harvard; her own convent education in Connecticut and then France; holidays spent winning tennis trophies and sailing her own boat and dancing to swing records. She even chewed *gum*! I had to refuse, though, when she offered me some from a little paper packet—I was afraid Lady Bosworth would see and report me to Aunt Charlotte for unladylike behavior.

The morning's riders and walkers eventually straggled in, damp and dirty, and made straight for the fire, followed shortly by the billiards players. It was, as Lord Bosworth predicted, all fun and games from then on. The boys were entranced by Kick, even though she wasn't beautiful, or even very pretty. She was sturdily built rather than ethereal, her face was square and freckled, her hair was even wilder than mine—but she was so lively and confident that none of that mattered. (There's probably a lesson somewhere in there for me. What a pity it's as difficult to change one's personality as one's looks.) Kick sprawled on the floor and poured out a stream of gossip and politics and bad jokes in her slangy, enticing American accent, and the boys laughed and argued and teased her back. The girls were equally impressed—they didn't even try to compete. It was amusing to see the two horrible girls become instant longtime friends of mine once they realized Kick liked me. ("Oh, but you should have seen *Sophie's* Court dress!" they cried. "Sophie, do tell Kick about that wonderful speech your brother gave at your coming-out ball!") The only one to ignore Kick was Geoffrey, who seemed to have fallen head over heels for Veronica.

"You're being very patient with him," I said to Veronica that evening as we dressed for dinner. "It must be such a bore for you, when he's so dreadful."

"Oh, I don't mind *very* much," Veronica said. "If Simon can bear it, I expect I can."

"What do you mean?" I said, putting my hairbrush down.

"Well, you know who Geoffrey *is*, don't you?"

"Yes, he's Toby's awful dorm-mate, the one who tried to get Toby to join the British Union of Fascists."

"Well, he seems to have lost interest in Fascism now, thank heavens for small mercies. If only he'd lost interest in hunting as well. Anyway, he's Geoffrey Pemberton."

"Who?"

"Oh, Sophie! His father's Sir Julius Pemberton, from the Foreign Office."

My mouth fell open. "Veronica FitzOsborne!" I gasped. "I can't believe you've actually been, been . . ." I couldn't even find the words. "Been *encouraging* that poor boy's attentions, just to get access to his father!"

"I haven't been encouraging him," she said. "I've simply re-frained from *discouraging* him. *I* didn't want to come to this stu-pid house party, but I'm not going to ignore an opportunity when it jumps up and down in front of me. Anyway, you didn't think he was a 'poor boy' a moment ago—you said he was dreadful."

"I am absolutely appalled," I said, deciding to ignore that last remark. "I just want you to know that I thoroughly disap-prove. And I suppose *that's* why you're wearing *that* dress."

"I'm wearing it because, firstly, you and Julia made me buy it, and, secondly, it's the one Phoebe laid out for me tonight. She spilled talcum powder on my black silk, and I wore the blue gown last night. Why, do you think it's a bit much?"

"You're practically falling out the top of it," I said, which was only a slight exaggeration. "Geoffrey will be struck deaf and dumb at the sight—or is that your intention, so you'll be spared another hunting monologue?"

"One can only hope," Veronica said, peering in the looking glass and trying to tug up the neckline of her dress. "Isn't it *odd*, the way males react to what are, after all, simply bits of flesh designed for feeding infants? I've had whole conversations in which men have spoken directly to my chest—as though they expected *it* to answer. But it's just biological determinism, I suppose, in which any sign of female fertility acts as a—"

"*Please* don't mention biology or fertility in Geoffrey Pemberton's presence," I begged her. "I can't bear to think of what the consequences might be. And here, take my wrap. You need it more than I do."

I kept a wary eye on Veronica all evening. However, I have to admit that her behavior was entirely proper and her dress no more revealing than the other girls', so it's probably just bad luck that Geoffrey has invited us to his country house for—

The ink blot obscuring my previous sentence was the result of a startling interruption. I'd decided to update my journal, and the Long Gallery proved to be much warmer than my bedroom (Lady Bosworth doesn't believe in fires being lit in guests' rooms; she thinks it encourages hibernation). I was perfectly safe in the Long Gallery, I'd thought, as everyone else was off riding or playing tennis or working on the vast jigsaw in the music room. So there I was, scribbling away in what I'd imagined was an empty room, when I suddenly heard a voice say, "Ah! Kernetin, I presume."

My head jerked up and I stared with astonishment at the middle-aged gentleman who'd appeared directly in front of me. He tilted his head, examining my page with interest. His gaze was so intelligent that I slammed my journal shut at once, for fear he might actually be decoding what I'd written (even though I knew that was impossible). But how could a complete stranger have known it was called Kernetin? How, for that matter, had he been able to approach me so silently? *Was* he a stranger, after all? Now that I came to look at him more closely, there was something familiar about that faded hair slanted across his forehead, those sharp hazel eyes . . .

I held out my hand. "Colonel Stanley-Ross," I said. "How do you do? I'm Sophia FitzOsborne."

He beamed at me, showing nice crinkles around his eyes, and shook my hand. "And you're just as clever as I'd heard! May I sit down? I'd ask to have a closer look at that marvelous book of yours, but I fear that really *would* be presumptuous. However, I cannot resist one enquiry—is that an abbreviated form of Kernetin that you were using?"

I acknowledged that it was. "I suppose you've seen Toby with the proper version."

"Yes, and that hard-hearted boy refused to teach it to me, on the grounds I was both a grown-up and a non-FitzOsborne. But now I see it's boustrophedonic—most ingenious!"

"I expect you come across quite a few codes in your line of work," I said, hoping to find out what exactly he did.

He twinkled at me. "Oh, it's a fascinating area," he said, giving nothing away. "And *speaking* of interesting communications"—he fished around in the pocket of his tweed jacket— "I've just come from Oxford and happened to drop in on my favorite nephew. He asked me to give you this." The Colonel handed over an envelope, my name written on the front in Rupert's careful, rounded script. "He was reluctant to send it to your aunt's house when you weren't there, seemed to imagine she might open it *herself*. What a suspicious boy he is! I wonder where he gets it from? And no, I haven't peeked, I promise."

"Did you see Toby at Oxford, too?" I asked, sliding the envelope inside my journal.

"I'm afraid not," said the Colonel. "It was quite early in the morning when I visited, about a quarter to eleven. He was still in bed."

"He claims to be working *very* hard," I said.

"Burning the midnight oil, I'm sure," said the Colonel. "But do you hear that? Tea approaches! Such a civilized custom, I do miss it whenever I'm away from England. But first, tell me—I've been absent such a long while—what is happening with Montmaray?"

I gave him a summary of our campaign activities thus far. "And the Foreign Office wanted to sweep the whole thing under the carpet!" I finished with great indignation.

He nodded thoughtfully. "And you wrote directly to Alexander Cadogan?"

"Well . . . I'm not *entirely* sure he received those letters," I admitted. "They may have been lost."

"I think *he'll* be amenable," said the Colonel, gazing into the fire and tapping one long finger against his lips. "Of course, it's the job of the Foreign Office to carry out government policy—which happens to include appeasement of Germany, at the moment—but there *are* a few dissenters . . . By the way, would that have been your cousin I saw in the music room, talking to Julius Pemberton's son?"

I said glumly that it was very likely.

"She's probably wasting her time with Sir Julius, although I've heard your cousin has exceptional debating skills. And the Pemberton men *do* have a well-known weakness for statuesque beauties . . ."

I gave the Colonel my Appalled Look, and he chuckled.

"Well, I won't encourage her. Have you approached any De-fence people?"

"Simon Chester's just starting on that," I said. I assumed the Colonel had met Simon at some stage, and he had.

"I can give him some names," the Colonel said. "I've already had a word with a couple of colleagues. Tiny cogs in the depths of Whitehall are being oiled as we speak, and soon they will begin to turn, and who knows what might happen . . . But where is Simon now? Oh, London. I'm driving up there myself this evening."

The Colonel seemed to lead an extraordinarily busy life. I wondered why he'd chosen to stop off at Lady Bosworth's for tea. Surely it couldn't have just been to deliver Rupert's letter and have a chat with me? But as soon as we arrived in the drawing room, he sauntered over to Kick and casually engaged her in a conversation that resulted in him being invited to the American Embassy for drinks the next week. *Mission accomplished,* I thought. He went over to have a brief talk with Veronica, nodded goodbye to me from the doorway, then clapped his trilby on his head and departed. It was odd, I realized, that I'd spoken with him so easily. I'd never even met him before. But then, he looked so much like Rupert. They both have very trustworthy faces.

Speaking of Rupert, I ought to copy in his letter—but that will have to wait. It is nearly one in the morning, and my fingers are too cold to move anymore.

7th June 1938

One would think that Aunt Charlotte would have been *impressed* with Veronica's and my behavior at the Bosworth house party. Veronica had captured the heart (or something) of a titled gentleman's eldest son; I'd made friends with the daughter of the American Ambassador; neither of us had mortally offended anyone, as far as we knew. But *still* Aunt Charlotte grumbled.

"A baronet's son!" she said. "When I keep introducing you to the heirs of dukes and marquesses! Well, I suppose Sir Julius is respectable enough, but they've such a tiny little place, barely a hundred acres. And really, Sophia, of all the ambassadors for you to get mixed up with! *Kennedy*—what sort of a name is that? Irish, I suppose, *and* Catholic! All those dozens of children, they sound *most* unsuitable."

The newspapers don't agree. They can't get enough of the Kennedys, especially Kick, whom they've now labeled "Most Exciting Debutante of 1938." And even Aunt Charlotte acknowledged it was a social triumph for us to be invited to the Kennedy girls' debutante dance, held at the American Embassy. I thought I'd become jaded about fancy balls, but my goodness! *Such luxury!* I'd never experienced anything like it. Flowers and food and entertainers flown in from around the world—and enough crown princes, dukes, and counts to satisfy even Aunt Charlotte.

"If only Tobias could have been there," she sighed afterwards. "Lord Dorset's niece looked *most* disappointed when she realized he wasn't with us—and was that the Spanish Infanta I saw talking to the Ambassador? What a missed opportunity for Tobias! Of course, I'm pleased he's taken my advice to settle down, but I do hope he isn't working *too* hard."

Well, that's one thing she doesn't have to worry about. He isn't. Rupert wrote and told me so. I shan't copy out all his letter, but here's the relevant bit:

As for Toby, he's doing no work whatsoever and is drinking too much, which isn't unusual—however, he's also stopped going out, appears to have given up eating, and seems completely miserable. I'm sure you know what (that is, who) is causing all this. Is there any chance you could come up to luncheon one day and talk some sense into him? Of course, I know how difficult it would be for you to get away. Please don't mention anything about this to your aunt— Toby said her last lecture was dreadful, and he really thinks she might take away his allowance if he gets into any more trouble.

Of course, you are very welcome to come to luncheon

any day, regardless of whether your brother comes to his
senses or not . . .

Then the rest of the letter was about how Rupert had released the dormouse back into the woods where he'd found her as an orphaned baby, and how he hoped she was managing to gather enough food and keep out of the way of owls.

Well, of course, I had to go up to Oxford, but how was I to *get* there without attracting the notice of Aunt Charlotte? And should I ask Veronica to come with me or not? Because I wasn't sure if she knew (or *wanted* to know) about Toby and Simon—or if she'd recovered from her intense envy of lady undergraduates.

Then, just as I was pondering this, Aunt Charlotte and Veronica were invited to luncheon at Sir Julius Pemberton's, and he said he'd send his car for them. And Parker revealed that his cousin had recently taken over the lease on an Oxford pub and that he, Parker, wouldn't be at all averse to catching up with his relative . . . It must have been Fate. At any rate, today Parker dropped me off outside Christ Church, where I found Rupert waiting with a stack of books and a one-eared cat.

"I hammered on Toby's door when I went off to my morning lecture," Rupert explained as the cat led us through a shadowed archway. "And then I asked his scout to make certain Toby was awake and dressed by luncheon, so it *should* be all right . . ."

We came out into a beautiful Gothic quadrangle with a sparkling fountain at the center. Veronica would have loved the architectural details, I thought—all the battlements, the turrets, the niches crammed with statues. She certainly wouldn't have been troubled by the sight of lady undergraduates, because every single person I saw was male, from the young gentleman in white flannels striding past swinging his tennis racket to a pair of withered-looking dons in billowing black gowns. Even the servants were men. We came upon one of them as we emerged from a staircase into a dim corridor.

"Ah, Mr. Stanley-Ross," he said. "Well then, you'll find His Majesty dressed, as per orders, but don't expect much more." He gave me a disapproving look that seemed to extend to the whole of womankind, then clanked off downstairs with his bucket.

Rupert sighed, pushed open a door, and ushered me into a set of large, cheerful rooms. Mild sunlight filtered through the windows, casting a gentle glow upon the plaster walls, the dark leather armchair, the invitation cards propped along the chimneypiece, and the empty wine bottles on the desk. Toby himself lay flat on his back on the rug, looking like a martyred saint— Saint Lawrence, perhaps, but without the scorch marks.

"Don't ask me to move yet," he murmured, his eyes closed. "There's an enormous lead ball inside my skull, and I've only just got it to stop rolling about."

"Well, what do you expect when you drink an entire bottle of champagne?" said Rupert.

"It wasn't the champagne," said Toby. "I never get a sore head with champagne. It must have been the brandy. Or that bottle of crème de menthe someone gave me—awful stuff, tasted like toothpaste . . ."

"Aren't you even going to say hello to your sister?"

"Oh! Sorry," said Toby, turning his head a bit and squinting at me. "Hello, Soph. Veronica isn't on her way up, is she? Please say she isn't."

Rupert offered me the armchair, having removed the cat from it, then leaned against the desk. We both crossed our arms and scrutinized Toby.

"You're extremely fortunate," I told Toby, "that Veronica had a prior luncheon engagement."

"What, with Daniel?" asked Toby.

"No, Geoffrey Pemberton," I said. "He invited her to meet his family."

"Pemberton!" cried Toby, lurching up, then clutching his head. "Ow!" He hurriedly lay down again. "Soph, I *warned* you about him! How could you let her? He's revolting!"

"Who's Pemberton?" asked Rupert, so I related the story.

"Your uncle thought it would probably be a waste of time, though," I said to Rupert. "Is he really in the Secret Service?"

"No one knows," said Rupert. "Sometimes we wonder if he's actually just a Foreign Office clerk with a vivid imagination. Toby, *do* get up."

Toby opened his eyes cautiously. "I'm still a bit seasick, I think. And, ugh, Rupert, your cat is *staring* at me again."

"'A cat may look at a king,'" quoted Rupert, although she looked more like Grimalkin than the Cheshire cat as she crouched on the chimneypiece, flicking envelopes to the floor with her tail and keeping her eerie green eyes fixed upon Toby. I'd forgotten that Alice in Wonderland had lived at Christ Church. Her father had been the Dean, or something like that.

"Yes, and Lewis Carroll was a Mathematics don," Rupert said when I asked. "We'll take you to see the Alice window in the Hall after luncheon. *If* your brother ever deigns to get up, that is."

"I think I prefer it down here," said Toby. "It gives one a whole new perspective on life, looking at things upside down. The world's far less cluttered. Soph, come and try it."

"No thanks," I said. "My life's all right as it is."

"Mine isn't," said Toby with an enormous sigh. "It's full of sorrow and suffering."

"Oh *God*," muttered Rupert. "I'm going to see about luncheon. Sophie, if you lose all patience with him, my rooms are two doors down."

"Dear old Rupert," said Toby after Rupert had stalked off, the cat making her stiff-legged way after him. "He's never been properly in love, that's his problem."

"*Rupert* doesn't seem to be the one with the problem," I retorted. "And if you are miserable, I don't see how getting drunk would make things any better."

"Oh, but being drunk is lovely," he said. "You've no idea. Everything turns fuzzy and golden." He stretched his arms over his head. "It can be awful *afterwards*, of course," he conceded. "Although, at least then my wretched physical self matches my wounded . . . What's the inside bit called?"

"Your mind? Your soul?"

"My wounded soul, yes," he said, clasping his hands upon his chest in a deliberately melodramatic gesture.

I huffed at him impatiently. Toby is so used to concealing his feelings under flippant remarks and frivolous pursuits that even now, in what I suspected was genuine pain, he had to make a joke of it. It was especially annoying that Toby's good looks seemed quite unaffected by his recent bout of debauchery. Even the weight he'd lost merely served to accentuate his cheekbones. I thought of how *I* looked when I woke up the morning after a ball, purple smudges under my eyes and hair like a gorse bush (when I was never allowed so much as a *sip* of champagne). It was immensely unfair.

"Oh, stop wallowing, Toby!" I snapped. "Honestly! When I think of how hard Veronica and Simon are working to get Montmaray back—looking up law books, writing letters, trudging round Whitehall—and here you are, lying about, feeling sorry for yourself!"

He sat up then, wincing a bit, and frowned at me. "Well, what do you expect *me* to do?" he said peevishly. "It's not as though they need me. Anyway, what are *you* doing, other than being driven round the countryside on outings—"

"Me!" I exclaimed, jumping up from the armchair. "When I'm not attempting to talk some sense into my *idiot* brother, I'm stopping Veronica and Simon from killing each other! *I'm* the one running messages between them, because they can't even bear to work in the same room! *I'm* the one helping them write their letters and doing their typing! *I'm* the one trying to keep Aunt Charlotte off their backs—"

"Sorry!" said Toby, reaching out a hand and tugging me down beside him. "I *know* you are. I know *they* are. I'm sorry, Soph, I really am. I just—" He took a deep breath. "I just feel so *useless!*" he burst out. "I know I can't do anything to help with the campaign, I'm too stupid and I'm stuck here, but at least I used to be able to . . . to entertain them. Make them laugh when things were getting too tense—"

"Them?"

"You know what I mean," Toby said quietly, bringing his knees up under his chin and hugging his shins. "Tell me. How is he?"

"He's fine," I said. I didn't need to ask whom Toby meant.

"He tells me not to come to London," said Toby, not meeting my eyes. "He says that he's busy working, but I *know* he goes off somewhere in the evenings. One of the footmen told me."

"Oh, Toby," I said, my voice softening. "It's not what you think—"

"So, he confides in *you,*" said Toby bitterly.

I considered breaking my promise and explaining about Simon's law classes, but it occurred to me that I had no idea what Simon did with his evenings. Perhaps his course had finished. Perhaps he *was* out with a girlfriend.

"Don't you think you're being a bit unreasonable?" I asked Toby as gently as I could. "I mean, do you really have any right to tell him what to do, or who to see, or—"

"Yes. I love him," said Toby. They were the most heartfelt words I'd ever heard him utter. They silenced me. I put my arm round him, and he rested his head on my shoulder.

"And that's all there is to it," he said after a while, almost succeeding in adding a note of levity to his utterance.

"But how do you *know?*" I wondered aloud. I knew I felt *something* for Simon, even now. At one stage, I'd even thought it might be love, but how could one tell? Perhaps it was easier to understand when one had shared . . . well, whatever Toby and Simon had shared. I suddenly felt very unworldly and innocent.

"One just . . . knows," said Toby. "It simply happens. Like being hit by a bolt of lightning, except more painful." He turned to me, suddenly intense. "It was only a bit of fun at first, just . . . uncomplicated pleasure. And I'd always liked him—well, you know how likable he is. And then, all at once, I *loved* him. If *only* I'd been serious about him, right from the start . . . But now, the more I try to show him that I mean it, the more he hates me!"

"He doesn't—"

"No, no, I know he doesn't hate me. I'd almost prefer it if he did. No, he's completely indifferent."

"I don't think that's true, either, Toby. He's very fond—"

"You know what?" said Toby, scrambling to his feet. "One of these days, he'll fall in love with some woman. Oh, I'm sure *he'll* be sensible about it. The one *he* chooses will be rich and well connected and beautiful, because that's the only sort of woman he ever notices."

My heart contracted, knowing this was true. So I wasn't yet over whatever it was that I felt for Simon—although I was profoundly grateful I didn't feel anything near as much as Toby did.

"And I'll be watching," Toby went on, "*praying* that she breaks his heart, *wanting* him to be as miserable as I am!" He loomed over me. "Soph, don't you see what a horrible person I am? Do you really wonder why I drink? When I'm drunk, I don't think those things. I don't think—I don't *feel*—anything at all. I'm *lovely* when I'm drunk."

"You really *are* an idiot," I sighed. "Don't you know everyone has wicked thoughts, all the time? Do you honestly believe your feelings are any worse than anyone else's? Why, I can think of at least one time when I wanted to— Well, never mind, but it was awful."

He frowned at me, clearly incredulous. It was probably a good thing he didn't realize it was he himself I'd wanted to hurt—and yes, I'd been in a jealous snit over Simon at the time. It was quite a tribute to Simon's charm, I suppose, that he had us all in a fluster over him.

I was also surprised that Toby hadn't yet discovered that one didn't *always* get what one wanted. In my experience, one *rarely* did. But then again, my brother had been born on the Sabbath day, "blithe and bonny, good and gay," with fireworks and feasts to celebrate his arrival in the world. I imagined that would set one up with rather high expectations for life.

"What matters," I said very firmly, "is not what one feels but how one *acts* as a result of the feelings."

I was going to add that it was also a good idea to consider *other* people's feelings before taking action, but my words of wisdom were interrupted by a sharp knock at the door. It swung open a few inches, and Rupert and the cat poked their heads around it.

"Well?" said Rupert.

"I've now seen the light," said Toby. "I renounce the Demon Drink. From this moment on, my life will be a shining beacon of purity and—"

"At least you're vertical now," interrupted Rupert. "Are you ready for luncheon, Sophie? We're eating in my rooms, if that's all right."

Luncheon was delicious—one of the benefits of saving the cook's cat from death by terrier, I expect. The cat devoured a piece of salmon, then jumped onto the table, peering at each of us in turn as we worked our way through melon, lobster salad with fresh rolls, and then meringues and coffee and tiny glasses of a liqueur that tasted of marmalade. The warmth of the sun, the cooing of the pigeons, the soft snufflings of the bandaged hedgehog asleep on Rupert's desk, all combined to lull me into a sense of drowsy well-being (although I suppose the Cointreau may have helped). The problems of the world seemed a long way away. Even Toby looked a bit happier by the end of the afternoon, I was pleased to report to Veronica when I finally arrived home.

"Good," she said, nodding.

"And how were the Pembertons?" I asked her.

"Bad," she said. Sir Julius had shown not the slightest interest in discussing Montmaray. "He's one of those very correct civil servants who'd no more question a departmental ruling than run naked through Whitehall. And I could see he was horrified that Geoffrey liked me. Not even Aunt Charlotte's money could compensate for me being a bluestocking *and* a Red."

"That would make you a deep shade of purple. What about Lady Pemberton?"

"Dead, years ago—probably from boredom. You've no idea how tedious the conversation was. Even Aunt Charlotte thought so. She put on her Queen Mary act—you know, looking down her nose at everything."

"That can't have helped our cause."

"No, but it never really had any chance of succeeding," said Veronica. She sighed. "Still, at least it's got Geoffrey off my back. He hasn't the imagination or the strength of mind to go against his father's orders, thank heavens. I almost wish . . ." She stopped.

"Go on."

"No, it would sound insufferably vain."

I laughed. "How could anyone accuse *you* of vanity? I've never met a girl less interested in clothes and hairstyles and makeup!"

She pulled a face. "Well, no, I'm not interested in any of *that*, although I quite understand why so many girls are. Their only hope for a secure future is to marry well, and men do seem to care what a woman looks like. It must have been even worse in centuries past. It's pure luck, though, whether one's looks happen to fit contemporary conventions of beauty. I'm not sure mine do now—"

"They do," I said emphatically.

"—but *if* they do, *if* how I look attracts even a few men, I've realized it feels very uncomfortable to use my appearance to . . . to further my own aims. So I was going to say, I almost wish I didn't have that option. Not that it worked particularly well with Geoffrey Pemberton."

"But you don't have any scruples about using your *brain* to convince others of your point of view," I noted.

"Well, I feel as though I've developed my brain, through reading and listening and thinking. It feels less of a gift, and more of a hard-won prize, than how I look."

"I think it's just as much a gift, being born with a brain that's *capable* of developing," I said. "I mean, look at Kick's sister." (Rosemary Kennedy is a little slow, poor thing, although she's a very sweet girl. And it's possible she only seems slow in comparison to her brothers and sisters, who are unrelentingly quick, sharp, and loud.) "Anyway, whatever you've been given, Veronica—looks or brains—I think it would be a dreadful waste for you to ignore them. I just wish you could transfer anything you don't want to me."

"Don't talk like that!" she scolded. "You're very pretty, Sophie, and there's certainly nothing wrong with your brain. And you've been blessed with a lovely temperament, so calm and gentle. Or *is* temperament a gift? Perhaps *it's* developed through hard work, too."

This is the sort of thing I could talk about for hours. I was going to say that temperament was surely related to looks and brains—that a beautiful girl was bound to be more confident than an ugly one, for example, and that only someone with brains could be effectively devious. But the gong rang to dress for dinner, and Phoebe arrived to help me do up the back of my gown. Then came dinner and sitting around in the drawing room afterwards—and it is only now, long after midnight, that I've found the time and privacy to take out my journal and write this down. However, I'm so tired from my long day that any further musings on the human condition will have to wait.

21st July 1938

Dinner at the American Embassy last night. Kick's elder brothers have arrived from the United States, and Veronica made quite an impression on Jack, the younger of the two, during cocktail hour. She must have spent at least twenty minutes deep in conversation with him, until she suddenly broke off and stalked across the room towards Toby and me.

"Do you know what that young man just *said?*" Veronica exclaimed indignantly, once she was within exclaiming distance.

"His sister's standing right behind you, you realize," warned Toby.

"Well, I don't hold girls responsible for the behavior of their *brothers,*" retorted Veronica, unable to refrain from shooting a contemptuous look in Simon's direction as he clinked glasses with the most glamorous of the Embassy secretaries. Kick poked her head out from the cluster of young men surrounding her and grinned at us.

"Jack just can't help himself with beautiful women," she said. "Go on, tell us."

Veronica crossed her arms and scowled. "Well, we were having a perfectly sensible discussion about European rearmament—although I do think he overestimates the influence of British trade unions in this economic climate—"

"Get on with it," said Toby.

"Well, and then he said something about 'you English' and he'd never even *heard* of Montmaray! And, as if that wasn't bad enough, he asked if I was a *Catholic*!"

"Are you?" said Kick. "I didn't know that!"

"I most certainly am not!" said Veronica. "I'm an atheist!"

"Gosh," said Kick. "Which one's that again? I always get it confused with 'agnostic.'"

"Oh Lord, please don't ask questions like that, Kick," groaned Toby. "Not unless you want a three-hour lecture on why the very notion of God is fundamentally irrational—"

"I'll pray for you, Veronica," said Kick, patting Veronica's arm, then disappearing back into her scrum of admirers.

I don't think Kick was joking, either. Last week, I went to her house to collect her on the way to Harrods, and just as she was putting on her hat, she realized she'd forgotten to say her rosary that morning. With a quick "Oh, Soph, you'll excuse me, won't you?" she dropped to her knees, right in front of me in her bedroom, and prayed away in silence for a good ten minutes. Watching her, I almost envied her unwavering faith in such rituals. Perhaps believing in God is part of why she's so confident. Although I suspect that's simply due to growing up in her family. Having Mr. Kennedy as a father would either frighten a child to death or make her tough enough to withstand anything. He certainly terrifies *me*. I had luncheon with the family when we came back from our shopping trip, and had to keep reminding myself that I'd faced far more unnerving situations and survived *them*. Hans Brandt dead with all his insides coming out, surely *that* was scarier than the Ambassador's ice-blue glare and razor-sharp tongue, I kept reminding myself. But (unsurprisingly) this didn't help my state of mind much. Mrs. Kennedy is extremely odd, too, so brittle that one expects her to crack apart any moment . . . Oh, but who am I to talk about odd families! Even the nicest ones, such as the Stanley-Rosses, have a black sheep or two. And Kick is a *lovely* girl, despite what Aunt Charlotte says.

Aunt Charlotte was just getting back from a dinner of her own as we arrived home last night, and she wanted to hear all the details of our evening. One good thing about our second Season is that Aunt Charlotte is a little more relaxed regarding letting us go places without her as a chaperone. I'm not sure if it's because Veronica and I have been on our very best ladylike behavior lately or because Toby's now around to escort us. (Of course, it's possible that our aunt was exhausted from the strain of supervising us and simply needed a rest.)

"Elizabeth Elchester says she hears Billy Hartington is making an absolute *fool* of himself over that Kennedy girl," Aunt Charlotte announced after herding us into the drawing room.

She perched on a sofa, spine straight as a poker, and fanned herself briskly. "Not that it will come to anything. Imagine, the heir to the Duke of Devonshire marrying a *commoner*! And, of course, with the Duke's poor grandfather having been murdered in cold blood by Irish Republicans—"

"It wasn't his grandfather. It was his great-uncle," said Veronica.

"—it's *completely* out of the question that an Irish Catholic girl could ever become the next Duchess of Devonshire," Aunt Charlotte went on, frowning at Veronica. "Particularly *that* girl. A gum-chewing American whose father splashes money around in that vulgar fashion." Our aunt turned to me. "I suppose she's gloating about having snared the most eligible bachelor in England."

"No, she's not," I said stoutly. "Kick has dozens of boys after her, she might not even have noticed Billy Hartington. Besides, her family would hate for her to marry a Protestant."

"Of course they would," said Aunt Charlotte. "They'd expect him to convert. It's all part of their Popish plot, you see, marrying English peers and bringing up the heirs as Catholics. Those Roman Catholics have never given up hope of reclaiming the British throne. It's Guy Fawkes all over again—"

Veronica opened her mouth, no doubt to explain the political context of the Gunpowder Plot, but Aunt Charlotte held up an imperious finger, decorated with diamonds and emeralds and a sapphire the size of a quail's egg.

"I do not wish to argue about it," Aunt Charlotte said, "and stop contradicting me, Veronica. It's most disrespectful of you. Besides, you're distracting me from my point—which is that this situation is entirely *your* fault. I told you last year that Billy Hartington was perfect for you. You really ought to have done something about it, saved the poor Devonshires all this worry . . ."

Our aunt might seem sane and sensible in comparison to her elder brother most of the time, but a distinct streak of lunacy becomes apparent whenever she contemplates Veronica's or my marriage prospects. Still, I'd rather she occupy herself with us than with Toby, who is showing his own streak of FitzOsborne contrariness at the moment. Thank heavens Aunt Charlotte hasn't yet discovered that he won't be going back to Oxford in the autumn. He got the letter from Christ Church on Tuesday.

"You've been sent down?" cried Veronica, snatching the letter from his hand.

"No, I have not," Toby said calmly. "I've simply decided I'm not suited to an academic—"

"You didn't even *turn up* to your examinations?" Veronica said faintly, her head bent over the paper.

"No point. Waste of time for me, for the invigilator, for the poor don who'd have to mark the exam—"

"Aunt Charlotte is going to have a fit," I said, looking over Veronica's shoulder. "Although . . . No, it's not as bad as it seems. They're offering you a second chance, Toby. You just need to work really, really hard next term."

"I don't want a second chance," Toby said. "I didn't even

want a first chance. I oughtn't to be there. It should be Simon, or you, Veronica—"

Veronica threw the letter onto my bed and walked out of the room.

"You really are the absolute *limit*, Toby!" I said, turning on him in a fury. I could just imagine how Veronica felt. "Tossing this opportunity away when you know how much it would mean to Simon or Veronica!"

"But that's why I'm doing it!" he said, blinking. "So that one of them can—"

"How can you be so *stupid?*" I shouted, almost stamping my foot. "Aunt Charlotte isn't going to let either one of them take your place!"

"We'll see about that," he said, setting his jaw in that stubborn way that Henry does. "Anyway, I'm just doing what you told me to do. I've stopped wallowing in misery. I'm taking charge of my life."

"*I* didn't tell you to, to . . ." I was going to say "ruin your life," but of course, it wouldn't ruin Toby's life. Plenty of gentlemen leave Oxford without taking a degree. It wasn't as though he'd planned to become a doctor or an engineer or a professor. The really infuriating thing was that I knew Aunt Charlotte would forgive Toby, sooner or later—probably sooner. It was possible he might actually succeed in coaxing her into funding Simon's higher education . . . but no, that was surely beyond even Toby's powers of persuasion. I scowled at my brother. "Well, what on earth are you going to do with yourself now?"

"Do?" he said. "I'm the King of Montmaray, isn't that enough? And I'm sure it'll be easier to rule Montmaray from here, compared to being cloistered away in Oxford. I can help you with the campaign."

I knew perfectly well that he just wanted to be closer to Simon, so I continued to glare.

"Oh, *Soph*," Toby said, in his most cajoling voice. It seemed to bend through the air and beckon me closer—but I resisted. "Now, don't look like that, darling. I really *do* want to help."

I suddenly remembered Rupert and asked what he thought of all this.

"He's a bit cross about it," Toby conceded. "But he'll come round eventually, he always does. He's so sweet, he's just like you. Now, you'll go and talk to Veronica, won't you, help her understand?"

"If I do discuss this with her," I said, "it'll be to make *her* feel better, not you!"

I sometimes feel like a one-person League of Nations, trying to mediate between all the feuding members of this family.

Then I went to visit Julia at her newly finished house in Belgravia this afternoon, and *she'd* just had a tiff with Anthony.

"He tells me it's *counter-revolutionary* to be presented at Court, even though absolutely everyone gets presented again once they're married—Mummy would've been mortified if I hadn't gone ahead with it—and besides, *he's* a viscount, for heaven's sake! What does he think Marx would have to say about *that*? Oh, darling, don't let anyone tell you that men are more logical than women, it's utter rubbish! Now, I thought I'd use this as my sitting room. Oh, do you like that carved screen? Isn't it gorgeous, it's my favorite thing in the whole room! It's Indian, and so are the miniatures over the desk. I had the chairs covered in that cerise silk to complement the curtains, and look, I found this carpet in the attics at Ant's family place, isn't it perfect in here? Let me show you the bedrooms . . ."

The house was a beautiful mixture of antique furniture and modern art, original oak paneling and bright silk curtains, freshly painted cream walls and lovely faded Persian rugs. I told Julia that if she ever grew bored or lost all her money, she could have a very successful career as an interior decorator.

"Aren't you sweet to say so! Do you really like it? I thought the house would *never* be done, but here it is, finally—only, of course, Ant complains the place is too big and cost far too much, and he hates my dear little Picasso sketch, says it doesn't look anything like a face. He's about as cultured as a football—my husband, that is, not Picasso, *he's* an absolute genius. You're staying for tea, aren't you, darling? Oh, don't worry about that, I'll telephone your aunt, and I can drive you home afterwards. We haven't had a proper chat for ages, and I need to find out all about your current admirers . . . Nonsense, darling, I'm sure there are dozens of them! Well, I do know at least *one* of them, but you can do far better than my awkward little brother—"

My face coloring to match the curtains, I protested that Rupert was neither awkward nor interested in me, and tried to change the subject. But Julia was, as usual, unstoppable.

"Frankly, it's a relief to find out he's interested in human beings. We were starting to think he'd end up marrying a badger or a tufted owl or something. Thank God Toby's at Christ Church, too, otherwise Rupert would stay locked away in his room with his books and his animals and never go out at all. Now, Sophie, tell me whom you're in love with. Then I can invite him over and keep throwing you two together . . . I know! We'll have a dinner party and play Sardines! I'll shove you both into a cupboard, and he'll be proposing in no time at all."

Given that Julia hadn't been sounding very enthusiastic about matrimony, I couldn't understand why she was so keen to marry me off, and I said as much to her.

"Well, I certainly wouldn't advise marrying *my* husband," she said. "Although perhaps *you'd* be more suited to— No, he needs someone like Veronica, bossy *and* interested in politics. I'm just bossy. Veronica's far too clever for him, though, she wouldn't have the patience to . . . Hmm, whom can we find for *her*? It's a pity Anthony Eden's still married—which reminds me!" Julia suddenly looked stern. "I hear you're at the American Embassy *all* the time these days!"

"Please, don't you start," I said. "Just because Kick's a Catholic—"

"Never mind about that. I'm talking about her brother. The

eldest one, Joe. Stay away from him. No, I'm serious." Julia leaned in, a rare frown creasing her perfect brow. "I'm warning you, he's NST."

"He's *what?*"

"Not Safe in Taxis. A friend of mine had to fight him off the other night, he wouldn't take no for an answer. Ripped her new Vionnet evening gown, too, she was furious . . . Oh, don't look so shocked, Soph, you need to know about this sort of thing! I don't suppose your aunt's told you *anything* useful. If only *I'd* understood the Facts of Life as a debutante, all the peculiar things that boys do might have made more sense . . . Tell me, is there anything you've been wondering about?"

Well! Thanks to Julia, I now know exactly how married women avoid having babies. Suffice to say it requires a round rubber object that one has to obtain from a doctor, except doctors refuse to hand them over or even discuss the issue till immediately before one's wedding day. The whole business sounds horribly messy, not at *all* romantic . . . although I suppose having a baby would be even more messy and unromantic. Anyway, it was very fortunate that Julia had finished her explanation by the time the footman came in to announce Simon had arrived.

"Good afternoon, Lady Whittingham," Simon said, giving Julia an unsmiling nod.

"Oh, Simon, don't be so stuffy," said Julia. "Call me Julia, for heaven's sake, and sit down, I'll ring for more tea—"

"I'm afraid we can't stay, my lady," he said. "The Princess

Royal asked me to collect Her Highness, as the family has an early dinner engagement this evening. Your Highness? I have your umbrella here."

"What was *that* all about?" I asked Simon once we were outside. "What early dinner engagement?"

"Why isn't Veronica with you?" he said.

"She had to look up something in the Reading Room at the British Museum. Parker dropped her off on the way. She said she'd take a taxi home—"

Simon opened the door of the Lagonda for me.

"Why do you ask?" I added. "Isn't she home yet?"

He went around to the driver's side and slammed his own door shut.

"Simon?"

"I don't think you ought to be visiting Julia Whittingham by yourself," he said, starting the engine.

I stared at him. "Why not?"

"Because I don't think she's a suitable companion for unchaperoned young ladies," he said very stiffly.

"What's *that* supposed to mean?" I exclaimed. "Julia's our *friend*! Our family's known the Stanley-Rosses for years!"

"I have nothing against the Stanley-Rosses," he said. "I'm merely pointing out that she's . . . Well, let's just say I wouldn't want my younger sister associating with her."

"I'm *not* your younger sister, so it's none of your business whom I associate with!" I snapped. "And how *dare* you insinuate awful things about Julia! She's a respectable married lady—"

"Really? So why were you the color of a beetroot when I walked in?"

"That's— What were you *doing*, listening at the keyhole?" I spluttered. "Anyway, who are *you* to talk about reputations? I'm sick of the way everyone talks about girls when boys do much worse and no one says a word about *them*!"

Simon opened his mouth to respond, then pressed his lips together. He looked over his shoulder at the traffic and jerked the car out into the street, and we drove back to Montmaray House in heated silence.

Veronica was in the library, staring at a fresh pile of notes, when I stomped upstairs. I'd been bursting to tell her what a hypocritical, infuriating busybody Simon had become, but looking at her, I had second thoughts. She'd certainly agree with me, but what I really wanted was someone to argue me out of my bad mood. There was no point increasing the general level of hostility in our household. So, instead, I told her what I'd learned about avoiding having babies. She put down her pen and listened with interest.

"Yes, I thought it must be something like that," she said after I'd finished. "What's it called again? A *Dutch* cap? Why do the English persist in naming anything connected with sex after *other* countries? Like French letters—although did you know Casanova called them 'English overcoats'?"

"Of course I didn't know that," I said. "I'm not even sure what they look like, and aren't they meant to be . . . well, not very reliable? But anyway, Veronica, doesn't the whole thing sound *too* disgusting? I mean, it makes me wonder whether Aunt Charlotte's right when she's so disapproving about the physical side of married life. It'd have to be utterly blissful to make up for all that mess." I thought for a moment. "Of course, novels do seem to suggest it *is* blissful. Otherwise why would Anna Karenina and Madame Bovary have bothered with adultery?"

"Weren't both those characters invented by men? It could just be propaganda, to make girls want to get married—or make them want to have affairs."

"Mmm. Well, it doesn't make *me* want to have affairs, look at what happened to poor them. Although if one believes romantic novels, a mere *kiss* is the height of ecstasy—"

"When, of course, it isn't anything of the sort."

"How would you know?" I asked. Then I looked at her more closely. "Veronica! Who . . . Oh, not Geoffrey Pemberton!"

"Ugh, no!" said Veronica. "Not that he didn't try."

"Then, who?" I demanded. "Daniel?"

"Er . . . ," said Veronica, checking to make sure the door was closed. "Yes."

"When?" I gasped.

"Well . . . today, actually. He met me at the British Museum. He had some books he wanted to give me, and he was near there, anyway, had a meeting at the University of London."

"And?" I prompted when she didn't say anything more.

"And . . . it just seemed to happen, when we were saying goodbye."

"But what was it like? What did you *feel*?"

She frowned. "Certainly not the heights of ecstasy. It wasn't unpleasant, though. I think I was too surprised to feel much. He looked a bit shocked, too. He did apologize afterwards."

"Well, he shouldn't have done *that*," I said.

"No, not in the middle of Montague Place," she agreed.

"I meant, shouldn't have apologized! But gosh, kissing in the *street*! Did anyone see?"

"Probably," she said, not looking very concerned about that. I consoled myself with the thought that she was wearing her oldest skirt and jersey rather than one of her smart, expensive outfits—less chance she might have been recognized.

"So," I said. "It seems he's serious about you."

"Do you really think so?" she said. "It might just have been the result of some temporary, physical urge—"

"Veronica," I said firmly, "I've been saying that he likes you—is in *love* with you—for absolute ages. And Daniel doesn't seem the sort to go around kissing girls without meaning it."

"I suppose not," she acknowledged.

"So you don't . . . you don't love him, then? Not even a little bit?"

"I was wondering about that," she said, in the tones she might use when pondering, say, the causes of the Franco-Prussian War. "How does one tell? I certainly *like* him more than anyone outside the family. He's so interesting to talk with, never boastful or patronizing the way men usually are. He's about a hundred times more intelligent and amusing than any of the eligible bachelors Aunt Charlotte keeps pushing at me."

"And he's a good person," I said.

"Yes," she said with a little smile. "Yes, he is, isn't he? And that's the important thing, isn't it?"

Daniel's appearance—his unremarkable features, his shabby clothes, the *surface* of him—wasn't even the smallest part of her considerations, and I wished *my* feelings were as unaffected by masculine beauty as hers. She made me feel rather superficial.

"Would you marry him?" I said. "If he asked you, I mean."

"Sophie!" she exclaimed, her eyes widening. "He doesn't want to *marry* me! He probably regards the very *concept* of marriage as an evil, bourgeois, capitalist plot! And in the event he did decide to marry, I'm sure his mother already has a nice Jewish girl picked out for him."

"But . . . doesn't that bother you?"

"What, you're saying I *should* marry him?" She started to laugh. "Perhaps I ought to propose to *him*?"

I wasn't quite sure *what* I was saying. Obviously, Veronica marrying Daniel was out of the question—yet I couldn't help thinking he'd be perfect for her. If only he were the son of a viscount, had a bit more money (or was less opposed to money in general), had been born Christian rather than Jewish . . . that is, if he were a totally different person. In which case, he wouldn't be perfect for her—in fact, probably wouldn't even have met her.

"You know, I'm tempted to invite him round for tea and introduce him to Aunt Charlotte as my fiancé," Veronica went on, still chortling. "Just to see her expression . . ."

I ought to be glad Veronica isn't heartbroken about it, but I couldn't help wishing that she *felt* more and *thought* less. I sincerely hope my first kiss is more exciting than hers. I'm not holding out for the heights of ecstasy, but a sensation other than surprise would be good. Somewhere less public than directly outside the British Museum would be nice, too.

Anyway, at least the conversation distracted me from my fury at Simon—for an hour or so. Toby noticed us both fuming throughout dinner and asked me what was going on. I refused to say anything, though, because I knew Toby would take Simon's side, despite it being ALL SIMON'S FAULT!

9th August 1938

Another Season comes to an end, and neither Veronica nor I is engaged to be married. Nor is Toby. What a surprise. Everybody has scattered—Julia and Anthony to visit friends at Cap d'Antibes, the Kennedys to a rented villa in Cannes, and Rupert to stay with a Scotch uncle who breeds border collies. Aunt Charlotte also decided to remain in Sussex for another week or two after the Goodwood race meetings were over.

Meanwhile, Toby, Veronica, and I arrived back at Milford Park to discover that Henry had grown another two inches and driven her poor governess to the verge of physical and mental collapse. (Miss Bullock is now on her way to a well-deserved holiday in the Lake District.) Estella had also grown considerably, mostly because she'd taught herself how to open gates and unlatch kitchen doors. She was discovered last week in the pantry making her way through a basket of summer berries, having already polished off a pile of freshly picked lettuce. The cook threatened to turn her into bacon, so Estella has been banished to the Home Farm for her own protection. We thought Carlos might be upset about it—the two of them had been inseparable—but it seems he's been making friends in the village. Henry reported that Mr. Herbert's housekeeper's dalmatian recently produced half a dozen puppies, all of them suspiciously jet-black and curly-haired.

"Carlos! You sly old dog!" said Toby.

Carlos looked up from attending to his paws and gave us a bashful grin.

"Mrs. Jones is awfully cross about it," said Henry. "She thought Dotty was just getting a bit fat, but then she found Dotty sitting in the laundry basket on the clean sheets, snarling if anyone went within three feet of her. She's usually so good-natured—Dotty, I mean, not Mrs. Jones. And then Mr. Herbert came back from evensong and found all these wet, wriggling puppies in the basket. They're so sweet, just like Carlos, except smaller, of course. I bet they'll be excellent swimmers—the biggest one's already tried to climb in the water bowl. We *can* take one, can't we? Jocko asked his dad if he could, and his dad said yes, as long as it wasn't a bitch, because he didn't want a pack of mangy dogs yowling round their house every six months."

All this reminded me that I needed to have a chat with Henry about the Facts of Life now that she's twelve, but it turned out she knew as much as I did, or possibly more, having spent so much time at the Home Farm watching the pigs and cows and horses. Henry is very unimpressed with the whole idea of periods (not that I blame her). If any girl manages to avoid them through sheer force of will, it'll be Henry.

Anyway, it is lovely to be back in the country—not just to see Henry, Carlos, and everyone else but to be out of London, away from Society. I don't get nearly as nervous about dances and dinner parties as I used to, but they're still a chore, each event being full of people we need to impress, people who might be able to help our campaign. I must admit that, despite our collective disapproval of Toby leaving Oxford, he's proving to be a real asset in this regard. For one thing, titles don't get much more impressive than "His Majesty," so even the most pompous civil servants, the stuffiest diplomats, the busiest Members of Parliament, pay attention to him. Between Toby's title and his boyish charm, Veronica's beauty and her encyclopedic knowledge of European history, and Simon's . . . well, Simon being *Simon,* we've made more progress in the past month than in the previous six.

Firstly, we've established that the Germans are still at Montmaray—and worse, have built a proper airstrip on the Green and anchored some ships off South Head. A pair of British pilots reported this to the Defence department in May, according to Colonel Stanley-Ross's sources. The pilots didn't see any soldiers there, but how would a pilot be able to tell? The Germans could be camped in the village, they could have repaired the damaged parts of the castle and moved in—

Oh, it makes me so *furious* to think of them there! In *my* bedroom, pawing through my things! Through *all* our things: Henry's old toys and Veronica's books; Toby's sketches; my mother's wedding veil and the FitzOsborne christening gown, lovingly packed away in layers and layers of tissue paper inside the old sandalwood chest in the Blue Room . . . To *think* of those men rifling through our personal treasures, stomping through the Great Hall in their filthy jackboots, hanging their disgusting swastika banners over our tapestries! I hadn't fully comprehended what their invasion *meant* till that moment in the Colonel's flat when he told us what he'd found out. I'd tried my best *not* to think about it—or, when it was unavoidable, to consider Montmaray's invasion only in the abstract. It was dreadful enough to remember the damage the bombs had caused, to know our poor animals had been killed, or worse, wounded and none of us there to help them.

It turns me cold to write this, even as the sun pours down over me, here on the terrace at Milford Park. My hand is actually shaking . . .

No, I want to finish this. I don't care how messy the writing is. So, yes, we have proof that the Germans have truly taken over Montmaray. But this is a *good* thing, it gives us ammunition for our fight. If it weren't for the statements and photographs those pilots provided, we probably wouldn't have been invited to meet with Winston Churchill. I expect it helped that Colonel Stanley-Ross is his first cousin, but still, Mr. Churchill seemed quite impressed with Simon and Veronica's arguments. It's a pity he's not a minister in the government, or even very influential (apparently, the Prime Minister loathes him), but surely it must help to have such a clever, determined man on our side? The Colonel also reported that there are several senior officers in the defence forces who are sympathetic to our cause— or, at least, alarmed by this evidence of German military aggression so close to England, and therefore very keen to do something about it.

With this (tacit) support in mind, we have tackled the Foreign Office with fresh vigor. Our aim is to convince Britain to apply strong diplomatic pressure on the German government. There's the usual bickering between Simon and Veronica over how to word our letters (especially difficult now, as we can't give away the identity of our intelligence sources), but things *do* seem to be progressing better than before. I am still very annoyed with Simon, though, so the two of us aren't really speaking to each other. It's maddening that he believes he has the right to tell me what to do! And worse, regards me as so weak-willed that I'm likely to be corrupted into shameless depravity by simply having *tea* with a lady of questionable virtue (which does not describe Julia, anyway). The problem with Simon is that it is not in his nature ever to apologize or admit he was wrong. However, *I* am behaving with dignity and restraint—in admirable contrast to *his* complete pigheadedness.

Speak of the Devil, here he comes up the drive. Now he's pulling boxes out of the car—he's still sorting through Mr. Grenville's files, but this must be the last of it, surely. How very irksome that Simon looks just as good with his sleeves rolled up

and his hair tousled as when he strolls into a Mayfair drawing
room in immaculate white tie and tails. Now Toby's running
down the steps to help him with the boxes. Well, *I'm* certainly
not going to join them.

Oh, bother, Simon's coming this way . . .

Later, in bed, unable to sleep. Spent an hour tossing and turning, then gave up and switched on the light again. There must
be a word for this feeling. Tumult? Except that makes me think
of tulips, which are very placid-looking flowers. It really isn't fair
that I should be forced to experience so many conflicting emotions in a single afternoon. Thank heavens I have the comfort
of my journal, even if my vocabulary is not quite up to the task
of describing my overwrought life.

Well, it turns out that Simon is able to bend a *little*. He presented me with a peace offering this afternoon, a souvenir of a
past conversation, something he thought I'd find intriguing. Of
course, he had no idea of its true significance—nor did I, at the
time.

"I noticed it as I was packing the last box," he said. "I took
all the bundles of personal letters to Montmaray House and
left them in the library, but I thought you might like to have a
look at this." He held out a slim volume, bound in cracked morocco, its edges nibbled by insects or mice. "I can't make out
much of the writing," he went on, "but you're better at reading
French than I am. I've no idea who owned it, although I assume
it was a girl, from the sketches. She must have been a

FitzOsborne—look, you can see the family crest stamped into the leather."

I took the journal with a token show of reluctance, but I felt a warm glow inside—due partly to this thawing of my relations with Simon and partly to being able to touch a tiny piece of Montmaray. It was as though I'd reached out across the ages and grasped the hand of one of my ancestors, a girl who'd slept in the same castle, perhaps even the same *room*, as I had. Turning to the first page, I gazed at the faded indigo ink with a rising excitement—which rapidly subsided. I couldn't understand any of it. The writing was perfectly legible, in the sense that the letters were of a familiar alphabet and were formed in beautiful copperplate script. I could even recognize a word here and there—*pomme* and *chien* and *livre*. It looked French—just not any sort of French that I had seen before.

"Perhaps it's an unusual dialect?" Simon suggested. "Or some ancient version of written French?"

"How old do you think the book is?" I asked, examining the cover.

"It's hard to say, but I don't think it could be from earlier than the 1850s," he said. "None of the records I saw dated to before that. And it could be much more recent, despite how it looks—it hadn't been stored very carefully. Well, there's a mystery for you to solve."

"Thank you, Simon," I said with a little smile.

"You're very welcome," he said. He stood up, took a step

towards the house—then turned back. "So, you're speaking with me again?"

"It appears so," I said. "That is, I've been saying words out loud in your presence—and you may even have been listening to them."

"Ah, Sophia, I *always* listen to you," he said. "I've learned from experience that it's very dangerous to ignore you."

I sighed melodramatically. "What a pity," I said. "It assists my plans for world domination, you see, if my rivals regard me as beneath their notice."

"Oh, you've been reading Machiavelli again?" he said. Then he dropped his teasing tone. "But, Sophia, I hope you understand that when I give you advice, it's not because I see you as weak or foolish or in any way less than me. It's simply brotherly concern."

"You're *not* my brother—"

"No. But I can't see *your* brother giving you any useful advice." Before I had a chance to bridle at this, he crouched down beside my chair. "Oh, Sophie!" he said. "Please don't be cross. It's just that sometimes I have access to information that you don't have. I can't help that."

"You were wrong about Julia," I said. "Wrong and insulting."

"I may have been insulting, but I know I'm correct in . . . in certain aspects. Look, how about we agree to disagree on the subject of Julia Whittingham? Can't we stop talking about her? I can't think of anything I'd like more, believe me."

"All right," I said. "And how about you agree to stop telling me what to do?"

"All right," he said, grinning. "Seeing as it's impossible to get you to do anything I want, anyway."

We shook hands solemnly to seal our agreement, then he went off to unpack his boxes. I remained seated on the terrace for a while, gazing out at the lake and smiling to myself. Then I looked down at the book again. Each page was filled with the same careful handwriting, interrupted by occasional pen-and-ink sketches. These were all delicate, whimsical studies of flowers—full-blown roses with tumbling petals, cheerful clusters of daisies, a single violet dwarfed by a smiling bee. I scanned the lines of script, but nothing made sense. Even the punctuation was odd. Some letters had accents; some didn't where they probably ought to have had them; capitals appeared in the middle of words; and there were no commas or full stops.

Finally, I got up, went inside to the library, and took down the oldest French dictionary from the shelves. I managed to decipher several more words, but the syntax was so bizarre, the words so unrelated in meaning, that I was no closer to comprehension than when I'd started—and I was certainly a great deal more frustrated. Then Veronica burst into the room, beaming and waving an envelope at me.

"From the Foreign Office, inviting us to a meeting next month!" she cried, dropping it on the table. "I really think we're getting somewhere now! And look, another letter from Carmelita. She came top of her class this term, her father was thrilled. Look at her letter, not one spelling mistake, and English her third or fourth language! Henry ought to be ashamed of herself . . . Oh, what's that you've got?"

I pushed the journal towards her. "Simon found it at Mr. Grenville's, but I can't work out the French."

Veronica sat down across from me and looked at the first page. "It's not French," she said slowly. Her smile had vanished. She turned the page. "It's in code."

"A code!" I exclaimed. "How exciting! Rather frustrating, though—I'm longing to find out what it says."

She gave me an odd look, far sadder and more sympathetic than I thought the situation merited, and continued to turn the pages.

"Well, perhaps we can decipher it," I went on. "How old do you think the journal is?"

She gave me an even odder look. "I suppose . . . it depends when she wrote it. It was probably just before she got married."

"*Married?* How do you know?"

"What?" Veronica said. "Well, I mean, she didn't take it with her to Montmaray, obviously, and yet there's the Fitz-Osborne crest on the cover. It must have been with her old things here in England. I imagine her family's belongings were sent to Mr. Grenville, after both her parents had died—"

"Whose parents?" I said. I was utterly bewildered. "What are you talking about?"

Veronica blinked. "Don't . . . don't you recognize the writing? And the sketches?"

"No," I said, tugging the journal away from her and peering again at the first page. "No, not really. Except—well, now that I think about it, this little picture of a bee reminds me of . . ." I put my hand over my mouth.

"Oh, I'm sorry, Sophie!" said Veronica, jumping up and coming over to put her arm round me. "I really am, but I thought you'd realized!"

"Are you saying . . . it's my *mother's* journal?" I stared at the book. "Is it *really* her handwriting? I don't remember what it looked like! I don't remember anything about her! Except this little picture of a bee, it's just like one that she drew for me. Remember, when I got stung in the kitchen garden, and I started refusing to go outside? She said bees weren't nearly as terrifying as I thought, and she sketched one with fuzzy legs and fat wings and an enormous grin . . ."

My eyes filled with tears. I'd kept the picture tucked into the frame of our bedroom's looking glass for ages and ages, till the paper turned yellow and tattered, and someone (probably me) threw it out. I'd thought I'd forgotten it. I'd thought I'd forgotten everything about her.

"*Typical* of Simon, upsetting people like this!" Veronica was saying. "Just *wait* till I get hold of him!"

"But he didn't know," I said, wiping my eyes. "There's no reason he'd recognize her writing. And we both thought the book was old, really old!"

"Store anything in a damp, rodent-infested basement for a couple of years, and it'll look like that. But it wasn't just the handwriting that told me." Veronica dropped her arm from my shoulder and moved away. "It was the fact that it was in code."

"What do you mean?"

"That was how Toby and I came up with the idea of Kernetin. Aunt Jane told us that when she was younger, she always wrote her journal in code—to stop her mother finding out things."

I was stunned. "I don't remember that at all," I said.

"You were quite young. Toby and I were seven, I think, so you'd have been five or six. We couldn't imagine *what* she might have wanted to hide from her parents! We dreamt up all sorts of dreadful crimes and kept hurling them at her, hoping to trick her into a confession. But she just laughed at us."

I gazed at the book, at this startling evidence of the hidden life of my quiet, mild-mannered, fading-into-the-background mother.

"Of course, she was far too good to do anything wrong," Veronica added hurriedly. "We knew that, really."

"Nobody ever talks about her," I said. "Toby never does. Simon and Aunt Charlotte barely knew her, so I wouldn't expect them to. But *you*." I twisted round to look at Veronica. "You were always so vague whenever I asked you about her. I thought you'd forgotten her. Or that she was so . . . so inconspicuous that no one ever noticed what she was like."

Veronica was shaking her head.

"Oh, no!" she said. "No, Sophie! She was lovely. She was so kind and patient, everyone adored her."

"But why didn't you *talk* to me about her?"

"Well—it seemed to bother Toby so much, anyone mentioning either of your parents." Then she sighed. "No, it wasn't only that. *I* didn't want to think about her, either."

She crossed her arms and glanced away, towards the windows. There was a long silence.

"She was always much more of a mother to me than my own was," Veronica said at last, very quietly. "When she died, I wished it'd been Isabella instead. Isabella and my father, both of them, I wished *they'd* been in that carriage when the bomb hit. They ought to have been—they were the ones invited to Seville. It was so unfair. Then I suppose . . . I suppose I was so horrified by it all, by what had happened, by the dreadful thing I'd wished . . ."

She shook her head again.

"It's my fault that you don't remember her, Sophie. I turned her into something dim and blurred. I tried to make her disappear." Veronica lifted a hand to brush impatiently at her eyes, then gave me an unhappy smile. "There, what would Freud have said about that?"

"Probably that the whole lot of us are in dire need of psychoanalysis," I said, getting up to hug her.

"Ah, but not you," she said, pulling back after a moment. "*You* don't need psychoanalysis, Sophie. You've got your journal. It must be the reason you're the only normal one amongst us."

"Normal!" I scoffed. As if I even know what "normal" is!

"The balanced one," said Veronica, carefully disentangling

her hair from where it had got caught in the clasp of my necklace. "The only calm, sensible FitzOsborne."

Then a footman came in to say Aunt Charlotte was on the telephone, and Veronica hurried off, although not before promising to help me decipher the journal.

I sat back down and looked at the sketch of the bee. *Poor little thing*, I thought. All it had to defend itself was its sting—and if it used it, it would die. I remembered the meeting at the Foreign Office, how I'd unwittingly extinguished all of Veronica's excitement about that. But I couldn't help feeling she'd be disappointed yet again, that the meeting would be futile, that we were helpless little creatures about to be swatted by the vast hand of the Foreign Office . . .

I felt very sad then. I feel sad *now*. Sad and lonely and forsaken. My mother seems further away than ever. I even spent an entire half hour earlier this evening feeling furious at her for leaving us to deal with all these awful grown-up problems by ourselves. As though she'd done it *deliberately!* Then I turned my anger upon myself for being so stupid.

However, at least writing this down has made me exhausted enough to sleep. It's nearly two o'clock in the morning—an hour when the whole world is silent, and dawn seems an age away, and everything is black and still and hopeless. But perhaps things will seem better in the morning . . .

They'll have to. They can't possibly seem any *worse*.

22nd September 1938

Veronica, Simon, Toby, and I met with Mr. Reginald Adams-Smythe at the Foreign Office this afternoon. Veronica and I weren't invited, but Veronica announced she was going regardless, and Simon didn't even attempt to stop her. I pretended to be Simon's secretary. I took down everything I heard in my abbreviated Kernetin, which is getting extremely fast but looks almost entirely unlike shorthand. (I saw Mr. Adams-Smythe's own secretary give my notebook an astonished, upside-down look.) At any rate, it means I can now write a proper, detailed account of the proceedings.

I'd expected everyone at the Foreign Office to be rushing about with grave expressions, because Hitler is threatening to invade part of Czechoslovakia, and the British Prime Minister has just flown back to Germany for more negotiations. Mr. Chamberlain is willing to try anything to avoid war, and no wonder, when all the newspapers are saying Germany's air force could reduce London to smoldering ruins in a matter of days (and one only has to look at Guernica to see what the Germans are capable of). However, the Foreign Office looked pretty much the same as the last time I'd been there. I even saw Mr. Davies-Chesterton standing in a doorway, although he made a squeaking noise and vanished as soon as he caught sight of us.

We were shown into a magnificent office on the second floor, where Mr. Adams-Smythe was installed behind a mahogany desk large enough for a game of Ping-Pong. Based on the furniture and the size of the windows and the number of staff kowtowing to him, I ranked him a good five or six notches above Mr. Davies-Chesterton in the Foreign Office hierarchy. After we were seated, Mr. Adams-Smythe had his secretary pass him a file. He surveyed this for several minutes while Toby beamed at the secretary, reducing her to a blushing, quivering jelly, and Veronica and Simon had a near-silent argument, culminating in her tearing a page from my notebook and scrawling him some urgent, last-minute note. Eventually, Mr. Adams-Smythe looked up, folded his hands on the desk, and invited Simon to begin, whereupon Simon outlined our problem and explained why it was in the best interest of the Foreign Office and the British Empire for them to assist us.

Perhaps it was Simon's legal expertise, perhaps it was the three days he'd spent rehearsing this speech with Veronica criticizing every aspect of his performance, but gosh, he was good! The secretary looked ready to applaud when he finished. Even Veronica seemed impressed. Then Mr. Adams-Smythe cleared his throat.

"Yes, a most unfortunate situation," he said. "We've had our people investigate this matter thoroughly since receiving your letters, and you'll be very pleased to know that—after much effort—we have resolved this issue."

We all held our breath and leaned forward.

"Ahem," he said. "You see, the problem rested on the ownership of this island of Montarey—"

"Montmaray," said Veronica.

"Er, yes, the property under dispute. Firstly, we needed to ask some very important questions. For example, did the German government have a legitimate prior claim to the area? Were there German-speaking residents who would be inconvenienced by your claim to this land?"

"*If* there are Germans living on the island," said Simon quickly, shooting a quelling look at Veronica, "they are there *illegally*. They're trespassers, taking advantage of last year's violent invasion of the Kingdom of Montmaray. This is all documented in the report sent to the Ministry for Coordination of Defence—"

"Ahem," said Mr. Adams-Smythe. "Yes. However—fortunately!—there's no need to bring *that* ministry into our discussion. Ha-ha! In light of current international events . . . Yes. Well. You see, we've been in discussion with the German Embassy about this matter, and they explained that their government purchased this island from its legal owner several years ago."

We stared at him.

"Its *legal* owner?" repeated Simon in a strangled voice. Toby placed a restraining hand on Veronica's arm, because she looked ready to explode.

"Yes, that's right," said Mr. Adams-Smythe. "Apparently, it's not uncommon, property ownership becoming confused over many years. An understandable mistake on your part! While your family may have been long-term tenants, the property *actually* belonged to the Spanish government. Not surprising, really, given the location of the island . . . Ah, yes, I see it's just off the coast of Spain."

"It's two hundred and ninety-three miles off the coast of Spain!" snapped Veronica. "The Isle of Wight is seventy miles from Cherbourg, but I don't see you handing *that* island over to the French!"

"Er, no," he said, momentarily wilting under her glare but then drawing himself upright. "Yes, but, you see, we have clear documentation of ownership of this particular island. Title deeds and so forth."

On cue, a young gentleman marched in with yet another file, which he presented to his boss. Mr. Adams-Smythe removed a piece of paper and waved it at Simon, who snatched it out of the older man's hand. Simon bent his head over the document, staring at it for so long that I was tempted to drop my secretary pose and lean over his shoulder to read it. He finally shook his head and passed the paper to Veronica. Toby and I exchanged frustrated looks but remained silent. (This had been the plan, for Simon to do all the talking unless we needed a burst of charm from Toby.) Veronica glanced up from the paper and gave Simon an intense look that I found impossible to interpret. Simon took a deep breath.

"This document," he said, "has obviously been manufactured by the Germans. It's a manifest forger—"

Veronica kicked him in the ankle. It seemed Simon hadn't interpreted her look very effectively, either. Then she passed him back the document with her finger pointing to a particular spot, and his eyes widened. He opened his mouth—then closed it, gave her a tiny nod, and eased back in his seat. I couldn't believe it. *Simon*, sitting back and allowing Veronica to take the lead?

Veronica gazed across the vast desk at Mr. Adams-Smythe. "You don't think this document has been forged or fabricated by the Germans?" she asked.

"Of course not," he said at once. "Now, really, one can't make unfounded accusations like that! Particularly in the current . . . Ahem! I assure you, our department has investigated this document most thoroughly!"

She nodded slowly. "So . . . you are saying that this island belonged to the Spanish government, and they sold it to the Germans a couple of years ago." Her tone was light, almost idle. Toby and I glanced at each other again. I had no idea where this was going, but for the first time, I thought it might end up somewhere we'd quite like to be.

"Yes, yes," said Mr. Adams-Smythe. "It's plain that—"

"Yet it appears from this document that the land was acquired by the Spanish government from one of its own citizens," went on Veronica. "Fairly recently, in fact."

"Ah!" he said. "Yes, I see how that might be confusing to one not familiar with Spain. However, with the tragic situation in that country, so many old landowning families having died out—in such cases, their property reverts to the Spanish government."

"Just to make things *quite* clear to me," Veronica said. "When you say 'Spanish government,' you're referring to the democratically elected Republican government? I mean, the British government hasn't secretly acknowledged Franco as the legitimate leader of Spain, has it?"

"Er . . . no," said Mr. Adams-Smythe, glancing at his young assistant.

"Good," Veronica said briskly. "You see, I recognized the name of this particular Spanish landowning family. A prominent aristocratic family—well known to those *familiar with Spain*. The Germans obviously did a tiny bit of research when they were fabricating this document, in order to make it seem more plausible— Oh, excuse me! It's *genuine*, isn't it? Your staff have confirmed that. Silly me. And everyone *knows* how honorable the Nazis are, it's unthinkable that they'd ever be deceitful! Anyway, as I started to say, this particular Spanish family *does* have a legitimate historical link to the island of Montmaray. Furthermore, the family has *not* died out. The late Duke's only daughter—indeed, his only child—married the King of Montmaray. Her maiden name was Isabella Cristina Margarita Álvarez de Sevilla y Martínez."

Toby made a small sound, which he hurriedly turned into a

cough. Simon was lounging in his chair with the air of someone watching a very entertaining show at the Theatre Royal.

"Er," said Mr. Adams-Smythe, looking around wildly. His assistant sidled up and muttered in his ear. "Ahem! Yes," said Mr. Adams-Smythe. "Correct. However, I'm afraid that his only child, being female, was unable to inherit, old Spanish law—"

"But surely that was one of the first acts of the Republican government?" Veronica said. "To abolish all those old laws oppressing women, to establish a State separate from the rules and traditions of the patriarchal Church? I think you'll find the Republican government hasn't any problem with women inheriting property—and you did say *they* were the true government, did you not? So the family's land wouldn't have been acquired by the Spanish government, not when the family had a legitimate heir."

"But, but," Mr. Adams-Smythe spluttered. "This is irrelevant to your claim! This Isabella Margaret de . . . de . . ."

"Isabella Cristina Margarita Álvarez de Sevilla y Martínez."

"Yes, that lady—she's not mentioned anywhere in your file! She's not part of your claim! And, and . . . well, *she* must have sold the land to the Spanish government!"

"She most certainly did not. I'd know if she had, because— Oh, did I forget to mention that she was my *mother*? Sadly, she's now deceased. And I'm her only child—her female child, it's true, but quite able to inherit her property, according to current Spanish law. There'll be no difficulty proving my relationship to her—one only needs to look at old pictures in *Tatler* to see that I'm her daughter. So *if* this document is correct, then *I'm* the legitimate owner of the island of Montmaray, and I certainly didn't authorize its sale to the German government, nor to any private German citizen. However, this debate is all theoretical, isn't it? Because we all know this document is fraudulent, don't we?"

She nodded at Simon and he leaned forward.

"We certainly do, Your Highness," he said, "and the question is, who fabricated it? It's horrifying to consider the British government might actually forge a document in order to discourage another sovereign nation from pursuing a legitimate grievance—"

"But, but we haven't done anything of the sort!" cried Mr. Adams-Smythe desperately.

"Then it's rather depressing to see the British government so willing to accept German lies," Simon said. "Truth and justice pushed aside for the sake of political expediency." He shook his head. "In any case, there's abundant evidence that the Fitz-Osborne family has owned Montmaray since the sixteenth century. Why, your own Queen Elizabeth the First acknowledged the FitzOsbornes as the royal rulers of Montmaray in her letter written in— In what year was it written, Your Highness?"

"I believe it was written in 1588, Lord Chancellor," said Veronica. They turned identical glares upon Mr. Adams-Smythe.

He blustered on a bit more, his assistant growing paler and paler, before Simon finally put them both out of their misery.

"Well, I think that's all for the moment," he said, getting to his feet. "Please do contact us as soon as you've worked out how you're going to rectify this grave error."

Then we swept out of the office, Veronica leading the way. Toby gave a great whoop of triumph as soon as we reached the corridor, causing disapproving heads to emerge from various doorways. Toby ignored them.

"The expression on that man's face!" he crowed. "And that flunky, I thought he was going to *faint* when you started going on about Spanish law!" He dropped his voice. "Was it true, what you said about Spanish inheritance?"

"Partly," Veronica said. "But as *all* of their argument was fraudulent, it doesn't really matter that I ignored a couple of key points of Spanish law."

"Well done, Your Royal Highness," said Simon, smirking at Veronica.

"Well done, Lord High Chancellor," said Veronica. "That speech of yours was not bad at all."

We started down the staircase.

"Of course, I wrote most of it," Veronica added. Simon rolled his eyes.

"Don't start up again, you two," said Toby. "Now we must celebrate! At once! Tea at the Ritz, I think."

"Celebrate?" said Simon. "Celebrate *what*? We still haven't achieved anything!"

We clattered out into the street and climbed into the car.

While we all knew Simon was right, it did feel as though there was *something* to celebrate, even if it was just the temporary cease-fire between Simon and Veronica. Besides, the chocolate cake at the Ritz is scrumptious—I wasn't about to miss out on that for anything.

We sped off to the hotel and were immediately shown to one of the nicest tables in the Palm Court (Toby is friends with the headwaiter). The string quartet was playing Vivaldi, the chandeliers were throwing armfuls of sparkling light against the marble columns and looking-glass walls and golden statues, and everyone gazed at us and murmured as we took our seats. Luckily, the four of us were dressed in our smartest day clothes, on account of the meeting. (I don't mind being stared at, as long as I look all right—which doesn't happen often.) As soon as we were seated, a waiter brought us tea and two tiered silver stands laden with pastries and sandwiches.

"I imagine heaven will be just like the Ritz," sighed Toby, taking an éclair. "And it will always be teatime there."

"What makes you think *you'll* end up in heaven?" said Simon.

Toby started to explain how wonderfully angelic he was, bringing joy to everyone he met, but I was distracted by a couple in the dimmest corner of the room—not that it was *very* dim, given the chandeliers and so forth. The gentleman had just taken the lady's hand and was giving her a look that Henry would have called "soppy." The lady was wearing a very chic suit of marina-blue silk that looked just like one of Julia's. Then she turned, and I saw it *was* Julia. I dropped my teaspoon, and Toby looked round.

"Is that *Julia?*" Toby said. "Who's she with?" He waved at her, and, after a quick word to the gentleman, she stood up and threaded her way over to us through the maze of tables.

"Hello, hello!" she cried. "Gracious, *look* at all of you! What's the occasion?"

"Who's that man?" Toby asked. The gentleman had now vanished.

"Just a friend," Julia said. "Ooh, you've got chocolate éclairs, how *unfair*, we just had scones—"

"A *friend?*" Toby repeated, raising one eyebrow.

"Now, don't be jealous, darling," she said, patting Toby on the head. "He's not your type. Is that champagne coming *our* way? Excellent, what are we celebrating?"

Veronica explained all about the Foreign Office, and Julia listened with a show of great interest. Simon busied himself handing round the sandwiches so he didn't have to participate in the conversation. Then a group of Julia's friends came in, and she jumped up and went over to say hello.

"Well!" said Toby, sitting back in his chair and watching her tip-tap across the marble floor in her beautiful Italian shoes. "If *I* were her, I wouldn't be organizing my romantic rendezvous at the Ritz. She might as well put an announcement on the front page of *The Times*. Poor Ant—although one can't really blame her. He's a dear old thing, but imagine being *married* to him."

"What are you talking about?" said Veronica, who'd been sitting with her back to Julia's table and missed all the references to the mysterious "friend."

"He's not talking about anything," said Simon quickly, frowning at Toby. "Sophie, would you like the last sandwich? It's ham, I think."

"No, thank you," I said, partly because I haven't felt quite right about eating ham since I met Estella, but mostly because I was so troubled over Julia. Not that holding hands with a gentleman meant she was having an *affair* with him, I reminded myself. Perhaps he was a cousin who'd had sad news—his best friend had died or he'd lost his job, and Julia was comforting him . . . Although he *had* been looking at her the same way that Daniel looked at Veronica. And Julia hadn't *said* he was a relative . . .

Oh dear! Poor Anthony, he probably didn't even *know*, he was so sweet and trusting and . . . well, I had to admit it, a tiny bit *dim*. And he did have that awful bristly mustache—kissing him must be like kissing a hairbrush. Perhaps if I could persuade him to shave it off, Julia might feel more kindly towards him and not be tempted to *do* anything . . .

And then there was Simon, who'd known all along. This was what he'd meant when he'd said she was an "unsuitable" companion for me. There wasn't a hint of "I told you so" from him, but still, I could barely meet his eye. Any sense of celebration evaporated. And not even the half glass of champagne that Toby insisted I drink helped cheer me up.

28th September 1938

I *knew* the Nazis couldn't be trusted! Those poor Czechoslovakians finally agree to give up the Sudetenland, having been bul-
lied into it by Britain and France, and now Hitler's announced
that's not good enough! He demands they hand over *any*
Czechoslovakian district containing *any* Germans, not just the
bits of land containing a majority of Germans, and he insists all
this territory be given up by the first of October!

How can he possibly expect anyone to agree to his crazy demands? Does he *want* a war? It looks increasingly likely. I nearly
cried this morning when I saw the men digging up Hyde Park to
make air-raid shelters. We all had to go and get gas masks on
Sunday, and they are horrible. The eyepieces fog up, and they
taste of rubber. Henry telephoned us from Milford, incensed that
the Air Raid Precautions people weren't providing gas masks for
dogs, although she was mollified somewhat when I told her
about the *Daily Mail* article on gas-proof kennels that I'd read.
Several London schools have already been evacuated to the

country, and Toby said there was a huge queue at the petrol station this morning. Aunt Charlotte, back in Milford now, sent a message for us to return to the country immediately, but we are ignoring her. There's still our campaign, as futile as it now seems, and we need to be in London in case the Foreign Office suddenly calls us in for another meeting.

Oh, and Chamberlain was on the BBC last night, giving a stupid speech. He promised to make the Czechs hand over their territory, and says he will never make Britain go to war "because of a quarrel in a faraway country, between people of whom we know nothing." He did, however, acknowledge that Hitler was being "unreasonable." *Unreasonable!*

Too furious to write anymore.

2nd October 1938

Phoebe told me off (in her mild, Phoebe-ish way) for refusing to go to the thanksgiving service at St. Mary Abbots this morning. I don't mind attending church in Milford, because the sermons are only about six minutes long (Aunt Charlotte starts glaring at Mr. Herbert at the five-minute mark), and it gives me a chance to catch up with village gossip afterwards. But I hardly ever go to church in London. I'm not very keen on God at the moment, anyway. If He really *is* all-powerful, if He really *does* care about the human race, then why hasn't He arranged for Hitler to get run over by a bus? Why on earth, I asked Phoebe, should I be thankful to God?

"But there's lots to be thankful for, Your Highness. We've got peace now!" Phoebe said. "Peace for our time, peace with honor, that's what Mr. Chamberlain said!"

It's a good thing she didn't say that in front of Veronica.

"Peace!" Veronica cried as we sat around reading the

newspapers yesterday. "Peace with *honor*! Has anyone asked the Czechoslovakians if *they* think it's peaceful or honorable? They weren't even *invited* to the meeting that carved up their country! And now Poland and Hungary are going to snatch up any bits that *they* can. Czechoslovakia has been thrown to the wolves."

"At least it gives Britain a bit more time to get ready for war," said Simon, frowning over *The Times*. "The armed forces here are woefully unprepared."

"Yes, I remember Mr. Kennedy saying that," said Toby. "Especially the air force—"

"Oh, I don't believe it!" interrupted Veronica. "Look at this! Chamberlain actually appeared on the Buckingham Palace balcony and waved to the crowds! What happened to the King keeping out of politics? How *dare* the King misuse his influence to support Chamberlain's political career!"

"The King's not supporting Chamberlain. He's supporting appeasement of Germany," Simon said.

"They're the same thing, and both are unconstitutional!"

"Well, you didn't mind the King getting involved with politics when you were writing letters to him about Montmaray," Simon pointed out.

Veronica scowled at him. Simon accidentally let slip about his law classes last night, and Veronica was so scathing about it that I suspect she is jealous (she's been trying to get Aunt Charlotte's permission to do a course at the London School of Economics but without success). Toby was also upset Simon hadn't confided in him, but (of course) covered it up with a flurry of jokes, so Simon snapped back. Hurt feelings all round then, especially after Toby and Veronica found out I'd known all along.

"Listen to this," I said, trying to distract them by reading from the *Daily Mail*. "'Our Cabinet Ministers became schoolboys again. They clambered about on the windowsills, whooped wildly, and threw hats in the air.'"

"This whole country has gone *mad*," Veronica said darkly.

While it *is* nice to know that London won't be bombed to bits tomorrow, I cannot share Phoebe's relief about this "peace." The poor Czechoslovakians! And if Britain cares so little for them, all those millions of people, why would it have the slightest concern for Montmaray? What will happen if—*when*—Hitler decides to take over the whole of Czechoslovakia and then moves on to the next country? Eventually, all of Europe will be under his control unless Britain and its allies do something to stop him. Will there be war, another world war? *Surely* there's another way. Shouldn't the League of Nations be doing something? All right, Germany isn't a member of the League anymore, but lots of other important countries are. They could all get together and take nonviolent action, couldn't they?

However, as the leaders of the world seem unlikely to heed my advice, I'm going to stop writing about current international events and do some more work on my mother's journal. I haven't got very far with my deciphering, though, because one needs to have some idea of what's being written about, in order to guess at the words. And how can I possibly know what my mother was thinking of when she was my age? Was she planning her wedding? Worrying about the Great War? Perhaps I should give up on it and write an overdue letter to Henry and Carlos instead. Or write to Rupert, now back at Oxford, he's a very soothing person . . . No, that will start me thinking about Julia, and whether she really *is* behaving as scandalously as Simon believes.

Bother. Sometimes I wish I could thrash all the troublesome thoughts out of my head, the way the maids beat our rugs clean each week. What would tumble out of my brain? Dust and dead earwigs and snapped-off pencil points, probably . . .

Fearsome row this afternoon. Aunt Charlotte arrived unexpectedly from Milford and found Daniel having tea with us at Montmaray House. It was all perfectly respectable—Simon and Toby were both there—but one would think she'd caught Veronica in *bed* with Daniel, the way our aunt carried on. Of course, Veronica didn't go out of her way to placate Aunt Charlotte (it occurs to me now that telling the blatant truth can be far more belligerent than telling a lie).

"Well, I wouldn't even have *met* him if it weren't for you," said Veronica unrepentantly after poor Daniel had been marched out of the house by Harkness, our large and frightening butler.

"What!" cried Aunt Charlotte, clutching her necklace in that way she does whenever she's forced to think about the "lower classes" (as though she can picture them snatching the jewels from her dead, white, aristocratic neck, as in the French Revolution). "I would *never* introduce you to such a person!"

"You interviewed him," Veronica said. "You sent him to Montmaray as our tutor."

"Well!" Aunt Charlotte spluttered. "I certainly wouldn't have done anything of the *sort* if I'd known what type of person he was! Taking an unsavory interest in the young ladies he was being paid to teach—"

"He stopped being my tutor five years ago."

"Not to mention being a Bolshevik," Aunt Charlotte went on. "*And* a Jew. He's unsuitable in *every possible way!*"

Unfortunately, she'd walked into the drawing room as we were discussing the horrific events of last week—the Night of Broken Glass, they're calling it. All over Germany, synagogues were set ablaze, Jewish shops looted, houses ransacked, dozens of Jews killed, tens of thousands of them rounded up and arrested.

"Have you heard from your uncle?" Veronica asked Daniel.

"Not a word, not since the end of summer," said Daniel. "Although my cousins are in Paris now. A Jewish refugee organization helped get them out—"

Whereupon he turned to find Aunt Charlotte looming over him in a towering rage.

I will give this to Aunt Charlotte—it took her about two seconds to realize Daniel was in love with Veronica, that he wasn't simply a random Communist we'd met through Anthony, someone who'd dropped in to collect donations for Spanish refugees. Our aunt is definitely a woman of the world. If she weren't so snobbish and sharp-tongued, I'd ask her for some advice about my own love life—specifically, if there's any chance of me ever having one. It's a good thing her world doesn't encompass men who fall in love with other men, or Toby would *really* be in trouble. Although, come to think of it, she'd probably forgive her golden nephew even *that* (provided he also agreed to get married and produce a couple of heirs, of course).

Anyway, speaking of Spanish refugees, I should note down the latest news. The Spanish government has promised the League of Nations that it will send all the international combatants home, and most of them have already left the war front. There's also been a big battle going on around the river Ebro since the summer. Initially, this seemed to be going well for the Republican government, but now Franco's forces have the upper hand. Daniel said it was a huge blow to Republican morale when Chamberlain signed that agreement with Hitler, because the Spanish government had been hoping everyone would join together in an anti-Fascist pact. So things do not look good at all. I'm just grateful all our Basque friends are now safely settled in either Mexico or Manchester.

Better go, I have to smuggle a letter out to Daniel on Veronica's behalf, as she's imprisoned in the house till Aunt Charlotte relents. It makes me feel like a minor character in Shakespeare— even though Veronica's envelope is far more likely to contain a memorandum on fund-raising for Spanish refugees than a perfumed billet-doux signed with a lipstick kiss . . .

Back from a house party in Yorkshire. The house was so enormous that the footman had to unwind a ball of string to show us
the way from our bedrooms back to the drawing rooms. It was all
far too grand (and cold) for me to enjoy myself. I suppose it was
nice to see proper, heavy snowfalls for once, but when I went
outside to watch the groundsmen clearing a path, I saw the lawn
underneath was black with coal dust. It must be an awful job for
the staff, keeping the place clean.

There were only half a dozen young people in attendance,
apart from Toby, Veronica, and myself, but luckily, one of them
was Rupert. It turns out he had some pigeon-racing connection
with someone in the household. Billy Hartington was there, too.
I sat next to him at dinner, and he spent the entire evening
telling me how wonderful Kick was. Which, of course, she *is*,
but surely he could have talked about *something* else, if only for a
few minutes. Billy didn't even seem to notice Veronica (and she
looked absolutely beautiful that night in a new silk Empire-style

gown, the exact color of crushed strawberries). So much for Aunt Charlotte's ambitions for Veronica to become the next Duchess of Devonshire.

The only reason we were invited to the house party was that the Countess who lives in the house had Toby in mind for one of her unmarried daughters, and the only reason we went was that Veronica was desperate to get away from Aunt Charlotte. Our aunt does nothing but nag Veronica now, an unrelenting tirade from breakfast to bedtime. I don't see how much longer it can go on before Veronica snaps. The only thing restraining her is Aunt Charlotte's usual threats to stop all our allowances.

"Please, *please*, marry this girl," Veronica begged Toby on the way to Yorkshire. "Then you can set up on a country estate far away from London and Milford, and I'll come and keep house for you."

"Marry someone yourself," said Toby, rubbing at the car window and peering out at the icy landscape.

"I'd be tempted to, if anyone asked," said Veronica glumly. "But the only proposal I've ever had was from Geoffrey Pemberton, and his father put a stop to *that* soon enough."

It really is depressing to think that the only way we'll escape our aunt's guardianship is by handing ourselves over to a man. I have a little more sympathy for Julia now—not that I approve of her current behavior, if she *is* having an affair. I haven't seen her since that afternoon at the Ritz, and I wouldn't dare ask her outright, anyway. But no *wonder* she was so determined to marry Anthony, regardless of whether she was in love with him or not!

He had money and a title, and he wasn't a violent drunk or a gambler or the Elephant Man . . .

Heavens, I'm becoming cynical. It must be because I turned eighteen last month and am now practically a grown-up.

Anyway, to return to the house party. There were a few unfamiliar girls there, this year's debutantes. They all made a rush at Billy, till they realized how boring he was being about Kick, then they turned like a pack of hounds upon Toby, but the Countess put them off with very severe looks. That left Rupert. He was so quiet that none of the girls paid him any heed at first, and then he and Toby wandered off somewhere by themselves on Saturday morning. But that afternoon, Rupert went out into one of the courtyards to put some crushed peanuts in the bird feeder. The shrillest of the debutantes was standing at the French windows and caught sight of him, a robin redbreast perched on his shoulder, a pair of chaffinches pecking in the snow around his feet.

"Ooh, look!" she squealed. "How *sweet!*" Then she and her friend rushed out to join him, frightening most of the birds away. Rupert was too polite to tell the girls off—he even helped one of them put some food on the platform. I scowled at the scene from the window.

"Annoying, isn't it?" murmured Toby in my ear.

I agreed wholeheartedly. "Poor little things, it's so hard for them to find food in winter—and then, when a nice human finally feeds them, they get scared off by a bunch of shrieking girls."

Toby chuckled. "I *meant* having to watch someone *else* discovering his charms. I told Rupert the girls would go mad for his Saint Francis of Assisi act, and look, I was right."

"It is not an *act!*" I cried, turning on Toby. "Rupert really *loves* animals— Oh, shut up!" Because Toby was smirking at me.

"What?" he said. "I didn't say anything." Then he sauntered off, hands in pockets, whistling the "Wedding March."

My brother can be so *irritating* sometimes—even worse than debutantes.

But speaking of weddings—one thing that *has* managed to distract Aunt Charlotte from Veronica this week is ghastly old Oswald Mosley. He's caused a scandal of his own, by marrying Diana Guinness. In *Germany*, with *Hitler* as his best man! Not only that, but it happened two years ago and they kept it a secret (no doubt for some sinister Fascist reason) until they couldn't hide it any longer because now she's given birth to his son. Apparently, Diana Guinness had been one of his mistresses for years and years, even before his wife died, even before Mrs. Guinness got divorced from her first husband (who is awfully nice; I danced with him once at a ball). Diana Guinness, by the way, is the sister of horrible Unity Mitford, the one who wears her swastika badge everywhere and is in love with Hitler. It's all *too* disgusting. But the good thing is that Lady Bosworth is Mosley's cousin, and now she doesn't know whether to pretend she knew all along or to be very disapproving like everyone else (which would demonstrate that she either didn't know what was going on or has no control over younger family members). It's rather nice to see her in such a fluster, because she found out about Veronica and Daniel and has been giving Aunt Charlotte "helpful" advice on the matter ever since. That's probably why Aunt Charlotte has been in such a poisonous mood lately. Daniel once told me that there's a word in German, *Schadenfreude*, which means "pleasure felt when observing the misfortunes of one's enemies." Trust the Germans to make up a word like that, but it does occasionally come in handy . . .

This afternoon, Veronica, Toby, and I were in Oxford Street doing Christmas shopping when we saw the most extraordinary thing. The traffic lights had just turned red when suddenly the road was filled with dozens of bodies, flat on their backs. At first, I thought they were *dead*, knocked down by the buses and vans. But how could so many have been knocked over at once? Then I realized that the men on the road were not only still alive but unrolling posters over themselves.

"Why, it's the National Unemployed Workers' Movement!" said Veronica. "Good for them!"

"But they'll get run over!" I cried as the traffic lights turned green. Fortunately, not one of the vehicles moved. Meanwhile, the men had started chanting, "We want work or bread! We want work or bread!" A few policemen turned up and started dragging the men, limp as half-empty sacks of coal, off the road. But as soon as each protester was dumped on the footpath, he crawled straight back to where he'd been lying.

"You know, they're using the same techniques as the suffra-gettes," said Veronica admiringly. "And I've read about Gandhi's supporters in India using passive resistance, too." I sincerely hoped she wasn't thinking of adopting similar techniques for *our* campaign—although I suppose they could hardly be any less suc-cessful than writing letters to Whitehall. At least these men seemed to have the support of the onlookers. Not a single per-son went to help the policemen.

"Well, all those men'll *have* jobs soon enough, the way things are going," said Simon, after we'd finally struggled our way home through the stalled traffic. "They'll either be making armaments or using them when war breaks out."

Simon is being very gloomy nowadays. I think he reads too many newspapers. Also, he and Toby have had another row, be-cause Toby has been disappearing for large chunks of the day and refuses to explain his absences. Meanwhile, Henry was cross that she and Miss Bullock had missed out on seeing the protest.

"I would have thought seeing giant pandas would be some compensation," I said, because they'd been on their way back from the Zoo at the time.

"Well, I could hardly see anything of the pandas—there were all these *children* in the way," Henry said. "So I went to talk to the leopards. Do you think, if there was a war and Regent's Park got bombed, that the zoo animals could escape? And live off rabbits and foxes and things?"

"More likely they'd live off *people*," said Simon. "All the dead ones." He really *was* in a black mood. It turned out that

Mr. Grenville's secretary had found another couple of boxes of old financial records—just as Simon thought he'd dealt with the last of them. I offered to help, but he just grunted at me and stomped off. Well, perhaps Christmas will cheer him up. Although, possibly not—he'll be spending most of it with his mother in Poole. Poor Simon.

In other news, Alice has written from Cornwall to invite us to her *wedding*. It was a bit of a shock, but she is only forty, not really too old to get married again—possibly even young enough to have another child—and perhaps she fell in love with a handsome silver-haired Cornish fisherman. (I am ignoring Simon's assertion that she simply wanted to secure British citizenship for herself and Jimmy, given all this talk of impending war.) Aunt Charlotte won't let us go to the wedding, of course, but we've sent a bone china tea set and blue linen sheets as our present.

Rupert has also invited us to spend New Year's at Astley Manor. Actually, his mother wrote to Aunt Charlotte to ask us, but Rupert dropped in yesterday, too. It was one of the rare days Toby wasn't out ("All this fog," he'd said enigmatically, frowning out the window), so we had a nice, long luncheon together, all of us.

We FitzOsbornes will spend Christmas at Milford, of course. It's at this time of year that I feel most nostalgic for Montmaray, I think. When we were children, it was such an exciting time— making clumsy little presents for one another, hanging paper chains and cardboard stars around the castle, going carol-singing in the village. We can do most of those things at Milford, and in many ways, it's *better* at Milford—the food nicer, the gifts more expensive (and useful), the decorations far more opulent (and there are servants to deal with the prickly holly and sweep up the pine needles under the tree). But somehow, Christmas doesn't seem as *real* at Milford.

It could just be that I'm too old for Christmas now. Even Henry is too old to get *really* excited about it. She is as tall as I am, and I can see she's going to turn into a beauty when she grows up, a female version of Toby. (It's very unfair that the FitzOsborne girls least interested in their looks have the greatest natural advantages in this area.) Henry is annoyed that Aunt Charlotte persists in treating her as a child, and she claims she is too old for a governess now. She's also taken to saying "When I was a child . . . ," as though that were a hundred years ago. For example, leaning over my shoulder yesterday, as I was trying to finish Virginia Woolf's *Three Guineas:* "When I was a child, I used to think that word—'fiancé'—was pronounced 'finance'!"

"Well, they pretty much amount to the same thing," said Toby glumly, because the rich Countess with the aging, unmarried daughter has been pestering Aunt Charlotte about Toby's "intentions."

"You ought to be honest with the girl," I told Toby. "Do it now, so she doesn't develop any false hopes."

"Yes, you're absolutely right," he sighed. "Will you write a nice, tactful letter for me?"

"No," I said firmly. "But I'll look over yours once you've written it."

And he has just finished the draft of it, so I'd better go and read it. I think he ought to post it next week, though. Poor girl, it wouldn't be much of a Christmas present for her.

Three Guineas is very interesting, by the way. It's all about how men want war and women want peace, and how powerless women are to change anything in the world—so when I said "very interesting," I suppose I actually meant "very depressing" . . .

10th January 1939

One of Daniel's comrades is involved with Aid Spain, which has
organized a fund-raising exhibition of Spanish art, so Veronica
and I took the underground train to Whitechapel to see the
paintings this afternoon. I don't know whether it was having to
go down into the tunnels or remembering that Jack the Ripper
had strolled along those very same streets not so long ago, but I
was feeling quite shaky by the time we reached the art gallery.
And then—the *paintings*! There was an enormous black-and-
white one by Picasso, full of disembodied limbs and screaming
faces, with a woman clutching a dead baby, and a horse with a
spear thrust through its belly, and another person being devoured
by monsters, or flames, or both. I don't really understand modern
art, so mostly I ignore it, but this particular painting was so over-
whelming, I almost needed to sit down (except I couldn't, there
were too many people). Then someone beside me said that the
painting was called *Guernica*. That was what it was about! And
I suddenly saw the *point* of modern art—that those twisted-up,

agonized figures of Picasso's showed the suffering of modern war far more effectively than any traditional painting could. *Guernica* almost seemed to vibrate with intensity, despite the lack of color—it brought to mind a wobbly newsreel image of soldiers at the front, or the ghastly type of nightmare in which one tries desperately to run away but can't move.

Then I looked at the floor below the painting, and there was a sprawling pile of men's boots, hundreds of them. That was part of the price of admission—everyone had to bring a pair of good, strong boots. The Aid Spain people were going to pack them all up when the exhibition finished and ship them to the Republican soldiers. But I couldn't help imagining there were chopped-off feet inside the boots, just like in the painting—that if I peered closer, I'd see scarlet blood oozing through the dark leather, pooling on the floor. I really *did* need to sit down then. Fortunately, there were fewer people around by that stage, and Veronica, turning to speak to me, saw my face going white. She grabbed my arm and made me sit against a wall, and Daniel went off to find a cup of water. It was all quite embarrassing, but the Aid Spain man seemed to think it demonstrated sensitivity and true commitment to the cause rather than feebleness, so I felt a bit better. And I really *was* glad I'd gone to the exhibition, because it was the first chance Veronica and Daniel have had to talk to each other in weeks, and she wouldn't have been allowed to leave the house without me.

I'm not sure what Daniel did to celebrate New Year's Eve (probably went on a protest march with the unemployed, knowing him), but Toby, Veronica, and I had a nice time at Astley Manor. Lady Astley was especially kind to me, sitting me down beside her after dinner and turning the focus of her gentle conversation upon me. Did I prefer living in the country or the city? Yes, it *was* easier for children, growing up in the country, wasn't it? Did I want a large family of my own? Yes, she could *see* I loved animals (Lord Astley's springer spaniel had just galloped into the drawing room, planted his muddy paws on my skirt, and licked me on the chin). It was a sure sign of a sweet personality, she thought, being good with dogs and children (by "children," I think she meant Henry; it was a good thing Henry wasn't around to hear this). And really (Lady Astley now looked over at Julia, who was lying on the sofa, flipping through *Tatler*), an amiable nature was one of the most important attributes of a happy wife.

"Men may be drawn to glamour and excitement at first," Lady Astley said, "but what they actually need is someone who'll be sweet and understanding, who'll tolerate all their little quirks and funny ways . . ."

Julia turned the page with rather more force than was required. She'd spent Christmas with Anthony's parents, and he'd decided to stay on there for another week or two. I had the impression Julia had been summoned back to Astley Manor by her mother for a "little chat" regarding . . . well, certain things. Julia's marriage, for one. Not that I could imagine Lady Astley triumphing in a battle of wills with Julia. Although, who knows, perhaps Lady Astley's placid exterior conceals an iron backbone and a Machiavellian mind?

I must admit that she did contrive to throw Rupert and me together quite often during our three-day visit (as though she'd decided that, yes, I *was* sufficiently sweet, rural, and animal-loving to make a good wife for her favorite son). Not that I minded, really. Rupert's a very restful person. It's almost like being with Veronica or Toby—I never worry about what I should say next, as he's quite comfortable with silence, and so I feel comfortable, too. We wandered around the grounds of Astley Manor, Rupert pointing out owls' nests, and a badger sett, and the fresh tracks of a three-legged stoat in the newly fallen snow.

One day, he asked a lot of good questions about Montmaray, and I found myself recalling all sorts of things I thought I'd forgotten—the orange flippers of the puffins disappearing into the sea as they dived for fish, for example, and how lobsters always have one large claw and one smaller one, and can be "right-handed" or "left-handed," just as people are. We also talked about Toby (Rupert was glad Toby seemed happier now, although Oxford was lonely without him) and about my writing (Toby—without my knowledge—had given Rupert a copy of my two *Evening Standard* articles on the Basque children). Rupert said they conveyed the refugees' situation much better than some of the proper journalists' articles in *The Times*, which was awfully nice of him to say, even if it wasn't true. He suggested that if Aunt Charlotte ever followed through on one of her frequent threats to cut off our allowances, I could get a job writing the ladies' page for a newspaper. I suppose I'd have to learn proper shorthand first, though. And proper typing.

The second afternoon of our visit, Rupert was called over to a neighbor's place to help with a mole that had been caught in a trap, so I went off looking for Toby (I already knew where Veronica would be—in the library, immersed in the late Lord Astley's memoirs). I found Toby sprawled across Julia's bed, reading *Woman and Home* out loud while she did her nails at the dressing table. She offered to do mine, but Aunt Charlotte thinks nail varnish is vulgar, so I regretfully declined.

"Listen," said Toby. "This is *so* educational. 'Many women do not know that *habitual constipation* is a major cause of frigidity.' Oh, and there's a helpful advertisement for Eno's Fruit Salts right beside it."

"What's 'frigidity'?" I unwisely asked.

"'A lack of interest in marital relations,'" he read with raised eyebrows.

Julia snorted. "I doubt it's due to constipation," she said. "More likely it's caused by husbands who haven't a clue what they're doing."

"Julia!" said Toby in scandalized tones, clapping his hands over his ears, then changing his mind and reaching for my ears. "Don't say such things! Not in the presence of innocent, unmarried girls!"

I heartily agreed, wondering if I'd ever be able to look Anthony in the eye again without blushing.

"Well, don't say I didn't warn you," said Julia, blowing on her fingertips. "Look for an older man, Sophie. A French widower or some such, that's my advice."

"Speaking of which, how's your *friend?*" said Toby.

There was a pause, during which Julia carefully replaced the lid of her crimson nail varnish. "We are no longer friends," she said at last. "Happy?"

"Very," said Toby. "Ant's been like a bear with a sore head lately."

"How would *you* know?" asked Julia, frowning at him.

"Oh, I see him around," said Toby, turning back to the magazine.

"Where?"

"Here and there," said Toby. "Round and about. Up and down—"

"*You're* the one he's giving flying lessons to!" cried Julia, jumping up. "I *knew* it! He tried to imply it was some woman, in a pathetic attempt to make me jealous—but I always knew better!"

"What?" I said, gaping at Toby. "How long has *this* been going on?"

Toby put down the magazine and gave me a slightly sheepish look. "A month or two. Don't tell Simon, will you?"

"Are you trying to pay him back about the law classes?"

"No, I'm trying to learn to fly," Toby said with dignity. "And I'm really quite good at it. Ant says I'm a natural. I should have my flying license next month if the weather holds up."

"But why do you want a flying license?" I asked.

"Well, it comes in handy if one wants to be a pilot in the Royal Air Force," he said.

There was a stunned silence. Julia and I stared at him.

"The Royal Air Force?" Julia said. "But, Toby, darling—"

"Surely you didn't imagine I'd ever want to join the *army*?" he said. "Those dreary khaki uniforms . . . And I get seasick, unfortunately, so the navy's out."

"But—" I started, then couldn't go on. Julia flung her arms around me.

"There, see what you've done, upsetting your little sister!" she cried. "Don't worry, Sophie, there's not going to be a war!"

Except I knew there was a very good chance (that is, a very bad one) that there could be. And until then, I'd mostly thought of war as cities being bombed, civilians being gassed, refugees fleeing on foot to the country. Foolishly, I'd forgotten the armed forces, the soldiers and sailors and pilots who'd be risking their lives for the rest of us. I thought of Toby and Simon, Rupert, Anthony, Daniel, all the young men I knew . . .

"Really, if there *were* going to be a war, they'd introduce conscription," Julia said firmly. "All they've done so far is try to get people to become Air Raid Precautions volunteers, that's all."

"Well, let's wait and see," said Toby, opening the magazine again. And he refused to discuss the issue any further, although I cornered him later and made him promise to tell Veronica and Simon about the flying lessons.

Then, that evening, Colonel Stanley-Ross came over for dinner. All the Stanley-Rosses fell upon him—I gathered he hadn't been around much lately. As soon as I got the chance, I asked the Colonel whether he thought there was going to be a war.

"Well, let's wait and see," he said, too, taking in my anxious expression and giving me a kind smile. "The League of Nations isn't dead, you know, Sophie. It's still working towards peace. Very few people want a war, even in Germany."

"If only Montmaray were a member of the League," Veronica said with a sigh. "Then we might have a chance of some international help . . ."

"Have you heard anything more from the Foreign Office?" the Colonel asked.

"The whole thing's been passed on to yet another committee," she said. "Not that they'll do anything to upset Germany, not while Chamberlain's Prime Minister."

"Don't lose heart," the Colonel said. "Just recall your triumph over old Adams-Smythe! They were still talking about that in the staff dining room the last time I was there. I don't know if he'll ever recover from the humiliation."

"What, the humiliation of being outdebated by a mere *girl*?" said Veronica. "Perhaps if the Foreign Office employed some female diplomats, it'd be a bit more effective."

"There'd certainly be fewer wars if *women* were in charge," said Julia, looking pointedly at Toby. "*Women* don't have ridiculous urges to fly off and be heroes . . ."

But then Lady Astley calmly ordered us to pay attention to the brandied chestnut pudding, a new creation of the cook's, and to consider whether it went better with the chocolate sauce or the caramel. And I was more than willing to divert all my thoughts towards that—away from other, less pleasant matters.

15th February 1939

Barcelona has been taken by the Fascists, and it looks as though Madrid will be the next to fall. And Hitler has just given a speech demanding back all the former German colonies around the world—although Chamberlain, the Arch Appeaser, claims that "it is not the speech of a man preparing to throw Europe into another crisis."

However! Wondrous, amazing news has arrived this afternoon at Milford Park! At least, it's *potentially* wondrous and amazing. I think.

Toby was out flying with Anthony at the time. Henry was upstairs arguing with Miss Bullock, Aunt Charlotte was off visiting the Bosworths, and Veronica and I were sitting about the library feeling bored and useless. Our Montmaray campaign seemed to have reached an impasse. I was wondering aloud whether I ought to write an article about Montmaray—I was sure Daniel would publish it in his newspaper if I sent it to him.

But what would that achieve? His two thousand or so subscribers were already passionately anti-Nazi, so I wasn't going to change their opinion, and besides, the sort of people who read *The Evolutionary Socialist* each week were not the sort of people who had any influence in the British government—or any other government, for that matter. Veronica was half seriously considering writing to Mr. Gandhi for some advice on nonviolent protest methods when Simon ran in, brandishing some papers at us.

"What is it?" said Veronica. "Oh, you've found another long-lost bank account. What a surprise. *Why* our family continues to pay Mr. Grenville's firm to look after our affairs when the records are in such chaos is quite beyond—"

"Look!" cried Simon breathlessly. "Look at where the money is going!"

"Switzerland," I said, reading over Veronica's shoulder. "So? Lots of people have Swiss bank accounts, don't they?"

He took a deep breath. "This account was set up in 1920, in order to send a fixed annual amount, raised from coal royalties, directly to a bank account in—"

"Geneva!" cried Veronica. "No! It can't be, not to—"

"The League of Nations! Look, I just found this letter from the League acknowledging the first payment. We must have been invited to join, way back in 1920, and we've been paying dues all this time!"

"But . . . but that's impossible," said Veronica faintly, staring at the letter. "If Montmaray were a member of the League of

Nations, we'd be in their official papers . . . They'd have voted to allow us to join."

"How do you know they didn't?" he demanded. "We'd need to look at the minutes of their early meetings. It would hardly have been at the top of the agenda, would it? They must have had a thousand more important things to—"

"But the League's an international bureaucracy!" she protested. "Full of professional administrators—and how could they fail to notice a huge sum of money being handed over to them each year?"

"Not a *huge* sum, not compared to all the money other countries pay," he said. "Perhaps they saw that it came from London and assumed it was part of Britain's contribution? Or they thought it was a donation from some English philanthropist, and it went straight into general revenue? And as Montmaray hadn't contributed any staff to the League, didn't send any representatives to the first Assembly meetings—"

"But *why* didn't we? Why didn't we *know* about this?" said Veronica.

Simon huffed impatiently. "Well! Look at how things were in Montmaray after the Great War, with the King being—"

"Insane," said Veronica, nodding. "And Aunt Charlotte probably authorized Mr. Grenville to sign any official papers that arrived at his office. You know how she thinks it's unladylike to take any interest in finances or government matters."

"The League of Nations has been accepting our money all this time," said Simon. "I can prove it!"

"They'll *have* to listen to us now," said Veronica, her voice catching his excitement. "Whether we're an official member or not—and perhaps we really *are!*"

She gazed up at Simon, her eyes shining.

"Simon," she said, "I could *kiss* you!"

"Please don't," he said hastily.

Well, *I* certainly wouldn't have minded kissing him, but I restricted myself to a heartfelt "Well done, Simon!" He put his arm around my shoulders and beamed down at me.

"Wait till Toby gets back," he said. "Wait till we tell him!"

Veronica had already snatched up a pencil and some paper. "Firstly, we need to write to the League of Nations, asking them to check their records—"

"And requesting a hearing at the Court of International Justice," said Simon.

"Wait—perhaps take it directly to the Council itself?" said Veronica, scribbling away. "Isn't that what Abyssinia did when Italy invaded it?"

"We'll need independent witness statements, though," mused Simon.

"Those pilots who took photographs of the airstrip and the German ships at Montmaray. We'll have to get in contact with the Colonel—"

"But it'll be argued that Montmaray is German property, that it was sold to them," said Simon, running his hand through his hair. "That's the official view of the British government.

What we *need* is proof that the Germans bombed the island in 1937—we need evidence of their violent attack."

"There's plenty of evidence!" said Veronica. "All of us are eyewitnesses."

"It won't be enough," said Simon, shaking his head. "We need—"

"Otto Rahn," I said.

They both looked at me.

"Herr Rahn will help us," I said. "He told me how sorry he was about what Gebhardt had done. He tried to warn us before he left the island. Herr Rahn's not a Nazi, not a proper one. He would *never* have agreed to them bombing our library."

Veronica looked down at her list. "Write to Otto Rahn," she said at last. "In . . . Berlin, wasn't it? Is he at one of the universities? Or perhaps we can get in contact with him via the Ahnenerbe, if he still works for them. I'll get Daniel to translate our letter into German—"

Bother. There's the car. Aunt Charlotte's back.

17th March 1939

Here we are, back at Montmaray House, deep in preparation for yet another Season. Aunt Charlotte's demeanor is that of a war-weary general, facing the enemy across the trenches for the third and (she hopes) decisive battle.

"I see the Mosley girl is making her debut," she says grimly, peering at the gossip columns of *The Times* as though they were military dispatches. "His *first* wife's daughter, of course. Well, the girl's pretty enough, I suppose, and she's inherited her mother's jewels. But she hasn't *your* looks, Veronica—and that reminds me, I must have Barnes get all my jewelry out of the bank. *All* of it this time, including the emeralds. Sophia, you'll need a turquoise ball gown to display them to their best advantage—please see to it. You may have the car this afternoon . . . Oh, not another Kennedy girl being presented at Court! How many more of them *are* there?"

I have to say that, while I understand Aunt Charlotte's increasing desperation to get us married off, I have more important matters on my mind than finding the right shade of silk to match the Montmaray emeralds. As predicted by everyone but Mr. Chamberlain, Hitler's forces marched into Prague two days ago. Czechoslovakia is now entirely under Nazi control. The Munich agreement, "peace for our time," is dead. Hitler's promises have been shown to be worthless. The next major move, according to Veronica, will involve Poland. She and Simon had an argument about whether Germany would invade some city in Lithuania first, but I'm not quite sure where it is, or why the Germans care so much about it. In other depressing news, the Spanish war is all but over, the British government having formally recognized Franco as the new leader of Spain three weeks ago . . .

Oh good, Aunt Charlotte's gone off to the hairdresser's. Except Simon's just walked in, looking grave. Oh dear, what's happened *now*?

An hour later.

"Listen, everyone," Simon began. "Toby, stop staring out the window and come over here. We need to talk. Things are looking very bad, war could be declared at any time. I think we need to consider if . . ." He took a deep breath. "Well, if we'd all be better off becoming British subjects." He raised his hand to cut off Veronica, who'd already started to speak. "I *know* we're Montmaravians, Veronica, and we always will be. But right now, Montmaray is officially German territory, and if Britain declared war on Germany tomorrow, we'd be classified as enemy aliens. We could be imprisoned or deported. I suppose we could explain we were refugees, but then we'd be officially stateless. The sensible thing would be for us to apply to become naturalized citizens of this country, right away."

"And we might need to be British subjects to join the armed forces," said Toby, looking unnaturally serious. "I mean, I will. And you, Simon, if you join up—"

"There might not be any choice about joining up, they're already debating conscription in Parliament," said Veronica. "But, anyway—"

"Which reminds me," interrupted Simon. "Sorry, Veronica—but, Toby, you need to speak to your aunt about your plans. She has no idea what you're doing—actually, neither do I. Are you planning to join the Royal Air Force? Or were you thinking of the Auxiliary Air Force? Either way, they'll ask you for proof that you're a British subject."

"Actually, I'm not sure they will," said Toby thoughtfully. "I mean, if there's a war, they won't really care, will they, as long as we're all fighting against the same enemy? Although . . . what happened in the last war, Veronica? What about all those Montmaravian men who fought in France with the British?"

"They fought under the Montmaravian flag, of course," she said. "But—"

"The problem is," said Simon, frowning, "that the Home Office is making it very difficult to become a British citizen now, with all these refugees starting to flood in from the Continent. Henry might just scrape in, as she's under sixteen and her aunt, her legal guardian, is British through marriage. But that doesn't help *us*. We weren't born in the British Empire, our fathers weren't born in the British Empire, none of *us* is married to a British subject—"

"Unless there's something you're not telling us about Daniel, Veronica," put in Toby.

"It *is* possible for the British monarch to grant us the rights of British citizens," continued Simon, "as a royal prerogative, but it seems unlikely he'd do so. Not after Henry's debacle at Buckingham Palace."

Veronica cleared her throat. "If I could *possibly* be allowed to speak for one moment? Thank you so much. As I was *trying* to say, I doubt there'll be any difficulties *if* we decide we want to be British citizens."

Simon gave her an exasperated look. "Veronica, I've just finished explaining that we don't meet any of the conditions allowing us to become—"

Veronica sighed. "Oh, Simon," she said, "all those hours spent poring over law books, and yet you've forgotten the Sophia Naturalization Act of 1705."

"The what?"

"Don't you recall the Electress Sophia of Hanover?" Veronica asked.

"Who?" said Toby.

"Sophie, *you* remember her," said Veronica.

"Um," I said. "Didn't her son become King George the First?"

"Exactly," said Veronica. (Of course, the only reason I

remembered her is that we share a name.) "The Electress Sophia was heir to the British throne, but she hadn't been born here. So an Act of Parliament in 1705 naturalized her *and all her Protestant descendants* as British subjects."

"Are you saying . . . ?"

"That the FitzOsbornes are direct descendants of the Electress Sophia of Hanover, yes," said Veronica. "Therefore, we are eligible to become naturalized British subjects."

"Are you *sure* we're descended from her?" asked Toby.

"Of course I'm sure," said Veronica. "Her youngest grandchild married our great-great—"

"Yes, all right," said Toby quickly. "We believe you."

"That's all very well for you three," said Simon. "But my surname is Chester, not FitzOsborne, and there's no proof I'm descended from—"

"Do try not to be so idiotic," Veronica said impatiently. "We know perfectly well who your father is. You're just as much a FitzOsborne as I am."

We all stared at her. Simon opened his mouth, then closed it again, turning rather pink.

"I didn't say I was *happy* about it," she added rather defensively. "And, anyway, this is all beside the point! Becoming a British subject would mean giving up everything—renouncing our titles, swearing allegiance to the British crown, all of it! I haven't any intention of pretending to be British just because there might be a war starting!"

"I agree," I said, but I was too busy taking down notes to say much more.

"Yes, you're quite right, both of you," said Toby. "Simon?"

"I . . . well . . . of course, I don't want to be British!" he spluttered, still in shock over Veronica's acknowledgment of him as one of the family. "But . . . but we still have to think about what we're going to *do* if Britain declares war on Germany!"

"Why don't *we* declare war on Germany?" suggested Toby. "Right now? We've certainly got reason to."

"We are *not* declaring war," said Veronica forcefully. "Not until we have no other option, till we've exhausted every diplomatic means. We are going to present our case to the League of Nations, the way any civilized nation would."

"Well, it'd help if we had a stronger case," said Simon, having finally pulled himself together. "I mean, we still don't have any independent witnesses—"

At that moment, the footman entered the breakfast room with the post (I think we were all rather glad about the interruption, the conversation had become so intense). He placed a large envelope in front of Veronica.

"Who's that from?" said Toby, peering over. "The British *Furriers'* Association? Why are you corresponding with them?"

"Oh, it's Daniel, incognito," she said, slitting the envelope open with her butter knife. "On account of him being banned from this household in any shape or form. I think he uses old envelopes from his father's office."

"You didn't hear that, Bert," said Toby to the footman.

"Of course not, sir," the footman said, with the barest hint of a smirk. "Shall I bring in some more toast, sir?"

"No thanks. You can clear away now—"

"Otto Rahn's written back!" cried Veronica. "Daniel's translated his letter!" She scanned the page as we all leaned in eagerly. "Rahn's resigned from the SS! And he's written another book, *Lucifer's Courtiers*—gosh, it sounds even more bizarre than his first book—"

"Never mind about his books!" said Simon. "What does he say about providing a statement against Gebhardt?"

"He says that he will. He says . . . Oh. He must have had a falling-out with his superior officers in the SS. He was sent as a guard to some concentration camp, and he says what he saw there . . . Hmm. He's opposed to war, to the way Germany's preparing for war. He doesn't approve of Hitler. Then there's an enormous paragraph about establishing a New Order of Pure Ones and working towards Universal Peace . . . Sophie, he especially asks to be remembered to you."

I took the page from Veronica and read it. "He sounds very sad. 'This new nation of Germany is no place for a man such as I.'"

"I just wish he'd sent his *statement* with this letter," said Simon after the page was handed on to him. "The League of Nations is asking for all our documentation as soon as possible."

"It sounds as though he's already started writing it," I said.

"But he wanted to send us this note first. There, didn't I *say* he wasn't a proper Nazi?"

And they all agreed I was very wise, and henceforth, they would always pay close attention to me. Not really. Still, it is very good news to hear how supportive Herr Rahn is. And when the League of Nations sees all our documents, reads what Herr Rahn has to say, they'll have to help us. *Surely* they will.

27th April 1939

We really ought to have expected it, after Italy invaded Albania at Easter, but anticipating bad news doesn't make one feel any better when it arrives. Yesterday Chamberlain announced that all British men aged twenty and twenty-one years old are to be conscripted immediately into the armed forces.

Rupert is twenty. Three of our footmen and a dozen other male staff at Montmaray House and Milford Park are of an age to be called up.

"Well, it's a good thing I've already applied to join the Royal Air Force," said Toby brightly at breakfast this morning. "Otherwise I'd feel quite left out of things."

Whereupon Aunt Charlotte burst into tears.

I don't know whether she was upset over Toby or at the prospect of losing so many good servants, but it was certainly unexpected. Veronica and I stared, dumbfounded, across the table at her, though Toby jumped up at once and put his arm around her.

"Now, there's no need to *fuss*," he said, fishing out his hand-kerchief. "Goodness, there isn't even a war on! It's just the government being sensible. It'll give all those poor unemployed men up north something to do. Three square meals a day and nice, warm uniforms—awfully kind of old Chamberlain to think of them."

"When I remember the last war," Aunt Charlotte wept. "When I think of your poor father, and yours, Veronica . . ."

As neither of our fathers died in the war (mine didn't even fight in it), I wasn't quite sure what she meant by that. Unless she was reminding us that Toby was the last living, legitimate male FitzOsborne, the one who was supposed to carry on the family name. As if summoned by my thoughts, Simon entered the breakfast room at that moment.

"Simon!" cried our aunt, catching sight of him. "Simon, you must join the air force, too! I . . . I *order* you to do so, to look after Tobias! He *can't* go off by himself, he's just a *boy*—"

Then she buried her face in Toby's handkerchief, and I did what I ought to have done immediately and rang for Barnes. She arrived within seconds, took in the situation at a glance, and whisked Aunt Charlotte off to bed, summoning tea, brandy, and blankets as she went. (Imagine if *Barnes* were called up. Our household would collapse, but the British army would become unbeatable.)

"Don't worry about poor old Aunt C," said Toby to Simon, who was still standing there, stunned at the unprecedented sight of our aunt showing any emotion other than annoyance. "She'll have forgotten all about it by tomorrow."

Simon sat down at the table, shook his head, and reached for the teapot. "Oh, but I take my orders seriously," he said. "I've no intention of letting you go off alone."

Toby's jaw dropped. "Simon! You can't even *fly*!"

"If *you* can learn, I certainly ought to be able to do it. How different can it be from driving a car? Sophie, could you please pass the sugar?"

"It's completely different!" exclaimed Toby. "It's in three dimensions. There's an up and a down, it's—"

"They'll bring in conscription for men aged up to twenty-five next," said Veronica soberly. "Soon half the country will be in uniform."

"Yes, it's much better to decide what one wants to do now than to have very little choice later on," said Simon, stirring his tea.

"But . . ." I hadn't seen Toby so flustered in a long while. "But it's safer for you here! And who's going to look after the girls if we're both away? And what about our submission to the League of Nations?"

"We'll deal with everything as a family, as we always do," said Simon. "Won't we, Veronica, Sophie? So, has the post arrived? Anything from Otto Rahn?"

Veronica and I shook our heads in unison, glanced at each other, then returned to our breakfast. There we sat, spreading marmalade on toast and reaching for the milk jug, while the world fell into chaos. Our unflappable aunt having hysterics, Toby coming over all serious and responsible . . .

Veronica picked up her newspaper and rustled it. "Typical," she said loudly. "Franco's announced the Spanish Civil War is over, King Zog of Albania's been forced into exile by the Italians, British attempts to build an alliance with the Soviet Union have stalled yet again—but *The Times* chooses to devote almost an entire *page* to the royal corgis!"

She was doing her best to return us to normality. It wasn't her fault that it wasn't really working.

25th May 1939

The most bizarre thing has happened. Aunt Charlotte has started reading the newspapers—not just the Court Circular and the gossip columns, but the bits in the middle about international politics. It's very disconcerting. Mind you, she only pays close attention to political events if they involve people she knows (that is, people with titles). For instance, the evacuation of Spanish refugees from camps near the French border drew her interest only because Lady Redesdale's eldest daughter, the Honorable Mrs. Rodd, had gone over there to help organize the ships to Mexico and Morocco. Still, even this rather narrow focus on politics has had a noticeable effect on our conversations. This morning, Aunt Charlotte was tutting loudly over some inflammatory remarks made by Mr. Kennedy (he is very pro-appeasement).

"Wants to keep America from interfering in European arguments, he *claims*!" said Aunt Charlotte. "More likely, wants to avoid all those sons of his being drafted into the army! Isn't that right, Sophia?"

"Oh," I said feebly. "Well . . ."

"Either that or he wants to keep his European business interests safe!"

Not that Mr. Kennedy's remarks are any worse than King George sending warm birthday wishes to Hitler last month. Still, it *is* becoming rather awkward, having conversations with Kick now. I try to avoid the subject of politics altogether, which isn't easy these days. Not that I've seen much of her lately, she's been so busy. She's on several Society committees, including the one that organizes the Derby Ball. The Kennedys also had King George and Queen Elizabeth over for dinner a few weeks ago, which must have taken an awful lot of planning. Unsurprisingly, we weren't invited to the royal dinner. I gathered Aunt Charlotte was still annoyed about this snub.

"And *now* Kennedy claims the Jews are complaining too much about Hitler," Aunt Charlotte went on. "For heaven's sake! It's not the *Jews* who are causing all this trouble in Germany!"

If only Veronica had been there to hear that! But she was at the Foreign Office, looking up League of Nations records. Aunt Charlotte still doesn't know much about our campaign, probably because we've been very careful to keep most of it a secret from her. Despite her newfound interest in politics, she'd vehemently disapprove of Veronica and me having any direct involvement in it, and she'd no doubt be able to find dozens of tasks for Simon to do if she realized he was "wasting his time" on the Montmaray campaign. Montmaray is something Aunt Charlotte has put firmly behind her.

"I have never been one to chase after rainbows," she said very repressively when Henry once asked our aunt if she missed her childhood home. "And you, Henrietta, would do well to follow my example!"

"But I can't just *forget* Montmaray," Henry said indignantly. "And I wouldn't want to, even if I could!"

"Of course you could," snapped Aunt Charlotte (she was in a particularly bad mood that day). "One can do anything if one really applies one's mind to it. In fact, one might say it is your *duty* to think in a sensible manner, as opposed to a foolish, sentimental, and futile one!"

This was one of the few times I was glad that Henry disregards most of what Aunt Charlotte says.

And this reminds me of another disconcerting thing—Aunt Charlotte keeps dragging me into embarrassing conversations about Toby and *his* duty.

"Now, what do you think of this Lady Helena?" my aunt said to me this morning after she'd finished tearing apart Mr. Kennedy. "The girl is absolutely besotted with Tobias, and I don't wonder at it, he's such a good-looking, charming boy. Her mother sounded thrilled about the whole thing when I sat next to her at Pamela Bosworth's luncheon party last week. But I asked Tobias about it yesterday, and he said, 'I've never really been attracted to blondes.' What *can* he mean? What does the color of her hair matter when she's the daughter of an earl and stands to inherit her mother's fortune?"

Aunt Charlotte tossed her newspaper at the table.

"Oh, I know he's still young, Sophia," she said with a sigh. "But your father was only nineteen when he married your mother. Of course, there *was* a war on at the time—that always lends a sense of urgency to romance."

My mother had been nineteen, too. When she was my age, she'd been engaged to be married. I can't imagine getting engaged at my age. That is, if anyone were to propose to me now, which I admit is fairly unlikely, war or no war.

"I really do *worry* about Tobias," continued Aunt Charlotte, shaking her head. "Not just about this ridiculous flying scheme of his— Oh, and I had some strong words with Mr. Chamberlain about that last night at Lady Londonderry's, I can assure you! 'Conscription is all very well for men with nothing better to do,' I said to him. 'The unemployed, the lower classes, and so on, but what about all those young gentlemen who have *responsibilities* towards their families? Have you thought about *that?*' He didn't have any reply, of course! Actually, he's not looking very well, Neville Chamberlain. Gaunt, far too pale. I told his wife she ought to ensure he gets out more in the fresh air. But you're distracting me, Sophia—we were discussing Tobias. Yes, I can't help feeling concerned about him. Surely he's fallen in love by now, once or twice? That's natural, isn't it, by his age? But no, he claims there isn't *any* young lady in his thoughts! He confides in you, though, Sophia. So tell me—*is* he in love?"

"Well, I really couldn't say . . ." I desperately searched for another topic of conversation. "Oh, look, Veronica's left her gloves on the—"

"Or perhaps I ought to ask Simon Chester about it," my aunt mused aloud. "Tobias seems to spend most of his time with Simon these days . . ."

I considered having a violent coughing fit, or fainting across the floor in a very histrionic manner.

"Not that it matters if he *is* infatuated with someone, of course," she went on. "Love is all very well, but in the end, the most important thing is to do one's duty."

I couldn't help protesting at that. "What, even if it makes one absolutely miserable?"

"Don't be so melodramatic, Sophia," sighed Aunt Charlotte. "Life is not a fairy tale. Love does not always lead to happiness ever after. And at least if one *knows* that one has done the correct thing, then one can hold up one's head proudly during . . . well, the less pleasant times."

I might have argued further, but poor Aunt Charlotte was looking rather sad, perhaps thinking of her own marriage, and I didn't have the heart. Anyway, the footman came in at that moment to tell me I was wanted on the telephone. I followed him out into the corridor and turned towards the library, but he stopped me with a little cough.

"Excuse me, Your Highness," he said very quietly. "I'm afraid the gentleman does not wish to speak to you on the telephone but in person. I took the liberty of asking him to wait downstairs, but if Your Highness does not wish to speak with him, I'll ask him to leave immediately."

"What gentleman?" I asked.

Bert glanced towards the open door of the drawing room and edged a little further away from it. "A Mr. *Bloom*, Your Highness."

"Daniel!" I whispered. "Yes, of course I'll see him! Oh, thank you, Bert! But won't you get into terrible trouble if—"

"Mr. Harkness is visiting the dentist," said Bert. "He's due back at eleven. If Your Highness would follow me . . ."

So I hurried off after the footman into the unfamiliar depths of Montmaray House, down uncarpeted stairs, along a dimly lit stone passage, into a tiny room that smelled of candles and boot polish.

"Sophie!" cried Daniel, jumping to his feet when he saw me. "Where's Veronica?"

"At the Foreign Office. Is something wrong?" I said, although it was obvious that there *was*.

"I came straight over, I didn't want to trust this to the post," he said, holding out a scrap of newsprint. "It was sent to me from Berlin."

It was in German, in that angular Gothic script that's so difficult to decipher, but I recognized the first few words. "*SS-Obersturmführer Otto Rahn* . . . Oh, Daniel, what does it say?"

He hesitated. "Sophie, I'm so sorry. He's dead."

I stared at Daniel.

"He died in a snowstorm in March. It must have happened not long after he wrote to us, just after he resigned from the SS. They found his frozen body in the mountains."

"No," I said blankly. Otto Rahn couldn't be *dead*. I could see him so clearly, telling me all about his Grail quest, the words tumbling out with such enthusiasm, such passion. He'd been so full of *life*. "No, I can't understand it, that can't be right," I said, shaking my head.

"Perhaps . . . perhaps he went walking in the snow and got lost," said Daniel. "The mountains can be treacherous—"

"But he was a healthy young man!" I burst out. "An experienced hiker! He knew the mountains well, he understood harsh weather, he'd gone on expeditions to Iceland! I can't believe he'd . . . You don't think it was an accident, do you?"

Daniel removed his spectacles and rubbed his eyes. "Sophie, I don't know who sent me this, but I think they must have discovered my address by going through his things. Perhaps it was a friend of his—but why would a friend send this anonymously? If it were a friend, surely he'd have included a note. And this page—it's from *Völkischer Beobachter*. That's a Nazi newspaper."

Daniel fumbled his spectacles back into place. He looked very anxious.

"Think about it, Sophie. Rahn resigns from the SS. He agrees to help a family who've been victims of Nazi brutality, who are planning to complain to the League of Nations about a high-ranking Nazi official. Immediately afterwards, Rahn disappears in the mountains—"

There was a knock on the doorframe and Bert poked his head around it.

"Excuse me, Your Highness," he said, glancing at the clock on the shelf above me.

"You have to go," I said to Daniel. "The butler will be back any minute. You can't be found here."

"I'll be in contact," he said, snatching up his hat. "But *please*, tell Veronica she needs to be careful. She'll listen to you. You *all* need to take care—"

"Yes, yes, of course," I said. A door slammed somewhere close by. "Go! Hurry!"

Bert hustled Daniel off, and I ran back upstairs. As soon as Veronica returned, I dragged her into my bedroom, the words spilling out of me so fast that I had to explain everything again once we were sitting down. She took the newspaper clipping from me and studied it, her face tightening.

"Do you think the SS found out about Herr Rahn's letter to us?" I asked her. "Could they have destroyed his statement, the one where he wrote down what happened to Montmaray?"

"It would certainly explain why we haven't received it."

"But do you think they . . ." I swallowed hard. "They *couldn't* have followed him, could they? And, and—"

"Killed him in cold blood? I doubt Gebhardt's conscience would bother him much, if he decided he needed to eliminate an enemy." She chewed her bottom lip. "On the other hand, it's possible that Herr Rahn decided he didn't *want* to live anymore, not in a Germany ruled by Hitler."

"You think he killed himself?"

"That's far more likely than him getting caught in a snow-storm and accidentally freezing to death. The medieval Cathars didn't have any objections to suicide, you know. They weren't like the Christians—they thought it could be a heroic act in certain circumstances. And we know he followed their beliefs."

"But even if he *did* choose to die, he only did it because the alternatives were so awful!" I cried. "To live under Nazi rule, to fight for the Nazis if war broke out—or else to be branded a traitor to his country. Oh, Veronica, we shouldn't have written to him! We *forced* him to make a choice!"

"No, we didn't!" she said sharply. "We don't know that at all. Remember, he'd fallen out with the SS before he heard anything from us. Yes, *perhaps* he'd learned about the bombing of Montmaray prior to our letter, perhaps he made an ill-advised complaint regarding Gebhardt. But there are plenty of other possibilities. Maybe they found out he had a Jewish ancestor. Maybe he broke off an engagement to some favored Nazi official's daughter. We just don't know. What bothers me now is—"

"That the SS have Daniel's address," I said. "They know where he lives, and that he was helping with the campaign."

She nodded. "But they can't do much to him when they're all the way over in Berlin and he's here."

"There's his uncle, though," I said. "The one who lives in Vienna."

"The Nazis might not connect Daniel to him. I'm not even sure if he and Daniel have the same surname," Veronica said, trying to sound reassuring but not entirely succeeding. She took a deep breath. "Still, at least Daniel's not planning any visits to Germany. And the Germans are hardly likely to send over a Nazi assassin . . ."

We stared at each other, our eyes widening.

"No, no, *she's* still locked up in Broadmoor," Veronica said. "I'm certain she is."

"I'd better get Simon to check on that," I said. So I did, and the Crazed Assassin was still behind bars. But it didn't make me feel much more secure.

17th July 1939

We used to have a little brass clock at Montmaray, on a shelf near the kitchen sink, and for many years it was our only reliable timepiece. One day, the goat barged into the kitchen and knocked the clock into the washing-up water, but until then, it worked beautifully. It was my job as a child to wind its key precisely seventeen times every Sunday evening—a number that had been calculated to keep the clock ticking for one week, thus far and no further. As I neared that magic number, the clock springs would squeak in protest, the cogs would groan, and it seemed that at any moment, the entire thing would fly apart, spraying the walls and ceiling with its sharp metal innards. That didn't ever happen, but I always held my breath as I turned the key. Perhaps one day I'd lose count, perhaps one day I'd apply a fraction too much tension . . .

That's how I feel now. The world has been wound up as far as it can go. The slightest pressure in the wrong place, at the wrong time, and everything will explode. We went to the

Independence Day garden party at the American Embassy, and even the Kennedys were having difficulties maintaining their cheerful American outlook on life. Kick, uncharacteristically somber, told me that Billy Hartington had joined the Cold-stream Guards, and Veronica had a long, gloomy discussion with Jack, who's been touring the Continent for the past few months.

"He says Britain's started its rearmament program far too late, that the Germans have twice as many aeroplanes and are churning out new ones twice as fast as Britain can. And do you know what *else* he said? That when it comes to winning wars, a totalitarian regime like Nazi Germany will always have the edge over a democracy! Because a dictator can force every citizen into the army or the factories, ban trade unions, outlaw strikes, take over the press, and flood the country with war propaganda."

"And what did you say?"

"I told him I'd rather die in a democracy than live under a dictator. And I reminded him about the League of Nations! I still have faith in diplomacy, in rational, intelligent negotiation, if it's backed by a strong commitment to sanctions and a power-ful international defense force."

"Then what did he say?"

"He asked me out to dinner at the Ritz."

She turned him down, of course. Aunt Charlotte would've thrown a fit if she'd ever found out.

Well, *I* don't want a war, no one does, but it's hard to advo-cate for peace when people like Oswald Mosley have comman-deered that side of the debate. He held a "Peace Rally" last night at Earls Court, and twenty thousand people turned up to listen to him rant about how "a million Britons shall never die in your Jews' quarrel." I've just finished reading the newspaper reports about it. Drumrolls, fanfares, waving banners, black uniforms, roving searchlights, howling spectators flinging up their arms in the Fascist salute—for a man who claims to love peace, Mosley certainly does a good job of using every military gesture and jingoistic cliché in the book (assuming the book was written by Hitler).

I wish I had Veronica's firm faith in the power of reasoned, diplomatic discussion to solve international conflict, but I'm afraid I am full of doubts and worries. I went over to Julia's yesterday, and she and her friend Daphne were trying to decide what to do if war does break out. Daphne favored enrolling in the Wrens, the Women's Royal Naval Service, because they have the smartest uniforms, although she conceded that nurses have a better chance of meeting men.

"Nursing!" said Julia. "Ugh, all those bedpans and dressings."

And blood, I thought with a shudder. I could never be a nurse.

"No, I think I'd rather drive an ambulance or chauffeur generals around or something like that," Julia went on.

"Girls used to work in factories in the last war, didn't they?" mused Daphne. "Oh, but those ghastly overalls . . ."

Anthony has joined the Auxiliary Air Force. Rupert failed the medical for the army—he has a heart murmur, from being ill as a child—but his uncle is trying to find him a position somewhere. David, Julia's eldest brother, is already a lieutenant in the Royal Wiltshire Yeomanry. They haven't heard from Charlie, Julia's other brother, in months, but they think he's still in Canada, and that's part of the British Empire, so *he'd* be drawn into a European war, too. (Poor Lady Astley, imagine how she must be feeling right now! Aunt Charlotte hasn't much to complain about, in comparison.) Even Phoebe's brother has swapped his Blackshirt breeches for khaki and is at an army training camp on the coast.

Oh, the afternoon post has arrived. Just a moment . . .

A leaflet from the ARP telling us how to put out a fire and explaining what all the different air-raid signals mean. Also, yet another letter from the League of Nations—we get one every other day now. It turns out we *were* voted in as a member of the League in 1920, even if no one paid much attention at the time, and they seem determined to make up for their two decades of neglect by bombarding us with paperwork. This latest invites our head of state to address the Council of the League of Nations, and it might even be quite soon if they hold an extraordinary meeting of the Council before the usual September one due to the current political situation. As the King of Montmaray is in Leicestershire doing an RAF-approved aerobatics course and the Lord Chancellor of Montmaray is very busy learning to fly in London, I'm not quite sure how we're going to manage this, particularly as Aunt Charlotte is about to drag Veronica and me back to Milford. I think our aunt has finally given up on this year's Season—most of the eligible young bachelors have been called up, anyway, and Toby is occupying all her energies at the moment. She is absolutely obsessed with him providing a family heir, sooner rather than later. I think she's afraid there'll be a war, and we'll all be killed, and the FitzOsborne name will die out. I wouldn't be a bit surprised if the next time Toby gets leave, she locks him in a bedroom with one of his more determined admirers and a bottle of champagne, in the hope that it'll force him into a hasty engagement . . .

21st August 1939

So, the League of Nations confirmed that they would be holding an extraordinary meeting this month, at which we would have an opportunity to convince the world to help us. But first, we had to get around the formidable obstacle of Aunt Charlotte and her obsession with Toby's marriage prospects.

"We shall have a house party, Saturday to Monday," she announced. "Whom shall I invite?"

Toby politely explained that he would be using his week's leave to travel to Geneva with Simon, Veronica, and me, in order to address the Council of the League of Nations.

"Nonsense!" said Aunt Charlotte. "Write and tell this League that it's not a convenient time, that you have a prior engagement. Besides, you know what I think of all this fuss you children have been making about Montmaray—it's quite futile, anyone can see that. Now, Lady Helena—"

"The League's an international organization with an unalterable schedule," Toby interrupted. "And I'm not interested in Lady Helena. I don't want to spend Saturday to Monday with her, and I'm certainly not going to marry her."

"Well, what about her sister?" said Aunt Charlotte. "Not officially out yet, but she's seventeen. Or there's Sir Nigel's daughter, you met her at the Hunt Ball, that tall, thin girl. Not very graceful on the dance floor, I'll admit, but one can't be too fussy. Her father has a good-sized place in Scotland, and her grandfather's a viscount. And then there's Lady Sarah—"

"Aunt Charlotte," Toby said, speaking very slowly and clearly. "Please listen to me. I am not interested in any of these girls."

His words finally sank in. "What? *None* of them?"

"None of them."

She stared at him in disbelief. "Tobias, these girls are the *cream* of English Society! Do you have any idea how much effort I have put into *finding* them, and investigating their *backgrounds*, and—"

"Yes, and it's very kind of you to take all that trouble, but I'm not interested in them."

"Well!" she cried, sitting down very abruptly. "If *these* girls don't meet your exacting criteria, then may I ask who *does*? Is there anyone you've ever *met* whom you might consider marrying?"

Toby thought for a moment. "Yes," he said. "Julia."

"Julia?" shrieked our aunt. "Julia *Whittingham*? But she's already *married*! And the *stories* I've been hearing about her lately, she's *completely* unsuitable—"

"I like her," said Toby firmly. "And as I can't marry her, I shan't marry at all."

It wasn't the best moment for him to take a stand on the issue, although I suppose it had to happen eventually. If only Simon had been there to calm things down! But he was off organizing train tickets and hotel bookings. So Veronica and I spoke up in support of Toby, and things rapidly progressed from bad to worse, ending with Aunt Charlotte informing us that she was cutting off all our allowances *immediately*.

"Well, it's a good thing I withdrew enough funds for our trip when I was in London," said Simon when he got back and found out what had happened. "And I've bought our train tickets."

"Never mind about that!" said Veronica. "How are we supposed to *catch* the train when we're locked up here?" Because Aunt Charlotte had confiscated the car keys and instructed the staff that we weren't to leave Milford Park under any circumstances. Even our post was to be scrutinized. Of course, she couldn't keep this up indefinitely, but it certainly threw our travel plans into chaos. We had a midnight meeting in my room to discuss it.

"I could ask Parker if he'd drive us up to London on Sunday night," said Toby. "But I don't want him to lose his job."

"If *only* Aunt Charlotte would let me keep pigeons," said Henry, sitting cross-legged on the end of my bed. "We could have sent a pigeon to Rupert—"

"Rupert!" said Toby. "That's it! We'll telephone him, ask him to drive us to the station!"

"How?" I asked. "Barnes has the key to the telephone room."

"Something will come up," said Toby confidently.

Unfortunately, it didn't. Ignoring all of Toby's protests, Aunt Charlotte sent an urgent invitation to Lady Helena, having correctly judged her the girl most likely to persist in the face of Toby's indifference, or even actual dislike. (Note to self: chasing after a boy when the boy has turned one down only makes one look desperate and unattractive.) Lady Helena arrived on Saturday morning with enough clothes for a fortnight's visit, but the only welcoming face was Aunt Charlotte's. Toby was ordered to take Lady Helena riding, to play a game of tennis with her, and to walk her round the lake to the folly, where the footmen had set up a picnic tea for two.

Meanwhile, Aunt Charlotte kept Simon occupied with a string of pointless administrative chores. She'd always treated him more as a valued servant than a family member, but it suddenly seemed to occur to her that his loyalties might lie with *us* rather than with her. In any case, she didn't trust him enough to allow him to use the telephone.

Veronica hid herself away in Phoebe's attic room, working on Toby's League of Nations speech, with intermittent help from me. Veronica was, of course, very good on the facts, but I convinced her that the speech needed something extra.

"We can't just lecture the Council," I said. "We need to make them *feel* for us. We have to tell them such a riveting, heartrending story that they won't be able to *stop* themselves from coming to our aid! Put in about all the young Montmaravian men dying in the war, and how devastated your father was."

Veronica gave me a dubious look but took up her pen again. Then I ran back downstairs, where I'd been loitering outside the telephone room, hoping one of the servants would leave it unlocked for a few minutes. Henry had already made several fruitless attempts to pick the lock with a hairpin.

"It always works in detective novels!" she said crossly. "There must be something wrong with your hairpins, Sophie!"

Things were getting really desperate by Sunday afternoon. Toby was due to address the Council meeting in Geneva on Tuesday, and our train left London on Monday morning. But, at last, an opportunity arrived, just as we'd sat down to tea. A maid came in with a telephone enquiry from the Earl of Dorset, about some horse he wanted to buy from Aunt Charlotte. While she was giving the maid her reply, Toby kicked me under the table, turned to Lady Helena, and started a very loud conversation about this year's Royal Ascot race meetings. As the French had won both the Windsor Castle Stakes and the Queen Alexandra Stakes, beating three of Aunt Charlotte's horses, the topic was explosive enough for me to sneak out of the room unnoticed. I reached the telephone room just as the maid left and found, thank heavens, that the door was still ajar. There was an agonizing wait while I was connected to Astley Manor, and then, finally, I heard Rupert's voice.

"Sophie!" he said. "How are you?"

"Fine, thank you," I whispered. "No—wait, not really. Look, I don't have much time, but can I ask you the most enormous favor? We all need to get to London tomorrow, and Aunt

Charlotte's got us imprisoned here at Milford, and she's taken away our allowances and the car keys and—"

"Oh Lord, what's Toby done now?" said Rupert. "No, forget I asked that. What time?"

"We need to be at Victoria Station by eleven, but we'll probably have to leave here quite early, before anyone's awake, and you mustn't tell anyone—"

"Meet you at five? On the side road outside Milford Park, near the lane that leads to the stables? I may not be able to get hold of my mother's car, but there's the farm van—"

"Oh, Rupert!" I said. "Perfect! You're absolutely *wonderful*. You've no idea how much I . . ."

My voice died away as I realized that the light filtering through the frosted glass door had suddenly become much dimmer. I whirled around. Barnes was standing in the doorway, a set of keys dangling from her fingers. I noted with alarm that her eyebrows had climbed so far up her forehead that they'd disappeared under her fringe. This, Phoebe had once told me, was a Very Bad Sign.

"Sophie?" said Rupert. "Are you all right?"

"Er . . . lovely talking with you, Rupert! Have to go now. Bye!" I hurriedly replaced the receiver.

"Now, now, Your Highness," said Barnes, shaking her head. "The Princess Royal gave *clear* instructions about use of the telephone."

"Well, yes," I said. "But—"

"But young love isn't bound by rules," finished Barnes dryly.

"Er," I said. "No . . ."

I tried desperately to think of some plausible excuse. But wait. Were her eyebrows lowering a fraction? To my amazed relief, I saw that they *were*.

"Oh, I was young, too, once," Barnes said. "And in love." She gazed past me. "A long time ago . . ."

I looked over my shoulder, but all I could see was a framed etching of Montmaray House, circa 1785, and I didn't think Barnes was *quite* that old. She cleared her throat.

"Well, I won't tell your aunt, not this time," she said more briskly. "But if this young gentleman has honorable intentions, he'll approach your aunt for formal permission to court you."

"Er . . . thank you. I mean, yes, he will. Right."

She lowered her voice. "I could even have a quiet word about it to the Princess Royal. *If* you and your suitor manage to conduct yourselves with restraint and dignity from now on."

What on earth had I got myself into now? But at least Barnes hadn't heard any of the travel arrangements. And the story did provide the others with some much-needed amusement, although I warned them that if they dared breathe a word of it to Rupert, my retaliation would be Swift and Painful.

We had a frantic packing session as soon as everyone else had gone to bed, then let ourselves out of the house before dawn this morning, as quietly as we could. All was dark, except for a couple of quick flashes of Morse code from Henry's room—

hopefully the "all clear" signal, although none of us could actually understand Morse. Henry had been deeply disappointed about having to remain at Milford but said she understood.

"I'm like the spy who's left behind enemy lines once the army retreats," she said.

"The most difficult and dangerous job one can have," said Toby solemnly, giving her the letter for Aunt Charlotte. This explained that we would only be away for a few days and would send a telegram from our Swiss hotel as soon as we arrived. Henry was to put off handing over the letter for as long as possible, at least till after luncheon. We weren't quite sure how much influence our aunt had over police officers or railway guards, but we figured we ought to be safe once we were at sea.

We found Rupert exactly where he'd said he'd be, sitting behind the wheel of a nondescript Ford van. He had a thermos of coffee and a gingham-lined basket beside him on the seat.

"Well?" he said. "Should I be wearing a wig and fake mustache? Are you on the run from the law?"

"Sophie can explain," Toby said, scrambling into the back of the van with Simon and Veronica. "Oh good, are those cinnamon rolls in that basket?"

I sat up front with Rupert and explained. This took a while. Then we discussed poetry, getting through quite a lot of Auden and Eliot and Spender, because the trip took hours. It's only a hundred miles from Milford to London, but the van made unhappy noises whenever we went up a hill, or down a hill, or round a sharp corner. Rupert said the poor thing wasn't accustomed to long journeys. We had two flat tires within half an hour, then had to stop to buy more petrol. We made it to Victoria Station with about fifteen minutes to spare.

"Good luck," said Rupert after we'd surrendered our valises to the uniformed porters. "Please *try* to stay out of trouble, won't you? And send me a postcard from Geneva, our butler collects stamps." Then we rushed off to board the Golden Arrow, which was huffing smoke impatiently at the faraway glass roof of the station.

"Well, *this* is more like it," said Toby, looking round at all the mahogany and shiny brass and plush velvet that made up our first-class compartment. "Much nicer than sitting on a bench in the back of a Ford van. Of course, it's all right for *some*, traveling up front with the chauffeur. I do hope, Sophie, that you and Rupert managed to conduct yourselves with restraint and—"

I gave Toby a warning look. He grinned, then yawned widely. "Oh! So tired. Is there enough time for a little sleep?"

"We'll be at Dover in ninety-eight minutes," said Simon, looking at his collection of timetables.

"And you need to practice your speech, Toby," said Veronica, rummaging in her bag for her papers.

Meanwhile, *I* have used our journey to write down all of this. I've just caught my first glimpse of blue sea, though, so I'll put my journal away for the moment . . .

Later, on the *Canterbury* ferry (just as opulent as the train but with more of a nautical theme). Toby says he feels seasick.

"I never know whether it's better to stay belowdecks, so I don't have to look at the waves sloshing around, or go up and get some fresh air," he moans. "How much further?"

I can't help quoting Lewis Carroll:

"What matters it, how far we go?" his scaly friend replied.
"There is another shore, you know, upon the other side.
The further off from England, the nearer is to France—"

"'Then turn not pale, beloved snail, but come and join the dance,'" finishes Toby automatically. "Ugh, *snails*, that makes me feel even sicker. Soph, why did you remind me of *them*? They're so slimy and—"

"You could practice your speech again," suggests Veronica, holding out the sheaf of now-crumpled papers. "It'll take your mind off how you're feeling."

"I think I *will* go up on deck," says Toby hurriedly. "Simon, join me?"

Off they go through the Palm Court. Veronica frowns at one of the pages, gets out her pencil, and makes yet another note in the margin. I don't think Toby's managed to get all the way through it yet—Veronica keeps interrupting to change the wording, then Toby accidentally omits a sentence or misreads a phrase and has to start again, whereupon Simon tells him to slow down or vary his intonation . . .

Oh, here come the Customs and Passport men. Very efficient of them, doing all the paperwork on board the ferry before we arrive in Calais. They're giving our Montmaravian passports very odd looks, though. Now Veronica is lecturing the Passport men about Montmaravian history, and they're backing away slowly. The clock's striking two, we'll be there soon . . .

On board the Flèche d'Or, the French version of the Golden Arrow. It suddenly seems quite remarkable to me that one can spend an hour or so on a ferry and then find oneself in a *completely different country*. This is my first time on the Continent (on *any* continent), so I am going to note down all my impressions very carefully. It seems warmer here than in England, but the sea smells the same. I wore my best suit today and was still worried I'd look terribly drab beside all the chic Frenchwomen, but the few ladies I've seen so far are no more stylishly dressed than those in London. That woman climbing up the steps into the carriage, for example, shapeless beige skirt and salmon-pink blouse . . . Oh, she's English, I just heard her complaining about the heat in pure Cockney. Well, I expect most of the train passengers *are* English. The men on the platform are slightly more exotic-looking. There are a lot of mustaches, and one man is sporting both a mustache *and* a beret . . . Now, *there's* an interesting man, tall and military-looking, beautifully cut dark suit, bet he had it tailored in Paris. He's rushing onto the platform, but too late, the guards are closing the carriage doors. He turns towards our window and—

IT'S GEBHARDT!

22nd August 1939

Not sure of the time, or even where we are. Well, I know where *I* am, sort of, but Toby's and Veronica's whereabouts are a terrible mystery. I'm going to write down everything, though, now that I have a spare moment. Just in case . . . No. *Must* keep thinking positive thoughts.

So—the train was about to depart from the station at Calais, and the four of us were leaning out, or against, the large open window of our compartment. Then several things happened, all at once:

1. Simon sneezed.

2. I realized why the man on the platform had caught my attention and yelped, "Gebhardt!"

3. Toby said, "Don't you mean 'gesundheit'?"

and

4. Veronica yanked us all down below the windowsill.

A whistle blew, the engine roared, and Simon hissed, "Quick, see what he's doing! Which one is he?"

"The tall one, white hair," Veronica said, peeking round the edge of the window. "He saw us! He's shouting at the guard on the platform . . . Wait, I think I recognize the man behind him, he's one of the soldiers who searched the castle!"

I risked a glance as the carriage trembled. I saw the platform had begun to move, falling away behind us.

"Yes, it's that red-haired man," I said. "Look, Gebhardt's limping!"

"Good!" said Veronica. "I hope that bite Carlos gave him got infected and they had to chop off his leg. That might slow him down."

"Wait, this is the Nazi officer who ordered the bombing of Montmaray?" said Toby, finally catching up. "What's *he* doing here?"

"Trying to stop *you*, of course!" snapped Simon. "Seeing as you're about to make a formal complaint about him to the League of Nations!"

"And Hitler wouldn't want yet more evidence of German aggression being aired at this Council meeting," said Veronica. "Not right now."

"Perhaps Gebhardt wants more revenge," I said shakily. Simon put a comforting arm around me, but it wasn't much help. The sight of Gebhardt had kicked open a box of sickening memories that I'd thought I'd locked away forever.

"Well, he can't stop the train, can he?" Toby said. "He can't do anything now till we get to Paris, and what's he going to do *there*, shoot me in cold blood in the middle of Gare du Nord?"

"You don't know him!" I said, turning on Toby. "You didn't meet him, you don't know what he's capable of!" And I couldn't help thinking of poor dead Otto Rahn . . .

"Gebhardt's utterly ruthless," agreed Veronica, chewing her lip. "And he wasn't in uniform. What if he works at the German Embassy in Paris? That might explain how he knew we'd be here. He must have got hold of the agenda for the Council meeting and guessed we'd take this train. And diplomats don't have to follow local laws."

"The police could refuse to arrest him," said Simon. "Besides, he hasn't done anything yet. It's not illegal to try to catch a train."

"What are we going to *do*?" I almost screamed. My rising panic was blocking all attempts at rational thought.

"Let's move to another carriage, for a start," said Veronica. "He saw which compartment we were in—let's not make it any easier for him."

We jumped up and made our way towards the back of the train as fast as the swaying corridors would allow. Veronica and I kept a nervous eye out for Nazis, but we didn't spot any other familiar faces. Fortunately, the train was far from full, and we found an empty compartment in a second-class carriage. We huddled there together, glancing up anxiously at each passing footfall.

"Right," said Simon in a low voice. "We need to figure out a plan. We arrive in Paris at Gare du Nord at about half past five. We're supposed to take a taxi to another station, Gare de

Lyon, and catch the southbound train to Geneva an hour later, but—"

"But that's what they'll be expecting us to do," I said. My mind was suddenly, miraculously, clear. "I think we ought to split up as soon as the train stops in Paris. Much harder for them to chase after two groups. Simon, where are those train timetables?"

"Toby's the important one," Veronica reminded us as Simon and I examined the timetables. "*He* has to get to Geneva in time for the meeting at two o'clock tomorrow. It doesn't matter if the rest of us are late or if we get—"

The carriage jolted and we all gasped, our gazes flying towards the window. But it was a stone on the tracks, or a splutter of the engine, nothing more ominous than that. The train gathered itself up and sped onwards. Outside the window lay the battlegrounds of the Somme, fields of white crosses and red poppies spread out over the shattered skeletons of a million soldiers. I could tell the others were thinking of the war, too—the last one as well as the one that was threatening to erupt at any moment. I forced myself to concentrate on the timetables in my lap.

"All right," I said. "The Simplon Orient Express leaves Gare de Lyon at half past ten this evening. Veronica, you and Toby take that. It doesn't go to Geneva, but it stops in Lausanne early tomorrow morning. How far is Lausanne from Geneva?"

"About forty miles, I think," said Simon. "The Swiss are very efficient, it couldn't be more than an hour or so by the local train. Or you could hire a car. I think they even have boats that travel down Lake Geneva."

"You'll be at the hotel in time for breakfast," I said. "Don't worry about waiting for your luggage when we get to Paris. Simon and I will manage that. Then we'll catch the first train to Lyon we can find, and . . ." I peered at the timetables, but no immediate solution presented itself. "Well, it's not far to the Swiss border from there. We might have to catch a train tomorrow morning. We'll meet you at the Palais des Nations in time for the afternoon session of the Council."

And to my amazement, the first part of the plan worked beautifully. My wild and fearful imagination had conjured images of Gebhardt blocking the railway tracks with his car, flinging grenades at the engine driver, even landing a Nazi parachutist on the roof of our carriage, but the Flèche d'Or slid unhindered into Gare du Nord at exactly 5:35 p.m., right on time. The instant the train came to a halt, Toby and Veronica hurled themselves out onto the platform and raced off towards the exit, almost bowling over a startled porter. I could only pray the Orient Express wasn't booked out, and that they'd manage to get tickets for that evening. Meanwhile, Simon and I took our time gathering up our possessions. We were the last passengers to step down from the carriage, having carefully scanned the platform first.

"I'm pretty sure the train from Calais is faster than any car," said Simon. "Although if Gebhardt *is* a diplomat, he's free to ignore the usual road rules."

"He could have telephoned ahead and arranged to have someone waiting here in Paris for us," I pointed out. I kept a tense watch as Simon collected our luggage, engaged a porter, found a taxi, and got us and the bags into it. Then we sped off down Boulevard de Magenta, Simon and I whipping our heads back and forth to see if anyone was following us.

"But, really, it makes more sense that Gebhardt would have told any accomplice of his to go straight to Gare de Lyon," said Simon. "All the Switzerland-bound trains depart from there."

"Oh, so we're driving directly into an ambush? That's *such* a comfort to know," I said crossly. The heat was stifling, my neck hurt from all the frantic head-turning, and not only was Gebhardt trying to *kill* us (or at least delay us in some extremely unpleasant Nazi manner), but he had ruined my first glimpse of Paris. One of the most beautiful and important cities in the world, and I was too anxious to take it in properly. I did see the top of the Eiffel Tower, somewhere off to my right, and the taxi driver pointed out the place where the Bastille had stood. But, all at once, we were there, at Gare de Lyon.

"You wait here while I go in and find out about the trains to Lyon," Simon said. "Gebhardt might recognize you—"

"We *want* him to recognize me!" I whispered back (because the driver was starting to give us very suspicious looks by then). "We have to draw him away from Toby and Veronica! They might still be in there, buying their train tickets!"

And I heaved my bag up and stomped off towards the station entrance while Simon was still fumbling through his wad of francs to pay the driver. I was so annoyed by that stage that I almost hoped I *would* encounter Gebhardt—perhaps I could drop my bag on his good foot and completely cripple him. The bag weighed a ton, because I hadn't been able to decide between several outfits, and I'd brought along *Les Misérables* (to read) and my mother's still-undeciphered diary (for luck). I plunked myself and the bag down near the doorway and peered around the station. Nothing. A few minutes later, Simon arrived, looking hot and bothered.

"Well?" he said.

"Not a sign of anyone," I said. "Friend or foe."

"There's a train to Lyon in thirty-five minutes," said Simon. "Here's your ticket, in case we get separated. Let's go and have a drink—there's a café over there."

Still no one appeared. Our train arrived; we boarded one of the rather shabby carriages, shoved our bags in the luggage rack, and sat down on the thinly padded bench. It was only after the train had begun to rattle off that I caught sight of our nemesis running onto the platform, looking in quite the wrong direction. I wrenched up the window, thrust my head out, and screamed, "Hello, Herr Gebhardt!" For good measure, I took off my hat and waved it at him.

"What are you *doing?*" exclaimed Simon, yanking me back inside.

"Luring him away from Toby and Veronica," I said, watching with great satisfaction as Gebhardt and his red-haired colleague started huffing and puffing along the platform after us. They came to the end of the platform, grew smaller, then vanished from our sight. "Gosh, it's just not his *day* for catching trains, is it?"

"You do realize that this is the *slow* train?" said Simon, sounding thoroughly exasperated. "He'll simply get back in his high-speed Mercedes-Benz and chase after us till we stop at some little town, then he'll storm on board and—"

"He only knows Veronica and me," I said. "He might have seen a photograph of Toby, but he doesn't know you at all. I think the two of us have a very good chance of getting away."

"Well, let's find somewhere else to sit," Simon said, raking his hand through his hair in agitation. "And do something to change your appearance."

We finally settled on the last carriage as the safest place. "There's a baggage car on the end—we can hide in there," said Simon, looking down the corridor.

"And we're right beside the doors," I said. "We can jump out onto the tracks if we have to." I'd taken off my jacket and hat, and hidden my hair under a scarf of Veronica's. "You keep an eye on that window, I'll take this one."

The train made several stops, more passengers getting off than on, but there was no sign of our pursuers. "Where are we now?" I asked.

"God knows," said Simon, peering out the grimy window. "I feel as though we've been traveling for days." The sun was slowly sinking, a blazing ball in an orange sky, but it didn't feel any cooler. The window beside me refused to budge, and the carriage was stifling. The atmosphere wasn't helped any by the ancient gentleman sitting opposite us, puffing away at a foul-smelling pipe. I leaned against the window, fighting my drowsiness with decreasing success. The train slowed down again . . . Another town appeared, then receded . . . The gentleman picked up his moth-eaten carpetbag and shuffled off down the corridor, to be replaced by a pair of old ladies in black dresses with white lace collars . . .

Suddenly Simon swore.

"It's them!" he hissed.

Instantly awake, I stared out the window. Gebhardt was talking to the guard at the front of the train, and the red-haired soldier was running down the platform, towards the last door of the last carriage—towards *us*! Cutting off our escape route, stopping us from getting to the baggage car!

"Quick, put your arms around me," said Simon.

"What?"

As the door to our carriage was flung open, Simon pushed me into the corner of our compartment and covered my body with his. One of his hands turned my face towards his, and I instinctively clutched at his shoulder, my other arm going round his waist. To anyone passing by, we were young lovers, overcome with passion on a sultry summer's evening. At least, I *hoped* that's what we resembled. My face pressed to Simon's neck, my heart hammering even faster than his rapid pulse, I heard the stomp, stomp, stomp of boots along the wooden floor. The noise ceased, mere yards from us.

"Don't look," murmured Simon into my ear. I could feel the tension in all the muscles of his back.

The boots made a scraping sound. Was the man turning

for a closer look at us? Then the footsteps started up again—moving *away* from us, towards the front of the train. A door slammed. Simon shifted his weight slightly, trying to look out the window. There were angry shouts from the next carriage—in French, not German. There was a thud and a series of heavy, rapid footfalls.

"Is that . . . ?" I whispered. Was Gebhardt on board now? There was no way we'd fool *him*. We braced ourselves, waiting for the blow to fall.

There was another thump. I heard the guard's voice and then a shrill whistle.

"They're both back on the platform!" said Simon. The engine groaned, and heaved itself forward. There was the sound of raised voices—the stationmaster yelling at the Nazis.

"Thank God the French hate the Germans even more than we do," said Simon. "Gebhardt probably thinks we left the train at the first stop."

"Right," I said rather breathlessly. "Well, you can get off me now."

"Oh, sorry," he said, doing so at once. I sat up and adjusted my scarf, which had become somewhat disarranged during our . . . entanglement. I wasn't sure if the experience counted as my first kiss (there *had* been some accidental lip contact), but it had certainly been exciting. Just not in the way I'd always hoped. It hadn't even been very private—the two elderly ladies were now gazing at us with great interest. I felt myself turning scarlet. One of them said something to me in rapid French.

"Er," I said. "*Excusez-moi. Je ne comprends pas . . .*"

They giggled and shot Simon sly looks, and one of them patted me on the knee. Then they offered us grapes and some little seedcakes from one of their many baskets. I gathered that they thought we'd eloped, that Gebhardt was my father or the redhaired man my abandoned fiancé. It was quite embarrassing, but the cakes were excellent, and I was starving by then. They asked where we were headed and gave us detailed directions for finding a hotel in Lyon that their nephew owned. Half an hour more of amiable (although rather muddled) conversation, and then they gathered up their baskets and departed, fondly wishing us *bon voyage* and winking at me behind Simon's back. A further half an hour, and Simon and I arrived at our destination. Not Geneva, unfortunately, just Lyon, and when we checked, we found there wasn't a train to Switzerland until eight o'clock the next morning.

"It's just as well, really," I confessed. "I don't think I could face another couple of hours on a train."

"Nor could I," said Simon. "Shall we try that hotel the ladies recommended?"

This proved to be fairly clean and within our budget, and (after further confusion, due to the hotel manager believing we actually *were* newlyweds) we were shown two tiny rooms connected by a door. We had a hasty wash in the bathroom down the corridor, then followed the manager's directions to a *bouchon* around the corner. This was exactly as I'd imagined little restaurants in France to be—red wallpaper, flickering candlelight, a tangle of dark bentwood chairs and tiny tables, a mustachioed waiter polishing glasses behind the bar.

"*Très romantique*," said Simon. "Perfect for a couple on their honeymoon."

I kicked him under the table. "Stop it," I said, trying to read the menu in the dim light. "What's 'andouillette'?"

"Sausages made from pork tripe."

"Oh. Then I think I'll have the salade Lyonnaise. And coq au vin."

The waiter brought us bread and a jug of water, then poured me a large glass of red wine before I could stop him. I was afraid it might be some terrible breach of French dining etiquette to ignore it, so I had a sip, and it was all right. But the food was *superb*. I really think the chef could have made even pork tripe taste divine. And it wasn't at all expensive, not compared to London restaurants. The glorious meal was almost enough to make me forget our troubles—almost, but not quite.

"Do you think Veronica and Toby have enough money?" I asked. "Simon, what if Gebhardt drove straight back to Paris? What if he waited at the station there, in case we'd doubled back, and then he saw Veronica and Toby?"

"I doubt he'd want to loiter around that station for another couple of hours, after the day he'd had," said Simon. "And even if he did, there wouldn't be much he could do on a busy platform. I'd like to see him try to drag Veronica off somewhere quietly. She'd raise absolute hell—and Toby speaks excellent French, he'd soon get all the guards and passengers on their side."

"But it's so awful, not knowing where they *are*," I said. "If only someone would invent telephones that we could carry around with us! Then Veronica could telephone us to say they were all right. Or we could telephone her . . ."

"They should train pigeons to track certain people," Simon said. "Then we could carry the birds around, inside special pockets in our jackets, and send the birds off with messages whenever we needed. You ought to get your suitor working on it."

I tried to kick Simon under the table again and missed, possibly because I'd finished my glass of wine by then. (I hadn't been certain I liked red wine, not at first, but it seemed to improve with each mouthful.) "Stop making fun of Rupert," I said sternly. "If it weren't for him, we wouldn't even have got this far today! There's nothing wrong with being wonderful with animals. Also, pigeons are extremely clever, so you shouldn't make fun of *them*, either. But anyway . . ." I frowned. "What was I saying?"

"How much have you had to drink?" asked Simon.

"I don't know. I think the waiter refilled my glass when I wasn't looking. Oh, yes—Rupert! Well, he's not my suitor. I like him very, very much, he's awfully sweet, but I don't feel . . . I just don't feel *romantic* about him."

"Good," said Simon, pouring me a glass of water. "Because I think you could do a lot better, as far as husbands go."

"Why does everyone keep telling me not to *marry* him?" I cried, throwing up my hands. "When we haven't the slightest *interest* in getting married to each other!"

"Shh," said Simon. "Drink your water. Otherwise you'll have a horrible headache tomorrow."

"I already have a headache," I muttered. "From being forced to think about *marriage* all the time. Simon, who are *you* going to marry?"

I think I may have been a little bit drunk, after all. But Simon only laughed.

"I'm afraid I'm not much of a catch. No money and no title."

"That's true," I conceded. "But you're clever and hard-working. And *moderately* good-looking."

"Why, thank you."

"Only moderately," I said, which was a lie. Every woman in the room, and at least one of the men, had been eyeing Simon, on and off, all evening. I glared at his most persistent admirer, a stylish brunette in the corner, then turned back to him. "Simon?"

"Hmm?" he said, tipping the rest of the wine into his glass.

"Have you ever been in love?" (I was definitely drunk.)

"No."

I stared at him. "Really? *Never?*"

"Never."

I took a deep breath. "Not even with . . . not even with Toby?"

Simon sighed and drank his wine.

"Toby," he said at last, "is a beautiful, charming, self-centered brat. He's frittered away opportunities that others would kill for, he's relentlessly frivolous—"

"That's not fair," I protested. "He's very serious about this air force thing." I didn't add that he was also very serious about Simon—I wasn't *that* drunk.

"All right, I'll admit Toby has hidden depths," said Simon. "*Very* hidden."

"It's not easy for him, you know," I said rather sadly. "Especially with Aunt Charlotte determined to marry him off. Do you think Toby could ever . . . ?" I trailed off, not quite sure how to phrase it.

"Oscar Wilde was a husband and a father," said Simon, reading my mind. "And don't think I haven't already pointed that out to Toby."

"But imagine poor *Mrs.* Wilde," I said, frowning. "I don't think it was very fair of that man, if he already knew that he was . . . Although I suppose one could like both men *and* women. After all, you do."

"I think I prefer women," he said levelly.

"Well, that's the more sensible option," I said. "Also, it's more . . . legal."

"True."

"And, anyway, women are nicer," I said. "Better dressed, not as aggressive—"

"Really? You mean Veronica's actually a *man?*"

"Very funny, Simon," I said. "You're just jealous of her."

"I am, a little," he admitted. "Or I used to be. Now it's closer to grudging admiration. At least Veronica makes the most of what she's been given. You can be damned sure *she* wouldn't toss away an Oxford education."

"Toby only did that because he hoped Aunt Charlotte would let you or Veronica go to Oxford in his place."

"Then he's an idiot," said Simon. "He ought to have known your aunt would never agree to that. Although I must say, it *was* rather clever of him, telling her he was pining away over Julia Whittingham, that *that* was why he couldn't consider marriage to any other girl. Not that it'll work in the long term, but it might give him a bit of room to maneuver."

"And you call *me* Machiavellian," I said.

"Ah, Sophie," he said, smiling at me—not with his guarded half smile, but a rare, unrestrained one. "You're *beyond* Machiavellian. Look at how you've cleverly got me to spill my secrets this evening. It's a good thing you're too drunk to commit them to memory, otherwise they'd all get scribbled down in that wicked journal of yours . . ."

Ha! Little does Simon know that I have an EXCELLENT memory for conversations! And I wasn't *that* drunk. I had a lovely, long sleep after we got back to the hotel, and not a trace of headache when I woke up. And I've managed to get all this written down since we left Lyon, having resolutely ignored the spectacular Alpine scenery speeding past the train window. Simon has asked several times what I'm writing, but I've told him to concentrate on watching out for Gebhardt.

Oh, now the Customs men are moving through the train, checking everyone's papers. We must be nearly at the Swiss border . . . Will write more soon.

23rd August 1939

So, we arrived at the Hôtel des Bergues, located conveniently close to the train station, offering a splendid view of the calm blue expanse of Lake Geneva.

And Veronica and Toby weren't there.

No, said the man at the reception desk, His Majesty and Her Highness had not arrived, and they had not left any messages for us. Except . . . Oh, he was mistaken, there *was* a telegram. I tore open the envelope. It was from Daniel, wishing us good luck.

"Don't worry," Simon assured me. "They've gone directly to the Palais des Nations, that's all. It wasn't as though they had any luggage to drop off."

We took a taxi to the headquarters of the League of Nations (although it turned out to be within walking distance) and hurried over to the main desk in the vast marble lobby to make our enquiries.

"One moment, please," said the elegant blonde behind the

desk. She picked up her telephone receiver and spoke into it in French, then English. Meanwhile, I stared around at all the cold white stone, at the heavy pillars and lofty ceilings. It was a secular cathedral, built for the glory of International Diplomacy rather than God. I could see the effect was meant to be dignified, but it came off as rather boastful and unwelcoming. The lady at the desk finally informed us that Madame Blair would speak with us in her office and that a clerk would show us the way.

"But could you tell us if His Majesty, the King of Montmaray, has arrived yet?" said Simon.

"He has not," said the desk lady crisply before turning to an Oriental gentleman waiting beside us.

Madame Blair was even crisper. "No, the delegation from Montmaray has *not* arrived, nor have I received any message from them. The afternoon session of the Council begins in"— she examined her tiny diamond wristwatch—"ninety-seven minutes. This is all *most* unfortunate. The issue of Montmaray is the first item on a *very* busy agenda. I expected to meet with the Montmaravian delegation at eleven o'clock sharp, to explain the procedure to His Majesty—"

"Something's gone wrong," I said. Simon put his hand on my arm and turned back to Madame Blair.

"The delegation was due to arrive in Lausanne at 6:26 this morning," he said to her. "Have you heard of any delays with the trains? Any . . . any accidents?"

"I have heard of no such thing," she said, drawing herself up and glaring at him. "Several gentlemen arrived from Lausanne this morning without reporting any difficulties." She snatched up a pen and held it over a typewritten list. "Now, I must know, at once, whether I need to make changes to the agenda—whether the delegation from Montmaray will be addressing the Council this afternoon or not."

"Yes," said Simon firmly. "Montmaray *will* address the Council this afternoon."

"Under what authority—"

"I am the Lord Chancellor of Montmaray," he said. "If the King is unavoidably delayed, *I* will speak in his stead."

He stared her down.

"Very well," she said with a sniff. She marched out to confer with her colleagues, then returned to escort us to the empty Council Room. She briskly pointed out Montmaray's place at the massive, semicircular marble table, raised on a platform at the front of the room. She explained the procedure whereby Toby (or Simon) would be introduced by the President of the Council, enter the room, and deliver his speech. She also showed me the stairs to the observers' gallery. Then she deposited us in a reception room, saying she would meet us there fifteen minutes before the Council session was due to begin.

The moment she disappeared, Simon sagged onto a sofa. "*I* can't address the Council!" he said to me. "Toby's got the only copy of that speech!"

"Never mind about that!" I cried. "Where *are* they? If Veronica hasn't sent a message, something really terrible has happened!"

Simon ran a hand through his hair. "All right. Let's . . . let's think about this logically. They've probably gone to the hotel—"

"We left a message for them there, at the front desk! Anyway, they'd come straight here! We have to do something! Tell the police or—"

"Tell them *what*? That a couple of people are running late for a meeting?"

"Then telephone the train station at Lausanne or . . . or . . . I don't know!"

The trio of gentlemen sitting in the corner broke off their conversation in Greek (or whatever it was) and turned to gaze at us disapprovingly.

"Look, let's go outside," muttered Simon.

We rapidly made our way out through the wide corridors, reached the main doors of the Palais des Nations—then came to an abrupt halt, racked with indecision.

"Perhaps I should go back to the hotel," said Simon. "See if they've telephoned—"

"No, no, they'd come directly here . . . Oh, Simon, *how* could Gebhardt possibly have got to them? They took a completely different route!"

"It's probably something else, a flat tire on the way from Lausanne . . ."

We paced up and down, hurling useless fragments of sentences at each other, and all the while, the minute hand of Simon's watch moved closer to two o'clock.

"Right," he said at last. "We've got ten minutes till that

woman comes to collect us from the reception room. I'll go back in. You take a taxi to the hotel and—"

"SOPHIE! SIMON!"

We whirled around. A dusty black car had pulled up on Avenue de la Paix, and Veronica was climbing out of the back of it. We raced over.

"Oh, thank God you're all right!" I said, flinging myself at her.

"Where's Toby?" Simon demanded, staring into the empty backseat of the car.

"At the police station in Lausanne." The driver reached over to close the door, and Veronica turned to him. "*Un moment, monsieur, s'il vous plaît!*"

"Gebhardt?" I said. "They caught him?"

"What?" said Veronica. "No, no, Toby got arrested in the men's room at the railway station—"

"WHAT?" Simon and I shrieked.

"What the hell was he *doing*?" shouted Simon.

"Oh, no, *he* wasn't doing anything disreputable, he just went to help a man who was being beaten up, but Toby got hurt—well, I think he did, he had blood on his face, although that may have been the other man's, it was all so confusing—and then the police arrived and hauled everyone off to the station. And when I finally found out where they were holding him, the policemen refused to listen to me—*typical* of a country that won't give the vote to women! They wouldn't even let me *see* Toby, and I didn't have enough money to offer bail, wasn't sure if they'd think I was trying to *bribe* them. Oh, and I forgot to say Toby had all our identification papers! And then it took ages to find a telephone, and I left a message at the hotel, but they said you were here . . . What time is it?"

"Time to go," said Simon. He took her arm and pushed her in the direction of the building. "Get inside. Sophie will show you the way. You need to deliver that speech to the Council. I'm going back to Lausanne to rescue Toby—"

"Speech!" said Veronica. "What are you talking about? Simon, *I* can't give that speech. Toby's got all the papers—"

"You wrote it!" shouted Simon, clambering into the front seat of the car. "You know more about it than any of us! Now, get going!"

He said something to the driver and slammed his door, then the car sped off. I grabbed Veronica's arm, suddenly aware of how pale and exhausted she looked.

"It's just that I didn't get much sleep last night," she confessed. "One of us had to keep watch for Gebhardt, and I wanted Toby fully awake when he addressed the Council today."

"You'll be fine," I said to her, tugging her back up the drive. "We've still got a few minutes, and I brought along some of your things, in case you needed to change."

I dragged her into the nearest ladies' room, where Veronica splashed some water on her face and pulled on a pair of unladdered stockings.

"Have you had luncheon?" I asked, pinning her hair up.

"I didn't even have breakfast," she said. "Everything was so chaotic, you've no idea. I was so worried about Toby—and you know how difficult it is to work out what's going on when one doesn't speak the language fluently. The only thing that went right was that we managed to avoid Gebhardt."

"That's because he was busy with us," I said, handing her my lipstick.

"What?" she exclaimed, wheeling around.

"Never mind, I'll tell you about it later," I said. "Here, you've got lipstick on your chin." I fixed her face, straightened her collar, brushed the dust off her jacket, then led her down the hall towards the reception room, wishing she'd been able to change into her new suit.

Madame Blair was waiting by the door, tapping her foot. "His Excellency the Lord High Chancellor of Montmaray—"

"Has been unavoidably called away at the last minute," I said. "May I introduce Her Royal Highness Princess Veronica of Montmaray? She'll be delivering the King's speech. Veronica, this is Madame Blair from the Secretariat of the League of Nations."

"What?" said Madame Blair, aghast. "But, but my agenda—"

"Gosh, look at the time," I said, taking Veronica's arm and marching her towards the door that led to the Council Room. I could see a dozen eminent-looking gentlemen slowly taking their places at the table, having entered the room from the other side.

"All right," I said to Veronica. "Now, the President of the Council will introduce you—"

Madame Blair shoved past us, bustled up to the table, and had a hurried conversation with one of the men. He frowned and wrote something on his pile of papers.

"—then you walk in and take your seat," I went on. "You're sitting over there, at the very end of the table. I think the President will talk about Montmaray for a few minutes before inviting you to stand up and give your speech. I'll be upstairs in the gallery—"

But Veronica hadn't taken in a word I'd said. She was staring at two gentlemen who were shaking hands at the far side of the room. "That's Joseph Avenol," she said, her eyes enormous. "The Secretary-General of the League of Nations!"

I glanced over. "Is it? Good. Anyway, I'll try to sit right in the middle—"

"It's *not* good!" she cried. "He's *terribly* pro-appeasement! I had no *idea* he'd be at this meeting; he's part of the Secretariat, not the Council."

Her gaze jerked away from the men, across to the towering windows with their forty-foot drapes, around the marble walls, up at the huge murals depicting Humankind engaged in various heroic acts. A uniformed guard shut the big bronze doors on the other side of the room, and the chatter began to die down.

"They're starting," I said. "You need to—"

"No," said Veronica, taking a step backwards. "I can't do this."

"What?"

"This is *insane*! I don't have any *notes*, I've never even given a speech in public before, they're expecting the *King* of Montmaray to speak!"

I was alarmed to see the panic in her face.

"Veronica—" I started.

"Just *look* at them!" she continued, twitching her hand in the direction of the Council. "Men, all of them old and distinguished, not a single, solitary woman at that table! Why did I ever think we could . . . ?"

She shook her head wildly. "They're not going to pay the slightest bit of attention to me, a *girl* from a place they've never even *seen*, someone who's not even listed on the *agenda*."

She took another step backwards.

"It's all been a waste of time," she said, and her voice was full of despair. "They aren't going to do anything to help us—"

"Stop that!" I said, grasping her arm. I glanced into the Council Room, where the President had just risen to speak, and I lowered my voice. "Listen to me, Veronica. They *invited* us. And we risked our *lives* to get here, for this one chance to tell our story. We've been working towards this for months, and all that time, *you* were our leader. Not Simon. Definitely not Toby. *You* were the one doing the research, chasing up the records, writing the letters—yes, I know Simon helped, we all did, but you started this, you kept it going, and *you're* going to finish it."

She stared at me, still shaking her head.

"They'll pay attention to you," I said, "because you'll *make* them listen. Look, I don't know what the Council will decide. I don't know if they'll help us. That's beyond our control. All you can do is walk through that door and tell them what happened to Montmaray. And that could never, *never* be a waste of time. How could it be futile to tell the truth, to ask that justice be done? Think of why we're doing this! Remember Montmaray, remember how the castle looked that last afternoon . . ."

I closed my eyes for a second. It was as though I were there again, amongst the smoking ruins, overwhelmed with grief.

"Even if Simon and Toby were here," I said, my voice wobbling, "we'd still want *you* to speak. Because you're the one who should explain Montmaray to the world."

"Your Highness!" snapped Madame Blair, from somewhere behind my shoulder. "The President of the Council has just announced your name! Are you ready?"

Veronica took a deep breath. The world waited.

"Yes," she said. "Yes, I'm ready." Then she bent down and kissed me, turned on her heel, and walked through the door.

I stood there for a moment, watching her take her seat, then ran upstairs. The gallery was only half full, and I found a seat in the front row, right in the middle. I peered over the railing, my heart pounding, and saw that the President of the Council was still reading out our submission to the League of Nations. He kept mispronouncing "Montmaray," putting the emphasis on the wrong syllable, the middle one.

"It's 'Mont-ma-RAY'!" I wanted to shout. Couldn't he at least have *checked* that beforehand? *That* hadn't been a last-minute addition to the agenda!

Meanwhile, Veronica was scribbling away frantically in her notebook. The Council had finished being astonished at her unexpected appearance and were now regarding her with expressions that ranged from benign condescension to bristling outrage. Veronica had been right. These men did not believe that women—or was it just *young* women?—had any place at the front of this room. Below me, facing the Council, sat row upon row of men in dark suits. I counted three lady observers in sensible hats. There were two female secretaries sitting at the desks placed directly below the Council table. That was it. My hands tightened around the railing. Virginia Woolf had been right, too—women weren't making the decisions about war, about peace, about *any* of the really important issues in the world. Even though we, just as much as men, suffered the consequences when the decisions our leaders made turned out to be the wrong ones. It made me want to hurl a copy of *Three Guineas* at the pair of elderly Council men currently muttering to each other and scowling at Veronica—except it was a rather thin book, and it wouldn't have done nearly as much damage as they deserved.

I suddenly realized that the President had stopped speaking. Veronica was standing up, gazing around the room. Her eyes met mine for a second, and I leaned forward, hoping she'd see all my love, all my faith in her, in my look. She half smiled, then glanced down at her hastily assembled notes.

"Gentlemen," she said. "And ladies." She nodded at the two secretaries. "The Covenant of the League of Nations is one of the most inspiring documents of our time. Truly, there is no greater aim than 'to achieve international peace,' no better hope than for 'open, just, and honorable relations between nations.'"

I was probably the only person in the room who noticed the slight waver in her voice, the uncharacteristic hesitancy before each sentence.

"But I need not quote further from the Covenant, not to those gathered *here*," she went on, with growing confidence, "just as I really need not remind you of the many times when the League has averted war. To mention only three of them: in 1921, peace and independence were restored to Albania after Yugoslavian forces withdrew; in 1925, Bulgaria and Greece were able to resolve their conflict without further violence; in 1934, Peru and Colombia signed a peace treaty. All thanks to the mediation of the League. And yet—"

She turned to the men at the table.

"And yet, here we are, a mere twenty-one years after the end of the Great War, the 'war to end all wars.' And the world is, again, on the brink of war. Why? Because there are several powerful, belligerent nations that are determined to ignore the principles of civilized society, that have torn up peace treaties, invaded their neighbors, and trampled on the rights of their own citizens."

She paused, leaned forward, placed one hand on the table—a technique I'd seen Simon use rather effectively in arguments with her.

"How can this *possibly* be happening while the League of

Nations exists?" she said. "Well—perhaps it's because the League, our international police force, has been too concerned with peace and not enough with justice."

There was some angry muttering below me. Veronica straightened and raised her voice.

"For those who have not had the opportunity to peruse the documents my nation has provided to the League, allow me to summarize our situation. Montmaray, an island in the Bay of Biscay, has been an independent kingdom since 1542, and a member of the League of Nations since 1920. It has never experienced civil war, never invaded any other country. The only time in recent history it has participated in international conflict was in 1917, when Montmaray offered assistance to the Allied forces at the Western Front. My late father, King John of Montmaray, raised a battalion. Most of the young, able men of Montmaray sailed to France under his command. Nearly all of them were slaughtered in a single day in the trenches. The best of our young men—our hope, our future—were gone, forever. My father never recovered from it. Our kingdom was devastated, very nearly destroyed."

She took a breath. The room was now silent.

"So—I understand about war. I know that the devastation goes on long after the treaties have been signed and the last soldiers shipped off home. I understand why anyone who'd lost a son, a brother, or a father in the last war would do almost anything to prevent another war. I understand the desire to appease these new dictators who make such noisy demands and stamp their feet so heavily. It doesn't seem such a high price to pay, does it? Giving them a bit of land, letting them have a few more aeroplanes and tanks than they're strictly supposed to own, turning a blind eye when they round up a few of their own Jews or Communists and throw them into concentration camps. After all, we *were* rather unfair to them after they lost the last war. And if they get what they want, they'll stop asking, won't they?

"But what does history tell us about such men? What does literature say? Let us turn to Shakespeare, who wrote: 'Why should Caesar be a tyrant, then? Poor man! I know he would not be a wolf, but that he sees the Romans are but sheep.'"

Veronica looked at the Council members.

"Gentlemen, two years ago, the Germans bombed the Kingdom of Montmaray. They knew that the only permanent residents on the island were women and children; that communication with the outside world was limited and difficult; that there'd be no rescue for the citizens of Montmaray. Yet a Nazi officer, SS-Obergruppenführer Wilhelm Gebhardt, sent seven bomber planes to destroy, firstly, the village and the village boat, and then the bridge that connected the sixteenth-century castle to the rest of the island, and then the castle itself. I was there that day. I survived, by a series of miracles, and so did my immediate family. We are the last remnants of Montmaray, living in exile. Our home is now a German military base. The Germans have built an airstrip, from which they launched attacks to aid Franco in the Spanish Civil War, in violation of international non-intervention agreements. They have warships anchored off our coast, perfectly positioned to attack France and Britain. And, although you may have difficulties believing this, the Nazi officer who invaded the island and ordered the bombing also tried to stop us from reaching Geneva to give our testimony today. Germany in 1939 is not a nation that respects the laws of civilized societies."

She looked down at her hands, now clasped on the table. Anyone else might have thought she was offering up a quick, silent prayer, but I knew better.

"No doubt you feel there are more important issues facing the League of Nations than the fate of a tiny island none of you has ever visited," she went on. "But consider this: whether it is Montmaray or Czechoslovakia or Poland that is under threat, the League of Nations was established to deal with *precisely* this issue. I quote Article Ten of the Covenant: 'Members of the League undertake to respect and preserve against external aggression the territorial integrity and existing political independence of all Members of the League.' Or, to put it more simply: Are you sheep, offering up your smallest lambs for slaughter, one by one, every time the wolf makes angry growling noises? Or are you a shepherd, prepared to do your duty and defend the flock?"

She turned back to the men of the Council.

"Gentlemen, each one of you represents a strong nation. Your heads of state command armies and navies. The League is not powerless; it is as strong as its members wish it to be. So— make a decision today that will go down in history as brave and just and right. Take a stand against greed and brutality. Honor your Covenant."

She sat down. There was a ringing silence.

I sat there in the gallery, tears sliding down my face, wishing the place were less like a cathedral, more like the theater, so I could cry out "Bravo! Bravo!"

But then, to my amazement, the woman seated directly below me began to clap. And the applause spread, through the ranks of the newspapermen, the observers in the gallery, the diplomats sitting behind the Council, even one or two of the Council gentlemen themselves, although they stopped the instant the President frowned at them. Veronica glanced up from her notes, looking rather taken aback. Then something in the middle of the audience made her eyes widen, and she smiled and shook her head slightly.

I wiped my face and leaned over the railing, but all I could see was the back of a fair-haired man, who was standing up and applauding vigorously. I'd thought for a moment that Veronica might have seen Simon or Toby. My worries about them had somehow been pushed aside while Veronica was speaking, but now they came flooding back. Had Simon found Toby? Was Toby seriously injured? Had Simon managed to convince the police to let Toby go? Had Toby actually been charged, and with what crime?

Awash with anxiety, I barely registered that the President was speaking again. A gentleman stood up to respond (and how

I wished they had little flags in front of them, to identify where they came from). It took a moment before I understood he was giving a speech *in support of Montmaray*! And then another stood, this one Belgian (I heard him introduced), and then another and another, each man censuring Germany in no uncertain terms! Even the *British* Council Member was sympathetic to our cause (if rather noncommittal). And then the President was proposing something—but I'd suddenly realized who Veronica's fair-haired supporter was: I'd caught a glimpse of his face as he turned to his neighbor. It was Colonel Stanley-Ross! What was *he* doing here? Except now I'd missed whatever motion the President had proposed. And the Council was voting! The hands went up— six, seven, nine, no, more than that—it was unanimous.

"The Council of the League of Nations," declared the President, "resolves to send a letter of protest to Germany, condemning Germany's actions against Montmaray and offering to mediate this dispute between the two nations."

We'd done it. We'd finally done it.

Veronica was beaming. I was half laughing, half crying. There was more applause, brief this time, then the President announced a short adjournment, and Veronica was ushered out the door. A dozen newspapermen charged after her, and I saw Colonel Stanley-Ross try to follow, his way blocked by all the others in the audience who were getting to their feet. By the time I'd made my way downstairs, Veronica was surrounded by a phalanx of reporters and photographers in the corridor. They were firing questions at her, and she was holding her ground and firing answers right back at them. I could see and hear her, but I couldn't get anywhere near her.

"*Manchester Guardian.* Is it true that the King of Montmaray has offered his services to the Royal Air Force?"

"Your Highness, *New York Times.* Does Montmaray recognize Franco's government?"

"Your Highness! Are you satisfied with the level of support Britain has given to your government in exile?"

"What do you think of Neville Chamberlain?"

"What's your position on the situation in Danzig?"

"Are you engaged to be married?"

Veronica turned an icy look upon this last reporter, and he took a hasty step backwards. "Why do you want to know that?" she said. "Have you fallen hopelessly in love with me?"

There was much appreciative laughter and more flashing cameras.

Then a reporter said, "Your Highness, what was Montmaray hoping to achieve from addressing the Council today? Hitler has gone back on previous agreements, ignored previous letters of protest—so will today's Council resolution make any difference? Will it *matter?*"

Veronica hesitated. The reporters leaned in, pencils poised over their notebooks. Then she lifted her chin.

"What we wanted," she said, "was to be heard. For the world to understand what has happened to Montmaray. The truth, gentlemen, *always* matters."

"Your Highness—"

"Thank you for your questions," she said firmly, "and good day to you all."

"Your Highness! *Your Highness!*" But the Colonel had finally arrived and was shoving his way through the newspapermen, scattering them like skittles. He bundled Veronica and me into a taxi and rushed us back to the hotel, where he'd taken a suite across the corridor from ours. There he made a flurry of telephone calls, and two hours later, Toby and Simon arrived—Toby looking rather bruised but otherwise unharmed.

"I'm *so* glad my nose isn't broken, after all," Toby said, collapsing onto the Colonel's sofa. "It really is one of my best features."

"If you care so much about your looks, why the hell did you get involved in a public brawl in the first place?" snapped Simon. But I knew, and Toby knew, that it was just Simon's way of showing how relieved he was.

"As if *you'd* have stood by, watching those bullies attack that poor little man," said Toby. "And they lured him in there in the first place, I saw it. Of course, *they* got off scot-free because one of them was the son of a very important councillor, while the poor little man got charged with public indecency."

"Yes," said Simon, "and *now* do you see what can happen to men who—"

"But never mind about all that," Toby said quickly. "Go on about what the Council said, Veronica."

"Well, then the Council voted," said Veronica. "And I knew

the decision had to be unanimous, and I was *sure* the French Council Member was going to vote against it, but somehow, the resolution got through." She heaved a sigh. "And yet, that reporter was right. What *will* a letter from the League of Nations achieve? Germany withdrew from the League in 1933, and Hitler doesn't seem to give a damn what the rest of the world thinks of him. And the Council refused to commit to any firm action if Germany didn't comply—"

"Now, now," chided the Colonel. "You're missing the point. Thanks to you, the world finally knows about Montmaray—or they will, once they read tomorrow's newspapers. And to get even a letter of protest out of that Council is an enormous achievement. I saw Avenol working away at the Greeks and Yugoslavs before the session started, urging them to show support for Germany."

"Joseph Avenol?" said Simon, handing Toby some more ice for his face. "He was there?"

"I wish *I'd* been there," said Toby. "In the audience, I mean, not speaking. Of course, I always planned to have *you* give that speech, Veronica. I knew you'd be ten times better than me."

"You should have heard the applause," I said proudly. "She was magnificent."

"No, I wasn't!" Veronica protested. "You should have seen me beforehand, Toby. I was petrified with nerves. If it hadn't been for Sophie talking me into it, I don't know *what* I would have done. No, actually, I do—crawled into the corner and crumpled into a heap. Sophie forced me out there, she made me remember why I was doing it."

"Sophie's very good at talking people into things," said Simon, nodding gravely.

"Or getting them to talk out things," said Toby, smiling at me.

"Yes, I've always said *she's* the one who holds our family together," said Veronica.

"So that's why we've decided it ought to be *you*, Soph, who faces Aunt Charlotte when we get back," said Toby. "The rest of us will go into hiding till you give the signal that it's safe to emerge from our secret bunker."

I pulled a face at him. "Was she *very* cross?" I asked the Colonel, anticipating the answer.

"Well, your sister valiantly held out for longer than you'd expected," he said. "Just to make sure you'd really got away—which only heightened your aunt's agitation. I believe the words 'boarding school' were raised, more than once."

"Poor Henry," I sighed.

"Oh, she didn't seem too worried," the Colonel said. "Although she did ask me how old she needed to be before she could apply to join the British Secret Service. I denied all knowledge of any such organization, of course."

"You ought to recruit Aunt Charlotte," said Toby. "Imagine the skills *she'd* bring to an interrogation."

"You seem to wheedle your way around her quite easily, young Tobias, most of the time," said the Colonel. "Oh—and I forgot to mention, I checked with our Embassy in Paris, and that Gebhardt fellow *does* hold diplomatic papers."

"So you were right, Veronica," said Simon.

"And you were right," she said, "when you figured the French police wouldn't be any help to us."

"However, I suspect the man may be on his way back to Berlin now, for his own safety," said the Colonel. "There's a limit to what the French authorities will tolerate within their own borders, diplomatic immunity or not. But enough talk for the moment! Baths and rest for everyone, and then you shall all have dinner with me. To celebrate your collective triumphs!"

And so, that evening, we dined on caviar and consommé and escargots à la bourguignonne and duck à l'orange and raspberry almond mille-feuille, seated amongst the diplomats, foreign ministers, and heads of state of a dozen or more nations, several of whom sent over their compliments and bottles of champagne. There were numerous toasts.

"To Montmaray," proposed the Colonel.

"To peace, liberty, and justice," said Veronica. "If it's possible to have all three at once."

"To the secretive and apparently limitless influence of Colonel Stanley-Ross," said Toby.

"To Sophia and all her quiet, indispensable talents," said Simon with his half smile.

"To family," I said.

Finally, Veronica admitted she could barely keep her eyes

open, and the boys rose from the table to accompany her back to our rooms.

"Sophie, would you care to join me for coffee in the lounge?" the Colonel said casually. "I won't keep you up long."

We found a set of armchairs in a dim corner, half hidden behind some potted palms, and a waiter brought coffee and a glass of cognac.

"Don't look so worried," the Colonel said. "I simply wanted to congratulate you in private. Knowing how modest you are."

I opened my mouth to protest that I hadn't done anything, and he gave me a fond, amused look. "Thank you," I said instead. I was just relieved that he hadn't brought me here to tell me to marry Rupert—or not marry Rupert.

The Colonel cleared his throat. "I also wanted to say that I believe your mother would be very proud of how you've turned out."

"My *mother?*" I put down my coffee cup to stare at him. "You knew her?"

"Oh, yes," he said. "I proposed to her. She turned me down, of course—very sensible of her. And I don't think she'd even met your father at that stage."

"Have you told Toby this?" I asked, still filled with astonishment. "I mean, that you knew her?"

"Well," he said ruefully, "I *did* mention her, when I first met Toby, the first time Rupert brought him home from school. But your brother was rather . . . Well, I can understand how he must feel. It must have been terrible, losing her at such a young age." The Colonel looked down at his swirl of cognac. "But I can see that you're different to Toby, so I thought I might . . . offer you whatever memories I had."

"Please," I said. "Tell me everything."

And so he did. He told me that she was clever and quiet, and had a wicked sense of humor that was only ever revealed to those closest to her. She adored Jane Austen and took herself off on a pilgrimage to Bath when she was sixteen. She detested the spectacles she needed to wear, then laughed at her own vanity. She went for long walks in the countryside with her sketchbook and her smelly old beagle. She dutifully practiced the piano for an hour each morning but had absolutely no talent for it. She was terrible at tennis and disliked riding, but played a lively game of chess.

"She hated sacrificing pawns, said she felt sorry for how small and defenseless they were—then, while I was busy snickering at that, she'd whip her queen across the board and checkmate me."

I laughed. "What did she look like?" I asked.

"Very much like you. Perhaps an inch or two shorter, and she was at a distinct disadvantage when it came to the fashions of the day. She was swamped in those long dresses, all those ridiculous pin tucks and frills and lace edgings. She always seemed on the verge of tripping over her hem. And I remember her hair was always falling down. It was the most beguiling thing I'd ever seen. I'd sit there, longing to be permitted to pin those curls back in place. Oh—and she always smelled wonderful, of roses and violets, all those old-fashioned scents."

I smiled. I loved those scents, too. "What else?" I asked.

"She was very kind. And tactful. For example, if she saw that someone felt embarrassed, she'd go out of her way to draw the others' attention away from that person, if that's what was needed, even if it meant everyone would attend to *her*—and she really seemed uncomfortable when others paid too much attention to her. She was happiest sitting back and observing, I think. She kept a journal—"

"I have it!" I burst out excitedly. "Here, with me, in Geneva! But it's in code and I can't understand a word. I'm pretty sure it was the diary she kept just before she went to Montmaray. Do you think you could have a look at it, figure it out?"

"I could try," he said. "But I'm not sure I'd be able to outwit her, even now. And I'm not sure I'd want to read about myself, aged eighteen—although, no, I'm sure she was kind about me, even in private. And of course, once your father came along, I doubt she wrote a word about anyone else. They were very much in love, right from the start."

"He was so handsome," I said. "I remember that."

"And good-natured," said the Colonel. "He was a thoroughly nice chap. Actually, Toby reminds me quite a bit of him. Very funny and confident, without ever falling into outright arrogance. Everyone liked him."

He sighed and gazed off into the dining room, where the waiters were drawing the curtains and snuffing out candles.

"Well," the Colonel said at last, "enough reminiscing for one night, I think. I'll see if I can dig out some old photographs for you, though."

"Thank you," I said, although the words seemed pitifully inadequate when he'd given me such a gift. I tried again. "You really can't imagine how wonderful it is to speak to someone who knew her. I remember so little of her."

"Oh, it's a pleasure, Sophie," he said, smiling at me. "One of those aching, tender pleasures, but nevertheless . . . I meant what I said, you know. That she'd be proud of you, of how brave and clever you've been. Of what you've done, and of what . . ."

"Of what we're about to do," I said when he failed to finish his sentence. I looked him straight in the eye. "There's going to be a war, isn't there?"

He put down his empty glass. "Why do you say that, Sophie?" he asked, giving the impression he was choosing each word with great care.

"Because . . . because that's what I was thinking today," I said slowly. "Watching the Council this afternoon. Thinking about how old and how . . . impotent those men seemed. I mean, I know the League has stopped wars before but not wars between really powerful countries. The League just stood by and let Italy invade Abyssinia, Germany take over Czechoslovakia . . . and now there's all this talk about Poland. You told me at the start of the year that the League wasn't dead. But it's dying, isn't it? I realized that today."

"It certainly isn't looking very healthy," he conceded. He

glanced around. We were the only ones in the room. "Sophie—I don't want to alarm you."

"There's nothing more alarming than not knowing what's going on," I pointed out.

"Well . . . it'll be in the newspapers soon enough, I suppose. You know, of course, that our one hope for peace, our one hope for controlling Hitler, is for Britain and France to make an alliance with the Soviet Union?"

I nodded.

"Well, there was a lot of discomfort in Britain at the very *idea* of us talking with the Communists. And that attitude hasn't helped negotiations at all, let me tell you. I've been in Moscow, trying to jolly things along. Still, it seemed highly unlikely the Soviet Union would ever consider linking up with Nazi Germany. Communists and Fascists are mortal enemies, they're violently opposed on every possible issue. Or so we thought. But on Saturday, Hitler and Stalin signed a trade agreement. Then, yesterday, the Soviet Union broke off talks with us. And worse, it seems the Soviets are about to agree to a military alliance with Germany."

"But then—" I said.

"Then Germany can march into Poland unopposed. Actually, the Germans and the Soviets will probably divide Poland up amongst themselves."

"And Britain's promised to help Poland, hasn't it?" I said. "If Poland gets invaded, Britain and France have to come to its aid."

He looked very grim. "Not only that, but once Hitler has no need to fear the wrath of the Soviet Union, he can turn his army and his air force to the west and the north. France, Belgium, Holland . . . England."

"When?" I whispered. "How long do we have? Months? Weeks?"

"Days," he said flatly. "That's why I came to collect you, that's why I've booked seats on that flight to London tomorrow morning. I didn't want you stranded here when war was declared."

"But—but you could be wrong!" I said desperately. "It could be another false alarm, like the Sudetenland crisis last year, when everyone was digging trenches in Hyde Park!"

"Sophie, I *hope* I'm wrong. But . . ."

He shook his head, then reached over and grasped my hand, knowing I was thinking of Toby and Simon, of all the young men already in uniform. We sat there in silence for a moment.

"Then—was it all a waste of time?" I said, struggling to keep my voice even. "Coming here, to Geneva? If the League is dying, if the newspapers will be full of Stalin and Hitler tomorrow, if Europe's going to explode into war any day now—was it all a waste?"

"Was it?" he said.

"No," I decided. "It wasn't a waste for *us*. It was important to try. It was important to *tell* people. And it showed us what we could achieve when we worked together, if we were . . . brave and clever and persistent, all those things you were saying."

"You're going to need those qualities in the months to come," he said. "We all are."

The few people who remained in the hotel lobby were wandering towards the doors. The staff were closing shutters, flicking off the electric lights, one by one. The Colonel and I stood up, and I pulled my wrap around my shoulders.

"I'll tell you something else," said the Colonel.

"What?"

"I'm very glad that you're on my side," he said with a smile. "You FitzOsbornes are formidable."

"Even in exile?"

"*Especially* in exile."

And then he held out his arm, and I took it, and we walked off into the darkness.

Author's Note

This novel is a blend of historical fact and imaginative fiction. Real people and groups mentioned include Horatio Nelson; Machiavelli; King Canute; Karl Marx, Engels, Trotsky, and Stalin; Mussolini; Amelia Earhart; King George VI, Queen Elizabeth, Princess Elizabeth, and Princess Margaret; President Franklin D. Roosevelt; Sir Oswald Mosley and the British Union of Fascists, also known as the Blackshirts; Lord and Lady Londonderry; Prince Rainier of Monaco; Lady Redesdale and her daughters Unity Mitford, Diana Guinness, and Nancy Rodd; Miss Betty at the Vacani School of Dancing; Monsieur Raymond; Greta Garbo; Queen Victoria; King James I and George Villiers; Oscar Wilde; the National Joint Committee for Spanish Relief, Aid Spain, H. W. H. Sams and Leah Manning; "Potato" Jones, "Ham and Eggs" Jones, and "Corn Cob" Jones; Lady St. John of Bletso; Queen Elizabeth I; Rosalind Christie, the daughter of Agatha Christie; the Archbishop of Canterbury; Göring; Hitler; William Caxton; Samuel Pepys; John Milton; Neville Chamberlain; Stanley Baldwin; Mrs. Simpson and the former King Edward VIII; Winston Churchill; Franco; General Mola; King Alfonso of Spain and the Infanta María Cristina; Archduke Franz Ferdinand; Lord Rosebery; the Duke of Devonshire and Billy Hartington; Earl Fitzwilliam; the Rector of Stiffkey; Ernst Toller; Thomas Inskip; Sir Alexander Cadogan; Anthony Eden; the

League of Nations; the Duchess of Kent; the Kennedy family; Lewis Carroll; Queen Mary; Guy Fawkes; Casanova; the National Unemployed Workers' Movement; the suffragettes; Gandhi; Otto Rahn; Vivien Mosley; the Electress Sophia of Hanover and King George I; King Zog of Albania; and Joseph Avenol. Where real, historical people appear in the novel, I have used their biographies, their own writings, and other evidence to try to make their actions and words as true to their known lives as possible. However, the FitzOsbornes, Stanley-Rosses, Bosworths, Pembertons, Elchesters, Adams-Smythes, and other characters are figments of my imagination.

While Montmaray does not exist, most of the world events described in the novel actually occurred. These include the bombing of Guernica; the evacuation of Basque children to Britain; the coronation of King George VI; Japan's invasion of China; Italy's invasion of Abyssinia and Albania; the War of the Stray Dog; the Anschluss; the signing of the Locarno Treaties; the Sudetenland crisis and the German invasion of Czechoslovakia; the Night of Broken Glass; the exhibition of Picasso's *Guernica* at the Whitechapel Art Gallery; and the protests held by the National Unemployed Workers' Movement. It should be noted that Sophie's knowledge of world events is often restricted to what she has read in the newspapers, and this is sometimes incomplete or slightly inaccurate (for example, while the newspaper headlines of the time stated that Hitler was best man at Mosley's wedding, Hitler was actually the guest of honor). Montmaray House, Milford Park, the village of Milford, and Astley Manor are fictional, but most of the other places mentioned in the novel are real.

Information about aristocratic life in 1930s England came from *In Society: The Brideshead Years* by Nicholas Courtney; *Black Diamonds* by Catherine Bailey; *Grace and Favour: The Memoirs of Loelia, Duchess of Westminster*; and *London: The Glamour Years, 1919–1939* by Susanne Everett. Several books by Anne de Courcy—including *1939: The Last Season; Society's Queen: The Life of Edith, Marchioness of Londonderry*; and *Debs at War, 1939–1945: How Wartime Changed Their Lives*—were invaluable, particularly for providing descriptions of debutante life and the Season. *Fashion Sourcebooks: The 1930s* by John Peacock and *The Private Life of a Country House* by Lesley Lewis were also helpful. *H. V. Morton's London* and *The Penguin Guide to London* by F. R. Banks supplied useful information about London.

Information about Sir Oswald Mosley came from *Blackshirt: Sir Oswald Mosley & British Fascism* by Stephen Dorril; *Diana Mosley* by Anne de Courcy; and *Harold Nicolson: Diaries and Letters, 1930–1939*, edited by Nigel Nicolson; as well as from Mosley's own writings, including *Fascism: 100 Questions Asked and Answered* and *The World Alternative*. Lynne McTaggart's *Kathleen Kennedy: The Untold Story of Jack's Favourite Sister* provided most of the information about the Kennedys, although I also used *Times to Remember: An Autobiography* by Rose Fitzgerald Kennedy; *Why England Slept* by John F. Kennedy; and *The Sins of the Father* by Ronald Kessler. The strange story of the Rector of Stiffkey came from several sources, including *The Age of Illusion* by Ronald Blythe.

The Long Week-end: A Social History of Great Britain, 1918–1939 by Robert Graves and Alan Hodge; *The Diplomats: 1919–1939*, volume 2,

The Thirties, edited by Gordon A. Craig and Felix Gilbert; and *Human Smoke: The Beginnings of World War II, the End of Civilization* by Nicholson Baker provided useful information about political events in Europe in the 1930s. Information about the Basque children came from various sources, including the online archives of Spanish Refugees and Basque Children (www.spanishrefugees-basquechildren.org). The United Nations Geneva website (www.unog.ch) and the online photo archives of the League of Nations (www.indiana.edu/~league) were also very helpful.

Quotes from the following books, newspapers, and magazines were used:

Julius Caesar by William Shakespeare (pp. 35, 39, 261, 262, 435)

Ballads and Songs by John Davidson, cited in *H. V. Morton's London* (p. 106)

"The Tragedy of Guernica" by George Steer, from *The Times* (London), 28th April 1937 (p. 118–19)

"Potato Toasted," from *Time* magazine, 26th April 1937 (p. 122)

Pride and Prejudice by Jane Austen (p. 170)

Seven Plays by Ernst Toller, cited in *Wild Mary* by Patrick Marnham (p. 194)

Alice's Adventures in Wonderland by Lewis Carroll (pp. 284 and 404)

"It Is Peace for Our Time," from the *Daily Mail,* 1st October 1938 (p. 340)

The Covenant of the League of Nations (pp. 433 and 436)

Toby also misquotes a line from Gilbert and Sullivan's *The Pirates of Penzance* on p. 39. And, yes, the opening words of *The FitzOsbornes in*

Exile pay homage to the first sentence of Dodie Smith's wonderful novel *I Capture the Castle*.

Thank you to Zoe Walton and Nancy Siscoe, for their patience and invaluable editorial advice; the hardworking teams at Random House Australia and Random House Children's Books (U.S.); and Rick Raftos and Catherine Drayton.